About the author

Michael Alty was born in Southport, Lancashire, England, in 1949.

He was educated in Preston and is a former scholar of Deepdale School.

It was in the summer of 1992, he became a Modern Language student at the Lancashire College in Chorley where he successfully obtained a vocational qualification from the London Chamber of Commerce, and before going on to study logistics engineering at the Nelson & Colne College in Padiham, Burnley.

He then went on to excel at St Martin's College, Lancaster, where he gained a diploma in the German language.

Michael joined the British Army in 1964 and served in Malta, Cyrenaica in Lybia, North Africa, Germany and Northern Ireland and afterwards was for twenty-five years involved in the Aircraft manufacturing industry at Warton, Preston, Lancashire where his language skills were used by BAE Systems to promote his work.

He, and his wife, Margaret, also a writer, are now living in Burnley, Lancashire and together writing full-time, hope their books will appeal to people of all ages.

Purple Patches

Michael Alty

Published 2019 by arima publishing

www.arimapublishing.com

ISBN 978 1 84549 743 9
© Michael Alty 2019

Typeset in Garamond

Swirl is an imprint of arima publishing.

arima publishing
ASK House, Northgate Avenue
Bury St Edmunds, Suffolk IP32 6BB
t: (+44) 01284 700321

www.arimapublishing.com

PURPLE PATCHES

An introduction

This is a story of a colourful Scottish family, who for thirty-two years lived in East Kilbride, Lanarkshire with the main character in the book, Robert Bruce Hamilton-Brown, a disgraced World War Two Royal Air Force non-commissioned officer, and a former buyer for 'Tindal's; the exclusive manufacturer of Gloves and Accessories in Glasgow.

The story, with a descriptive historical background begins as a poignant reminder that greed, avarice, envy and jealousy are indeed carnal sins which seem to be apparent everywhere in today's so-called modern society, and in essence, it doesn't cost anything to be nice.

My name is Henry James Hodgekiss and my wife is called Elizabeth Marion, formerly Balfour. We have a fifty-two-year-old daughter, Lesley who's been working in the Far East for a number of years as a professor of modern languages and we have been retired for several years, living in a comfortable town house in Waverly Court, a tiny muse in Westminster, London.

One of my sisters-in-law is called Leonora Duncan *née* Balfour; everyone in the family calls her Nora for short. Nora is sixty-eight years of age and works as an artist and businesswoman, living a comfortable lifestyle in St. Ives, a small town in the West Country.

I was for a time an Executive Officer with the Civil Service in London and my office in Whitehall was next to the Admiralty buildings in Trafalgar Square. My wife, Elizabeth, who much prefers to maintain her privacy and keep her anonymity, is an ex-chartered accountant and worked for a well-known bookmaking outfit off the Strand in Aldwych.

My story begins when Christopher Balfour, my brother-in-law and his wife Hazel drove from Streatham on a visit in May this year. He brought with him a large cardboard box containing two canvas field post office delivery sacks, of the type used in the Near, Middle and Far East. Inside these button-down bags were several drawings, picture portraits, a photograph album, letters, diaries and a scrap book belonging to my wife's late step-father, Robert Bruce Hamilton-Brown.

Christopher had this idea we would be interested in the contents of the boxes because there were references to the Royal Air Force, and because of Elizabeth and I being versed in the art of writing novels we could possibly use it to our advantage.

Christopher also mentioned there was a trunk up in the attic inside their home, where lengths of quality cotton curtain material, an Indian silk sari, and a lady's wristwatch in a satin presentation case are stored; the question remained who was to be the recipient of all this clutter in the wake of my wife's step-father departing this life.

It was late in the afternoon when Christopher and Hazel departed No 4 Waverley Court and this was when I began to empty the two boxes, spreading the contents out neatly onto the wooden flooring and into some assemblance of order starting with a tatty old 'Union Jack' flag which had probably seen better days when waved by Dr. David Livingstone or Stanley himself.

The second remnant to be uncovered from one of the two mauve overseas postal courier bags was a novel written by my wife's stepfather, Robert Bruce Hamilton-Brown which quoted a song, later popularised by the famous Italian singer, Dean Martin, which goes:

"When the deep purple falls
Over sleepy garden walls
And stars begin to flicker in the sky
Through the mist of a memory
You'll wander back to me
Breathing my name with a sigh
In the still of the night
Once again I'll hold you tight
Though you're gone
And I'm so far away
For as long as you care for me
Lovers we will always be
Here in my deep purple dreams"

In a letter from the late Alistair Campbell of No 21 Brook Street, Glasgow addressed to Robert Bruce Hamilton-Brown of No 6 Holloway Road, Streatham, South London dated the 16th August 1993, 'I am in receipt of your surprise novel "Purple Haze"; the lyrics to the song are very apt and the poem, "The Seven Verses", with your note at the end written in India in 1941, is not attributed to any author. I was never sure you were in Burma or indeed sailing around the vast Indian Ocean during the war, Robert; the attention to fine detail, I feel is not your own and it most certainly wasn't Rudyard Kipling.

'You mention the time is 08.00hrs. "I am leaning on the starboard bow," you write, "watching the new day, slowly but with the certainty of destiny, leave the womb of night. There is something sacred about this hour, which defies description and can only be felt with the same intense unrealism as one feels infinite things.

"To port, to starboard, and as far astern as the horizon, the sea stretches forth, a solid mass of indigo blue, broken only on the surface by countless millions of wavelets brought into being by an indescribably pleasing Southern zypher.

"The sun, now over the horizon brings to this vast area, a vividness of light and colour which in its perfection, creates a world of total enchantment. We sail like painted ships upon a painted ocean. Aloft from the mast head, against an azure canopy, our gay coloured signals fly in the breeze, astern our white wake, like a boiling cauldron gives way to a near blue and finally gives way without distortion merges into the surrounding blue ocean.

"No artist, even with a palate of all the known colours could produce such a scene. Always the element of life and light escape the stroke of the brush, leaving us with but a mortal creation. Mortal, as those who share this scene with me are mortal. Arrayed as toy soldiers it would seem, in many coloured uniforms, with no end of meaningless markings and motifs, carrying with them the crude weapons of war which glitter in the sun. All are bound for distant destinations there to create havoc and death, in keeping with the logic of our times. Alas we are creatures but of a second in eternity behaving as though we were eternity itself. Written

3

on the troop ship in the med on the way to India 1941; can you return my writings sometime? Your good friend: Robert Bruce Hamilton-Brown."

'Your "vivid lives", Robert, written fifty-two years ago aboard a troop ship brings such a memorable war-time sea passage to life. You seem to have been in that time of all-pervading danger, a more overtly religious young man. Your "Knockers at the Gate" and "Sentry Go" won't be to everyone's taste and certainly not to mine; Robert Bruce Hamilton-Brown in those evocative times always on the prowl for GORE!! Remember "Marmion" by Sir Walter Scott, Robert? Poor benighted Marmion; all the Douglas's were villains and not to be trusted.

"The hand of Douglas is your own, Robert
And never shall in friendly clasp
The hand of such a Campbell grasp
And in the midst of the battle
Morag could hear your death rattle
Among the screams of the dying
She fell to her knees crying"
"Oh, what a tangled web we weave
When first we practice to deceive"

'You abandoned me, turned your back on your best friend along with my sister Morag, Robert Hamilton-Brown, and for this I will never forgive you. I'm glad to have had the insight into the core of the young Robert, and indeed feel that your impertinent approaches are still there, albeit moving more slowly. Morag, had she still been alive would, I am sure, have used your novel to kindle the fire and then to watch the pages slowly burn and witness the smoke rise to endless eternity. Meanwhile, it is my intention to find a dark place in the attic in which to store the book, somewhere out of arms reach and for it to join one's lifetime of acquired junk and some of the photographs I took of you on board The Good Ship T.S.S "Athenia" on Thursday 16th July 1931, remember? It is truly amazing, Robert, how a person can be in two places at the same time;

you were seen in the flesh by one of my colleagues sitting in the buffet bar on Preston railway station in January 1942. The fox hunting scene which was elegantly wrapped around your girlfriend's shoulders later became a talking point at the Y.M.C.A and promulgated me to be an associate member of the Animal Rights Movement.

'I trust that your wife, Beatrice Balfour is also in good health but, without apology, I feel gracious not to have met her. Looking at a snap-shot of us both by a lake in Montreal I leave you to ponder over your consistent misdoings, some of which happened a long time ago and some that prevail to this day. Of all the tables and chairs there are in this world, Robert, why oh why, *didja* have to sit down at mine? Alistair.'

Leading Aircraftsman Robert Bruce Hamilton-Brown 1011007 was called up to serve in His Majesties armed forces in July 1940 until April 1946. He reluctantly walked through the gates of RAF Padgate, Warrington Cheshire before being posted on a long stay at RAF Kirkham, Lancashire. He wasn't on-board a troop ship in 1941, it was a lie contrived to impress his colleagues, friends and family he was a big man, larger than he actually was and, ironically, voiced by his own petard found himself sailing on the troop ship "*Reina del Pacifica*" on November 15th 1943, bound for the Far East to join the Intelligence Section 261 Squadron RAF India Command; the Commanding Officer being the "Menace" meander. The fickle finger of fate had been pointed at him once again.

'Oh! I do like to be beside the seaside,' he made known to his brother Hadrian who had moved away from Scotland to live in Melbourne, Australia a couple of years previously.

Oh! I do like to be beside the seaside
I do like to be beside the sea!
I do like to stroll along the Prom, Prom, Prom
Where the brass bands play:
"Tiddely-om-pom-pom"
So just let me be beside the seaside
I'll be beside myself with glee
And there's lots of girls beside,

5

I should like to be beside
Beside the seaside!
Beside the sea!

"I Do Like to be beside the Seaside" is a popular British music hall song written and popularized in 1907 by John A. Glover-Kind and made famous by music hall singer Mark Sheridan who first recorded it in 1909. It was, for a long time, used as a signature tune by the entertainer, Reginald Dixon MBE, who was the resident Wurlitzer organist at the Tower Ballroom in Blackpool, however, unlike Hamilton-Brown, Reginald was called up to join the RAF as a flying officer and served admirably from July 1940 until his demobilization in April 1946. After his war, Reginald Dixon returned to the Tower Ballroom to resume his entertainment career until his retirement in 1970.

From the North, South and Central piers situated along Blackpool's *'Golden Mile'*, the twenty-six year old Robert Hamilton-Brown would stalk his prey; vulnerable young women with a flair for a Scottish tongue and what seemed to be his ability to bore them with third-rate poetry and offering them cigarettes from the rear of a ceramic laughing cow, a novelty he bought from Woolworths during his first visit to Blackpool in 1940 from RAF Kirkham. He was a purpose-built machine of jealousy, an embarrassment, raddled with avarice, a traitor to his country and to the British Empire, somehow managing to escape being scrupulously vetted by the authorities prior to his call-up. The man with the *'Golden Gob'*, a voyeur who disliked people and referred to women as being aliens from another planet; totally illogical, dangerous, and possessing brains the size of a pickled onion frequently visited strip clubs and infamous burlesque revue theatres and bars on Blackpool's promenade; to drool over half-naked girls and achieve excitement for his own personal gratification. After paying one shilling and sixpence, the entrance fee to a gaudy establishment, he walked along a dimly lit passageway before climbing a set of stairs to gain access into the theatre's small auditorium. The five-minute scenes included an Egyptian theme showing a nude Cleopatra playing a harp, a buxom Red Indian squaw sitting cross-legged outside a wigwam knitting a sweater and a Hindu belly dancer from Bispham, cavorting in front of a crudely painted backdrop of the *Taj Mahal* by moonlight; his preference being a stocking-clad nineteen-thirties facsimile of Bette Davis; reminiscent of Arthur & Company's '*White Heather*' hosiery. The unlicensed premises had been known to have been raided by the police, and members of the audience and cast arrested for indecent exposure, but however, this was soon to be rectified and resolved when a local councillor was caught fiddling around inside a large cardboard bucket filled with toffee popcorn.

Before Hamilton-Brown was called up to join the RAF, he thought the erogenous zones were somewhere between Wigan and Warrington and the world, full of pickled onions and not oysters. In the summer of 1942 there was a strong American presence in Blackpool and it wasn't uncommon to see 'Willis' jeeps and Ford military two-ton trucks parked up outside the '*Silver Sword*', an Arabesque revue bar and theatre on Central Drive.

'Would you like a *Camel?*' one of the American airmen asked Robert.

'Where have you parked it?' was the obvious reply. Over-sexed, over paid and over here was one way of describing the American invasion to the North West of England.

And when one of the belly dancers had allowed him to visit her back stage for extra mural activities, he declined the offer and said: 'thank you very much, but I have a moonlight serenade with Glenn Miller upstairs at the Freckleton CO-OP'; a wind-up gramophone being a very poor second to a twenty-two-piece Army Air Force band. Hamilton-Brown, in his hour of need had been known to reduce himself by listening in to the speaking clock:

"When you're feeling lonesome and blue,
Not having anyone to talk to
Then phone up the operator's time
Just to hear a voice of some kind
She said on your third stroke it will be three o'clock
She said that for over an hour and then he was hung up."

The atmosphere in the '*Silver Sword*' auditorium was similar to a '*Smokey Joes*' bar, empty 'LUCKY STRIKE' packets everywhere and one had to tread warily lest one became stuck to the floor with spittles of penny arcade bubble gum. It was when military forage caps were being exchanged for "Kiss me Quick" hats, and nylon stockings being bartered for something just as quick around the back; the RAF and Royal Military Police, the American 'SP', Shore Patrol would intervene brandishing three-foot long baseball bats to bash Uncle Sam over the top of his head. In those days if Jerry or the Japanese didn't get you, then, you could be damned sure the Salvation Army would; a great prelude before going into battle with a massive headache caused by a tin box. There was a story abound that during a thousand bomber raid on Dresden, the navigator of a B52 Flying Fortress opened up a stick of Blackpool rock to find it was made from a sawn-off piece of broom handle; the aeroplane, after taking a great deal of flak from Jerry also took five hours to limp back to its base in Lincolnshire.

Fish and chips, meat and potato pies everywhere, row upon row of hamburgers, hot dog sausages and buns stacked up neatly behind steamed-up sheets of Perspex and the smell of caramelized onions wafting down the promenade. All of which designed exclusively to go, wrapped up in newspaper and publicly enticing respectable holiday-makers to become pigs; ration books became somewhat of a joke to the towns' inhabitants; however, guesthouse landladies became very rich charging extra for pork sausages to be put on to a breakfast plate. It is a known fact that the town of Blackpool dispenses more tomato ketchup, brown sauce, Colman's mustard and mayonnaise per capita than any other seaside holiday resort in the world; Berlin being the exception if Britain and America had been lucky enough for it to be surrounded by the Baltic or Caspian Sea.

Ah, Blackpool, inspired by the Eiffel Tower in Paris is one of the better fleshpots in England's green and pleasant land; As a boy, I can remember happiness, the mechanical clown sitting on a chair behind a glass cabinet at the entrance to the fun fair; rocking backward and forwards, laughing loudly similar to a demented hyena. I can also remember vividly, the Tower Ballroom and its circus, the zoo, the Aquarium and the Winter Gardens, dancing to British dance band leaders, Jack Hilton, Larry Brennen and Charlie Parker; ah, those were the days. I can also recall the Hall of Mirrors inside the Fun House, some concaved and some convexed where holiday-makers wearing plastic translucent *Pack-a-Mac* raincoats and *Rain Mate* hats would try to make themselves look slim after eating their way through enormous mounds of steak and kidney pudding, chips and mushy peas.

As part of Adolf Hitler's 'Operation Sea Lion' plan; the German invasion of Britain, the Nazi leader's intention was to turn this exclusive holiday and mobilization centre into being used for rest and recuperation for his troops; this was completely outrageous because he was always in bed and missed all of the fun, especially the morning of 6th June 1944. He also wanted a Swastika flag to be placed on top of the tower to warn the population in the Isle of Man that it was going to be their turn next to put the kettle on; it is of little wonder why the Manx flag is remarkably similar in comparison to a Swastika. They didn't starve either because of the abundance of herring which were opened up, their guts ripped out, the remains smoked and then made into kippers and, if that wasn't enough, they could always make gourmet meals from the fish and feed it to the cats before being entertained by a resident comedian, called, Norman Wisdom.

A Blackpool open-top landau mush once told me that during the war an American GI asked him the name of the Plaza he was driving on? After telling him it was the Pleasure Beach, the soldier replied, saying:

'Back home in the United States of America we have beaches five times the size of this.'

'Bullshit!' was the driver's reply, tinkling his bell to muffle the response.

'Hey man, what is that diner over there?' was the next question now waiting for an exaggerated comment as the GI sat regally, emblazoned with medals, on a black leather seat when the carriage passed by the Central Pier.

'It's a fish and chip shop.' the driver said, divulging the information without extra charge.

'In the United States of America, we have fish and chip diners six times the size of that.'

'What a load of Tommy rot.' the driver told him before pointing up towards the top of the tower on North Shore and continuing to say: 'And before you ask me what that thing is up there, Mac, it is a vinegar bottle for one of your fish and chip shops.'

'Hey man, where can a guy buy a decent steak around here?'

'Why don't you try Chicago?' the driver said, snaffling a ten-dollar bill from his hand.

Chapter One

Princes Dock, Glasgow, Scotland - Thursday 16th July 1931

The last minutes before departure: the announcement for all guests to leave the ship had been given; tearful embraces had been made and the final flurry; a mixture of excitement and apprehension, as friends and relations prepared to disembark, to file down the gangway and on to the ground to wait, subdued by now, to wave goodbye. The passengers, equally as silent, stood at the rail looking down at those below and remaining there as the quayside fell slowly away from them, the space between widening until they became small blurred shapes on the land they were all leaving behind for another country across the Atlantic.

For the young seventeen year-old Robert Bruce Hamilton-Brown the nine day voyage to Quebec was the prelude to an adventure which would take him and the Scottish Delegation of the Young Men's Christian Association the distance of several thousand miles, beginning in Quebec, continuing with a month of travelling, visiting, Montreal, Toronto, Cleveland U.S.A and New York City, via Washington where men build their business temples even higher.

"The Anchor-Donaldson Liner, the Good Ship T.S.S. *"Athenia"* will sail on the evening of Thursday 16th July from Princes Dock, Glasgow at 10.15 p.m. Liverpool will be reached soon after noon on Friday, after which the last port of call is Belfast, where the vessel arrives late the same evening. The ship will arrive in Quebec, Canada on Saturday, July 25th. The return sailing will take place from Anchor Line Wharf, New York on the T.S.S *"California"* on Saturday August 22nd at noon."

On the quayside stood Robert's father, William Hamilton-Brown and to his right was the family housekeeper, Miss Patricia McPherson, the daughter of a marmalade and jam manufacturer in Dundee, who, for some strange reason, became William's wife later that year. And, next to her were his twenty-six-year-old son, Hadrian, and Robert's childhood sweetheart, sixteen year-old Morag, the sister of his best friend and confidant, Alistair Campbell. Mister and Mrs Campbell were there too waving to their son who was now leaning forward off the rail on the port side of the ship taking photographs with his brand new 'Kodak' concertina camera, in between blowing kisses to his family.

Friends and family of The Scottish Delegation were also on the quayside watching a dock worker unravel a capstan before the rope was hauled up onto the deck.

This was the beginning of 'THE FIRST WORLD (Y.M.C.A), YOUNG MEN'S CHRISTIAN ASSOCIATION ASSEMBLY AND WORLD CONFERENCE (1931)', consisting of 936 World delegates and was held in Toronto, Canada beginning July 27th 1931.

The brotherhood were tasked before embarkation to make up their own diaries showing details of the voyage, itineraries, distance charts; a series of blank pages for autographs and photo frames. The Y.M.C.A at work in Great Britain; its motif, a hollow red triangle, similar to the hazard warning signs one sees on motorways and the highways of life. It was of interest to note that Robert Hamilton-Brown had pasted on the first page of his diary an artist's impression of the T.S.S *"California"* signed on the top two corners by the Master and Chief Officer of the *"Athenia"*. It was when the ship passed through the Belle Isle Straits, Robert became somewhat embarrassed when a senior member of the delegation looked at the artistry in his diary and pointed out to him that he was sailing on the wrong ship; this was typical of the young and naive, Hamilton-Brown who seemed to know it all and knew nothing; a young man with an anti and post meridian problem with his trousers, who ate luncheon at dinner, supper at noon and breakfast at midnight. Robert prematurely discontinued with further entries to his diary on Saturday July 25th the day he arrived in Canada; his last entry read: 'Glorious morning, I can now see the Province of Quebec. It is quite a change to see land. Saw about six whales this afternoon, interesting to see the coastline. Can see little villages scattered within a timber land in the background. Houses of French design. I experienced a brilliant lightning storm this afternoon. Saw white porpoise at Fathers Point.'

Members of The Scottish Delegation on-board consisted of twenty-two attending boys, and The Young men's assembly, consisting of eighteen members, including seven wives; two members were to join up in Toronto.

The aim, as outlined in the itinerary stated: "The party starts out on 16th on what will be one of the memorable experiences of our lives. Many of us will be visiting the great American Continent for the first time, and our travel and contact with people and places will be full of interest to us. It is all bound to be of the highest educational value.

Moreover, we are charged with the responsibility of representing Scotland at the World Conferences of the Young Men's Christian Association. These Conferences are being held for the first time on American soil, and the preparations for them have been thorough and comprehensive. They are likely to be some speech-making for the Movement, and full of significance for the youth of the nations.

We shall be meeting the representative young men and boys of fifty countries and shall enter with them into a unique fellowship. We shall share with them in shaping the future policy of our World Brotherhood in a day of intense and challenging opportunity.

We, therefore, set out with hearts full of hope, and with the earnest prayer that this adventure may have the rich blessing of God upon it."

The outward track chart of the Atlantic Ocean showed 2,994 nautical miles to Montreal, Quebec from Glasgow, Scotland, calling at Liverpool, England; the voyage taking in ten days of travel.

The return arrangements, however, were far more complicated because of American embarkation formalities in New York.

Vessels on the return journey usually sail from New York about noon. Delegates are advised to call at the Anchor Line Office, 25 Broadway, New York, directly they arrive in that city - certainly not later than first thing on morning of sailing. They will thus be able to check time of embarkation, secure their cabin numbers which have been definitely reserved, procure a supply of baggage labels, and generally be advised on details.

All passengers embarking at United States ports are to be in possession of Customs Permits prior to embarkation. These are obtained at the Barge Office, The Battery, New York, but consult the Anchor Line officials; the object of the permit is to satisfy the authorities that no American Income Tax is chargeable. There is no trouble attached to securing Permits, but it must be done personally.

The homeward track chart was fractionally different from New York U.S.A to Glasgow, Scotland and for most of the passengers on board the Anchor Line *"California"* could take in the sights of Quarantine, The Ambrose Lightship, Fire Island Lightship, The Nantucket Lightship, Malin Head, Moville and Greenock.

Captain James Black, the ship's Master, and J. M Clarke, the Chief and first officer ordered their ship T.S.S *"Athenia"* to be put into full steam ahead, sailing out from the murky waters of the Clyde and steering towards the Atlantic Ocean and the Irish Sea.

Alistair and Robert shared cabin number 149 on the starboard side next to an exit door leading out onto Deck 'A'. The accommodation was adequate for the nine-day trip to Quebec; however, Hamilton-Brown was not amused when he discovered he had to share washroom and ablution facilities with a multitude of single male passengers. Being allocated a two-berth cabin wasn't aesthetically pleasing to Robert, the Chancer; a significant bounder who during the first night chose to leave his first letter to Morag on the desk for his companion Alistair to read when he went out onto the deck to throw up over the side. In later years, when he was sailing the seven seas on his way to India, Robert was known to have said: 'If, I were to go it alone in a Fairhaven lake rowing boat, I would reach Calcutta far quicker than the Troop Ship *"Reina del Pacifica"*.

And Robert was known to have sung to his comrades in the airmen's mess:

"You tak the high road and I'll tak the low road
And I'll be in Durban before ye
For me and ma true love, we'll never meet again
In that bonnie, bonnie pub
On Loch Lomond"

This was quite interesting because unlike the *"Athenia"*, Robert in November1943, had no idea which route the *"Reina del Pacifica"* was going to take on its way to the Far East.

A poem, called 'Night Thoughts' was inside the letter to Morag; it is a verse written by the Scottish poet, Fred. W. Holton:

Night Thoughts

How often have I dared to swear?
That, wild horses could not tear
Apart the two of us!
Yet why did I, the other night,
Surrender you without a fight
To a corporation bus

From this moment on the relationship between Robert and Alistair was somewhat soured and it became evident that there was a battle raging inside the Douglas camp, dissent amongst its lower ranks. Alistair in later years wrote: 'of all the tables and chairs there are in the world, Robert, why, oh why, didja have to sit down at mine?' this had been when they were taking their lunch break at Clyde Bank Grammar School.

Robert Hamilton-Brown began his diary of the trip, Thursday July 16th. "Sailed from Princes Dock, 10.15 p.m about; passed the T.S.S *"Transylvania"* on the way out. Alistair Campbell, leaning over the side taking photographs of the Clyde. It's a wonderful sight to see the Clyde lit up at night and to observe the valley works bathed in floodlight; quite cold tonight, turned in at about midnight. A few members from the Y.M.C.A Scottish delegation are suffering with sea sickness."

The poetical thoughts became evident when he describes the dreams he had during the first night on-board the *"Athenia"*; his journal continuing with, "Didja?" by, Karla Juul:

Didja ?

Didja ever sleep in the woods at night
An' have yer heart near stopped with fright –
Didja ?

15

Didja hear the coyotes' mournful cry
An' little footpads stealin' by –
Didja ?

Didja listen hard an' hold your breath
An' try an' lie as still as death –
Didja ?

Didja hear the snap o' a fallen twig
An' feel sure 'twas broke by somethin' big –
Didja ?

Didja 'magine if yu'd try to look
Yu'd see two eyes just like a spook –
Didja ?
An' so yu'd close yer eyes real tight
An' try an' sleep with all your might –
But didja ?

Didja wonder when yu' woke at dawn
An' the woods were filled with sounds of morn;
The peep of birds an' the rustle of grouse,
An' the chatter of squirrels that made them rouse;
An' you looked around on God's green world,
At the camp-fire smoke as it upward curled,
An' the smell o' the fryin' bacon so good
Made yu' glad yu'd slept out in the wood;
Didja wonder, when things looked so harmless and bright,
What's made yu' feel so scared in the night
Didja ?

He continued to write in his diary the following day: "The steward called us at 7.15 a.m. It was a fresh morning and breakfast was at 7.45. Passed the Isle of Man at about 9.15 a.m. heading for Liverpool; had luncheon at 12.45 p.m. Approaching Liverpool's Albert Dock at 2 p.m.;

the river Mersey is about six times as wide as the Clyde; ships, docks, cranes, and buildings on every side. We anchored opposite the Canadian Pacific Dock and took on passengers from tenders. Up anchor and turned about 4 p.m. Some rain in afternoon before making for Belfast. I made for the ship's library; the books quite old, some written by Francis Bacon and some printed by William Caxton himself. However, found a cosy corner to bury my head in words of wisdom."

Later, my thoughts were that Norman Wisdom had a great deal to answer for. Robert writes: "Reading makes a full man; there need be no loneliness – no friendlessness if we make friends of the great minds locked up in books, always ready to talk to us."

The scratching of Robert's fountain pen was beginning to annoy fellow British passengers who were sitting in the library trying to achieve a moment of silence away from the raucous Canadian tombola crowd on Deck 'B', he continues to write: "By early evening, the ship was rolling badly, strong wind blowing and the sea very rough; the skyline blue and not a cloud to be seen as The Good Ship "*Athenia*" sailed off the coast of Ireland."

Robert, for the first time on-board the ship, wore the '*Jock frock*', his provocative Scottish highland kilt; the distinctive green Douglas tartan ostentatiously parading along the decks, elevating nautically in the fresh breeze, occasionally swaying in time with the roll of the ship; a vulgar *skin doo* protruding out from one of his socks just waiting in metaphor to cut someone's throat. The irony of it all was that Sir Walter Scott may have been hiding in a lifeboat just waiting for the ideal opportunity to jettison Robert overboard and then to see him ride away and disappear into the back of the blue beyond on the crest of a wave. Then, there was the drone of Scottish bagpipes coming from the engine room; it was interesting to learn, however, that one of the attending young men from the delegation had brought the pipes with him to annoy the French after the British army, commanded by General Wolf, stormed the Heights of Abraham in Quebec in 1759. The piper was confined to the bowels of the ship because of a series of complaints by the ship's Bingo crooner concerning the noise.

It was on Thursday July 25th the ship held its fancy dress ball in the concert room. The evening began with tombola; the bingo caller who was called, Jimmy Murdoch was wearing a huge bonnet, a 'Tam-o'-shanter', a brimless wool cap with a bobble in the centre which could only be described as an over-sized Scottish pancake; a red and white gingham sarong, a table cloth surrounding his waist, and a pair of rolled down knee length woollen socks were untidily worn on top of his size ten-inch ammunition boots.

'And for all you ladies, six and four, key to my door, six and nine, sixty-nine.' he would call out; it was amazing how many times those numbers were used during the voyage. Ironically, that particular evening there was a man dressed in a tutu, purporting to be a ballet dancer who won a full-house.

It was at 4.00 a.m that morning, the steward called Alistair and Robert to see a rogue iceberg. The weather conditions out on deck were extreme; very cold, misty and the sea very rough. Angus McKenzie, the steward, was hoping Robert would catch a cold or contract pneumonia as the iceberg floated gracefully by underneath an early morning moonlit sky; his wish in retribution for not serving Robert's afternoon pot of tea at the correct temperature.

At day break, the sun made an appearance astern the ship, bringing the huge block of ice more into focus; an orange glow shimmering on the side, making it look like a well-sucked Fox's glacier mint as it majestically and silently moved in a southerly direction.

Many photographs were taken that morning, but unfortunately, Robert had forgotten to take the lens cap off his camera and in the afternoon was forced to search inside the ship's souvenir shop for a suitable glossy postcard, depicting a rogue iceberg; preferably one without a polar bear superimposed and sliding down a crevasse into the water.

Robert and Alistair returned to their beds only to be called at seven-fifteen by McKenzie; the man with the silver-plated coffee pot who could gain access to cabins faster than the ship's cat.

After the voyage to Quebec was over, Robert Hamilton-Brown would tell a story about being nervous and having to watch his back every time he went to the washroom to take a shower in case a senior Y.M.C.A delegate would insist on picking up his bar of *Pears* soap.

Chapter Two

At breakfast the first morning - Friday 17th July

The round tables in the huge restaurant began to fill up with passengers at seven forty-five; the captain's table in the centre of the room was the focal point surrounded by high-backed chairs; the geography of the seating arrangements in the restaurant seemed to be in an order of the all-important privilege and class.

Alistair and Robert were sitting at table number five, a long table next to one of the bulkheads. The twenty-two junior members of the delegation were seated at the same table opposite to one another, with one senior member at the head; the table arrangement was similar to an officer's ward room that one would expect to find on-board a Royal Navy battleship. The "soda-pop" and "penny whistle" club, as it was called later, waited patiently for one of the stewards to arrive with a pot of coffee, the prelude to a hearty Scottish breakfast, consisting of a variety of cereals, boiled eggs, and of course a plate of sliced fried sausage, black pudding, fried eggs, bacon and *Heinz* baked beans in tomato sauce; tea, warm toast and miniature jars of *McPherson's* marmalade and jam were to follow.

It was in Nov 1993, Robert Hamilton-Brown mentioned to his wife, Beatrice: "little did I know that fifty years ago, I would be sailing into the Irish Sea from Liverpool on-board a troop ship bound for India and twelve years earlier I was to be a passenger on the T.S.S "Athenia" following the same route into the Atlantic on my way to Canada; classic case of *déjà vus*, wouldn't you say?" he added.

Seated at the Attending Boys' table were:

Nairne, Stanley	Parker, Lauchian Ross
Allan, Joss Christie	Reid, Hugh Murray
Buchannan, John Macalister	Reid, Jan Laird Farmer.
Dawson, John Easton	Roxburgh, William.
Hamilton-Brown, Robert Bruce	Campbell, Alistair
Hudson, Robert Murray	Shaw, Robert Wilson.

Mackenzie, John William	Shepherd, John Alfred
McEwan, Tom	Smith, Alexander.
McLaren, Hugh Cameron	Steven, Neil McNair.
Martin, William	Tindal, John.
Crawford, John	Service, Quintin Miller.
Mr Thomas	W Swanson

And seated at the Young Men's table were:

Lightbody, Mr. & Mrs. Henry.

Donaldson, Mr. & Mrs. H.J. (Stowaways)

Duncan, Mr. & Mrs. Robert.

Gavin, Mr. Hugh Drummond.

Johnston, Mr. Duncan.

Kaye, Mr. & Mrs. Bertram David.

Macdonald, Mr. & Mrs. J. A.

Murdoch, Mr. & Mrs. John.

Norrie, Mr. & Mrs. G.O. (Stowaways)

Shields, Mr. Malcolm. Irvine.

Swanson, Mr. Thomas. W.

It was a brisk fresh morning as the ship sailed past the Isle of Man at 9.15 am, heading for Liverpool. The smoking room on the port side had a piano and was used shortly after breakfast by members of the delegation to sing hymns, chants and Scottish songs; other passengers on-board, who wished to contribute to the harmonies, were cordially invited under the proviso, they didn't try to upstage senior members of the delegation.

The ship rang out with music beginning with a battle hymn written by G.J Webb:

> "Stand up Stand up for Jesus,
> Ye soldiers of the Cross
> Lift high his royal banner
> It must not suffer loss

From victory unto victory
His army shall be led
Till every foe is vanquished
And Christ is Lord indeed

Stand up Stand up for Jesus
This trumpet call obeys
Forth in the mighty conflict
In this his glorious day..........."

'It must be the baked beans they all ate for breakfast.' a member of the ships' crew was heard saying.

'One day I will call it a day, but on that day, I will suddenly become famous, and then it will be far too late.' Robert Hamilton-Brown wrote in one of his diaries after listening in to a radio report during the war years of Russian Red Army troop movements which followed the German defeat in Stalingrad. 'Oh, the German army will never learn.' he said to one of his fellow RAF buddies, Leading Aircraftsman, Keith Reynolds.

'Napoleon Bonaparte hadn't taken into account severe weather conditions when he retreated from Moscow and subsequently was defeated in the battlefields at Waterloo.' Hamilton-Brown went on.

Robert, in metaphor, was literally stopped in his tracks when he was stationed at RAF Kirkham after Keith Reynolds said to him: 'Now I know why I had so much trouble trying to get on-board one of the trains in London.'

If fate was Robert's destiny he was surely there, singing hymns and chanting songs with a semi-religious voice which stayed with him all through his life, persecuting the English, disliking people and demonizing the Catholic Church; if Hadrian's Wall was in Berlin and the Brandenburg Gate in Carlisle, then he would have been a member of the *Stasi*, East Germany's Secret Police Force.

The Soviet Russian leader, Marshal Joseph Stalin was Robert's hero and Lenin, his mentor; paradoxically, there is enough ammunition to posthumously take L.A.C. Robert Bruce Hamilton-Brown to the Tower of London and shot for treason or banged up for the rest of his life.

His job in the RAF was as a 'Silent Peeper' and intelligence radio listener, reporting on troop movements, primarily, in Western Europe and apart from the British Army's General Wingate, he was undoubtedly the busiest man in the Far East.

In a letter to his first wife, Norma on November 11th, 1943, he writes:

"My dear Wife,

By the time you receive this letter, I will have sailed into the blue.

I go, not without protest, because with all heart, I wanted to be with you, but then greater issues than our personal lives are at stake. I don't mean, a vaunted Empire, a stupid king, or a blood-stained flag. Nay, infinitely more, the freedom of the peoples of the world is threatened with a thousand years of darkness. Art and culture, decency and honour, are being violated before our eyes and the women of the world are being raped. I go in the hope that, in some small way, I may be able to bring to a close, this age of pain and suffering. I go in the wake of the Great Red Army and the people of Soviet Russia.

I have pledged myself to be faithful to you, only death can see that pledge.

Pray for me in this uncertain hour, pray for all the people presently in the theatre of suffering. May it be, perhaps, we all may find a place in the warm sunshine, where under a shady tree we may rest, and watch the day drop like a ripe fruit, into the lap of eternity, and all around there will be peace?

By the time you receive this letter, I will have vanished into the blue. I go not without protest, because I know so well that much of what we are called upon to make sacrifice for, is but the pious utterings of a fascism class who are warmongers in time of peace, and would be peace-makers in time of war.

I have no illusions as to the exact position of the working classes who hold vested interests in this class-ridden society; nevertheless, if a true socialistic foundation of life is to be established, this conflict must first of all be terminated in their favour, even if it means for the present, a defending of the bad against the worst.

I go, in the wake, and with the vision of the Great Red Army, and the Soviet peoples, to assist them in the liberation of subjected peoples everywhere.

I go, strong in my determination to bring about an end to see forms of fascism, imperialism, vested interest, class privilege, and all such products of individual and collective greed.

I go because of us, Norma, because of my love for you, because of the many immortal things we have known and buried away above the night, away above the dust of the dead Gods, alone.

The "call" is our call, Norma.

The "call" is us, Norma, written by one who never doubted our existence.

O' divine and sacred one, pray that we may be spared, to know a short season together on this earth, pray that our souls maybe one of immortal love, and as night falls, may we know that peace which passeth all understanding.

My love is yours, my soul yours, yes, and should the logic of our time demand my life, that must I also give, but not for a slogan, or a class or sentimentalism, but for you, for us, for our faith, for our vision, for our hope, for those who die to free people everywhere. Robert.

November 11th, 1943 Draft No 5599, 105 P.D.C. Blackpool"

The great paradox of Hamilton-Brown's communist and socialite leanings was that Soviet Russia was an atheist country, the inner circle, non-believers of the Holy bible and associate biblical records. Stalin's army were to become known as the most ruthless soldiers in the world, bayoneting women and children as they swept through Northern Germany in 1945; who helped the American First Army to massacre thousands of German troops by blocking up entrances and exits to underground barracks after drowning them with fierce gushes of water, and latterly he built a fence higher and longer than the Great Wall of China to keep Slavonic speaking peoples in, and the rest of the world out.

Marshal Joseph Stalin murdered millions of his own people because of their unorthodox, anti-communist and Christian beliefs; the soulless river banks of Saint Petersburg representing the largest graveyard on earth, extending five miles long. Somewhere to rest their weary heads after a hard day's work; mixed with concrete and clay they lay forever.

This was what Hamilton-Brown in his moments of so-called wisdom believed; his theatres of suffering and personal sacrifices, to whom were they meant?

Joseph Stalin remarked: "You remove the man, you remove the problem!"

"The World's Debt to U.S.S.R." an article by George Bilainkin, was pasted in Robert's scrapbook in January 1944 and read:

"So long as man moves freely over our universe so long will the world feel an eternal debt to the U.S.S.R. for the flexible heroism of those who saved humanity from a thousand years darker than the Middle Ages; for the defenders and victors of Stalingrad were the defenders of all Western civilization, and the United States of America. Month after month the siege of Stalingrad waged, until nearly all the lone stacks and crumbling walls that remained of the Red City were under Nazi domination.

"Suddenly the future of the entire world rested in the almost frozen hands of those tired, shivering Russians.

"Do we dare, even now in the certain sight of victory, to think, without trembling, what would have been the inevitable sequel to the fall of democracy's citadel with Stalingrad under the Nazi flag?

"The Germans, losing hundreds of thousands of slave troops, would have raced down the Volga, would have captured seven-tenths of Russia's oil supply in the Caucasus, would have cut off Persia, would have reached Afghanistan, and would have stood challenging the door to India, the Empire's brightest jewel.

"Triumphantly, the Nazis might have joined hands with Japan. Egypt, the heart of democracy's bastion, might have been captured and the war of the world continued for seven years.

"Today the world salutes Stalin, historic military genius; Stalingrad his namesake city, the Red heroes of Stalingrad who changed world history by giving their lives on civilization's altar at the call of Soviet Russia's leader.

"Great Britain again salutes the Anglo-Soviet alliance, a treaty which shall give concord to men begging to be left to think, speak, write and work in peace."

Another newspaper article, describing Lenin and his doctrine was pasted in Hamilton-Brown's scrapbook during the same month and read:

"Lenin, the civilian who never wore a uniform became a master of military strategy and defeated the seasoned generals of many armies, including the German." Robert mentions Lenin's proclamation, "The Socialist Fatherland is in Danger; the first call for a "scorched earth" policy is to be in the Ukraine.

"Exert every effort to prevent the enemy from capturing the country's wealth. On retreating, destroy all railways, blow up and set fire to the railway buildings, and send all rolling stock-railway cars and locomotives to the East, into the interior of the country. All stocks of grain and other food, as well as all valuable property in danger of falling into enemy hands must be destroyed. Do everything in your own power to hinder the enemy advance. Set ambushes for him. Use firearms and cold steel against him.

"Make sure your rear is safe, and to do that, exterminate all spies, profiteers, marauders, hooligans, counter-revolutionary agents and senior members of the Y.M.C.A. who insist on you bending down to pick up their soap; they must be shot on the spot."

"England the Unready," an article written by F. O'Hanlon of Worthing, Essex, and sent to the 'CAVALCADE' newspaper in February 1944:

"Thank God for H.G. Well's article and CAVALCADE for publishing it.

Two years ago, I wrote that the question is whether Stalin can win the war before Churchill loses it. Churchill has some brilliant qualities, but he is the world's worst strategist and unfortunately, he thinks he is the world's best.

Eloquent orations and glorified with Cook's Tours with battalions of W.A.A.Fs and W.R.E.Ns do not win wars. In January 1943, we were assured that large-scale plans for attacks on the Continent had been made at the Casablanca circus next November. If Churchill remains in his present job, shall we be given another oration explaining why nothing has been accomplished in 1944, but that wonders will happen in 1945.

Churchill must give up the job of Minister of Defence. Ernest Bevin is the best man for the job, for he is the only one with the guts to sack Grigg, Amery, Hoare, Maitland, Wilson, Brooke and the die-hards of the War Office.

Russia's Contribution, Mr. Churchill thought it most natural that Russia, our Soviet friends and Allies whose problems were of a different nature did not appreciate the complications and difficulties which attended all amphibious operations on a large scale. But Mr. Churchill added another moving and sincere tribute to his repeated eulogies on the Russian achievements. "The advance of their armies from Stalingrad to the Dniester River, with vanguards reaching out towards the Pruth, a distance of 900 miles in a single year." stressed Mr. Churchill, "constitutes the greatest cause of Hitler's undoing. Not only have the Hun invaders been driven from the lands they have ravaged but the guts of the German Army have been largely torn out by Russian valour."

Meanwhile, Reuter reports on January 4th, 1944 of U.S.A.'s Plans for Commercial Imperialism: Senator E.C Johnson declared yesterday in the "Rocky Mountain News" Denver, Colorado, "The Great Powers of the United Nations would divide the post-war world into spheres of influence. While the United States had no territorial aspirations, "it secretly hopes to develop commercial imperialism on a gigantic scale." He predicted that Russia would dominate the Baltic States, northern Balkan States, Poland, Czechoslovakia, Germany and France. "Britain would dominate Norway, Holland and Belgium, including the latter's colonies and it would also dominate the Dark Continent and the Mediterranean States of Spain, Italy and Greece."

He added that Britain would have "the unique task of fighting communism within her sphere of influence and at the same time co-operating closely with Marshal Stalin." Japan would be reduced to her original islands and nationalistic China would be encouraged and expected to favour white nations by granting valuable trade concessions. Britain, Russia and the United States would exercise a sort of joint over lordship in the orient. Senator Johnson added there would be a post-war world division and foreshadowed Britain's Difficulty.

Norma Mulholland, who became Hamilton-Brown's twenty-six-year-old wife just one week before his departure from Blackpool, couldn't understand a single word of his illegible scribbling on unlined paper and she will be remembered before she died in the summer of 1946, saying: 'I wonder where Robert keeps his investments because they are certainly not in his trousers.'

Robert, the self-appointed Bolshevik revolutionist, had the habit of correcting people by continually slapping his thigh and afterwards rummaging around in a trouser pocket to find pieces of paper which contained investment details and how much they were worth. His aim in life was trying to impress his colleagues, so-called friends and family, and for those who went against him were called bovine names that one usually associates with farm yard stock.

It was my wife and Robert's step-daughter, Elizabeth Grace Balfour from his second marriage, who in later years said: 'he is the only person I knew who could peel an orange in his pocket and then went on to quote some of the lyrics to four Beatles songs; wonderful words and music written by John Lennon and Sir Paul McCartney and are called: "Mean Mr. Mustard", "Revolution", "You never give me Your Money" and of course, "The End".

> "Mean Mister Mustard sleeps in the park
> Shaves in the dark
> Trying to save paper
> Sleeps in a hole in the road
> Saving up to buy some clothes
> Keeps a ten bob up his nose
> Such a mean old man -
> Such a mean old man

His auntie Jean works in a shop
She's a go getter
Takes him out to look at the Queen
Only place that he's ever been
Always shouts out something obscene
Such a dirty old man
Dirty old man"

*

"You say you'll change the constitution, Well, you know we all want to change your head.
You tell me it's the institution, Well, you know, you better free your mind instead.
But if you go carrying pictures of Chairman Mao,
You ain't going to make it with anyone, anyhow.
Don't you know it's gonna be alright, alright, alright, alright"

*

"You never give me your money
You only give me your funny paper
And in the middle of negotiations
You break down"

*

"And in the end
The love you take is equal to the love you make"

Chapter Three

Sea sickness on-board the Anchor-Donaldson Liner "Athenia" on Friday, July 17th, 1931

Robert Hamilton-Brown had written in one of his diaries:

"The ship's pharmacy was busy today; the vessel rolling from side-to-side during a very heavy rainfall and high gale-force winds as we headed west off the coast of Ireland."

Robert somehow managed to continue to write and contribute to his diary but that was until he had the pleasure of meeting fellow passengers, Miss Alison Rankin, an Anglo-Scottish Canadian College student from Montreal, Canada, *Mademoiselle* Francoise La Cheminant, a French Canadian, also a college student from Montreal and a young mathematics and geography school teacher, Miss Victoria Brunswick from New York City. He continues to write underneath the dates:

Saturday July 18th.

"Rose at 7.15 am feeling even sicker; ship rolling badly. I didn't go down to breakfast but had a bowl of soup and a roll for dinner at seven. I was sick again after luncheon and went to my bed early. However, it was a lovely day with a fresh breeze blowing."

Sunday July 19th.

"Lovely day, but the sea is still rough. Put on my kilt today. Took a few snaps today. Lay on deck in the sun. Played 'Hunch cuddy' during the evening and ate a light dinner in the restaurant. I went to my bed relatively early."

Monday July 20th.

"Lovely day, fresh breeze blowing, and I am feeling much better today. I played 'Bridge' all morning. The delegation practiced a few Scottish songs during the afternoon for Toronto. I went to bed relatively early."

Tuesday July 21st.

"The sea is very rough today; strong winds blowing. The sky is very blue and not a cloud to be seen. Lay on deck in the afternoon. I was not feeling too great."

Wednesday July 22nd.

"It is a dull morning and has turned out to be a lovely day. I am still feeling very light and lay on my bunk all afternoon. Another delegation practice this afternoon and I am hoping to see *Belle Isle* tonight. I went down to a concert and enjoyed some very much. Lying off *Belle Isle*; fog is very thick. I am feeling much better."

Thursday July 23rd.

"Steward called us at 4.00 am to see iceberg; this is the first I have seen. I took photographs of some. We are now sailing through *Belle Isle Straits*. It is a lovely morning. Had photographs taken of the group at the stern of the ship today and then we were all taken through the engine room, it was a wonderful sight. Met Alison Rankin during the afternoon and took her to the fancy dress ball held in the concert room at night. Introduced to Francoise, Alison's seventeen-year-old school friend and fellow passenger. It was a beautiful sunset and saw Northern Lights."

Friday July 24th.

"It is a glorious morning and I am feeling extremely tired; my legs feel as though they belong to another part of my body. I can now see the Province of Quebec and is quite a change to see land. Saw about six whales this afternoon. It is interesting to see the coastline where I can see little villages scattered within a timber land in the background. Houses of French design. I experienced a brilliant lightning storm in afternoon and saw white porpoise at *Father's Point*."

*

There was nothing more to report in Robert Bruce Hamilton-Browns Y.M.C.A. World Conference diary; pages to this day remain blank, which were from Saturday July 25th up to, and including Monday August 31st, 1931. However, I revealed in August 1999 when my mother-in-law died of pneumonia and chronic arthritis in Streatham aged eighty-six that another diary which belonged to Hamilton-Brown, was found in a locked trunk in the attic of No 6 Holloway Road, closely guarded by two communistic 'stool' pigeons called Stan and Len. One of Robert Hamilton Brown's favourite jokes in later years, apart from the ceramic laughing cow which dispensed cigarettes from a hole in its backside, was to say: 'Did you hear about the guy who knocked on the door of the Russian Embassy in London and asked if Len was in?'

Another one of his jokes was to say, the reason why Russian men don't wear underpants is because their *Chernobyl* will fall out. It was quite some time before the penny dropped and only after a delectable Russian lady courier called Kate Chekhov, based in Malta, eloquently explained to me in English, how the punch line came about. Kate said she had great difficulty comparing the words: 'hustle' and 'hassle', and then she went on to say: 'A Maltese "Sleazebag" of a man who was standing at one of the tables in a casino asked, if I could tell the difference between sex and conversation because if I couldn't he said I would have to lie down so he could talk the pants off me.'

So, I said to Kate, 'what on earth promulgated him to ask you that question?' to which she replied:

'He thought I was on the game, and before sending him away with a *pea* in his ear, I said to him in no uncertain terms, not to hustle me because I was playing roulette and he was not to hassle me ever again.'

It was during an afternoon swim in the hotel pool, I asked Kate: 'Why is it that Russian women can't pass by a mirror without checking themselves?' She replied by saying:

'It is because we *"Muscovites"* are so incredibly beautiful, and what you see today, may not be in evidence tomorrow.'

'I suppose it is a bit like the German people;' I said to her, glancing up to see two enormous Bavarian slap dancers trying to empty the pool; 'eat and drink all you can today because it may not be there tomorrow; this is what they say and why most of them are so obese.' I added.

Needless to say, my wife, Elizabeth, was not amused when she returned from Angel's hairdressing salon in Valletta to find me cavorting with a Russian doll in the deep end, and it was early the following morning when Kate Chekhov became a passenger on the next *Aeroflot* flight back to Moscow. I suppose this was only to be expected, especially when your wife's brother-in-law is the Hon. Alfred Joseph Mizzi, Member of the National Executive Malta Labour Party and has the power to make foreigners disappear where there is an abundance of ready-mix concrete to fill in another Maltese hole in the ground.

Interestingly, there were a few Belgium people who disappeared off the island without trace when the new motorway was built in1992.

'Having had your ears lowered makes it easier for you to listen in at ground level.' Elizabeth pointed out before continuing with her threats to feed me to the sharks if I so much as looked at another woman.

'Does that include Natasha, the hotel's Bulgarian breakfast waitress?' I asked, inadvertently knowing full well Natasha and I could possibly end up off the coast of Sicily with a Great White following on behind.

Elizabeth, adding more Maltese ambiance to the holiday atmosphere by asking:

'Do you know what you do with Russian budgies, Henry, if they can't shut up and stop looking at themselves in a mirror?'

'Send them back to Moscow?' I replied.

'No, darling, you put a cover over the cage.'

*

The contradictory entries written on the pages of the two diaries confirmed what Alistair Campbell had known for years that Robert Bruce Hamilton-Brown was a charlatan, a bounder and a serial womanizer. The man with the golden sporran, who was into compounding of interest when he lent money out to members of the delegation for double amounts back. It wasn't uncommon to see him fiddling with scrappy bits of paper with an 'I owe you five pounds' written in bold across the top in indelible ink. In later years it was thought he had an off-shore bank account in Jersey and more wealth stashed inside a bank in the tax-free haven of Geneva in Switzerland. Elizabeth and I often wondered why several bars of *Toblerone* milk chocolate were in evidence in No 6 Holloway Road, Streatham; he said he had a craving for Swiss confectionary, but it was revealed that they were a mountainous collection of complementary praline bars handed to passengers on-board flights returning to London from Zurich.

The night of Thursday 23rd July during the fancy dress ball Hamilton-Brown had another '*Jock Frock*' kilt admirer; Alison's friend, Francoise who was dressed up as a belly dancer.

Alison had visited the ship's fancy dress outfit locker room early that evening and chose to be a cat wearing bright red lipstick and whiskers painted on her face with an eyebrow pencil. This was what Hamilton-Brown wanted, a cruise of a life-time, taking in more sights than he had expected.

During the course of the evening, Jimmy Murdoch, the ship's entertainer, gigolo and floating embarrassment, announced the winner of the fancy dress competition and it was no surprise to the participants that Hamilton-Brown won first-prize, an engraved 'Anchor Donaldson Line' silver spoon, for being the prick of the evening when a judge, a homosexual choirmaster from the University of British Columbia in Vancouver, Canada took great delight in watching Robert's kilt ride up high when he performed the highland fling and screaming like a demented hyena. It was of little wonder why the voluptuous Alison Rankin came second, and the provocative Francoise came third after they were considered by a man dressed as a nun to be twenty-five to one contenders to win the competition.

Meanwhile, Alistair Campbell having decided not to participate in a rude and erotic maritime demonstration similar to the *Lido* and the *Follies Bergère* in Paris was standing in the wings with his arms tightly folded waiting for eight bells to toll heralding the time and before going to the restaurant to have his cocoa supper.

The school teacher from New York, Victoria Brunswick, caused a sensation when she danced to a Charleston number, "*Black Bottom*", wearing a costume consisting of a skirt made of a string of artificial plastic bananas and little else. Her erotic dancing and near nude performance were driving Murdoch to the brink of insanity when later caught knocking on the door of a swab deck locker in the First-Class accommodation after the ball was over.

Having read Robert's diaries, my interpretation of the entire evening was to recall the Scottish poem, penned by Innes Tarquin Farquhar, the spin-doctor to Robert the Bruce at the battle of Bannockburn on June 24th, 1314.

Ode to a Prick

There once was a bird that sat on a thistle

Pricked its arse and made it whistle

Understandably, Alistair, the fancy-dressed Lord Kitchener, was not amused when later that evening, he saw Robert disappearing into a cabin situated on Deck 'B', rolling one hand around a curvaceous scantily-clad backside and the other holding on to the tail end of a black and white cat. That night Hamilton-Brown, with the exception of the ship's stoker, was undoubtedly the busiest man on-board when he accidently rubbed shoulders with Victoria Brunswick when he was walking unsteadily back to his cabin.

The banana lady from 'All Saints' proprietary school in Brooklyn was travelling alone and had somehow managed to change into something more respectable, a tiny "cloche" hat here, a velvet "cocktail frock" there, *Gold Stripe Adjustable* silk stockings, exclusive 'House of Miller' burgundy suede high-heeled court shoes; the buckle effect done with interlaced strips of patent, ideal for little women who live at that terrific New York pace. A matching handbag completed the outfit and befitting a lady living alone in a delightful apartment on Fifth Avenue, 59th Street, in prestigious uptown Manhattan.

'Travelling alone is very trying, don't you think, Robert?' Victoria said, checking the time on her recently acquired diamond encrusted *Cartier* wristwatch which had been given to her as a present for her twenty-first birthday. 'Staying in the Park Lane Hotel in Piccadilly, London for six weeks can be so tiring and such a bore, don't you think, Robert?' she continued to say and at the same time trying to stop him from falling asleep. 'Would you like to have a nightcap in my cabin? I have a large bottle of gin and some tonic water, if you so desire.' Miss Brunswick so eloquently asked in an uptown fast pace Manhattan accent.

'It's a wide world, this, but no matter where you are tomorrow you will find "Canada Dry"; the Champagne of Ginger ale.' Robert was able to say, trying to impress her with his temperance and advertising skills.

'I like young men who don't smoke and drink, they are more vibrant and energetic.' she said, pulling his tartan tie and hooking him into her First-Class cabin.

'Tell me, Robert, is that a gun in your purse, or are you just pleased to see me?' she said, quoting one of May West's famous lines. 'And, aren't you that regular Scots person I saw in the London '*Daily Mail*' Atlantic Edition newspaper; the man with the bag?'

'Sadly, yes.' he replied, having forgotten the ordeal of the ship's Daily Mail press photographer insisting on him wearing his kilt; the '*Daily Telegraph*' or the '*Times*' media would have been the better option to hide his loose change.

'Well, in that case, Robert, I will just have to find out myself just exactly what is up those nine yards of moth-eaten tableware.' she suggested, before lighting up a '*Lucky Strike*' cigarette with a view to fumigating the ship.

'When you smoke, one has to consider ones Adam's apple; don't rasp your throat with harsh irritants.' Robert advised.

One must agree with all I said, he was thinking. Victoria had told him she had been smoking Lucky Strikes for an extremely long time, and had always liked them, but she also liked the way they were advertised. The advertising seemed to her to be the truth, and it wasn't always bonking, knocking somebody or something!

'Don't worry yourself unnecessarily.' Victoria said admiring his sporran, wondering what was in it and more importantly what was behind it. 'Just relax and eat some shortbread, Horton's fast-frozen ice cream, or something.' she added.

'No thank you, Victoria, I have already eaten........'

'.... and, why do regular Scots persons carry knives around with them, protruding from their socks?' she interrupted, inquisitively.

'I think it has something to do with skinning rabbits, keeping wolves away from your tent door and warding off queers in Central Park and muggers in the Subway of New York City.'

'Did you know, Robert that New York City has the tallest erection in the world, it is called the Empire State Building?'

'I am going to Canada and the United States of America with a purpose, not to look at erections.' Robert said, in no uncertain terms and without further explanation.

'I thought the porpoises were in the ocean, following the ship which is currently steering on a course of 49.16 N and 65.14 W towards Quebec.' she, so knowledgably conveyed to him.

'There is something to be said about geography teachers,' Robert said, continuing with his unintelligible mumblings. 'It must give you a good sense of direction.' he added.

'Well, it does help to know where one is going and as for your Great Britain, it is a place that never looked better looking back.' she said, looking at herself in Robert's highly polished black patent leather highland dress shoes.

'The Scottish Delegation will be spending the remainder of the conferences in New York and we are all hoping to arrive on Monday, the seventeenth of August by train from Washington.' he added, unfastening a new device on the top of his shirt called a button.

'Well, in that case, all you boys had better come up and see me sometime.' she suggested, quoting another one of the famous actress's classic lines.

'Would you like us to visit you, one at a time or all at once? Robert replied.

It wasn't until the early hours of Friday morning Robert returned to his cabin battered and bruised from his experiences on Deck 'B' and Alistair made a point of reminding him it was their second-last day on-board the "Athenia" before arriving in Montreal, Quebec on Saturday and he needed his sleep.

Chapter Four

A bridge so far and far too long

By daybreak the ship had changed course and was now sailing along Canada's St Lawrence Seaway towards the St Lawrence River; the Province of Quebec clearly visible on both port and starboard sides. Leaning back against the rail at the stern of the ship one could see the Notre Dame Mountain range to the left and the Lauren tide Scarp peninsula to the right.

The distance remaining to the port of Cosmopolitan Montreal was approximately eight hundred nautical miles, allowing enough time for Robert to visit the ship's barber shop to have a much needed short back and sides haircut, having been told he looked like a Neolithic black-haired orang-utan which had somehow managed to board a ship bound for Canada, and twelve years later succeeding to escape the Glaswegian jungle by jumping over Hadrian's Wall en route to India.

The restaurant was pleasantly full of passengers wanting their breakfast and for Robert, it was an embarrassment to see three ladies, two of them completely unaware of what had been happening inside another First-Class cabin in the early hours of Friday morning.

'There are no prizes for guessing what you got up to last night, Robert, and I hope for your sake Morag doesn't get to know any of this because she will have your nuts on a skewer and roast them alfresco on our summer grill.' Alistair said to him over the breakfast table.

'Well, she won't know, will she, unless someone tells her?' Robert nervously replied.

'Unless you have forgotten, Morag is my sister and I don't want to see her hurt because of an insensitive bounder like yourself.'

Apart from the snap, crackle and pop noises coming out from a bowl of *Rice Crispies*, breakfast was eaten in complete silence.

The ship's barber was called Frederick Wormhole, an ex-cider apple grower from Taunton in Somerset. He asked Robert if he had enjoyed the fancy dress ball the previous evening because from where he was sitting in the concert room, he could see most of what was going on between him and two refined young ladies of good pedigree.

'I thought the name pedigree was attributed to an impeccable breed of dog?' Robert said to Frederick when he thought the word 'breeding' would have been a far better choice.

'It is, sir.' said Frederick when he parted Robert's hair with a large steel comb which wouldn't have been out of place inside a veterinary clinic.

Robert was sitting in a chair facing a mirror, the bevelled reflection spoiling his image by too much late-night revelling and over-indulgence: soda pop, Horton's ice cream, Weenies and more than enough glasses of tonic water to power a bright red Moffat fire engine.

Frederick went on to say that he enjoyed a *russet* in the gusset himself, also a *Billy-do* in the loo, a *hustle* in the bustle, a *scratch* in the grass, a *raclette* in a basket and a *double firkin* up the jerkin worn by a buxom young West country maid carrying two pales of milk suspended from a wooden yoke.

Frederick's rosy cheeks resembled two Sainsbury's '*Pink Lady*' apples which had fallen to the ground the previous evening after seeing Francoise La Cheminant cavorting around the concert room in a spectacular performance of the "Arabian Nights".

'Do you know? I once had the pleasure of cutting Fred Astaire's hair; well, I think it was him because of his black patent leather shoes; you know, the ones with the holes that leave speckled marks on your feet when it rains.' Frederick so descriptively told Robert in a *Wurzel* accent that one relates to giant hay stacks, pitch forks, cow sheds, manure and concentrated compost heaps. 'On the other hand, it could have been that other dancer, Jimmy Cagney.' he said, continuing with an element of confusion.

'But James Cagney doesn't look anything like Fred Astaire, and, furthermore, he could have been neither of them.' Robert so expertly mentioned.

'Well, yes,' Frederick replied, nodding his head like a seaside donkey. 'Anyhow, he was accompanied by a good-looking woman with ginger hair who couldn't stop foot tapping outside the salon.

'He was probably an American gangster who was going over to

London for his holidays.'

'It looks as if the ship will be arriving in Montreal a little late, tomorrow.' Frederick just happened to mention when a loud vibrating noise was heard followed by a crunch emanating from the engine room. 'Don't worry, sir,' Frederick said as he turned the swivel chair around to brush droplets of unwanted hair from Robert's '*Harris Tweed*' sports jacket. 'It always happens at this point of the journey when one of the ship's propellers gets caught up in a bunch of seaweed and a deep-sea diver has to go down to sort out the problem.'

'Ah well, that is a comforting thought, I suppose.' Robert said with a sigh.

'What is a comforting thought, young sir?' Frederick asked.

'I thought the problem could have been worse; we may have collided with a rogue iceberg in the Atlantic and ended up rowing back to Glasgow.'

'Or up the creek without a paddle; is that what you mean, sir?' Frederick said with an air of sarcasm coming from his lips. 'And, I wouldn't go wearing your kilt either; there are a lot of hungry seagulls flying around out there.' he added.

Robert leisurely spent the day playing cards with some of the delegation and after dinner, the evening ended with singing around the piano; Jimmy Murdoch tinkling the ebony and ivory keyboard of a baby *Steinway* for all it was worth. "Putting on the Ritz", "Daisy Daisy", "*Auld Lang Syne*" followed by, "We'll meet again", popular tunes of the day to bring to an end the first part of The Scottish Delegation voyage of discovery.

*

At eight o'clock, the following morning the ship was sailing along the St Lawrence River with scenic views of Quebec City to the right. With less than one hundred and thirty-nine nautical miles to Montreal, one of the world's greatest seaports, the ship was expected to arrive sometime around noon.

The Anchor Donaldson Line, "Athenia" had travelled one-thousand nautical miles inland as it sailed underneath the newly-completed Montreal harbour bridge over two miles long and costing $20,000.000 dollars, connecting Montreal with the South Shore. Its main span, one hundred and two feet above harbour level allows full clearance for lake, river and ocean shipping.

The shipping of the Atlantic and the Great Lakes and the railway traffic of half a continent converge upon Montreal where huge Atlantic liners berth with ease beside the magnificent piers of the cities fifteen-mile harbour front.

One can also see river vessels of the Canada Steamship Lines, Limited shooting Lachine Rapids en route from Upper Lakes to Saguenay River and, situated on the harbour front, one can gaze in amazement at the world's largest cold storage warehouse, erected and operated by Montreal Harbour Commission.

The itinerary for the Scottish Delegation included a one-night stay in The New "Y", Montreal's new Y.M.C.A. building, in the heart of the city, before leaving for Toronto by train the following day.

Following Canada's strict Immigration and Customs procedure, a brand-new silver-grey bus and two shiny black Ford motor cars were waiting outside the Anchor-Donaldson Line offices to transport the Scottish Delegation to the Y.M.C.A building in Drummond Street and the married accompanied members to the Ritz-Carlton Hotel in the heart of Montreal.

In 1931, a thirty-five-vehicle garage was on Côté Street near the company's headquarters. The bus network also grew in 1931 with services to Longueil and St Helen's Island via the new Havre Bridge.

Walking or driving along Drummond Street from St. Catherine or Sherbrooke, you will find The Montreal Y.M.C.A, the oldest on the North American Continent, established in 1851 and re-modelled in 1931, with the addition of the Evening College and Residence Building on Stanley Street.

For Robert Hamilton-Brown, the new "Y" was hardly a home for a young man away from home or the ideal opportunity to be alone;

however, in one of the more comfortable single residence rooms which were situated on ten floors, he could find solitude reading poetry, rehearsing presentations and practice singing to impress the Y.M.C.A. World Conference in Toronto.

The rooms were well furnished with comfortable beds, upholstered chairs, writing desks, telephones and attractive rugs that harmonize with the general colour scheme; a beautiful, colourful and harmonious place for young men to live. However, on each floor, airy washrooms are equipped with modern showers, wash-basins and mirrors and soap dispensers to save one having to bend down to pick up ones *Palmolive* soap. A special trunk storage room was also provided to hide unruly residents who insisted on you having to retrieve the latter. This was the place where good and odd fellows get it together; the "Y" has always been a club where both little and big boys can come and enjoy themselves and it is where a friendly welcome awaits you.

"Take a cool dip in the sparkling, clear water of the new "Y" Pool," the residents say.

'This is a spacious pool where no bathing costumes are allowed or permitted.' A member of the Y.M.C.A. Business and Professional Men's Club was heard saying to Robert in the new lobby. 'There was a crowd in the pool today, and how they enjoyed themselves. I saw a fellow standing around the pool who didn't know how to swim, but the instructor will make a good swimmer out of him in a very short time.'

The new lobby surprisingly has comfortable leather chairs and Chesterfields to invite fellows to stretch out their legs and take it easy. Any one of the delightful nooks and corners is just the place for a quiet chat or an idle half-hour's pleasure listening to the new radio.

Attractive Old English oak panelling, comfortable up-holstered furniture, floor and table lamps, rugs, draperies and a cosy fireplace, combine to produce an effect of good taste and restfulness. Here is a place where a man or boy may meet and talk with congenial friends, where wholesome discussion and interest in life provide an atmosphere of youthfulness and good will.

'Would you like some candy, Robert, or a bite from my peppermint stick?' Mr Jules Morgan, a director of the Canadian Pacific Railway asked him.

'No thank you, sir, I have just eaten, and besides, I don't accept sweets from teetotal strangers.' he quickly replied.

Robert Hamilton-Brown, a stranger strolling through this spacious well-furnished room wasn't impressed with the familiarity and over-friendliness of some of the older residents.

There was the new Health Service room under the direction of an experienced Swedish masseur with specialities, which included, powerful infra-red and ultra-violet lamps, Electric Cabinet Baths, Electric Chairs, Needle Showers, Massage Tables and other scientific devices; all designed to kill you in an instant.

The Cafeteria is on the ground floor where if you haven't eaten there, there is a real treat in store for you. You may gain access to this place of good things by the Stanley Street entrance, or through a corridor leading from the main lobby.

Near the Billiard Room is a large soda fountain and luncheonette, where you may get a quick lunch without the formality of going to the Cafeteria. Here are comfortable chairs and walnut-topped lunch tables, where fellows sip delicious thick malted milk and eat scrumptious steak Canadian sandwiches; the buffalo grill with jacket potatoes and fresh muffins was extremely popular after one had removed the horns from the beast and dusted it down.

It was at seven-thirty p.m., the telephone melodiously tinkled in Robert's residence room. It was Alison Rankin with her friend, Francoise La Cheminant giggling childishly in the background similar to a demented school girl in a playground just before the break-up for Christmas.

Alison Rankin, the red-haired vampire from Talon Street West, Montreal was behaving like a nymphomaniac on death row, and together with Francoise, her Anglo French belly-dancing assistant from Pinewood Avenue East, were trying desperately to entice Robert to join them for an evening stroll around Dominion Square, taking in the Basilica of St. James, Montreal's Roman Catholic cathedral, a one-third size replica of St. Peter's in Rome; its oval oratory towering seventy-six point eight metres above the city. The oval dome is a favourite spot for pilgrims who seek peace and solitude amongst the pigeons having climbed what seemed to be a never-ending stairway to heaven. And, for the tired, weary and worn out tourists who prefer a much darker side to life; the crypt is also quite popular where they can happily stretch out *sous-sol*, in the basement, to rest their weary heads among replicas of the dead; Pope Pius VII being the favourite. A Benedictine nun sitting inside the entrance hall was quite happy to relieve visitors of some money in exchange for a map telling everyone where the emergency exits are situated just in case a couple of over-sexed pyromaniacs in the crypt decide to set fire to her home; Alison Rankin and Francoise La Cheminant being no exception. And, for the tourists who find the entire place a complete and utter folly, a signpost can be found in the grounds of the building to tell them the distance to the Vatican in Rome.

At seven forty-five, Robert, on his way out from the Stanley Street entrance, mentioned to Alistair he had a headache, brought about by too much excitement and said he preferred to go out for some fresh air instead of joining in with a Hallelujah chorus about to sing the "Battle Hymn of the Republic".

This story, along with another tale he told later that evening was as convincing as the Loch Ness Monster being the star attraction at the Kelvin Hall Circus in Glasgow.

A shiny black Ford model A Cabriolet motor car belonging to Alison's father and driven by his chauffeur, Clive Dorian, was waiting outside the Y.M.C.A. building in Drummond Street to take Robert to Dominion Square where the two young ladies had been anxiously waiting to greet him.

It was a hot summer evening as the vehicle sped off down Sherbrooke Street West, passing by the Vista, showing its Art Gallery; the Erskine United Presbyterian Church, the Château and Arcadia Apartments.

The much-cherished American built car pulled up outside the Basilica where Alison and Francoise were sitting on a stone wall, legs crossed, facing the right-hand side of the road.

'Why, it's the man with the bag; Christmas is here again!' Alison said to

Francoise when Robert's sporran became caught up with the car door handle.

Francoise, equally surprised, was fiddling around inside her bag to find some loose change to pay the nun on guard behind the main door.

'It is so hot tonight and you must be hot too wearing that Scottish wrap-around travelling rug, Robert.' she said, wafting a glossy magazine from side-to-side in front of her face to keep her cool; the American film actor, Errol Flynn being the big attraction on the centre pages.

'Well we'll have to do something about that, won't we?' Alison said, making her way to a flight of stairs leading down to the Crypt. 'But first, we have to avoid the man that swings the thing.' she added.

'Who is the man, and what is the thing?'

'Why, he is the bloke who makes all of the smoke.' Alison replied.

'Where are we going?' Robert asked.

'You may very well ask,' Alison replied turning around occasionally to reassure him they were in God's house and not in Count Dracula's castle.

'I really shouldn't be here.' Robert said, breathing in the musty smells emanating from the crypt. 'I am a member of the Church of Scotland, and my father would be appalled if he were to find out I had changed my allegiance to the Church of Rome.'

'Don't worry, Robert.' Alison insisted. 'It's a bit like going to a coffee shop; the aromas all smell the same to me.' she added.

Robert began an attempt to impress the girls beginning with a recital of one of Robert Burn's famous poems, "Ode to a Haggis", by stabbing an innocent stone sarcophagus with a jewel encrusted letter opener.

'Are we going to listen to poetry this evening, Robert, or are we going to get down to business?' Alison asked, with her arms folded and looking up towards the limestone ceiling.

The evening progressed with the lighting of a few candles to illuminate and jolly the place up. This was when a stone lid on a coffin moved to one side and a tramp, an American boxcar 'Holy Willie', who was hiding himself away in a bourgeois town, poked his head out from the top and said:

'Can't anyone get any sleep around here?'

He, like many others, was a rolling stone and laid his hat wherever he roamed.

The two young ladies quickly adjusted their long grey pencil skirts and, after buttoning up their white high-neck ruff blouses, ran up the stairs with the speed of a thousand gazelles, leaving Robert to close the coffin by moving the lid back into position.

Robert, sliding his *skin dhu* down one of his long woollen socks, followed Alison and Francoise up the long narrow staircase, and standing on the steps of the Basilica he could see them speed off along Dominion Square in the highly polished Cabriolet.

At ten-thirty pm, Robert Hamilton-Brown returned to the Y.M.C.A. building having walked around the City for at least a couple of hours, burning up the last remnant of energy in his body. He entered the supper room where Alistair was sitting alone at one of the tables in the cafeteria.

'Where have you been till this hour, Robert?' Alistair asked inquisitively. And, what may I ask, is all that white stuff on the back of your kilt?' he added.

'Dust from the road, Alistair, just dust.'

Chapter Five

Jean-Talon Station, Montreal, Canada – Sunday morning 26th July 1931

Jean-Talon railway station (*Gare Jean-Talon*), also known as Park Avenue Station, is a former Art Deco railway station located in Montreal, Quebec, Canada. It is located on the northern end of Park Avenue and its main entrance faces Jean-Talon Street. It is situated in the Park Extension neighbourhood of the borough of Villeray-Saint-Michel-Parc-Extension.

The Canadian Pacific Railway built Jean-Talon station, which was designed by architect Colin Drewitt and opened in 1931. It was inaugurated in the presence of Camillien Houde, the mayor of Montreal at that time.

In its time, all trains headed towards Quebec City, Ottawa and the *Laurentians*, and it was an important stop for passengers until the early 1950s.

The central portion of the building became an Indigo Books and Music store which was then replaced by Société des alcohols du Québec store.

Transportation systems at the Jean-Talon railway station included The Canadian Pacific Railway, Canadian National Railways and the Metro station.

The trans-Canada Limited, stellar train of the Canadian Pacific Railway was the fastest trans-continental express to North America. This was an all-sleeping car train which crossed the Dominion from Montreal to Vancouver.

The International Limited, crack all steel trains of the Canadian National Railways operated daily between Montreal, Toronto, Detroit and Chicago; the fastest long-distance train in the world. This was the train, Robert and his fellow members of the Y.M.C.A Scottish Delegation boarded at eleven forty-five am, *en route* to Toronto, arriving early evening the same day.

At exactly midday, the train slowly pulled out of Jean-Talon Station to begin a spectacular six-hour journey to Toronto, passing through mountainous terrain where nowhere in America, outside of the Province of Quebec, does the traveller encounter scenes that preserve the spirit and customs of the Old World; the journey takes in villages on the Montreal-Quebec Highway where one can see bake ovens, windmills and wayside shrines beside the road; vistas of superb natural beauty.

The train to Toronto, traversing three hundred and forty-four miles; five hundred and fifty-three point nine-four kilometres, in six hours, raced over the Victoria Jubilee Bridge; the City's C.N.R's connection from Montreal Island with the South Shore of the St. Lawrence, Eastern Canada and the Atlantic States.

Billowing out from the engine was black smoke wafting furiously above the train, resembling the plume on top of a Trojan helmet; the steam emanating from the side of the huge cast-iron wheels was like looking at contaminated cotton wool rising to pollute Canada's idyllic mountain paradise.

The all-important reservation numbers were systematically checked by a C.N.R. inspector whose black bushy eyebrows commanded the upper part of his forehead. He wasn't amused when Robert showed him a flimsy Glaswegian Underground ticket; this being his idea of a little joke that morning, but it was to be short-lived when the inspector decided to change his seat number and had him sitting next to two real live Native American Red Indians who were called, Joe Wet Blanket and his wife Simone, the Laughing Cow of the *Saskatchewan* tribe.

Joe explained to Robert he was a staff sergeant and a communication expert in Canada's Royal Corps of Smoke Signals and that he and his wife were going to visit a Wild West Show in Buffalo. Robert got on very well with Joe because they smoked a pipe, read Tit-bits and shared each other's American '*Black Cherry*' tobacco.

'Staff Sergeant Wet Blanket doesn't sound quite right, somehow, especially in His Majesties Armed Forces.' Robert laughingly said to Joe.

'Ah, but when I joined up, I changed my name to Smith; by totem pole.' he sarcastically added.

'And your wife's name; is she called Smith as well?' Robert asked.

'No, she is still the same as she always was.' Joe remarked, jokingly.

'*Och aye*; I know the feeling.' Robert put in before reciting one of his ridiculous poems.

> "On yonder quay there stood a coo,
> I turned around she were nae there noo"

'My wife and her family are from the Native American Crowfoot tribe, somewhere between Canada and The United States.' Joe informatively put in choosing to ignore his adolescent sense of humour.

'It could have been worse; they could have been called an Indian Elephant Foot tribe.' Robert inferred with a cheeky grin on his face.

'An Indian Elephant, what is an Indian elephant?' Joe asked.

'An Indian elephant during its lifetime walks around the world two and a half times and cannot stop eating.' Robert explained.

'Sounds a bit like my mother-in-law.' Joe replied.

Robert became extremely nervous when Joe produced a large bowie knife during the journey to dissect a water melon the size of a World Cup football; the vivisection taking only a split second to complete.

'I read somewhere, that Red Indians were extremely good at transplanting hair.' Robert said as he gazed at the rolling prairies; yellow in colour, occasionally being discoloured by the passing of 'Big Chief' Darkened Cloud, which was to remind him of a poem written eleven years later, in 1942 and penned by Fred. W. Holton called Uplands; the first verse beginning:

> "Across the shoulders of the rolling hills
> Sour grasses blanch and spring.
> Threading their flanks, a thousand timeless rills
> Gleam grey and ceaseless sing.
> Cloud shadows chase
> In endless race
> Across the shoulders of the rolling hills"

'Yes, it had something to do with the British, French and American armies interfering with our homeland,' Joe, so sadly said. 'and having to put up with sitting in front of a fire eating Kentucky Fried Chicken on a Reservation; I just hope to God we don't rub shoulders with that Colonel Saunders in Buffalo. And do you know, Robert, we are really getting pissed off travelling ten miles just to see the movies' sweetheart, Mary Pickford, stretched out on a track waiting to be run over by the ten forty-five train from Montreal to Vancouver.'

'I thought that you lot didn't worship our God and instead of making the sun shine you were all hell bent in making it rain.' Robert said.

'Ah, but that was before the 'White Man' came along and began polluting the atmosphere; and now I am a Christian and go to church on Fridays, Saturdays and Sundays to stand up for Jesus.'

'And what happens during the rest of the week?' Robert asked.

'I go to Canada's chicken ranch and get my leg over.' Joe replied in a very low voice so Simone Laughing Cow couldn't hear.

'You wouldn't be interested in buying a second-hand sporran, Joe?' Robert asked; 'It will match your blue suede shoes.' he added.

Suddenly, it was time for lunch, heralded by a C.N.R. catering steward bashing the living daylights out of a brass gong in the restaurant.

The starters in the menu were a choice of spicy deep fried *goujons* of Southern fried chicken, French onion soup with *Gruyère* cheese and well-burnt *croûtons*, or *Escargot* filled with an off-putting pea green gunge; a type of garlic and *champignon*, mushroom *pâté*. The main courses were: *Faux Filet* of incredibly black Aberdeen Angus Steak, served with French fries, half a tomato and piping-cold corn bread; *Lapin*, rabbit served with fresh carrots, garden peas and garlic; a wet runny *Emmental* cheese *omelette* served with mixed salad, a miniscule *Quiche Lorraine Individuelle* or an *Alaskan Pavé de Salmon* saturated in a detergent called, *Crème de Persil*, parsley sauce topped with a slice of lemon. And, for dessert, *glacés*; a choice of vanilla, strawberry or chocolate ice cream; all served with a chocolate flake which was melting and fast disappearing down the inside of the glass.

The French Canadian waiter, Bernard Lapin had been busy serving bottles of *"San Pellegrino"*, *Eau minérale naturelle*, French natural spring water and '*Canada Dry*' tonic water to the tables and apart from *Coca Cola*,

Root, Nettle and Ginger beer served in ice buckets, there were no signs of any alcohol amongst the diners as prohibition had been in place for many years in the American and Canadian territories.

Robert, who was sitting amongst three members of the Delegation, chose and then ordered a starter, the *Escargot*, twelve medium size translucent snails signifying the twelve disciples of Jesus temporarily entombed in twelve miniature nautilus-shaped coffins filled with garlic and mushroom pesto and a glass of soda-pop; lemonade, resembling a kind of green *crème de menthe* cordial; the colour being the same to match the garlic and mushroom paste was also ordered to join a colourful array of culinary expertise specially prepared by C.N.R. Railways.

For the main course, Robert, patriotically ordered the *Faux Filet* of Black Aberdeen Angus Steak much to his disappointment when every morsel took him ten minutes to chew and later came to the conclusion he would need to be on the train for at least twenty-four hours in order to eat it.

Besides the inedibility of the steak, the chips being the wrong shape and a superfluous portrayal of a boring half-baked sun-dried tomato. Robert later complained to the train manager that the lavatory paper was too harsh for his refined bum.

'How do you serve the steak, Lapin?' Robert asked Bernard.

'Do you mean the beef, the rabbit or me, sir?' Bernard replied looking very disgruntled.

'I mean the *Faux Filet* of Black Aberdeen Angus Steak, you ignoramus.' Robert asked, beginning to sound very low on tolerance.

'Dead, sir.' was the reply.

'There is a hair on my plate, Lapin.' Robert said, pushing the food quickly away to the centre of the table.

'Keep your voice down sir, because they'll all want one.'

'And why is there no air conditioning in the dining car, Lapin; have you got a fan?' Robert asked as he tried to continue with his wining and dining.

'There is a door leading out onto the track, sir.' Bernard calmly replied.

The dessert Robert had chosen was the Vanilla Ice Cream Sundae with a chocolate flake which had disappeared forever into a thick creamy abyss.

'Where is the chocolate flake, Lapin?'

'Don't worry, sir, it is down there somewhere.' Bernard said, pointing his finger towards the bottom of the glass dish.

The newspapers were brought into the dining car by a boy wearing a Ratter type cap. "*The New York Tribune*" Chicago, headlines read:

"Held for Ransom"

"John Lynch, kidnapped gambler, has appealed to Al Capone, racketeer, to use his influence to affect Lynch's release. The kidnappers demand $250,000 dollars for his release and refuse a compromising offer of $50,000 dollars. They threaten to kill Lynch unless the full sum is paid."

Meanwhile, another article read:

"Troops called out in Spain, eight thousand troops with machine guns and artillery have been sent to regions in Spain to quell unrest"; the more serious part of the news being the American National League Baseball Scores.

Robert, surprisingly, bought one of the boy's newspapers instead of waiting to find a free copy which had been discarded by passengers on arrival in Toronto. Ironically, there was an article referring to his Royal Highness the Prince of Wales; "The Need of Men To-day is Greater Than Ever", perplexing problems of how to give youth training.

It was highly significant that the Prince opened the Union Station at number 65 Front Street Toronto on the 6th August 1927.

'Would you be so kind as to put out that bonfire, sir,' Bernard asked Robert, politely. 'The other diners cannot see their food for the smoke.'

'On which side of the window are you referring to?' Robert replied before getting up from his seat to go to the lavatory.

On his return from the Wesleyan Church, Lapin said to him: 'there was an article in yesterday's newspaper saying Paris is to have a cookery museum. Books, rare collections of old menus, manuscripts and almanacs for gourmets dating back to the Romanoff's and Louis XII of France; "The Art of Cooking Meat," and is in manuscript form prepared by

Pierre Petit.'

'It is a pity he is not on this train.' he said, chewing the meat over and over in his mind. And can you recommend a dry cleaner in Toronto, Lapin, because my kilt needs a good steam clean?'

'Why don't you stand on the platform by the side of the engine when we arrive at Union Street Station?' Bernard said with a cheeky grin on his face.

The train arrived in Toronto on time. It was six-thirty precisely when Robert and the rest of the delegation stepped down onto the platform where porters were busying themselves stacking suitcases and trunks on two-wheeled trolleys before loading them into a canvas- covered truck waiting outside the station.

The most direct line to and from the Union Street Station to the University grounds was the street car marked BAY, destination, Caledonia Road, for the University.

All delegates were assigned rooms according to the plan of the Programme Committee so in order to group persons of different nations together for fellowship purposes.

The lodgings were at the Wycliffe College, St. Michael's and for delegates accompanied by their wives and families who cannot therefore be assigned to the College residence, were alternatively located in a nearby boarding house and hotel. For the Scottish Delegation of the First World Y.M.C.A. Assembly of young men and Third World Assembly of Y.M.C.A workers with boys, this was to be their homes for the next seven days.

Dennis Thatcher, the husband of Margaret and the first woman British Prime Minister said, in later years: "Canada is a lot of to-do about sod all"; this was how Robert described the vast expanse of Canadian countryside when he got on the wrong bus at the Union Street Station and found himself sitting in a wild-life sanctuary park with only a grizzly bear, coyotes and a red-coated Royal Mounted Policeman to keep him company.

Chapter Six

The Y.M.C.A. Assembly in the Convocation Hall of the University of Toronto, Monday 27th July 1931

Robert Bruce Hamilton-Brown was given his green assignment card which he was supposed to adhere to for the duration of his time spent at the University; the unlucky House Group numeral seven had been crudely written in blue ink and on the top, was his name, just in case he forgot. The card was also endorsed, appropriately with the letter 'D' and, together with other bits of paraphernalia, an informative handbook describing the campus and its facilities. He was also given a diary, an autograph book and a small triangular-shaped brown and yellow Y.M.C.A. 1931 flag, to be placed on the top of a wooden scouting pole. Needless to say, the flag was never flown because the rigid pole had been utilized in metaphor for other purposes; namely, assisting a young real-live Apache Red Indian, Billy Two Rivers, in a scalp-hunting exercise when an all too familiar Y.M.C.A. Group Leader chased him around the University campus with an extremely large Bowie knife.

A programme, plus a daily bulletin describing the list of events, was handed to him giving information in detail of the location of all group activities and committee meetings and, most importantly, announcements.

The delegates, including visitors, wives, and families of delegates, were to take meals in Hart House, the Men's Club of the University of Toronto.

'We are to take breakfast in Hart House at seven forty-five.' Alistair informed Robert who was preoccupied brushing horse hair from the inside of his cavalry twill trousers.

'You did say Hart House, Alistair?'

'Yes, I did, and where *didja* go to last evening when we arrived at the Union Street Station?'

'As you know, I got on the wrong bus and then found myself in a wild-life park with birds, trees, flowers, insects and animals to keep me company.'

'You seem to be making an impact already, Robert. You have only been in Toronto for a few hours and you appear to know everything and everyone.'

'In the park, I met a policeman called Gordon Copper Nickel junior, and after dismounting his horse he showed me his whistle and then gave me a ride to Wycliffe College.'

'Well, you know what they say.' Alistair said with a sigh.

'No, what do they say?' Robert replied.

'A Canadian Mounted Policeman always gets his man.'

'I suppose you think my ordeal in the park was a hoot; really funny?' he put in.

'It could have been worse,' Alistair said. 'You might have been carried off by Black Foot.'

'And who may I ask, is Black Foot?'

'You know, the fellow we once knew at Clydebank Grammar School before he went to live in Moffat.'

'*Och aye*, I remember now, he was called Hamish McDonald, an odd fellow who insisted on sitting on his own and was madly in love with the poet and dramatist, Oscar Wilde, who had been dead for at least twenty-eight years and was banged up for being queer.'

'God played a nasty trick on him when he was born.' Alistair said, without placing any blame totally unbiased to our Great Laird.

'Who had a nasty trick played on him; Oscar Wilde or Hamish McDonald?'

'After breakfast,' Alistair pontificated, 'the entire delegation will have a free morning to get to know each other, but that won't include you, Robert, because it would seem you know everyone already, and after luncheon there will be a General Committee formed from the Boys' Workers' Assembly when each nation should be represented by two delegates and one older boy.' he went on, quoting the Handbook Guide to Robert, line for line. 'And then, at four thirty, there is a garden party in Victoria University Ground given by the Toronto Y.M.C.A. to the visiting delegates.' he added.

'Well, that will be fun for a wee while, won't it, because I am thinking of going into town to do a wee bit of sightseeing?' Robert said.

'Quite frankly, I don't know why you bothered to come on this trip, Robert; you don't seem to want to join in with anything.'

'You are quite right, Alistair; it was my brother who was supposed to attend the Y.M.C.A. Assembly, and not I.'

'Why isn't he here then?' Alistair asked.

'He was suffering with Elephant's foot and couldn't have made it up the gangway of the ship.'

'Oh, we're back to elephants again, are we? And, I sincerely hope you will honour us with your presence when you attend the Opening Session of the Assemblies in the Convocation Hall this evening, Robert; it is imperative you go because the President, Dr. John R. Mott is presiding.'

'What presents? I have no intention of buying any presents, or souvenirs for that matter, and when I was at Junior School, I knew a girl called Mott.' Robert said, jokingly. 'I never got around to seeing her box though.' he added, with a boyish laugh; the decibels loud enough to penetrate the walls of Wycliffe College.

The Breakfast Hall was a maze of congenial joviality starting with "For what we are about to receive make us all truly thankful"; 'the *'Quaker Oats'* porridge, bacon, beans and a grit tasted like shit, but you could live on it.' Robert said to his brother when he returned to Glasgow. A popular song during the conference went something like this: "It's bacon and beans most every day, and you might as well be eating prairie hay, *yippee aye yippee, yippee yippee aye*"; however, the Scotch pancakes served with *Maple 'Joe' Syrup* were exceptionally delicious at breakfast time, but then, Robert's perpetual whinging continued when he said, they looked and tasted like over-sized mammary glands that one could douse from a seepage of sap which had the appearance similar to Tate & Lyle molasses, a sugar refined syrup.

It was at one of the mahogany bench tables in Hart House, Robert mentioned to Alistair he would give anything for a *Forfar Bridie* to add to the *victuals*; a Scottish meat, onion and potato pasty.

It was at this point, Alistair was quick to recommend that Robert refrained from wearing his Douglas kilt because there was a burning desire of it being set alight by a very weary and angry Campbell.

At four-thirty, the garden party commenced with local dignitaries in attendance. Honourable George S. Henry, Premier of Ontario, His Worship W.J Stewart Mayor of Toronto. J.A Machado, the President of the National Council of the Y.M.C.A. in Canada and wives of the aforesaid, all wearing summer outfits to fit the occasion.

It was a hot afternoon and not a cloud in the sky when Alistair mingled and talked amongst his fellow delegates and the occasion was going to be a pleasant and momentous experience for him until....

Robert came back from "The Queen City" centre prematurely when he realized he had forgotten to take his wallet which had been discreetly, albeit unnecessarily hidden underneath his mattress in the dormitory at Wycliffe. He was hoping to purchase for investment, a small ceramic oil lamp from Eaton's, a newly opened store, but then on his next visit into town he found the shop was *fermé pour congé*, closed for a short break, and there was a sign on the door also informing prospective customers that they wouldn't be open until the following Monday; this was typical of the seventeen year-old, Robert Bruce Hamilton-Brown, if he had brains, he would be dangerous.

The neatly tended gardens behind Burwash Hall in Victoria University was literally full of visitors from around the world and one couldn't help hearing the unmistakable clicking of heels and to detect the odd duelling scar on the faces of East Prussian, Austrian or German delegates; also, the distinctive dark penguin suits and the odd top-hat which fell to the ground when members of the Japanese contingent rendered an *ojigi*, a traditional bow to fellow delegates on campus.

It was during one of the conference days Robert asked Alistair what the Japanese word *ojigi* meant. He explained it's a bit like O'Reilly without the Guinness.

Robert, always ready for a quick reply said: 'My father was exceptionally good at the Gee-Gees, especially the three-thirty at Ayr.'

'You're back early.' Alistair said. 'Did you buy anything interesting, or did you manage to find something more interesting, preferably wearing a skirt?'

'*Och aye*, you will have your *wee* joke; you are a regular '*hoots man*', aren't you, Alistair. And, you will be pleased to learn, I did buy something special; it's a pretty little American oil lamp and I bought it as a present for Morag.'

'That is truly interesting, Robert, but tell me where did you find the money to buy it because this afternoon when I went back to Wycliffe College for a shower, I found your wallet by the side of your bed.'

'*Agh*, that was *nae* problem, I had some loose change in my sporran.'

'Here, would you like a glass of fresh orange juice?' Alistair asked.

'When you're about to die, it's no use taking vitamin 'C'.' Robert nervously replied.

'Why, are you thinking of leaving us?'

'There seems to be a lot of umbrellas around here, especially among the older members; are we going to be in for a storm?' Robert had to say. 'Take that chap over there, the one who looks like a *Sumo* wrestler from Tokyo; I bet he has a *Samurai* sword hidden in his umbrella?'

'Don't be so stupid, Robert, he is the Principle of the much-celebrated HKU, the University in Hong Kong.'

'Thank you for retrieving my wallet, Alistair, I thought I had left it in the shower room.'

Dinner was served in Hart House at six-thirty. During this time Canadian well-burnt Buffalo steaks were served with jacket potatoes, string beans and the traditional muffin; alternatively, one could brave the German *Bratwurst*, char grilled sausages, the French *Hache de Beuf*, raw mince beef or the *Sushi*, Japanese stir fried rice dishes with things on sticks; all dishes were individually cooked in the cafeteria annexe with culinary expertise by *International Chefs de Cuisine*; a French Master Chef, complete with a gold-plated medallion suspended from a blue, white and red ribbon orchestrating each performance.

Robert despaired when he asked one of the chefs in the restaurant if he cooked Scottish *Haggis* with *Neeps*. He was told politely to keep his voice down because of a senior Japanese delegate, who was waiting patiently in the queue for his crab meat soup may have designs on using his cleaver.

After an hour of gastronomic deliberation sitting around a table, the meal for everyone was finally over and for Robert, the flaming steak had been eaten, the rattlesnake consommé drank and the *pomme tarte*, apple pie with custard *Anglaise* pushed to one side because of his ongoing hang-up towards the English.

The Opening Session of the Assemblies began with an Address of welcome by the Honourable George S. Henry, the Premier of Ontario and this was followed by the President of the World's Alliance Young Men's Christian Associations, Dr. John R. Mott who recited the words to a prayer, specially knocked up for the World Conference by Dr. Mott and began with a prayer:

"A Prayer"

"Father, who hast made of one blood all nations of men to dwell upon the earth, grant me to see in all thy children my own brothers and sisters; and move them to claim me as their friends.

Break down all barriers and bridge all chasms that divide us from one another. Heal the wounds inflicted on spirits by callous or careless speech or deed; and with thy sunshine dispel all bitterness.

Cleanse me from every pollution of pride or prejudice; and from all the sin that separates me from thee and from my brothers and sisters; and melt away all petulance and selfishness. Make a well-spring of loving-kindness flow continually within me, so that those of all nations and races who thirst for fellowship may stoop and, drinking, fine refreshment.

Strengthen the might of thy Spirit of justice and mercy among all peoples and especially inspire with courage and good-will men and women who guide the policy of states and who shape the thought of mankind.

Increase the sovereignty of the Son, Jesus Christ, the Prince of Peace, in the hearts and minds of the youth of the world, until the walls of the Holy City, where there shall be no more war, embrace thy children of all peoples.

Give to each of us the spirit of a child, that we may enjoy the happy

59

comradeship of the Kingdom on earth as it is in Heaven.

Glory be to the Father, and to the son, and to the Holy Ghost. As it was in the beginning, is now and ever shall be. Amen..."

The prayer seemed to have gone on for hours, interrupted only by Hamilton-Brown's snoring and the bouts of armour-piercing loud coughs which emanated from the nine God- fearing Russian Delegates who, out of respect, were standing to attention at the rear of the galleries, each one holding a Y.M.C.A. Handbook Guide, specially prepared for the delegates attending the 1931 World Conference. It was not so surprising that twelve years later most of them were executed by the startling development of an Atheist regime orchestrated by Marshal Joseph Stalin.

Dr. Mott continued with a powerful opening speech; The Significance of the 1931 World Conference, explaining that the Young Men's Christian Association, stretching over three-quarters of a century has made a great contribution to the constructive forces of the world and moreover, all over the world there are multiplying and solemnizing signs that some of the oldest and most powerful religions, traditions, and social sanctions are relaxing their hold, especially on youth. Again, the business of stagnation, financial depression, and widespread unemployment in so many parts of the world make today a far greater demand upon the services of an organisation like the Association Movement than at any time in history except in the midst of a World War; the world is indeed facing a "World Crisis".

During the summing up by Dr. Mott a shout was heard coming from the galleries, it was Hamilton-Brown having one of his regular nightmares, only controlled by two muscular and heavily-armed ushers who had no choice but to escort him to Hart House for an early cocoa supper.

A small shop situated inside the restaurant was continuously maintained and this was where newspapers, magazines, cold drinks, sun-dried tomato sandwiches and aspirin could be purchased quite cheaply; 'Argentinean', 'Vanity Fair' and the American 'Pretty Boy' magazine were only accessible by climbing up to the top shelf with the aid of a pair of wooden step ladders.

For Robert Bruce Hamilton Brown, several used copies of the magazine, 'Vanity Fair' sedatives, tranquilizers, and a copied key to the heavily fortified front door to the halls of residence in Wycliffe College were his only means of escapism during, what he called; a week of organised hell.

The twenty-five-year-old silent movie and Hollywood actress, Mary Astor became one of Robert's favourite pin-up gals after he had seen her glamorously flaunting herself inside a New York film magazine. The pictures depicted her on the front and centre pages had been clinically removed by Robert with a pair of vanity scissors and placed in a prominent position inside the door to his six-foot metal locker, the convenience of this being it was conducive to him having a pleasant and good night's sleep.

I can recall Mary Astor taking on the role of a murderess and temptress, Miss Brigid O'Shaughnessy after calling herself Miss Wonder lick in one of my favourite American films, "The Maltese Falcon" starring Humphrey Bogart as Sam Spades, which was produced in the 1940s; her early appearance and the fast elimination of Miles Archer, Sam's partner in the film, was gripping and caused my ice cream to fall from my hands onto my trousers; Brigid, also came to a sticky end during the epilogue when she was destined to take the fall.

Why is it, I am thinking, that most of the pathetic and sad female characters in history were called Mary? It must have had something to do with instability, if you pardon the pun.

At eleven pm, the heavy doors with their mock medieval ironmongery were securely locked making it difficult for late-night revellers to gain access to the building. For those managing to enter the building from the outside, they would find it impossible should they want to go out again and most certainly have clashed with the house matron, Mrs Jane Shipley with features resembling a brown leather Gladstone bag and a voice louder than the Clyde Bank fog horn.

A free newspaper stand had been placed inside the entrance to the building and one of the headlines read 'Economic Blizzard Continues' China invades Manchuria, Japan; the International outlook looks increasingly blacker and blacker.

Meanwhile, apparently in Germany, the existence of six million unemployed provided a tremendous economic source of discontent to add to the already considerable political grievances. Communism was beginning to spread and scare the middle classes.

At ten o'clock the chimes from the Soldier's Memorial Tower clock at the University of Toronto should have rang out; the tower had been waiting patiently in the grounds of the campus for several years for the facia and clockwork mechanism to arrive, and to this day it waits and waits and further waits.

Robert, full of his own discontent made his way back to Wycliffe College knowing that a war on an International scale was looming over the horizon, and Stalin, the 'Man of Steel' was behind his iron curtain waving a red flag stained with his own people's blood.

Chapter Seven

Tuesday morning, July 28th

The morning began with a bang when two copper boilers in the laundry room annexe exploded due to an absence of water; the noise of the combustion was enough to awaken the dead.

Robert Hamilton-Brown shot out of bed at approximately one thousand four hundred and sixty feet per second, similar to the muzzle velocity of a British military.303 bolt action sniper rifle and he was not amused when his sleep pattern became disturbed by a Chinese coolie specially employed by Wycliffe College to attend to the delegates' washing.

At six o'clock, a moustachioed, Chang Wan complete with pigtail was running around the campus hysterically hoping to find someone who could fix the unfixable because his home for the next six days was in danger of going up in flames. The strands of Chang's long black wispy moustache seemed to touch each step of the stairway leading up to the front door of the university.

The gas burners which were supposed to be underneath two huge containers hadn't been turned off and when the fire engine eventually arrived, destiny had already taken its course; the entire building was completely destroyed and Wishee Washee's washing and ironing enterprise had come to an abrupt end. However, as it happened, when he and his Widow Twankey of a wife, Lyn Wan, who, after eating a fortune cookie, trapped one of her fingers in a mangle before she and Chang opened up Canada's first Chinese Cantonese restaurant, 'The Lucky House' in Hutchison Street, Montreal but, one can take this with a large pinch of salt. The delegates and students thought he was a throw-back from the Klondike Valley because of the gold nuggets he had as replacements for his two front teeth.

The fire damaged laundry was scattered all over the once neatly tended lawns and the only recognisable garments were a pair of pink silk cami-knickers belonging to the wife of a senior delegate and a pathetic looking kilt which belonged to Robert Hamilton-Brown.

It was during the afternoon when all of the rubble was being systematically shovelled into the back of a muck wagon, a rickety old horse and cart, especially designed for this momentous and historic occasion, Robert, the Abanazar of the day, said to the driver:

'Hey, Mush, I didn't see PC Pong when the fire brigade arrived; ach well, you might as well tak the sporran as weal; its nae maer good ta ma noo.'

It was at breakfast in The Great Hall in Hart House when most of the Scottish delegation wore their kilts, Robert became very annoyed when Alistair asked if he had found a dry cleaner in Toronto to wash and iron his much coveted nine yards of green and black inter-woven cloth.

'I did, and I can see it's going to be another one of those days, and oh, how I wish I was back in the nether regions of bonny Scotland.'

'Don't you mean the heather regions belonging to the Highlands, Robert? I wouldn't call Glasgow the most picturesque of places in the world because the city has more pubs per capita of beer drinkers than the whole of the British Isles.'

'We come from Scotland the Brave, Alistair, not from *Sassenach* Britain who has harboured the English since the Queen Boadicea who, on several occasions attempted to invade our country, and as far as I am concerned, the buck stops at Hadrian's Wall.'

'Would that be on your way up to Scotland or on your way down, and you did say buck, didn't you Robert?'

'Of course I did, what else did you think I meant to say?'

'And now, let us see, after breakfast we have the morning worship conducted by the Reverend G.C. Pidgeon.' Alistair said, reminding Robert of his duty to start the day with a necessary soul cleansing exercise.

'Agh, not another pigeon, they and the cats kept me awake for most of the night.' Robert replied looking up towards the high ceiling in Hart House to hear more cooing sounds coming from the roof.

'And then, the morning sessions continue with the Introduction to Group Discussions; "Materialism and Christianity" followed by Problems of Young Men; and you know all about that, Robert, don't you?'

'Well, if they want the benefit of my wealth of knowledge and advice, they have only to ask.'

Sitting on the bench seats next to the boy delegates were the older members and their wives who were taking breakfast.

'Is there something on your mind, Robert, because you seem to be constantly looking over at the tables opposite to ours?'

'Yes, there is, Alistair, how perceptive of you to notice. There is something puzzling me, and for some time now I have been wondering how forty delegates including seven wives who travelled from Glasgow to Quebec on-board the T.S.S. "*Athenia*" could suddenly be reduced by four; since we arrived in Quebec, there have been only thirty-six people sitting at the tables.'

'Here we go; Inspector Hercule Poirot is at it again. Next you will be saying we have left a body behind in the ship's library and it is possible that the ones you say have disappeared may have been abducted and are now sitting outside a wigwam in Medicine Hat.'

'It is not my fault if I am highly intelligent with an imaginative mind and have a strange affiliation for the written word.' Robert said with overwhelming confidence.

'You're not exactly Agatha Christie, are you Robert?'

'Agatha Christie wears a skirt, Alistair, you should know that.'

'You were wearing a skirt yesterday, but where is it today, I wonder?'

Robert Hamilton-Brown was at it again when later he compared the official Y.M.C.A. World Conference Scottish Delegation Attending List to the names mentioned in his rather crude personalized knocked-up diary. There was an obvious abnormality, an anomaly amongst the senior delegation ranks because there were four people more in his journal than were on the official list. This to Robert was indeed bizarre, he thought, and there could be sinister connotations, if not, serious backhandedness behind this conundrum of fluctuating probability of numbers.

Robert enthusiastically ticked the names of the Scottish Delegation with a HB pencil, sometimes with a much-chewed eraser fixed on the top he would rub out a mistake or an unnecessary attempt at nervous graffiti.

The exercise in the elimination of names was now complete having kept his bedside light on for several hours trying to systematically figure it all out.

The conclusion he had arrived at was that there were four passengers; a Mr and Mrs H.J. Donaldson and Mr and Mrs G.O. Norrie, who were either stowaways on-board the T.S.S. "Athenia", sleeping in lifeboats or cabins occupied by fellow delegates and had the privilege of dining courtesy of the "Anchor-Donaldson Line" or they were a figment of everybody's imagination. The question remained; where were the two couples? They hadn't been seen since their arrival in Quebec. Were they still alive or not? Because, according to Robert, people do not vanish into thin air.

It transpired that Robert was quite correct to assume there was something wrong and to question the strange disappearance of the two couples. He later found out that Mr. Steven Boswell, the organizer of the trip was corrupt and bent, arranging for Donaldson and Norrie to travel with their wives to Canada, mingling with the Y.M.C.A. delegates on a low-cost block-booking basis. They were to visit their relatives in Toronto and then spend three weeks travelling around America, returning to Glasgow on Saturday 22nd August, sailing on the T.S.S. "California" from New York. All these findings, Robert kept to himself after rubbing shoulders with Donaldson and his wife in the Royal Alexandra Theatre, located near King Street and Simcoe Street, Toronto where H.M.S. Pinafore, one of the comic operas composed by Sir Arthur Gilbert and W.S. Sullivan was being performed.

During the interval, Donaldson had the idea to bung Robert a considerable sum of money to keep his mouth shut and not to tell anyone what was indeed going on. It was not until Hamilton-Brown had persuaded and guaranteed him and Norrie a safe passage back to Glasgow they handed over more money to him once the ship had up-anchored in New York.

It transpired that Robert on his return to Scotland made more money when he blackmailed the organizer of the trip; threatening him with excommunication from the organizing body and instant dismissal from the Sunday afternoon Y.M.C.A. Presbyterian's table tennis league.

Oh, they'll never learn.' Robert said with a sigh as he counted out the first of his spoils whilst sitting gracefully on a harsh wooden seat in one of Wycliffe's gentlemen's washrooms.

*

Toronto or "The Queen City", as it is known, is the second largest centre of population in the Dominion and one of the great cities of the North American continent. Its metropolitan population is roughly eighty-thousand and it lies on the north shore of Lake Ontario which is one of a chain of great lakes and rivers stretching half way across the continent. It is the capital of the Province of Ontario and is approximately in the same latitude as Cleveland, Detroit and Chicago but somewhat farther south than London, Berlin, Paris, Vienna, Budapest and Moscow.

Toronto has a favoured location and enjoys an equal climate. It has the finest harbour on the Great Lakes, with the waterfront extending ten miles.

As an educational centre it occupies an outstanding position with the University of Toronto as the centre. Affiliated with it and covering a considerable area of city space are notable colleges and schools.

Canada is, of course, young as nations go. There is a youthful spirit about her people. Her admittedly great natural potentialities are matched by the spirit of faith and confidence of her people.

Meanwhile, still in The Great Hall in Hart House, Alistair asked the obvious.

'And what sort of mischief are you going to get up to today, Robert? At two pm, there is a demonstration and an exhibition in Alumni Hall and the Recreation Grounds of Victoria University. The theme is pencil sketching North American Indian Arts and Crafts, working with beads, feathers, leathers, etc; the instructor and leader is called Chief Bullock.'

'You did say, Bullock, didn't you Alistair?'

'Yes, Robert, I did. What other name did you think I said?'

'I don't think I will be in attendance, Alistair, to learn how to make a

Tom-Tom drum from a discarded cocoa tin, a tepee, a cone-shaped Red Indian tent constructed from the hide of skinned Buffalo, and a feather duster made from an unfortunate bird that could fly over the campus between two and four o'clock this afternoon.'

'When I was young, Robert, I attended a nursery in Glasgow and knew someone called Tom Tom'; he was the son of a piper who stole a pig and away he ran; I never did get the opportunity to bang on his drum.'

'I suppose you think that was very funny?'

'Come on Robert, lighten up; go along and you never know, he may teach you how to make leather gloves or a pair of suede moccasins, surely that will put you in good stead after you leave school and join the *Glovers*, 'Tindal's' of Glasgow.'

'Chief what's-his-name may show us how to make a toupee from those hairy things hanging on a line stretched out between two totem poles in the Recreation Grounds of the University, but the *Apache* and *Sioux* tribes only discovered the wheel two hundred and fifty years ago when they saw the first covered wagon being pulled up for speeding along the prairie.' Robert said, feeling sorry for those who had the misfortune to be serving with General George Armstrong Custer during the attack on the Little Bighorn River in 1876.

'You never give it a rest, do you, Robert, if it isn't the English getting up your nose, it's the Roman Catholics in Scotland, and if that isn't enough, it is a knowledgeable North American Indian who is getting up your nose and in the firing line.'

'Do you know, Alistair, I am sick and tired with the amount of bible-punching that is going on around here; they begin at nine in the morning and don't let up until gone ten in the evening; is there some kind of psychology or brain-washing exercise being transmitted through our brains; I believe, there is, and who wants to know about the bearing of Natural Science on the Christian Conception of Life in Czecho-Slovakia?'

'The Czechs, I suppose, Robert, are just as much entitled to their opinions as we are.'

'Ah, but they haven't got a life, have they, living amongst all that poverty and communistic governmental restriction. And, how come most of the Czecho-Slovakian Y.M.C.A. delegates from their contingent in Canada seem to have more money than the lot of us put together?'

'That is because the thirty-nine members of the delegation are Russian-backed and come from good families in Dubrovnik and Prague.' Alistair said, making it absolutely clear who was funding the trip.

'I suppose, this is why they can't speak a word of English and get confused when they make an attempt at singing, "Stand up, stand up for Jesus" in pidgin English; those poor souls think it is Joseph Stalin who is being idolised in the song and not the son of our God.'

'Is there anything else you would like to complain about before I begin to eat my *Scots Porridge Oats*?' Alistair asked.

'Yes, as a matter of fact, there is, Alistair,'

'Go on, Robert because you are going to tell me anyway.'

'Well, if it wasn't for the Pilgrim Fathers sailing over to America on the *"Mayflower"* in the seventeenth century and setting up shop in Newfoundland and New England, the Scots wouldn't have gone to all that trouble fighting against the French in Canada and the Southern States of America, and you, Alistair wouldn't be eating *Scots Porridge Oats* with cream and maple syrup because the oats would be named after the 'Shakers'. And did you know that the Quakers sailed over to the new-found land, two-by-two with only one feline on-board, and this would account for the noises one can hear on the roof when one puts the cat amongst the pigeons.'

'And what do you have to say about the North American Indian tribes; wouldn't they have an answer to all this irregular chit-chat, Robert?'

'The 'White Man', namely the Union soldiers, raped, pillaged and murdered thousands of Red Indians and set fire to their homes on the reservations in Canada and North America; I don't think they were too pleased at being assaulted by cavalry soldiers wielding sabres stained with blood.'

'How lonely are the brave, Robert? I don't think I'm hungry anymore, and, is there a gentleman's room around here because I'm about to throw up.'

Robert, by this time had had enough discovering how to achieve a strong body by watching what he ate, how he ate and how not to eat too much. He also learned how to breathe deeply in the not too pure campus air and to exercise regularly and moderately and get plenty of rest; how to keep clean, inside and out, by frequent washing, brushing of teeth and regular elimination of waste.

They were teaching him how to discover a clear bright mind by being open-minded and willing to learn, developing a desire to know the truth and to crave knowledge in order to be a genuine, cultured gentleman, capable of filling his place in life.

The Y.M.C.A. World Conference also taught Robert how to develop and maintain a pure heart which had already fallen by the wayside. They didn't, however, teach him how to be true to his ideals and develop a passion for love, self-gratification and mutual service, to which Robert, paradoxically, had unthinkable letters after his name; the letter 'W' however, immediately springs to one's mind.

They taught him how to discover real friends by being a close friend to those about him, remembering to treat everybody as you would want them to treat him; all this is creating Life-Long Memories which are being formed now.

Alistair, who was about to pebble-dash the walls of the lavatory because of Robert's unique powers of suggestion and descriptive oratory skills at the breakfast table, could not take any more and to be reminded of close friendships and love would have been far too much for him to handle.

Chapter Eight

The boys, young men and friends of Toronto are invited to attend this evening's celebration.

Following a series of academic deliberation and discussion between Robert and his leaders as to how he was going to spend his time during the afternoon was indeed anyone's guess and to test the brains of the psychoanalyst, Sigmund Freud or the physicist, Albert Einstein; however, it was obligatory to do something, if only to pick one's nose, scratch one's head or poke one's neighbour with an artist's paint brush.

Alistair, along with other members of the delegation elected to go on a Nature Study, a "Youth's Adventure with God"; an afternoon outward bound course to learn how to light a fire by the side of Lake Ontario; catch freshwater salmon and whistle at the birds; this to Robert was the epitome of a waste of time because of the shortage of extra mural activities and short skirts around the camp.

Robert decided to join a handicraft class with the emphasis on painting in oil and water colours; the pencil sketching was an optional side-line demonstrated by Chief Bullock himself. There were also parquetry, soap carving, art metal work, and photography, linoleum block-printing and pottery-making classes being held next door to the artist's studio.

'I didn't come all this way to be taught how to make a terracotta cup and saucer; the Romans did that sort of thing when they were bored out of their skulls having thrown one or two Christians to a hungry lion.' Robert said to one of his leader friends. 'Haven't you got classes, where I can sit down and learn how to make a lot of money and be rich, and very, very rich?'

'There is the *"The Bankers"* Club offering morning, afternoon and evening sessions only to give limited time to an educational programme.' a business and professional man suggested. 'The courses include accountancy and book-keeping, advertising, business arithmetic, business correspondence, business English, presentations and public speaking.

'I don't know about the business English because I would much prefer if I spoke in Scottish.' Robert so proudly put in.

'As you wish, Robert.' Mr Kellogg said, tongue in cheek. 'You know, inside the echelons of the Y.M.C.A. it doesn't matter what dialect or language you speak; it is more to do with hidden depths, skills and eating the right kind of cereals for breakfast.'

Robert Bruce Hamilton-Brown, not for the first time had the idea he was heading for the big time and going places. It was namely, the New York Stock Exchange, where he could learn how to increase his fortune by turning his investments into real money. What he didn't seem to realize was that the American Stock Market at that time was very volatile, similar to a fairground roll-a-coaster; what usually goes up in value eventually comes down and sometimes with a crash; even the hotdog served with onions, sauerkraut and hot chilli peppers, which Robert bought from a vendor in Times Square ended up splattered on the sidewalk when far too much tomato ketchup was applied full-length along the top after he was hustled on Broadway.

'Hi Honey, is that a rocket in your pocket or are you just pleased to see me?' Bubble gum Samantha said, pointing a long red scratchy fingernail up towards her suggestive red lips. 'Hey, I'll buy you another hot dog, one that doesn't fall to the ground and then we can go and get some action?' she proffered to Robert.

'What kind of action do you mean, knees bend, arms stretched, rah rah rah, or what?'

'If you want some New York explosive action, Honey, I'm game for anything and just around the corner there is an apartment block where they rent rooms by the hour.' continuing with her street knowledge and where to find the lay-lines around North Manhattan.

'I think five minutes would do it because I have a bus to catch.' Robert was quick to put in.

'Gee honey; are you a regular Tarzan, a Superman or someone who can do it in less than an hour?' she so bravely asked when her pimp came along and asked whether they were going to have an all-night conversation or get down to an hour of one-to-one business.

After Robert had said to the refined 'Western Oriental Gentleman', retail business was on the agenda for tomorrow and not that evening, he was immediately threatened with a Saturday night special, a silver snub-nose imitation *Colt* hand gun; the piece specially designed for lighting fires, rolled-up cigarettes and frightening little old ladies, that sort of thing.

'Just where are you from man?' Bugsy Malone said and was now beginning to sound nervous at Robert's Scottish aggressive tone of voice.

It was then Robert said that he was from Scotland and was visiting 'The Big Apple', New York before going back to Glasgow and, following a forced amicable tête à tête, the gun-packing Gunsel said to him: 'gee man, I just knew already, you were from Canada.'

'Yes, and I knew already, you both weren't into real estate.'

The Place of Sex in the Christian Life was not part of Robert's thoughts, ethics and ideals and did not come into the equation, especially when he had to pay for it.

Alistair returned from the gentleman's wash room looking a little pale and somewhat green around the gills.

'Are you alright Alistair?' Robert asked knowing that he wasn't.

'Ach, I think so; it must have been the fried breakfast I ate; the beans play havoc with my digestive system.'

'Yes, I know the feeling: beans, beans, the musical fruit, the more you eat, the more you toot.'

'Was that supposed to be funny, Robert; you are beginning to sound like a regular hoots man without a kilt.'

'If you will excuse me, Alistair, I am just going to buy a newspaper from the shop, there must be something important to read because everyone seems to be buying a copy of today's 'New York Herald Tribune'.

The headlines read 'Economic blizzard continues in Europe'.

"Trade tends to run in periodic waves of boom and slump, and now following the collapse on Wall Street, values of stocks and commodity prices everywhere fell rapidly. Unemployment figures are leaping upwards. Countries, including Germany, are finding themselves deprived of loans from America. In Britain the socialists have had to give way to a National Government, which is nevertheless soon forced off the gold standard and will be compelled to abandon Britain's historic policy of free trade.

Meanwhile, the Nationalist Socialist Party Leader, Adolf Hitler, a house-painter by profession, whose ideas are crude in the extreme is being swept rapidly into power and he has already attempted a ridiculous coup d'état; the lenient German republic, however, had only imprisoned him for a short time."

Robert, having returned with his newspaper said to Alistair:

'Now I know why the Y.M.C.A. German delegation are so incredibly fit and are hell bent in wanting to join the army.'

'Come on, Robert; try to impress me with your recently acquired wealth of global knowledge.'

'That's how they get into their tanks; they just hop on to the turret, point the gun barrel towards Moscow and off they go; it's of no use being the fittest corpse in the ground if Marshal Stalin digs their bodies up and decides to kill them again.'

During the art session Robert asked his tutor which was the best drawing in the class; his surrealistic coloured pencil drawing of Field Marshal Lord Kitchener or the efforts and energies created by other members in the group depicting a fruit bowl containing a pomegranate, a couple of plums, a prickly pear and what looked like a banana which had been made from molten wax.

Robert's tutor, Mr Walter Wall, emphasised to him that the class wasn't a competition, and everyone was unique in their own way and the best did not come into the equation. Walter reminded him that the Flemish artist Vincent Van Gough was very controversial in the way he painted and compared his heavy-handedness with Robert when he used his skin-doo instead of a palette knife.

At precisely three forty-five, Robert and Alistair had their afternoon tea in Hart House Quadrangle. He mentioned to Alistair that his day teacher was a Mr Walter Wall, the name being like a Wall-to-Wall Street carpet and he had a strange aversion towards the nineteenth century Dutch painter, Vincent Van Gough, who, odd as it may seem, churned out paintings quicker than a Leicester Square pavement artist.

'And, why is it that every time you go to see a ship's doctor, he almost invariably asks to see the backs and the palms of your hands?' Robert asked.

'Maybe he thinks you are Jesus, or someone important enough to get him out of bed in the early hours of Saturday morning to see to a common cold, also it is possible, he could have thought you may have been able to walk on water.'

'How, the bloody hell, Alistair, do you think we got here in the first place?'

'I suppose, I asked for that one, Robert, but you do seem to emulate him from time to time.'

'Ach, Jesus and I are mates but, he was a hard act to follow, especially when he fell out with the Roman Empire and ended up being nailed to a wooden cross. And from what I have heard and read at the bible reading classes in Sunday School, Jesus wasn't alone, he had a few thousand of his followers to keep him company; if he had played his cards right he may have had enough wood for his carpentry and joinery business to last him for the remainder of his life.'

'You don't give it a rest, do you Robert; always trying to benefit from people's misfortunes.'

'That's why the Americans built the New York Stock Exchange, at No.68 Wall Street,' Robert replied; "To maintain progress and insure prosperity, every modern nation must provide a central market place for its public securities." – Napoleon Bonaparte.

'So, why did Jesus upset the money lenders when he kicked over six-foot tables in the markets and synagogues of Jerusalem all those years ago?' Alistair asked.

'That was because he was horrified by the current exchange rate between the Italian Lira and the hardest currency in the world, the Jewish Shekel.'

'You know, Robert, you can talk your way out of a Woolworths brown paper bag; that is the real truth of the matter.'

'If that is what you want to say Alistair, then so be it.'

It was at that precise moment Robert felt a finger poking him in his back. It was Walter Wall, who had been standing behind him all the time.

'I have been listening in to your constant dribbling and blasphemous defamations concerning me and our good Lord and Master, Jesus Christ, Hamilton-Brown, since I had the misfortune to walk in here to take my afternoon tea.' Mr Wall said, 'and, quite honestly, I would much prefer if tomorrow you would volunteer to be a target in Chief Bullock's archery class for beginners.' he added.

'I was once given a bow and arrow as a present but, they were very short-lived when on Christmas morning I missed the cat and instead, hit my dad between the eyes and needless to say, he was never the same once the sucker was removed by plastic surgery in Glasgow General Hospital; well, it gave the doctors and nurses something to do in between swigging back bottles of *Moet* champagne and eating the best *Cadbury's* Chocolates.'

'If I were you, young sir, I would stick to your poetry because that is what you do best, namely bore the pants off everyone around you.' Wall said, continuing to chastise Robert in the best way he could.

'Did you, know, Alistair, that nineteen-hundred years ago, Jesus of Nazareth was reputed to be the first Jewish Convenor of the Carpenters and Joiners trade union movement in Israel and that is why, to this day, there are eleven disciples and a boss man sitting at conference tables drinking free *Jaffa* orange juice and natural *Sinai* desert spring water, specially bottled in Dewsbury, Manchester.'

'But, the children of Israel vacated the Holy Land a long time ago, never to return.' Alistair had cause to put in before telling Robert of a Jewish neighbour who took it upon himself to break into the family's shed to borrow the garden roller. 'We were visiting the Scottish Highland Games in Braemar at the time.' he added.

'Ach, don't be too sure, Alistair, the Jewish people will return to their homeland one day soon, and the 'Star of David' will be seen flying once again over his royal City, Jerusalem.'

'Not from what I have read in the *'New York Herald Tribune'* newspaper, this morning,' Alistair said. 'There is a certain amount of unrest in Europe, namely Germany, who say their troubles are being caused by Jews and communists and Adolf Hitler has promised that if he should be returned to power, he will restore Germany's might and stop her humiliations at the hands of Britain and France. He is also planning a solution to Germany's ethnic problems and from what I have read so far, there won't be any Jewish people left to hoist their flag.'

'Anyhow, that finger poke in the back which Mr Wall kindly gave me could have been worse.' Robert said.

'What do you mean exactly?'

'To put it bluntly, and not to put a finer point on it, the weaponry could have been a Roman *Gladius* sword specially designed to cut and thrust into the side of a Christian.'

One of the senior Italian fellows, a Y.M.C.A. delegate from Tuscany who was called, Giovanni Giorgini asked Robert if he knew the distance between Italy and Canada?' This was a classic case of the likeable Giovanni being in the wrong place at the wrong time when, Robert with a timely deliverance said to him that all roads lead to Rome and suggested he go out into the street, turn left at the traffic lights and start walking towards Rochester.

'Tell me Robert,' Alistair asked, going to buy some chocolates to take back home to Scotland. 'You know, the ones which are on special offer in the university shop and have a maple leaf and a grizzly bear depicted on the front of the box?'

'Well, I might, but it all depends on how much I have left in the coffers after forking-out to buy a new set of underwear to replace the ones which went up in smoke this morning.'

It was several years later in Streatham, Robert Bruce Hamilton Brown revamped the song, popularised by the American country and western singer, Jim Reeves, which goes:

"Moonlight and Roses
Bring wonderful memories of you
My heart reposes
Inside a chocolate box coloured in blue
June light discloses
Loves golden dreams sparkling anew

Moonlight and Roses
Bring beautiful thoughts so true."

'I trust you will be with us this evening at evening song and after prayers there is a special classical musical gala arrangement performed by the University of Columbia Symphony Orchestra, conducted by Sir Anthony Burton-Collins; the emphasis being Brahms and List.'

'No, already I think I shall give this one a miss; I would much rather get Brahms and List somewhere else, preferably in one of those Jitterbug venues down the road.'

'You know, Robert, a cat has only nine lives, but they are no use when you're dead.'

There were four young men, Alain La Conte, Kurt Schmidt, Charles (Charlie) Edge, Bruno Bateson and a multitude of Canadian friends who were invited to the university that evening to make sure the world-wide Y.M.C.A. members appeared to be comfortable in their town.

The visitors from the City of Toronto after introducing themselves suggested to Robert that they visit the *'Notorious Night Club'* at No 230 Richmond Street West, Toronto.

'Is this place where they dance to sheep-dipping music?' Robert asked Kurt Schmidt, a young aeroplane apprentice mechanic who came from Bremerhaven in Germany before leaving with his parents to live in Canada.

'Don't you mean head-dipping music?' Bruno Bateson put in, a lumberjack type of person with a beard similar to Blackbeard the pirate.

'I think you will find it will be the Swing, the Foxtrot, the Big Apple and the Jitterbug they dance inside the club; the frequenters to the *'Notorious Night Club'*, especially the women do not stoop as low as that.' Alain La Conte explained in a French accent which sounded typically Parisian.

Alain, a graphic artist who had worked for a Toronto newspaper for two years put forward the idea that if Robert wanted to visit a hoedown they could visit the *'Golden Lasso'* in Pearl Street, where, if one so desired could witness a 'Lucky Strike' cigarette being extracted from a cowboy's mouth by just one crack-away from a twenty-foot long bullwhip.

Charlie Edge, a twenty-one-year-old Canadian-born market gardener from Rochester in the South of Toronto, became very excited with the idea of swinging young ladies around a dance floor and climbing up the walls likened to James Cagney and said:

'Come on you guys, what are we waiting for; let's go!'

Chapter Nine

The "Notorious Night Club", 230 Richmond Street West, Toronto

'Howdy Dude folks, I'm your man.' Burt Newman, the club's friendly doorman from Calgary, Alberta said as the famous five stepped over the threshold of the "*Notorious Night Club*" to deposit their hats and coats in a waiting cloakroom.

'How do you do?' Robert responded giving the doorman the impression he was happy to make his acquaintance. 'He's one of them,' Robert said to Charlie Edge, a slight man with a brain the size of a *petit poi*, a garden pea.

'No, he's one of those.' Charlie replied with a boyish look on his face. 'And one should not mock the afflicted, especially when one has to leave the establishment with a good- looking doll on his arm at four o'clock in the morning.' he added.

'If you step out of line by drinking too much soda, he'll give you a bunch of these.' Bruno Bateson said, waving a working man's fist in front of Robert's face just to remind him that if his genealogical background was to follow him on to the dance floor, there could be reprisals from the French who always sit together in a corner smoking distinctively pungent *Gauloises* cigarettes and playing cards.'

Robert asked Alain La Conte, later that evening, 'Why do Frenchmen always gather around tables to drink endless cups of coffee?' Alain explained that it was because they have lengthy discussions about the price of miniscule cups of Canadian *Café Noir* and who is going to pay the waiter.

'In Germany, we always know how much to pay because we have a reputation of banging on the tables.' Kurt Schmidt was pleased to tell everyone in his company.

'Yes, well, we all know about that, don't we, Kurt?' Bruno said giving his black beard a bit of a stroke.

'I can remember all too well when we went to the "*Golden Lasso*" last weekend.' Charlie said, reminding Kurt of his sexual behaviour in the car parking lot with Billy-Joe Baker; a six feet-two inches tall American cow girl cum line-dancer from Detroit.

'We were supposed to be going to the Country and Western Club for a knees-up not a blow by blow account of what happened in the car park; I would suggest in future you button up your Levis before getting into my limousine.' Charlie Edge said, continuing to fan his wad of ten-cents-a-dance tickets underneath Kurt's nose which sported a typical Germanic Charlie Chaplin-style black moustache.

'Billy-Joe and I would have stayed inside to watch the final shoot-out, but there were no tables available.' Kurt sarcastically explained.

Robert, the precocious intellectual who liked to listen to his own voice, made a comment to Alain when he tried to impress him by saying:

'I like the way the French roll their 'R's and drop their 'H's when they attempt to speak in the English language.'

'I suppose it's a bit like Bruno dropping his dungarees after a near miss collision with a great 'Red Wood' in Toronto's Forest of Dundee.' Charlie said with an exaggerated smile.

'You've got to treat French people like sensitive flowers.' Kurt said, with a botanical knowledge which was second to none. 'A red rose becomes a crimson weed if it is not nurtured with a firm hand under artificial sunlight.' he added.

'What the hell are you talking about, Kurt?' Bruno asked, inquisitively.

'I am talking about the French army, who had the audacity to settle here after defeating the English Red Coats at Quebec; the *Normands* are now civil servants living in Canada and I am a foreigner paying taxes to people wielding axes.

'You still haven't answered my question, Kurt; what has all this got to do with flowers which are going off?'

'Well, you see, the French need a clip around the ear now and again, administered preferably down inside a dungeon where it is cold, damp and dark.' Kurt Schmidt so graphically explained.

'You seem to forget I am a Frenchman.' Alain said disdainfully after listening to Kurt's anti-Semitism comments.

'You seem to forget, Alain, that if it wasn't for your football referee swallowing his whistle in the trenches during The First World War, we Germans would have won handsomely on Christmas Day.'

'Tell me, Robert, why hasn't your friend volunteered to come with us?' Charlie Edge asked.

'It is because he would sooner sing hymns and count his blessings around a piano; Alistair has this theory that the more money he puts into the offertory box on Sundays, the more closer he is to God.'

'But it is only Tuesday, Robert.'

'I know and thank God for that.'

'He's not another one of those, is he, Robert? Bruno put in.

'You mean an odd ball who thinks he is lucky when he loses a shilling and finds a pound.' Robert asked.

'Yes, I suppose you could say that.' Bruno quietly replied when he saw Burt, the club's Wild Bill Hickok and doorman, casually mincing his way over to where the French people had taken up residence.

The tune made famous and sung by Fred Astaire, "Puttin' on the Ritz" was played by Toronto's eighteen-piece dance band, named "The Rainbows" and its charismatic leader, ironically, was called George Rainbow. Couples, after dancing to the "Big Apple", the "Foxtrot", the "Swing", the "Waltz", "Jitterbug" and "Tap", precariously made their way back to the candle-lit tables to take in some much-needed rest and recuperation before getting up again for a traditional smooch underneath a glittering silver ball.

'Hey you guys, this is not a casino.' the doorman said to the asexual card sharks seated in a corner who had about as much interest in broads than a bunch of castrated buffoons; 'if you want to play poker, then I suggest you go visit *"The Golden Lasso"*; there are plenty of Mavericks in there just waiting to relieve you and your dough.'

'Would you guys like to go downstairs for some soda pop?' Bruno suggested, rubbing his hands in anticipation and giving everyone the impression he was thirsty and couldn't wait to break the law by going against the prohibition. 'We have a special knock, Robert, which we use to gain access to the closely guarded bar; it sounds something like "Dancing cheek to cheek" with a difference; that is, we only use our hands to bang on the door not a ten-pound sledge hammer wielded by over-enthusiastic dragnet officers.'

'What did Mike Hammer receive as a present for Christmas?' Charlie asked jokingly.

Following a series of I don't knows, the answer came as a bit of a surprise when he said:

'He received a sledge.'

'Come on you guys, let's go hit the bourbon; the bottles were specially flown in last week from Chicago but unfortunately half of the batch went missing when the plane crash-landed near to a police station on the outskirts of Niagara Falls, and rumour has it there wasn't a cop to be seen for several days in the local town of Buffalo.'

'Did you know that in 1923 an aerial rum-runner crashed near Croton, New York?' Charlie Edge divulged. 'In it was found one hundred and fifty bottles of Scotch and Irish whiskey, apparently being conveyed from Canada. And did you know, a coroner's chemist in Chicago, testing samples of liquor seized by the police, found wood alcohol in many of these samples?'

'I wondered why my glass of Scotch whisky tasted like maple syrup.' Robert said, allowing Charlie to benefit from a lesson in diffusion.

'And here's me thinking my bourbon tasted like dope; a stretching agent which aircraft manufacturers put on the wings and fuselages to stop aeroplanes from crashing.' Bruno so knowledgably put in.

'My goodness, is that Marlene Dietrich I see sitting at the side of the dance floor?' Robert said before walking down a wide marble staircase towards a small penny arcade.

'No, it's Mary Astor.' Charlie Edge interrupted.

'No, No, it is Sarah Bernhardt, the Jewish actress.' Kurt Schmidt insisted on saying as he slid down the spiral staircase, legs apart hoping to arrive at the bottom quicker than his unfit partners.

'I think you have got her name wrong.' Alain La Conte said when he himself eventually arrived at the foot of the stairs looking at Kurt disapprovingly. 'Sarah Bernhardt died with a big smile on her face a few years ago; she apparently had an eye for the ladies and had only one leg to stand on.' Alain went on.

'Well, it could be neither of them.' Bruno Bateson put in when he clocked Celia Johnson coming up from the ladies' downstairs powder room.

'Agh, they all look the same to me, especially when they put all that white stuff on their faces.' Robert said, continuing with his decadent and repugnant attitude problems.

It was when Johnny Kipper, the under-cover barman in the, 'The Black Hole of Calcutta' divulged the woman's name, everyone was taken aback after learning she was called Gloria Aspinwall, a twenty-four-year-old crumpet and scone manufacturing heiress from Bradford, Pennsylvania and not Queen Mary from England.

Everyone inside the bar was more than keen to return to the dance floor when Johnny Kipper seemed to vanish like a gambler's lucky streak when he was tipped-off about the Canadian Mounted Police raiding the premises.

'It will never cease to amaze me how a horse can get down these stairs.' Charlie Edge said and beginning to sound intelligent for the first time that evening.

'Tell me, Robert, how do you win so much money from the slot-machines?' Bruno asked, as if he didn't know already.

'It is quite simple,' Robert replied, sealing his tightly closed lips to emanate a recently patented zip-fastener, 'I bend the glass to slow the wheels down and somehow, by chance, they stop at the machine's lucky numbers; triple seven.'

'Did you know,' Charlie Edge asked Robert. 'Here in Canada, we have Kodiak grizzly bears which are nine-feet tall when standing on their hind legs?'

'That's very interesting.' Robert replied with a precocious smile upon his face. 'I have a Kodak box camera at home; I wondered why the strap broke?'

From that moment on, things began to settle down, but that was until Robert made a beeline for Gloria Aspinwall, the unquestionable belle of the ball.

The song and dance tune popularized and made famous by Fred Astaire, "Something's got to give" was now being played by the Rainbow orchestra and after the haze of cigarette smoke had slowly dissipated from around the dance floor Robert could see Gloria at the table drinking champagne from a translucent glass high-heeled slipper, specially designed for the club's notoriety and vulgar extravagance.

'May I have the pleasure of the next dance?' Robert asked nervously. 'I will have the pleasure if you've got the time?' he diplomatically added.

'Maybe I'll have the pleasure, if you've got the time?' she said yawning and then checking the time on her white and gold diamond-encrusted *Cartier* wristwatch.

'And may I introduce myself.' Robert insisted on telling her. 'My name is Robert Bruce Hamilton-Brown from Scotland.'

'Well, you don't say.' Gloria said, proffering a hand for him to shake; her gloves accentuating the slim bony lines of her fingers.

After Gloria had introduced herself to Robert and had seen a pair of his odd socks riding up loosely around his ankles, she declined the offer to dance to the Viennese Waltz; the socks, apparently, had been salvaged from the washhouse explosion that morning and were retrieved from a grass verge on campus.

'May I sit down at your table?' Robert asked, surreptitiously shining one of his short brown leather Gringos on the back of his white cavalry twill trousers.

'If you insist.' Gloria replied, looking around graciously to see who was taking in the scenery.

'Would you like to listen to one of my poems?' Robert asked, fumbling around inside his jacket pocket to find a scrappy piece of paper with a verse which was called: "Flowers of Anxiety" and began:

"Bring not the bluebells
Growing wild on yonder fells
Bring not the gilded lily
Abound in distant valley
Bring not the posies and the roses

The sweetness of the pea
But bring me your love and that is all
Until after the winter when snowdrops fall"

'Do you know, Robert; that is bordering on classic poetry?' Gloria said, patronisingly. 'And by the way who the hell, may I ask is Lily?' she added.

'Oh, you mean the flowers in the verse; it was something I knocked-up on the T.S.S. "*Athenia*"; the ship I sailed in from Glasgow to Quebec.'

'I bet you did: why don't you go visit Toronto's '*Zoo de Jerks*' or a '*Dude Ranch*'; an old style 'wild west' country club where they have sheep, horses and cattle to keep you company?' Gloria suggested when Robert insisted on sliding his recently acquired cowboy boots up and down on her leg under the table.

'I have a poem which you may or may not like to hear.' she said.

"You seem to me a bit of a toff
Why don't you grab your coat and just buzz-off?"

'You think you have the monopoly in being Scottish, don't you Robert?' Gloria said when he wiped his nose with a haberdashery shop remnant, an off-cut which one could be excused for turning into a Douglas tartan handkerchief. 'Well, I will tell you there are at least four thousand people in Toronto whose origins began by "The Bonny, Bonny Banks of Loch Lomond". My great grandfather was Scottish and a baker by trade; it was shortly after he came to live in America he made his fortune by baking pancakes, crumpets and scones, and rumour has it, he made the first cream doughnut and sold it to a Red Indian in exchange for his toupee. My father tells of him being a great pioneer living in a Mid-West back yard with only a flintlock pistol to keep the coyotes, wolves, rattlesnakes and Mohawk Indians at bay."

'He must have been a great man; making all that dough in his back yard.' Robert said in all sincerity.

'I meant to describe my great-grandfather in metaphor.' she said, looking at Robert as if he were the biggest jerk who had ever stepped foot on North American soil.

'Metaphor; is that somewhere near Bradford, Pennsylvania or New York.' Robert asked with an air of sarcasm.

'And, would you kindly extinguish your pipe, the smell is giving me a headache.' she demanded, bringing him more into focus after the dark grey smoke was eventually quelled by him continually tamping a knife on the surface of smouldering tobacco.

'Yes, certainly, Gloria, I used to smoke *Craven A* cigarettes, but they were too harsh and rasped my throat and turned my fingers bright orange; one also has to consider one's Adam's apple.'

'I know the feeling.' she said, looking down at an unbuttoned fly in Robert's trousers.'

'Smoking; it's such a filthy habit, isn't it?' Robert uttered without meaning a single word he said.

'I have a Scottie dog, called Chips and last week I lost him until he turned up in the paper.' Gloria said without thinking.

'Yes, I can imagine.' Robert replied when Gloria gave him the advantage of rhetorical superiority. 'And which Fish and Chip shop in Toronto would that have been?' he asked.

'I think you had better go and join your friends; they seem to be having a whale of a time.' Gloria said when she spotted a million-dollar trooper walking into the room and trying to look like Gary Cooper.

"It don't mean a thing if you ain't got that swing", Robert said to Gloria, and afterwards reminding her that she had two holes in her suede peep-toe high-heel shoes.

It was ten minutes past four when Robert entered the dormitory of the University's Wycliffe College of St Michaels.

'Tell me, Robert where have you been until now?' Alistair blearily asked him.

'Just dancing Alistair; just dancing.'

Chapter Ten

Wednesday morning, July 29th, breakfasting in The Great Hall, Hart House

'Will you be staying for dinner this evening, Robert or have you got other engagements?' Alistair asked at the breakfast table. And talking about engagements, Robert, I have just received a telegraph from Morag asking me how you are because she tells me, she hasn't received any communication from you since we departed from the quayside in Glasgow.'

'Unless you are sufficiently informed, Alistair, it takes at least two weeks for correspondence to arrive on the shores of the so-called British Isles by ship and a further three days for it to be sorted in Mount Pleasance Post Office in London.

'What about the Trans-Atlantic airship *Graf Zeppelin*, LZ 127 which takes just a few hours to fly from Lakehurst Naval Air Station, NAS USA to Friedrichshafen in Germany?' Alistair pointed out so accurately.

'But Morag doesn't live in Germany, Alistair.'

'Agh, but you see, as we speak there is a polar flight of the *Graf Zeppelin* which departed from Friedrichshafen five days ago for a research trip around the Arctic Circle, (*Polarfahrt 1931*). This adventure had been a dream of Count Zeppelin twenty years ago but unfortunately could not be realized at the time due to the outbreak of World War One. The polar flight, Robert, is to take one week and plans are in operation for the airship to make a rendezvous with a surface vessel and then to transfer and to take on-board the airship, souvenir mail, letters and postcards specially franked First-Day Covers of this historic journey.'

'I still cannot see the point you are making, Alistair.' Robert said wondering what he was going to say next.

'Well, it is quite simple; a matter of logic which you seem to be lacking at the moment. If you were to post a letter to Morag next week, Robert, it should have arrived through our letter box in Glasgow yesterday.'

'Oh, yes, I get your logic.' Robert said, scratching his head and allowing more dandruff to fall on to the table.

'And did you know Robert, next week we are going to visit the World's largest rigid airship manufacturers, the 'Goodyear' *Zeppelin* Corporation at Akron, near Cleveland, Ohio and that will be interesting, won't it?'

'And did *you* know, Alistair, that when we were three years of age, these things shaped like huge lead pencils were used to fly over the English Channel towards Britain and then bomb the shit out of London; the drone from the five engines during a dark smoggy night was enough to drive anyone crazy, apparently.'

'Yes, I did know that, Robert, and now the Americans have constructed an airship for army and navy purposes, and provision is made for storage of five warplanes within the hull; the storage compartments being seventy-five feet long by sixty feet wide and planes can be lowered or raised through a T-shaped opening during flight by means of a trapeze.'

'It sounds like Kelvin Hall Circus, Alistair, and I suppose the next piece of information you are going to tell me is the reason why the *Graf Zeppelin* made the Europe-Pan American flight last year (*the first around-the-world flight of the Graf Zeppelin*) was because America has designs on bombing the shit out of Japan on a first ever nonstop flight across the Pacific Ocean, calling at Tokyo's *Kasumigaura* Naval Air Base. We,' Robert continued to pontificate, 'in Britain, are building similar airships but, like everything else the English seem to do, they are always the slowest boat in a convoy.' he said with an undeniable hatred for anything made south of the Border.

'But the British R101 airship was destroyed by fire during its inaugural flight last year.' Alistair had to put in.

'That catastrophe could have been avoided if the manufacturers of the airship hadn't run out of 'No Smoking' signs in a highly inflammable area; it was either that or someone was careless with a box of matches.' Robert replied, tempering his *Meerschaum* pipe in to a glass ash tray, giving the carved effigy of John Brown a headache at the same time.

'I think there are moves afoot to build an airship in Scotland.' Alistair said with a quirky smile.

'Well, there you go, Alistair, the Scots produce better engineers, pioneers, inventors and bridge builders than anyone else; I suppose we have the Romans to thank for that. Also, we make the best swords, *claymores*, *skin dhu* and *dirks* in the world.' Robert boasted.

'And I suppose the Romans were responsible for the manufacture of those lethal weapons too?' Alistair said.

'No, no, it was the Vikings.' Robert replied. 'And, if it wasn't for Wilkinson's military swords and H.W. Phillips inventing meat choppers, we wouldn't have the razor blades we so desperately need.' he added looking at two days growth of beard covering Alistair Campbell's spotty complexion.

'I'm growing a beard.' Alistair said in all seriousness.

'I'll put it in the local press.' Robert replied. 'But, don't tell everyone because they will all want one.'

'Does that include Mrs Shipley, our resident dragon house matron at Wycliffe College?'

'Only, if you want.' Robert said, as he munched his way through a piece of bread the size of a front door step spread generously with strawberry jam.

'And, Robert, would you kindly remove that disgusting looking pipe from your mouth; you light it, wipe it or hide it away inside your pocket.' Alistair demanded assertively.

'Don't you like my new ivory *Meerschaum* pipe? Robert said. 'It has a deep-carved tobacco bowl, depicting John Brown, Queen Victoria's Scottish boyfriend; see, he is wearing a *Tam o' Shanter*, a wee bonnet made from ebony wood; well that's what it says on the wee box; notably, ebony and ivory go together like harmony.'

'Let me see.' Alistair said, looking closely at the mobile furnace in more detail. 'It was made in Hong Kong, Robert and as you can see it is clearly embossed on the underside; I think your *Wishee Washee* friend, Chang Wan, in what was the laundry room, has a lot to answer for because it is the second one I have seen around the campus this morning.'

'Gloria, my delectable dancing partner last evening didn't seem to mind me smoking a pipe; the unmistakable aromatic smell of American Black

Cherry tobacco was sending her crazy, Alistair.'

'How long have you known this Gloria what's her name?'

'Och, a wee while.' Robert said as he checked the time on his gold-plated 'Timex' wristwatch.

'Just how long is a piece of string? And what does she do, when she's at home.' Alistair replied inquisitively.

'When she is not scrubbing floors in the kitchen, she makes crumpets, scones and pancakes, that sort of thing.'

'Morag is going to wipe the floor with you, Robert, if she ever finds out about your inexcusable two-timing experiences.'

"It don't mean a thing if you ain't got that thing"

'What is the thing, Robert?'

"The way I held my knife, the way we danced till three; no, no they can't take that away from me".

'I shouldn't have thought anyone would want to; are you alright, Robert? I can always call a doctor. You didn't take the dagger, your Celtic inter-woven black wood and pewter special *skin dhu* along with you last evening, did you? It is of little wonder you weren't arrested; just, who do you think you are, Mac, the knife? And do I detect a hint of alcohol on your breath?' Alistair added, sniffing around underneath Robert's nose.

A cocktail, consisting of a *Crème de menthe cordial*, fresh orange juice and a tinge of ginger to add to its exotic flavour was Robert's only means of escape and evasion following Alistair's breakfast-time questioning.

'Tell me Robert, are you going to see this scrubber, again?'

'No Alistair, I would sooner make love to a Rottweiler or have it off with Jane, Mrs Shipley; she gets in and out of bed more times than Gladys Mary Smith gets out of Dracula's coffin.'

'She's not another one of your floozies from the *Krypton Factor*, is she?'

'No, Alistair, her stage name is Mary Pickford; she is one of Hollywood's greatest film stars.'

'That's an interesting point, Robert, because Mrs Shipley comes out at night too and last evening she asked me if I had seen you. And another aspect to this brief encounter was she was holding a tin which contained a home-made coffee cream cake and a pair of neatly folded trousers placed over her arm.'

'Och I, Mrs Shipley volunteered to wash and iron my grey worsted *trews* after they had wrapped themselves round a flagpole and I had to pay a fireman a *quarter* to hand them back.'

'And where does the coffee cream cake come into all of this?' Alistair curiously asked.

'I told her I would be more than happy to read some of my poetry to her on her day off.'

'You never give it a rest do you Robert, it's a wonder you haven't followed in William Gilbert Grace, the cricketer's footsteps, and made the first century.'

'Agh, there is time yet.'

'Anyway, I volunteered to take the cake and the bundle from her possession, Robert, and you may find that the moths have attacked your trousers during the night and the rats have invited themselves to a coffee morning.'

'I have written a poem, Alistair, it is dedicated to her and I shall recite it at the earliest opportunity. It goes something like this:

'Hot Pants
An audience full of *bruisers*
Came to watch a tight pair of *trewsers*'
On the stage these pants well worn
Took on a life all on their own
They twisted and turned it was such a big giggle
As a bit went up and down in the middle
Some would say that was the reason
To watch someone's trousers all summer season
Why! Why! Why came from a 'Smiler'
She was just another frustrated 'Delilah'

'One never knows, Alistair, there may come a time when someone will strut his or her stuff in an area the size of Wembley Stadium. And, did you know, Sir Robert McAlpine, another Scotsman, built the Empire

Stadium in Wembley on the twenty-eighth of April nineteen twenty-three?'

'He must have been knackered to have constructed a building of that magnitude in just one day, Robert.'

'Don't be a *hoots man*, Alistair; he was back in Scotland laying the tarmac on the roads leading to the isles.'

'But that is the Adam's family you are talking about, Robert; they work with the black stuff; hence tar-macadam.'

'Well, they were both good friends and came from the same place; 'Bonnie Scotland'. Have you ever been tar-macadamized, Alistair?'

'No, but I am familiar with a person who had it done on his eleventh birthday. You're not going to recite that rude poem to Mrs Shipley, are you, because a cat has only got nine lives but it is of no use to it when it is dead.'

'No, Alistair, I was only testing your reaction.' he said with rapprochement, re-establishing friendly relations by giving himself the opportunity to make amends by reading another poem from inside his jacket pocket, called: "Rellies in Wellies".

Rellies in Wellies
Little 'Bo Peep' lost her sheep
And didn't know where to go
A farmer took her by the hand
They found them in New Zealand

'And why, if I may ask the question, do Wellington boots appear in your poem?' Alistair said in total confusion.

'I was referring to the general footwear belonging to a couple who emigrated down under; they wear those to stop them from getting their feet wet.' Robert replied convincingly.

'It is good that Edward, the Prince of Wales, cannot hear you because he would certainly lock you up in the tower and throw away the keys.'

'Agh, he's not the Prince of Scotland though, is he Alistair? Stuart Charles Edward 'Bonnie Prince Charlie' was our man at the top, wouldn't you say. It wasn't our fault the '*Froggies*' confiscated his passport and he was permanently exiled in a castle devoid of eating shortbread for the rest of his life.'

'This isn't true, he wasn't the man at the top, but a 'Young Pretender'; he deserted Scotland to join his mates in France and afterwards organised reprisals against the English.' Alistair said, trying to set the record straight. 'But there weren't to be any reprisals, Robert, because the French thought he was too ambitious and an incoherent fool.'

'And after assembly, how are you going to spend the morning, Alistair? That's if you don't mind me asking.'

'I think I shall spend the remainder of the morning in the library where I can find peace and solitude amongst the books waiting patiently on the shelves to be read; most of my closest friends are there; George Bernard Shaw, Lord George Gordon Byron, Oscar Wilde; the list is endless. Tell me, Robert do you know Oscar Wilde?'

'Not readily, Alistair, but I may have his telephone number.'

"No one is as blind as those who cannot see" Alistair said quoting Shaw. 'And after assembly, Robert, how are you going to spend your precious time because Mrs Shipley is taking the day off.'

'I shall be playing 'bridge' in the halls of recreation with three members of the Scottish delegation.'

'Don't you mean 'poker', Robert? I can remember your bridge parties on-board the "Athenia"; you seem to have more money in your pockets now than when we up-anchored in Glasgow, and why, may I ask is the *Ace of Spades* lying on the floor?'

'It must have fallen out from one of my sleeves.' Robert said after magically producing a joker that was hidden at the back of his ear.

'And, when we visit the 'Goodyear' *Zeppelin* factory in Akron next week, Robert, I suggest you leave your matches with Mr M.B Vilas who is to be our host at his home at number 2289 Stillman Road, Cleveland, Ohio until Monday morning August tenth.'

Chapter Eleven

A day of leisure in the Recreation Hall at the University

"Manners *maketh* man" whilst, big boobies and make-up, *make up* a woman, Robert was eager to say when John Crawford seated to his right made a very big mistake by generating and making-up his own rules of poker to suit him and his pocket.

Alex Smith, another sucker, sitting opposite to the poker-faced and sleight-of-hand Hamilton-Brown, was saddened when he lost twenty Canadian dollars in less than one quarter of an hour playing cards at a table in the recreation hall next to Heartbreak House.

Stanley Nairn, usually a confident bridge player was seated to Robert's left suddenly became another member of the Hamilton-Brown 'I owe you club' when he lost his money at poker. Robert was quick to offer loans to his fellow players at a reasonable rate of twenty-five per cent compoundable interest and personal profit per week until the full amount was paid back to him.

A semi-religious German Y.M.C.A delegate who continually boasted during the morning coffee break being held in the Quadrangle of Hart House that if Herr Hitler ever came to power, he would overturn the money tables in the Jewish shops and markets, and then torch every Synagogue in Western Europe.

Robert pointed out that the New York Stock Exchange in Wall Street would be a lot better off if he were to keep his big mouth shut and piss off back to Germany.

Further to this, Robert called him a sour-face kraut and that his gold teeth were in danger of being knocked unconscious before flying back home to Berlin inside a LZ 127 *Zeppelin* airship.

'Did you know, Muller? The price of a *Graf Zeppelin* and barrage balloon is going up; it is all due to inflation.' Robert asked.

'I shall report you to the angry; the brown shirts and the Gestapo, our secret police back home in the Fatherland.' Klaus Muller said, giving Robert the impression he wasn't amused at his proposals.

'You don't frighten me, Muller because I am familiar with the fascist movement in Great Britain, also Germany's not so secret police; thugs with guns that's what they are.' Robert said with a savage look upon on his face. 'Go and eat some bratwurst sausage or something equally as bad.' he added.

The disheartened Hitler Youth went away completely disheartened wishing he had never got up that morning to eat a hearty Germanic breakfast, especially laid-on for him and his fellow Y.M.C.A delegates.

'I have a poem for you.' Alistair announced. 'It was written by Scottish poet, Fred. W. Holton and very appropriate towards your attitudes and perpetual hatred towards certain minority groups here at the University; it is called "A little Wetness behind the Ears"

'I wouldn't call the German delegation a minority group, Alistair; they seem to be taking over the entire place, anyway; Theodor Pianoff will sort them out this afternoon when they play football with the Russian Orthodox team on the sports and recreation field in the back campus of the University.'

'And, if you don't mind me asking.' Alistair anxiously enquired. 'Who is Theodor Pianoff?'

'He is the referee and plays the piano and harmonium for the older members in the Convocation Hall of the University; he is the guy who pulls out all the stops.'

'The poem goes like this, Robert':

A Little Wetness behind the Ears
"Water, water, lovely water
Of the elements the wettest
Some will love thee, some endure thee
Others simply detest

Let me sing a song about thee
For we cannot do without thee
Wondrous water!
Fills the river, cools the liver

When its icy, makes you shiver
Brings rheumatics, hydrostatics
Drives the weather to acrobatics
Comes in spring and comes in springs
Good for ships and other things

H_2O, how you flow!
Makes the trees and flowers grow!
Aqua purer, there's nothing surer
In each medicine and curer
Though you mean so much to men
Ne'er poet lifts his pen
In thy praise, the silly fellow
Prefers to lift a large umbrella

Many are thy works and wonders
Comrade of the winds and thunders!
Rusting metals, filling kettles
Washing bottles, making pot-holes
Floating sharks and arcs and barques
With 'Monkey Brand' removing marks
Water, water, lovely water
Do we love thee as we *oughter*?
You've never failed throughout the years
All too wet behind the ears"

'Well, yes; that was fairly good, Alistair, but it doesn't scan.'

'Neither do your poems; they are like birds that seem to have lost their direction.' Alistair graphically pointed out. 'And why, do you keep on slapping your thigh, Robert; have you got an affliction?'

'I do it to keep the flies away.' Robert said as he watched a rather disgruntled Klaus Muller tripping over a coconut mat in front of the door before visiting the toilet; the motif which said 'Welcome' was certainly not in keeping with his constant hatred towards the entire German race. 'I don't suppose he'll be having coffee in the Quadrangle again, Alistair because I spiked his drink with a high-dosage of aspirin; enough to power the largest of airships back to Berlin.'

'And as you are talking about flies, I would suggest you check your trousers.' Alistair said when Robert burst into song with "Something's gonna give". 'Why is it Robert, you always seem to appear insecure and emotionally upset, always having a go at anyone who has the misfortune to tread along the same path as you?'

'Well, they either go this way, that way or the other way, the choice is entirely theirs.'

'I just knew you would come out with something outrageous like that, and no anti-depressant in the world could sort your problem out.' Alistair said with all sincerity.

'How is it then, I have just volunteered to give some of my tablets away without prescription?'

'I can hear Theodor Pianoff playing the piano in the Convocation Hall,' Alistair said choosing to ignore him and tapping on a mahogany table to the music of Handel's Messiah; the Hallelujah Chorus.

'He wants to Pianoff back to Russia, but not before he has shown one or two of the German players a red card and sent them off from the football field,' Robert said. 'And then perhaps, we can all get some peace and quiet around here.'

'Here we go again; you have no culture, no morals, no ethics, nor an ear for good music.'

'George Rainbow and his dance band "The "Rainbows", sounded extremely good last night when they played *Putt'n on the Ritz*.' Robert replied, tempering his pipe once again with an implement which looked like a *Gretna Green* Smithy's anvil on the top of a chromium-plated pen knife.

'You didn't get up and have a dance did you, Robert?'

'But, of course; one just puts one leg in front of the other and away you go. I had a dancing tutorial outfit given to me for Christmas, which consisted of pieces of tissue paper cut into the shape of gigantic feet. The box, closely resembling a Bertrand Ling magic set without the top hat and cane, and one was supposed to scatter all this stuff on the floor and follow in the footsteps of Fred Astaire and Ginger Rogers; it wouldn't have been too bad if the manufacturers hadn't made the mistake of putting too many left feet into the box. And, to make matters worse, there were a couple of music sheets for one to sing along with as one glided when they were guided from the lounge into the kitchen.'

'The Chinese have got a lot to answer to, especially around here.' Alistair said, mimicking a coolie transferred on to the side of a *willow pattern* teacup and saucer.

'Och aye, they owe me for some kit I lost in the fire.'

'You did say kit, Robert, didn't you?'

'Yes, I did, are you going deaf?'

'Tell me, Robert, who gave you such a desirable present like that?'

'Edwina Robertson; remember, Alistair, she was the one-legged table tennis champion from the Young Women's Christian Association in Glasgow.'

'Yes, I remember; she kept falling over when you deliberately put the ball into a spin.'

'Edwina and I won the Sunday Presbyterian table tennis championship league, and the silver cup still resides on the mantelpiece back home, and no one can take that away from me.'

'I don't suppose anyone would want to.' Alistair replied falling about in fits of laughter.

It was after Robert had composed himself following a series of remarks thrown at him by Alistair which had somehow managed to penetrate his brain, when there was a telephone call for him in the foyer.

The telephone call was being made by Gloria Aspinwall, the upper middle-class blonde- haired American broad who Robert had failed to impress the previous evening. She was desperate to speak to anyone who would care to listen to her and indeed her problems, and if it was only Robert, 'The Bruce' Hamilton-Brown she didn't mind, because her Scottie dog, Chips, had escaped from her apartment once again into one of Toronto's busiest thoroughfares; St. Claire Avenue.

Robert asked her whether the dog was wearing an identity disc to which she remarked it had one attached to a tartan collar, but the address on it was her home address in Bradford, Yorkshire, and following a lengthy discussion as to how the dog could walk and swim a distance of approximately three thousand five-hundred miles he came to the conclusion she was never going to see him ever again.

She told Robert her evening in the "The Notorious Night Club" was spoilt by a Canadian *gigolo* who would insist on her going back to his apartment for a cup of coffee; his tiny flat was a tip and there were several unwashed cups lying around all over the place. Gloria continued to say that Chips may have disappeared just before sun-up when he was due for his early morning walk around Queen's Park. Robert asked, inquisitively, at what time she arrived back to her apartment, to which she replied that it was seven o'clock precisely.

'Would you like to call round to my place this morning for a cup of coffee, Robert?' Gloria desperately asked, probably feeling even more distraught by Robert's continual questioning.

'I don't think so, Gloria, you seem to have served up more cups of coffee than a British Lyon's Corner House waitress and, as for the dog, I would suggest you join it and go back to Pennsylvania.'

The dog was seen later that morning rambling through the campus of the University and it was when Robert noticed one of the Y.M.C.A. Chinese, U.S.A delegates picking him up to look at his collar he realized Chips could have ended his days inside a cooking pot; *chow mien, one-hundred year-old eggs* and *rattlesnake* soup being just three of their favourite Oriental dishes.

Robert retrieved the mutt without problem having convinced the Chinaman, Michael Mao, a throw-back from the Ming dynasty, that the dog belonged to him and he had only to look at the collar to see that the tartan was the same pattern as his Douglas tie.

There was a distinct smell of jasmine, frankincense and opium permeating all around the grounds of the campus and it was when he saw Chang Wan rearranging his washing line outside the laundry room in Wycliffe College to alert prospective customers of his presence, Robert knew he was the one responsible for supplying narcotics to some of the more adventurous students.

100

The next task Hamilton-Brown undertook was to nervously deliver the dog safely back to Gloria Aspinwall's place of residence.

There were no pets to be allowed inside the university buildings or indeed to stroll around the campus grounds unaccompanied. Robert passed on the responsibility of looking after Chips to eighteen-year-old Michael Mao under the condition it would still be in one piece and not dissected when he returned from making the dreaded telephone call.

He perused through the telephone directory in The Great Hall and found her name alphabetically at the beginning; Toronto 63047 was the unmistakable telephone number of her apartment at No 36 St. Clair Avenue.

Robert, after slowly and hesitantly dialling the number, held the black Bakelite receiver up to his ear.

Gloria answered the phone immediately and began the dialogue by saying:

'Oh, it's you again.'

'Yes, it's me,' Robert replied with a sigh. 'Also, I have retrieved your dog; it was found by a Chinaman.'

'My dog was roaming around in China, Ho Lee Fuck, how strange.' Gloria confusedly replied.

'No, Chips was found by Michael Mao, a Chinese delegate from Bay Street in San Francisco.'

'Now, you are telling me Chips was found in California; are you mad, Robert?'

'You don't seem to understand, Gloria, the dog was found by Michael when he saw it wandering around the grounds of the university campus this morning.'

'Oh, my darling Robert, I just knew you could be good at something. Why don't you bring him to my apartment and then you could have some cocoa or something a little stronger. In fact, I will organise a cab to bring you both back for lunch.'

After he had agreed to Gloria's terms, Chips was reluctantly handed back to Robert when an instant love affair developed between him and a blonde-haired dog.

'Robert,' Gloria asked him when he finally reached her apartment, 'having come all this way to British Columbia from Bonnie Scotland, what is it you desire the most?'

'Don't tell me you are serving *haggis*, *tatties* and *neeps* for lunch because that will be a turnip for my book.'

Chapter Twelve

Thursday morning, July 30th, breakfasting in The Great Hall, Hart House

Appropriately, the itinerary for Robert that morning was quite simple; to get his head down on someone's pillow and to try and correct a much-neglected sleeping pattern which had caught up with him after subjecting his body to several days of self-gratification and sexual abuse.

It was just before breakfast Robert was advised by one of the senior Scottish delegates, a Mr Donald Johnston, to go and visit the university's resident Egyptian physician, Dr. 'feel good' Amir Temmam, because he was suffering from advanced chronic insomnia after complaining to him that he was unable to achieve a good night's sleep because of the pigeons.

'I trust you had a good night's sleep because Jane Shipley was looking for you again last evening.' Alistair asked when Robert was about to sit down to eat his breakfast from a stainless-steel tray.

'*Agh*, no; doesn't that woman ever give up.' Robert replied as he violently bashed the top of a boiled egg with an E.P.N.S. silver spoon.

'Mrs Shipley is only looking after your welfare Robert and you can't blame her for that, can you?'

'Does the welfare include inviting me to her rooms at two o'clock in the morning; she is married with a husband, Alistair, and Mr Shipley is a keen fisherman who prefers to paddle a canoe on Lake Ontario than hang-around in the grounds of Wycliffe College.'

'You seem to know more about Jane Shipley than the rest of us put together; tell me Robert, have you a problem with your trousers?'

'Yes, it is my flies; the holes are far too big for the buttons, but don't you worry, Mrs Shipley will sort it out.'

'Sort what out?'

'The button-holes, Alistair, the button-holes.'

'And, where were you until one o'clock this morning, Robert Hamilton-Brown?' Alistair asked.

'Taking care of a dog, Alistair; just looking after a dog.'

'You do realize Morag is going to kill you when we return to Glasgow.' Alistair said, predicting his sister's reaction when she hears of Robert's sexual antics.

'For goodness sake, Alistair, I was only returning Gloria's dog after it was found roaming around the grounds of the university campus.'

'And that took you all of at least twelve hours, did it?' Alistair asked and now scowling at him. 'Yesterday, we had fish for lunch and a roast bison sandwich for dinner,' he continued to say.

'*Agh*, but I had the finest Russian caviar for lunch and roast turkey for dinner.'

'Tell me, Robert, what did you give to the dog?'

'The same Alistair, it was just the same.'

'And where were you until the early hours of this morning, Robert?'

'Just dancing, Alistair, I was just dancing.'

'You seem to be doing a great deal of dancing of late my friend; you're not on the turn are you?'

'No, of course not, whatever gave you that idea?'

'It's that picture of Salvador Dali you have hanging up inside your wardrobe that is puzzling me; the one with him sporting a well-groomed bespoke moustache with more wax than a Vatican candle.' Alistair said, pointing his finger at nothing in particular.

'He is one of the world's greatest surrealistic painters; I only wish I could draw and paint like him.'

'Just stick to your trains, boats, hot-air balloons and planes, Robert; they are more in-keeping with your trip back home and who knows, all of this occupational therapy just may help you obtain a good night's sleep.'

'That's bordering on poetry, Alistair, "Just stick to your trains, boats, hot-air balloons and planes and a giraffe that went up in bloody flames".'

'What are you referring to now, Robert?'

'A "Giraffe in Flames" is a famous painting by the Spanish artist, Salvador Dali and it is currently being exhibited in the *Louvre* galleries in Paris.'

'That is not politically correct, Robert, I don't like to see animals going up in flames.'

'Well, what about that roast bison sandwich you ate for dinner last evening; the bovine beast had been rotating on a spit all afternoon.'

'I would have thought you may have been friendlier with the French Bohemian artist, Toulouse-Lautrec; an unimportant miniscule of a man, but a large coat fitted him perfectly. And rumour has it, he was a pervert, and like you Robert, frequented music halls, particularly the *Follies Bergère* and the numerous cabaret review parlours in Paris, but strangely, but not so strangely, he had a problem with his easel when it continually fell over as he painted frilly-clad well-proportioned bottoms. He also had a good vantage point to see the epitome of rude exhibitionism; perched high on top of a tall wooden bar stool, and so the story continued, but was very soon short-lived when one of the high-kicking dancers brought him down to size.'

'Did you know that Toulouse-Lautrec was a good friend of Oscar Wilde, Alistair?'

'Yes, I read that somewhere at school; he was banged up in France and died of a mystery illness, which is what you will be subjected to if you don't stop putting it about.'

'How many times do I have to keep on reminding you that it is my brother who is supposed to be here and not me and quite honestly, Alistair, I again, do not know what you're talking about.'

'And, what on earth did one get up to yesterday, Robert, please pray tell me because it was unusual to see you looking quite so smart in appearance.'

'*Agh*, Alistair, if you go *oot perpen dicken*, there's always a cat that's good for the *licken*.'

'You are totally disgusting, Robert Hamilton-Brown; you know that, don't you?'

'*Och* well, if you really want to know, and if curiosity kills the cat then I will tell you.'.....

.....'The driver of the cab, Barney Gibson, dropped me off outside an apartment block in St. Clair Avenue, which is where Gloria Aspinwall rents the building's spacious penthouse suite on the fifth floor.

'I could tell the dog was glad to be home because as soon as I stepped out from the nearside door of the black Henry Ford limousine, Chips raced towards the elevator in an attempt to raise the roof before I did.

'Entering the apartment from the hall on the fifth floor was similar I thought, to an explorer coming out from the periphery of a jungle, having waded his way through thickets of over-grown tropical plants, shrubs and wild flowers.

'It was, as you well know, Alistair, a very hot afternoon and after I had twisted the *robinet* clockwise to tinkle the melodious door bell, Gloria immediately opened it, greeting me with a wicked smile upon her face.

'She was wearing a white tennis skirt; the shortest one I have ever seen and definitely not the type to wear at the ladies' open; her crisp heavily starched-to-death white blouse seemed very tight, covering what seemed to me a thirty-eight-inch chest; the buttons ready to pop at any second. Once we were seated, I was given extremely generous glimpses of creamy flesh as she crossed and re-crossed her shapely sun-tanned legs. The epitome of this sportive display were her white plimsoll shoes and blue cotton socks to match her virginity and mood, both of which were soon to be rectified on a *chaise-longue* in front of the fire.'

'I thought you said, Robert that it was an extremely hot and sticky afternoon with temperatures well into the nineties?'

'Yes, that's right, and Gloria had to turn on the ceiling fan to cool us both down.'

'*Och, I did ni cam oot* on the last banana boat, Robert.'

'And *I did ni* know we grew bananas in Glasgow.'

'You seem to be getting to know this young woman quite well, Robert.

'*Aye*, but Rome *was ni* built in a day, Alistair.'

'But then, the Roman city of Pompeii was destroyed in an instant by a pyro-plasmic explosion caused by a volcanic eruption and now, I suppose you're going to tell me, Robert, you recited one of your poems to her?'

'*Aye*, it was the one about Mary, Queen of Scots and how she lost her head, but that was until someone found it inside a linen basket.'

'You don't expect me to believe all of this rubbish, Robert, and I find most of what you say of late quite bizarre and diabolical to say the least.'

'Yes, you are right, Alistair, I'm only trying to get you going.'

'You will have to try better than that if you want to get me going.' Alistair said as he peered out through a broken stained-glass window to see a trash-can man, carrying out trash as fast as he can. 'There is a garbage wagon parked outside the Hall, Robert; just do us all a great favour and jump on the back.'

'The truth of the matter is, Alistair, she was about to go and play mixed-doubles with some of her friends and this was after she had phoned me during our coffee break in the Quadrangle yesterday morning.'

'*Agh*, I bet she was, and tell me Robert, why is there an impression of a tennis racket on the backside of your trousers, you're not going funny on me again, are you?'

'No of course not, Alistair, it was when I was about to position myself in front of the swimming pool to drink *Canada Dry* and soak up the sun, I inadvertently sat on it.'

'Well that, I am sure, would explain why the back of your trousers look like either a made in the U.S.A. waffle-iron or a Canadian steakhouse chip-making machine.'

'Yes, that is correct, Alistair, absolutely correct.'

'If you had been given advanced pre-warning, you could have taken your swimming costume to her flat so that you could pretend to be sailing back home to Glasgow on the T.S.S, "*California*".'

'That did cross my mind, but then I remembered the swimming costume was another item which ended up sprawled out on the grass at Wycliffe College. She has a maid, as well, Alistair.' adding more fantasia puppetry into the conversational scene.

'It's a pity she couldn't have looked after the dog while your friend was out painting the town red.' Alistair quickly replied.

'Her daily help is called Francis.....'

'And don't tell me, she is from Assisi in Italy.'

'No, but you were nearly correct in your assumptions, Alistair; she is from Pescara on Italy's Adriatic coast. She has the longest legs I have ever seen; you know the kind which are supported by White Heather Hosiery and go right up to one's.....'

'.....now, Robert, I think you have gone far enough, don't you?'

'Don't spoil it for me, Alistair, I haven't finished yet. I once knew a lassie, who would insist on calling *ma* dick, Peter, when she was in *ma* bed. But, alas, there *wa nae maer* room for the three of us, and so I kicked her *oot.*'

'Next, you're going to tell me, the maid was wearing the wispiest of waspies', of the type that go up and down when one is served with afternoon tea and cucumber sandwiches.'

'How did you guess?'

'And did she wear a hat?'

'Yes, but I told her she could leave it on.'

'She sounds a bit of a slut to me, Robert.'

'*Och aye*, "A we shag, me shag, and in *ta* bed *wi* go".

'It is truly amazing, *Nebuchadnezzar*, how you have managed to survive with your life thus far without wearing spectacles.'

'You know that there will come a day, in the not too far distant future, when one will have ones eyes tested and be fitted with slithers of celluloid micro-optics instead of wearing a pair of strong bifocal binoculars with lenses like glass paper weights.' Robert was so clever to prophesise.

'It's not my fault I was born with a lazy eye.'

'*Agh*, but it doesn't stop you from peering out through a bullet-holed stained-glass window, does it, Alistair.'

'This maid of hers; does she have a boyfriend?' Alistair asked.

'Yes, she has; he is a barrow boy and sells blue and white striped pyjamas in a market in Pescara.'

'Well that's bad luck; I'm still waiting for you to tell me, Robert, just how your day was *really* spent yesterday.'

'There is so much for me to tell, but right now I'm feeling rather tired and need to go back to Wycliffe to catch up on some sleep.'

As soon as Robert put his head down on the pillow, he began to reminisce about what had happened the previous day.

*

No 36 St. Clair Avenue, fifth floor apartment.

'Hello, Robert it's good to see you again.' Gloria said coquettishly before picking up the dog to sniff his smelly coat. 'My maid, Mrs Anderson, usually answers the door but as luck would have it, today is her day off and, I'm sorry if I look a mess, it's because I'm not used to slaving in a kitchen; cooking all the food, washing dishes and cleaning floors isn't my idea of having a nice leisurely day in your company, Robert. Shall we go out and have our lunch *alfresco*; I know a little restaurant on the outskirts of the town, it is called 'Lorenzo's' near to Fort Bradley. The plumber came this morning to fix the swimming pool on the roof because there is a blockage caused by large four-leaf clover leaves blowing over from the park, which was a pity as I was hoping we could sit around the pool and have some tea or something.

'Yes, going out for a sensible meal, that will certainly make a change from eating Chinese *Chop Suey*, German *Bratwurst* sausages and Anglo-French Canadian Buffalo grilled steaks at University.'

'The restaurant serves Buffalo grilled steaks as well, Robert, but at Lorenzo's, they just remove the horns and dust it down.'

'In Scotland we have venison which is the delicious red meat that comes from the deer.' Robert just about managed to put in, having been barracked with unnecessary chit-chat for the past five minutes.

'Yes, I know all about reindeer,' Gloria replied. 'Santa Claus travels on one every year and in Canada and North America we have the elk, a rather ugly beast with huge antlers, which decorate walls on top of shooting-lodge fireplaces.'

'An elk must be an extremely clever animal to be able to paint and decorate walls before it becomes the main ingredient inside a tin of 'Baxter's Royal Game Soup'.'

'But before we go out, Robert, I must emphasise that I don't want to listen to any more of your poetry because I am like Sleeping Beauty; I would find it difficult to stay awake.'

The poem that was hiding in Robert's trouser pocket bore no resemblance to the one he had mentioned to Alistair at breakfast the following day and should have read: "Mary Queen of Spots".

Mary Queen of Spots
"Oh, Mary, Mary quite contrary
How does your garden grow?
With lots o' seeds and plenty o' weeds
And pretty maids all in a row"

'I will give Chips a quick wash and brush-up and then we can all go *oot* for that wonderful meal that you are so looking forward to, Robert.'

'Just how far is this restaurant of yours, Gloria?'

'Oh, not far, Robert; it's about twenty miles down the road from here, I will call Barney Gibson, my trusty cab driver, to take us there.'

The waiter was called Stephan Peabody Junior and on arrival he asked Robert where he came from, and after telling him he was from Scotland he replied by saying: 'Did you drive all the way?'

Standing alone in the distance one could see Fort Bradley, a couple of canoes bobbing up and down in the still waters of Lake Ontario, and Robert was half-expecting to see it being attacked at any second by a bunch of unruly Red Indians who had just fallen out with a *Madame* from inside a chicken ranch next door to the restaurant.

Fort Bradley, established by Thomas Bradshaw as one of the military posts for the protection of the new frontier was built by Colonel John Flounders in 1803 on what is now part of the City of Toronto and named after the protector of the North American prairie lands, General Archibald Drummond, a local Canadian war hero.

Lorenzo's, however, is an Italian restaurant and was established in 1918 following the Great War in Europe and it is now famous for its delicious coffee and an extensive range of ice cream.

'Good day to you, and to Miss Aspinwall.' Peabody said, as he showed Gloria, Robert and Chips, the dog, to a table outside of what seemed to be a huge octagonal log cabin. 'Nice to see you again, Gloria; tell me how is Bradford, Pennsylvania; is it still there?'

'Well, the city was still there three weeks ago but I'm not quite so sure now.'

'You seem to be familiar with the waiter, Gloria.' Robert inquisitively asked.

'Oh no; one should not get familiar with servants.' she replied with a grin stretching to a size similar to the mouth of the Saint Lawrence River.

'Here is your menu, Gloria, but I have no need to tell you what is on it, do I?' Peabody said, giving one the impression that sometime in the past she had been sexually intimate with him.

'It must be great to find romance on your menu.' Robert concluded.

'Would you like an aperitif, Robert?' Gloria asked.

'Yes, give me your best shot, Peabody.' he replied.

Chapter Thirteen

The dreaming continued with what really happened......

The diagnostic effect, the power of suggestion, and a couple of sleeping tablets prescribed by the university doctor gave Robert the opportunity to achieve a better night's sleep, albeit somewhat late after devouring a hearty breakfast; this promulgating him to get up at around three-o'clock that afternoon just in time for afternoon tea in the Quadrangle.

"Roll me over, in the clover, roll me over, lay me down and do it again"; this characteristic song, together with a series of snorts, whistles and "z......".noises began to reverberate through the halls of residence in Wycliffe College and it would now seem, if he had taken up Mrs Shipley's more than generous offer to join her that morning for a cup of coffee, he would most certainly have been evacuated to the nearest hospital.

He digressed back to where he was sitting in Lorenzo's restaurant taking in and enjoying magnificent displays of creamy flesh, namely, Gloria's more than ample cleavage which was spilling out over the table.

'Tell me Robert, what you would like to eat?' Gloria asked pulling out her white blouse with both hands before blowing down the front of a tight-fitting bodice to keep her body cool; the top revealing undulating bosoms which moved like water lilies floating on top of a babbling brook.

'I would prefer to have the *Western Omelette* served with *Potato Chips* and *Creamy Cole Slaw*.' Robert replied, giving everyone the impression at the next table that he was incredibly hungry when he rapidly devoured the Ready to Serve *Hot Corn Bread* which was immediately brought to his table.

'And what would you prefer for an *entrée*, Robert?' she further asked beginning a game called *footsie* underneath the table.

'I would like the *Jellied Consommé Madrilène*, what is it exactly?' he patiently asked.

'It's a kind of thick French onion soup that looks like dirty brown fish pond water and has tadpoles, frogs and bits and bobs floating around on the top.' Gloria quickly responded before continuing to say:

'Wouldn't you prefer something else; like me for instance, Robert. I think, after we have eaten I will take you into the reservation park, there is no one around at this time of day; it stretches for miles and apart from stray Native North American Red Indians, an odd grizzly bear and a mounted policeman who thinks he is the aviator and wild west showman, Colonel William Frederick 'Buffalo Bill' Cody, we will be alone to do whatever we please. I have already asked Gibson to pick us up from the restaurant at five o'clock and so we will have plenty of time to get down to things.'

'And what are your plans regarding Chips?' Robert asked.

'Oh, there's no need to worry about those, there will be enough on your plate for both us and Stephan Peabody Junior will take care of the dog until we get back. And, what would you like for your dessert?'

'I think the *Honey Glazed Chilled Melons* with two red cherries would be nice, and if *ya* want bread and the *drippen*, *tis* good for the finger *licken*.' Robert suggested.

'If you want.' she immediately replied.

"If she goes down in the woods today, the teddy bears will have a picnic". Robert could have imagined as he wiped his forehead with a paper napkin to hide unwanted perspiration.

'And, tell me something else Robert, have you a girlfriend back home in bonnie Scotland?'

'*Agh nae*, Gloria; it's of *nae* use having lead in *ya* pencil if *ye havnai* got anyone *tae* write *ta*. And, why is it that everyone is called Junior around here?'

'It is because all the good-looking seniors keep dying off.' she replied disapprovingly.

'I'm not in the least bit surprised.'

'The Mounted Policeman wouldn't be called, Gordon Copper Nickel junior by any chance, would he, Gloria?'

'Yes, how did you know that, Robert?' she inquisitively asked. And there's no need to worry about him.' Gloria continued. 'He's as queer as a Confederate bank note.'

'My goodness me, Gloria, no wonder he insisted on showing me his woggle.'

Gloria settled down to begin her lunch starting with *Spicy Chicken Goujons* followed by an express *Caesar Salad*; a piping hot dessert, consisting of, *Apple Pie* and *Vanilla Custard* which could only be described as midsummer torture, was brought to the table by none other than the restaurant's chef and boss, Frankie Lorenzo himself; the man with a hand-held brass blow lamp which can incinerate a piece of *entrecôte* or a Scottish Borders grazed *rib eye* beef steak in less than one second.

'I have been blessed with a rapacious appetite.' Gloria said, slowly licking the last trickle of vanilla ice cream from a small silver electro-plated dessert spoon. 'I really can't stop eating, nibbling and putting things into my mouth.' she added.

'Yes, I know the feeling, Gloria.' Robert replied.

'You haven't brought that stupid pipe along with you, Robert?' Gloria asked, staring at a black leather pouch which contained his smoking paraphernalia; a pen knife, American 'Black Cherry' tobacco, slim cotton pipe cleaners and a "Notorious Night Club" book of matches.

'Yes, a pipe is part of my equipment.' he hesitantly replied.

'Yea, I have heard you Scotsmen have lots of equipment. Shall we go for that walk now, Robert, because I'm coming on with indigestion?'

'Okay, Gloria; I'm ready if you are.'

'But first of all, Robert, can you do something with those buttons inside your trousers?'

The dog was handed over to Peabody in a way he was familiar with because he had seen it all before on several occasions and that Robert's visit to the restaurant was of little surprise.

'See you later, and don't do anything I wouldn't do.' Peabody said as Gloria and Robert walked along to a gate leading into a vast rich wilderness of nothing in particular.

'I have handed over your compendium of pipe-smoking equipment to Stephan because if one is accidently careless with matches in the forest, it could cause a blaze, equable in size to the Great Fire of London.'

'Point taken, Gloria, I don't want my arse to be burnt twice in one week.'

'Why, what was the first time, Robert?'

'It was when my friend and fellow delegate, Alistair, threatened me with extreme violence because of my in-clan descent attitude towards the Campbells; they are like wild animals, heathens and beasties, and, it is they who have an attitude problem and not me. His sister, Morag, is a bigger problem, especially at a *Ceilidh* and the Scottish country dancing clubs and taverns where she will insist on wearing a tartan sash over one of her long white dresses, leather pumps with criss-crossed laces and a black velvet bonnet with the largest grouse feather protruding *oot frae* the top; *och aye*, you *cannai* make a silk purse *oot frae* a sows ear.

When we *gae oot* she will say: "Will *ye nae cam* back again?" And I will say: *Och, I was nai* aware I was *awa* in the first place; I was only *gan tae* the lavatory.'

'I thought you said you didn't have a girlfriend, Robert.'

'*Och, ye cannai* call her *ma* girlfriend, Gloria, she's like a cat dancing on a hot tin roof when she does the Highland Fling, and as for the sword dance; it's a pity that the two crossed ceremonial *claymores* were lying down on the highly-polished wooden floor and not standing up and pointing toward the ceiling.'

'I take it, you don't like this, Morag what's-her-name?' Gloria asked.

'The name is Campbell.' Robert replied with a more than angry smile.

'When I was a child,' Gloria interjected. 'My family and I ate 'Campbell's' condensed cream of tomato soup; we didn't like that either and my mother could make a small can last an entire week.'

'It's funny you should say that Gloria, my mother could do the same with a can of 'Baxter's Scotch Broth', lentil, potato, oxtail and the 'Royal Game Soup'; we *didnai* eat 'Campbell's' soups on principle because we were scared of having splinters of antler stuck in the back of our throats.'

'I suppose that would have been better than having a dagger thrust into your Scottish "Brave Hearts".'

'I must say, back home in Glasgow, Morag is very good at dancing to the "Gay Gordon's".' Robert put in.

'Don't tell me Copper Nickel Junior was there as well?' Gloria asked.

'*Och, nae*, he *wouldnai* get in through the front door. *Tak yer* partners for the "Gay Gordon's", the *compère* will say before an accordion player begins the first chord on his harmonious squeezebox to start the ball rolling.'

> "A Gordon for me
> A Gordon for you
> If you're *nae* a Gordon
> You're *nae* use to me
> The Black Watch are *braw*
> The Seaforths *an all*
> But the cocky wee Gordon
> Is the pride of *them all?*"

'It all sounds good fun to me.' Gloria said when hackles rose up from the back of her *wee* neck.

'*Agh*, not really Gloria, it's as funny as a broken leg.'

'I thought I made it quite clear to you, Robert, that under no circumstances any of your poetry would be read out to me this afternoon.'

'*Och*, that *wasnai* poetry; it was something that was knocked up in a barrack block toilet.' Robert so knowledgably explained.

Gloria and Robert walked precariously along a rickety old jetty and found a canoe which was in need of urgent repair. There were a couple of holes punctured in the side probably caused by tomahawks being thrown at it during an Indian attack on Fort Bradley.

'Come on Gloria, I will paddle you over to that deserted island in the distance; there seems to be a stretch of land where we could possibly sunbathe.'

'Okay, I'm ready when you are; ladies before gentlemen.' she said with an air of reluctance and caution as she stepped down from the jetty to position herself at the front end of the boat.

Robert followed Gloria with the intention of sitting behind her but, fate was abound when he lost his balance and immediately fell into three feet of water.

'Oh Robert, you're all *drippen* wet!'

'*Agh, I cannai gar oot* the water.'

'*Och,* I *didnai* know you had been to Australia.' Gloria sarcastically replied and before asking Robert. 'And, what are *ye* going to *didgeridoo* before *ya cam* on *we* the flu?'

'Do you mind, Gloria, I'm supposed to be the Scottish poet around here, and not you!'

'*Och,* ye *cannai tak* a joke?'

Robert had somehow managed to wrap and impale his body around one of the firmly embedded rotten-wood posts underneath the end of the jetty before lifting himself out of the water. Meanwhile, Gloria with the aid of the paddle set off from the jetty into more shallow waters where the canoe came to a halt, wavering amongst multi-coloured pebbles; this stretch of shore-line being deserted and apart from a fawn, a blown-up rubber crocodile and a lowly otter scurrying by to return into one of Canada's largest swimming pools, there were no human beings in sight but, that was until she heard the distinctive sound of horses' hooves: clip clop, clip clop, cliperty clop, coming down a pathway towards the river.

Robert, who was now standing sodden-wet next to Gloria thought he was safe but when he caught a glimpse of a "Gay Gordon", perched high on top of a Royal Canadian Mounted Police saddle, he became mortified.

'*Och,* I *cannai* believe it.' Robert said to her after he had pulled a bedraggled handkerchief out from his trouser pocket.

'What can't you believe, Robert?'

'My investment papers and poems are all wet.'

Gordon Copper Nickel Junior dismounted the seventeen hands of a handsome Anglo North American thoroughbred stallion with great expertise to shake Robert's hand and say:

'We meet again, Robert, this must be my lucky day.'

'Somehow, I don't think so, Sergeant, we would much prefer if you left us alone.' Gloria said to the six foot-two inches of something which looked like a bright red '*Swan Vestas*' means of ignition called a match.

'Could you possibly give me a light for my cigar, ma'am?' Copper

Nickel asked.

'Sure, here is my lighter.' Gloria said, producing a brand-new silver Dunhill cigarette lighter from her black patent-leather handbag. But, be careful with it because I filled it with petrol this morning and it leaks like bloody hell.'

'I am on my way to '*Ranger Bill's Cabin*' to have something special to eat for afternoon tea; I would be delighted if you could accompany me to the station; there are fresh water salmon and cucumber sandwiches on today's menu.' Copper Nickel said, mounting his horse which he named, 'Thumper the Jumper'.

'Thank you but, no thank you, Sergeant; we have eaten already.' Gloria replied.

'Well, that's a pity, Miss Aspinwall; you don't really know what you are missing.' he said as he prepared to go forward, holding on to the reins like a jockey who was about to jump a fence at the famous Aintree Race Course.

'Most people call it luncheon; Copper Nickel calls it truncheon.' Gloria said with no regret.

'Tell me, Robert,' Copper Nickel said with an element of surprise. 'Has it been raining because you look like a drowned beaver?'

'No, sir, I was just washing my hair.'

Sergeant Copper Nickel went away, changing the gait of the horse rapidly from a steady trot into a long-sliding one.

'We will now have to return to the restaurant.' Gloria purposely suggested as she looked up at a saturated Robert Bruce Hamilton-Brown standing directly in front of her with traces of blue fountain pen ink running down his arms. 'Stephan Peabody Junior will have to lend you some dry clothes before we return to the apartment.' she added.

'Please don't tell him how I became wet, Gloria, because I have had quite enough liquid refreshment for one day.'

'Oh, and by the way.' she said, enhancing Robert's knowledge of the vast expanse of land which Sergeant Copper Nickel had to cover on horseback. '*Ranger Bills Cabin*', is a Royal Canadian Mounted Police outpost in the Forest of Dundee and its recreation and sportive centre is run exclusively by Constable William Currie, a Lone Ranger with rather strange ideas.'

It was when they returned to Lorenzo's, Stephan Peabody Junior took Robert to one side and said:

'Oh, you're all wet, young sir; when you visit Miss Gloria Aspinwall, it sure as hell pays to take your clothes off, especially when you go into water; follow me,' Stephan continued to say. 'I will have you spruced up and spick and span in no time.'

'My, you're looking extremely smart, Robert; what a transformation.' Gloria said ten minutes later, looking at the brown pin-striped Italian tailor-made suit, a white cotton shirt with a separate collar and a red and blue striped silk tie which belonged to Frazer and Dean Dress Hire in Toronto. 'And after dinner this evening you could take me to the "Notorious Night Club" where we could dance the night away.' she suggested, rubbing a hand up and down a shiny arm. 'And, don't forget to bring your pipe-smoking equipment; I may want to borrow it tonight.'

At this point, Robert stirred from the deep sleep prematurely leaving his dreams more to be desired when the lights went on in the dormitory. The curtains were drawn back by Mrs Shipley and Robert in no uncertain terms was advised to get out of bed because laying there all day wouldn't be conducive to a good night's sleep.

It was around three-thirty when Robert stepped foot into the Quadrangle in Hart House for his afternoon cup of tea and home-made sponge cake.

Alistair immediately informed him that five minutes earlier, Gloria had been to the University and was asking about his whereabouts.

The lady was informed by the doctor that Robert was suffering from exhaustion and was in bed at Wycliffe College and if she so desired, to go visit him there.

'Bloody hell, Mrs Shipley is on the prowl and she doesn't seem to be in a very pleasant or congenial mood this afternoon; knowing my luck, she's bound to bump into her.'

'You didn't sit around a swimming pool all afternoon, did you Robert?'

119

'Och, no, we went for a wee walk and I showed her how to make fire by rubbing two pieces of wood together, in the hope of burning down the entire wastelands of British Columbia.'

'I take it you don't like Canada, Robert?'

Chapter Fourteen

Friday, July 31st "What a difference a day makes, twenty-four little hours".....

After breakfast in Hart House, Robert took solace in Christian worship at the Convocation Hall where a joint service with the young men's assembly was to begin with the hymn: "Abide with Me", written by W.H. Monk and is generally sung in moderato and goes:

"Abide with me, fast falls the evening tide
The darkness deepens, lord with me abide......

The theme of the Worship Service was "The Place of Sex in the Christian Life" with Mr Roy Dickerson, U.S.A. presiding.

For Robert, this was a golden opportunity not to be missed when he sat down on a wooden upright chair in the front row and listened to what he later told Alistair, was the biggest load of mumbo-jumbo and unadulterated clap-trap he had heard in years.

'You have to lead your life with reverence and conduct yourself with respect, Robert Bruce Hamilton-Brown.' Alistair so eloquently pointed out to him.

'*Och*, so this explains why the Reverend Roy Dickerson has six children and a wife that left him for a man who looks like Douglas Fairbanks Junior.'

'Well, from what I have gathered, when God said go forth and multiply, Robert, you were definitely first in the queue.'

'*Agh*, I *would nae* say that, Alistair and, I *would nae* know where you got that idea from because the theme for the worship service on Wednesday was "Boys who need not be Ashamed" presided by the National Secretary of the Y.M.C.A. England, Wales and Ireland; Dr. Richard Hotshot-Bagley, and he has a reputation for being an expert in picking up soap in the men's shower room.'

'Tell me, Robert, when did you last have sex?'

'You should know that, Alistair, it was the night I took Morag back to your house and you were trying to recreate the Victorian Forth Bridge with your Number Thee series 'Meccano Set.'

'*Och*, don't give me that, Robert; since we have been in Canada, you have acted like a ferret down a rabbit warren.'

'And what about my so-called antics on the good ship T.S.S. "Athenia", Alistair. 'Don't they deserve a mention?'

'*Och aye*, Beelzebub has certainly got a devil put aside for you, Robert, that's for sure, and it goes without saying.'

'Well, why did you mention it in the first place?'

'Because you asked me to, Robert; it's because you asked me.'

'We have only three more days left in this institution, Alistair.' Robert said just to remind him lest he had forgotten. 'It makes you wonder which lunatics are running this asylum.'

'They are Dr. John R. Mott, the Y.M.C.A. President, he is in charge.' Alistair replied and further adding: 'And then there is Russell G. Dingman, the Boys Workers Assembly Chairman and Dr. Erich Strange, the Young Men's Assembly Chairman.'

'Would you buy a used car from those three, Alistair? You've only to glance at their photographs in the Handbook to realize there is something odd about them.'

'Someone has to be in charge, Robert, especially when delegates keep disappearing into forests where they are rescued and then, delivered to the university by bent Mounted Policemen.'

'If you don't mind me asking, Alistair, what sort of recreation are we going to be involved with today; basket weaving, embroidery or painting the Forth Bridge?'

'I was thinking I might just join Mr. Walter Wall's art classes, being there is now a spare seat in the back row. And, have you decided what you are going to do this morning?' Alistair insisted, thinking Robert may have already decided to pay Miss Aspinwall another visit.

'I may pop into the poetry reading class which is being held in the Convocation Hall; I could give the delegates the benefit of a quick rendition of one of my poems before going into town.'

'And then after the art class.' Alistair put in. 'I may just go for a run around the campus because when I die, I want to be the fittest corpse in the ground.'

'When I die, Alistair, I would like to be buried alongside Mary Astor.' Robert replied checking the hour on his rectangular-faced Timex wristwatch.

'I don't think that would be a wise idea.' Alistair said, without hesitation. 'You may suffer from asphyxiation.'

The poetry reading commenced at ten-thirty precisely and began with a blind young man; an American Y.M.C.A. delegate, who, after reciting one of his poems brought tears to almost everyone's eyes, but, with one exception; namely, Robert Bruce Hamilton-Brown. The poem was called "Blindness" and began:

> "Blindness"
> "Show me the morning
> Show me the night
> Show me the stars that twinkle o' so bright
> Show me the happiness when sadness made to call
> Show me the sunrise when darkness began to fall
> Show me the garden that was full of roses
> Show me the daffodil, tulip and poses
> Show me the ice and show me the snow
> Show me the fire and its rich golden glow
> Show me the way with life's helping hand
> Show me the castle which was built in the sand
> Show me the reason why it came to be
> No one's as blind as those who cannot see"

'How could one follow that?' A Russian Orthodox delegate was heard saying. There was no need for applause because silence was enough.

Robert, producing a rolled-up bundle of papers from his trouser pocket selected a poem which I am sure everyone in the Convocation Hall wanted to hear. The poem was called, "King Harold".

> "King Harold"

"King Harold out-riding on his horse
Came a cropper on a golf course
At a watering hole he was made to fall
When he was hit by a stray golf ball
Harold mounted his horse in a couple of ticks
The time on his watch read 1066"

This was followed by a different type of silence which promulgated some members of the delegation to make a quick exit towards the lavatory.

'I have another one for you all to enjoy listening to this morning.' Robert said, trying his best to ward off any coughs and splutters which were about to head his way. 'This poem is one I knocked up; I'm sorry, penned last evening while having my cocoa supper. The poem is called, "Robin Hood" and, I would suggest you leave the applause until I have finished reading.' he added.

"Robin Hood"
"Robin Hood took off his boot
He had some trouble with his foot
Under an Oak Tree it was a disaster
When he tried to put on a corn plaster"

'Have you a day-time job back home, Robert?' Dr. Hartington-Smyth, the university's principle lecturer and head of the poetry reading class asked. Hartington-Smyth, who had more lines on his forehead than Darlington railway station, continued to jibe Robert by saying: 'Because, if you do have a day-time job, I would suggest you don't give it up to become a poet.'

'*Och*, he may be a doctor *o'* letters but, he *wouldnae* know a good poem if it was *ta* hit him in front of his *wee* face.' Robert later said to Alistair in the Quadrangle coffee shop lounge.

'Tell me Robert, Alistair asked puzzlingly. 'Can you explain why you constantly threw three sixes when we played backgammon on board the T.S.S. "Athenia"?'

'*Agh*, I was just lucky, Alistair, just lucky.'

'And why have you brought a suit carrier with you, are you planning on shipping out, Robert?'

'*Och*, no, I am going into town to have my suit dry cleaned; there is a dry-cleaning company that boasts a twenty-four-hour service and so when I collect it tomorrow, I will be ready to join the mass exodus to Cleveland on Monday.'

'This dry-cleaning company *wouldnae* be situated in St. Clair Avenue, by any chance, would it Robert?'

'No, no, Alistair, it is nowhere near Gloria's apartment, if that's what you are referring to?'

'It's a pity she *didnae* come back yesterday afternoon; she could have saved you a journey to the dry-cleaners.'

'*Aye*, that's true.' Robert said, giving it plenty of thought.

'And, at what time can we expect you back this evening?'

'It will be around midnight, Alistair, around midnight.'

'Just where is this dry-cleaning firm, Robert, Alaska?'

'No, Alistair, it isn't, it's in Chicago where the Mafia go to have their brown and white pin-striped suits dry-cleaned.'

'Don't let the side down, you're Scottish, Robert; it's in your genes.' Alistair said, reminding him once again of his behaviour and to button up his flies before he went out.

'I *didnae* know the whole of Scotland was in *ma* jeans, Alistair?'

*

No 36 St. Clair Avenue, Toronto

The black taxi which Robert had hailed from outside the University of Toronto was to take him to St. Clair Avenue via, Bay and Avenue Street and with the suit-carrier slung over his shoulder he got into the lift and went up to the fifth floor feeling completely rejuvenated with replenished energy similar to a marathon runner who had just taken a dosage of anabolic steroids.

The double elevator doors, following a short tinkle of a bell, parted in the centre leading out into a jungle of artificial flora and fauna, growing oranges, lemons and over-ripe second-hand rubber bananas which could have started their life in a Goodyear factory in Cleveland.

Robert twisted the round Bakelite *robinet* which was positioned to the left of the front door to alert the daily help, Mrs Anderson, or Her Royal Highness, Miss Gloria Aspinwall herself. And, to Robert's surprise the door was eventually opened by Stephan Peabody Junior who was standing just inside the entrance, mouth agape and minus a pair of shoes.

'May I come in, Stephan; I have brought your outfit back and was hoping Gloria would deliver it to you.'

'I'm sorry, Mr Hamilton-Brown, but no, you have come at a rather inconvenient time.'

It was when Robert heard a voice coming from one of the back bedrooms asking Stephan to come back to bed because she didn't want to buy a new Ewbank carpet sweeper, he thought now was the right time to leave the block.

Gloria's dog had somehow managed to escape the excitement and the bedroom farce once again and was last seen heading for Union Street Railway Station.

Meanwhile back at the ranch.....

Robert arrived back in the University of Toronto half-an-hour later and was immediately confronted by Alistair who asked:

'You are back early, Robert, has she let you down?'

'Och, no, I told you, Alistair I was going to the dry-cleaners and now I'm back just in time for lunch.'

Lunch that day was being taken in Burwash Hall; the student's dining room of Victoria University.

The main meal was a choice of either, Cauliflower Cheese with lashings of bread and butter, or a Steak Canadian Sandwich with capers, mayonnaise and an onion relish. There was a wild soup for starters; lentil, fennel and cream and, for a dessert, a waffle spread with chocolate or peanut butter.

Robert picked up a tin tray from a piled-up rack at the back of the queue waiting to file down in front of a self-service presentation counter; the steam wafting up towards the ceiling when one of the cooks removed the lids on top of the Bain-Marie and vegetable containers. He thought this to be the ideal time to join in with some of the young and impatient American delegates by making banging noises with his tray as he shuffled his way along the side of a ledge in front of the hot-plate counter.

'I don't see any Chinamen in here today, Alistair; they are probably missing their staple diet of boiled rice, fried bean sprouts and egg noodles.'

'Chinese Oriental cuisine which has *Cantonese, Sichuan, Peking, Mandarin* and American *Chop Suey* dishes on its menu is totally different to what we have been accustomed to, Robert, and Cauliflower Cheese and Haggis would definitely not be on their list of things to eat.'

'Why is it, Alistair, that in the French dictionary, they define a baguette to be either, a Chinese chopstick, a pole-vaulting stick or a knitting needle? The simple answer to this question is, my dear friend, he went on without waiting for an answer,' that the Concise English Dictionary has three times the amount of words as opposed to a French one, and when one asks for a condiment in a Paris restaurant, the staff don't get the wrong idea and throw you out.'

'But you don't like the English or the French, Robert.'

'Yes, I know, but combined with the French, English, Welsh, and Irish provinces, Scotland must rate to be one of the richest nations in the world.'

'I'm *nae* surprised, Robert because you don't spend a penny, do you? You know a nation has only got money when they are seen to be spending it.'

'*Agh, ya can nae* blame the Scottish five-pound note on *tae* me, Alistair; no one South of the Border wants the damn thing, and this is why we find it difficult to get rid of them.'

'Well, at least *ya* must be doing something right.' Alistair said but not entirely agreeing with every word Robert said. 'China has lots of languages and wonderful sights to see one of the Chinese delegates

Michael Mao was telling me yesterday. Chinese people and foreign tourists can walk for miles along its Great Wall.'

'It sounds very much like Berwick on Tweed and Hadrian's Wall without the ice cream.'

'I'm so looking forward to the farewell party tomorrow evening, Robert, aren't you?'

'*Och aye*, I *wouldnae* say yes and I *wouldnae* say no, but on the other hand I would *nae* miss it for the world.'

'Agh, I know you have a few aces up your sleeve. Robert, but just how many hands do you have?'

'Enough, Alistair, I have just enough for now.'

Chapter Fifteen

The Farewell Party in the Convocation Hall, Saturday August 1st

"Rule Britannia, Marmalade and Jam, Five Chinese Crackers up your backside, bang, bang, bang, bang-bang".

Mrs Shipley was the first person to greet Robert, the 'Bruce' Hamilton-Brown on his way to the University breakfast room in Hart House the following morning.

'Good morning, Robert, I trust you had a better night's sleep and you are all fit and well for this evening's entertainment.'

'Yes, three of my new-found friends who live in the town will be in attendance this evening, and it is hoped they will liven the place up.' Robert said, referring to Charlie Edge, Kurt Schmidt and Bruno Bateson. 'These local friends of mine will, I am sure, disassociate with some of the 'Holier-than-thou' delegates who seem to be milling around here; these include the Chinese, your regular 'Yellow Fellows', who, until I arrived in Canada, I thought worshipped a Buddha, an over-weight 'Michelin Man' with bigger tyres around his waist than a London Transport bus and, bigger tits than the Hollywood film actress, May West. Suddenly, these bald and slitty-eyed Y.M.C.A. dragons from the Orient are Catholics and join in with Western hymns, songs and chants; it was only yesterday I heard two of them singing the French-Canadian song, "*Alouette, gentille Alouette*". That goes for the Japanese delegates too, they seem to have a fixation on carrying long things hidden away inside their trousers.'

'That reminds me, Robert.' Mrs Shipley said, pointedly ignoring his rhetoric. 'I must do something with the button-holes in your trousers; they look positively disgusting.'

'I trust it is the button-holes you are referring to, Jane?' he replied, hoping she would immediately take control of the situation and for him, to leave it entirely in her hands.

'Tell me, Robert, why do you refer to the Chinese delegates as 'Yellow Fellows'?

'It is because they come from a place very close to the centre circle, the outer rim around the earth which is nearer to the sun than anywhere else.'

'This sounds very complicated to me, Robert, you must be very clever.'

'It's just a matter of logic, really, Jane.' he said with a smugness that was enough to baffle Einstein. 'The Chinese men go bald early as well; it is their diet, far too much rice, Pot Noodle and *'Tsingtao'* beer.'

'You know, I won't be able to go to the Farewell Party because I'm a woman and I won't be allowed in.' she said, nodding her head up and down like a seaside donkey. But if you would care to come to my rooms you can take your trousers off and then you will see what I can do.'

'And what about your husband, is he not at home?'

'Oh, don't you worry about the plumber; Wilber has gone fishing with his friend by the lake and won't be back until five-o'clock.'

'Well, that's okay then, but I can't stay for long because of having to eat breakfast in Hart House.'

'And, you needn't concern yourself, Robert, about eating in Hart House because after you have given me your trousers, we can both have breakfast together in my little apartment down the hall.'

Minutes later, Jane Shipley was sitting in her easy chair, her eyes firmly fixed on the opening in Robert's tight-fitting trousers. She was fiddling around with the buckle on his black leather belt when Wilber, her husband, suddenly burst in through the door.

'And who the hell are you?' Wilber asked when Robert's cavalry twill trousers fell down to position themselves untidily around his ankles.

'Bruno; Bruno Bateson.' Robert nervously replied when he was confronted by a large coppersmith's hammer and more than enough Elastoplasts and triangular bandages to fix the holes in the side of a canoe.

'I'm the one who is supposed to be the fly fisherman around here, Jane, and not you.' Mr Shipley attempted to make clear; his blood pressure rising by the second. 'And would you, young sir, kindly leave my apartment because I don't want to be the first university plumber and odd-job man to have pulverized one of my wife's boyfriends.'

Mrs Shipley's husband had changed his mind about going fishing that morning because his canoe had gone missing from the end of a jetty on

Lake Ontario.

It was during the party that evening as revelling and disorderly mess pranks were taking place, Bruno Bateson, after making a face mask from a brown paper bag, decided to put it on his head to avoid being recognised.

Mr Shipley was called in to replace a couple of electric light bulbs which mysteriously exploded having been knocked out by a catapult; the persons responsible being American delegates wearing blue denim dungarees and wire braces in their teeth.

Shipley, full of rage and anger, had taken it upon himself to find the culprits and on entering the Convocation Hall, called out: 'Bateson, where is Bruno Bateson?'

'I'm here.' came the reply as Bruno was about to leapfrog over his best friend Charlie Edge; hunch cuddy being one of Hamilton-Brown's favourite indoor games when he leapt on to the back of his friend, Kurt Schmidt to mischievously piggy-back inside the building, quoting one of London Scot's poems, penned in 1836 which incidentally, was called, "hunch-cuddy-hunch".

How fine is the muscular action?
So highly conducive to hunch
Oh! Hyena's glances are sweeter
Than all the corners of wealth

'Oh, you are, are you, take that you bounder.' Mr Shipley hollowed, shouting at him loudly and hitting out at him with a tin tray. 'And that will teach you to mess around with my missus.'

Bruno, who was now suffering from a severe headache and mild concussion, had somehow managed with difficulty to get up from the floor before taking off his crude paper mask.

'You are not the same person who was in my apartment early this morning; I'm very sorry young man.' Mr Shipley said, repeating the apology over and over again.

'Of course, it wasn't me, you fool; I would be hard up to grace your room: I've got moral standards and ethics to consider, unlike one person I could mention in here.'

'Good morning, Robert.' Alistair said when Robert walked into the dining room in Hart House the next morning and plonked himself down on a black wooden bench seat in front of the large rectangular banqueting table. 'Did you sleep well last night because you seem to be a little late in arriving for breakfast?'

'It was Jane Shipley, Alistair; she has fast become a pain in the arse. Remember you were telling me how she could fix the button-holes in my trousers? Well, this morning, she tried to do exactly that, and I said to her just what the hell do you think you are doing, I have a bus to catch.'

'That was very commendable of you Robert, and I think this little fairy tale will be omitted from my list of every-day things I have to tell Morag when we arrive home.'

'I suppose she is wondering how we are getting along?' Robert said looking over towards the hot plate where breakfast things were being cleared away in preparation for lunch.

'Yes, I suppose she is, Robert, and I can imagine Morag weeping on her pillow every night and probably wondering how many lies you are going to tell her?'

'I can remember, when I was very young, Alistair, my mum would sing to me one of those tear-jerking lullabies, and then I would lay my head down sorrowfully on the pillow and cry *ma* little *wee* heart *oot* because my mum had crept out of the house until the early hours to bonk the pants off the milkman.'

'Tell me Robert, what is bonking?'

'It's a bit like playing table tennis.' Robert quickly responded; 'One starts off with one ball and ends up with two.'

'You know, you really are the pits, Robert, telling me all these inaccurate sob-stories.'

'*Agh, weel,* it's you who started it.'

'After breakfast, we have the morning worship followed by religious education; the theme for this morning being, 'Morality and Ethics in today's Modern Christian Society'.' Alistair was to remind him.

'I don't need *nae* education because I'm just another brick in Hadrian's Wall.'

'You did say brick, Robert?'

'Yes Alistair; a wee brick.'

'I suppose you had better salvage a few leftovers from what is remaining from the lavish breakfast we all had this morning; I recommend the porridge with maple syrup and cream, and that should keep you going for a *wee* while.'

'*Och aye*, it's better than nothing, Alistair, and *a couldnae gan oot we* oot any breakfast.'

'And, where do *ya* think *ye* are *gan* this time?'

'*Ta* collect *ma* dry-cleaning.'

'Tell me, Robert, how old do you think Jane Shipley is?'

'I would say *aboot* twenty-three; twenty-four, Alistair.'

'I always thought your eye-sight and mathematics left a great deal to be desired, Robert.'

'*Och, give* or *tak* one or two years; it *doesnae* matter.'

'The woman, for God's sake, is forty-two years of age Robert, can't you see?'

'Well, I may be needing spectacles, Alistair, but there is nothing wrong with my mathematics and the ability to make money.'

'Do you realize, Robert, you are the only person I know who can peel an apple inside his pocket.'

'Yes, Alistair, I do have the ability to do that, amongst other things like counting up my loose change.'

'And, if you are still planning on having something to eat this morning, Robert, then I would suggest that you forget it because the porridge has just been cleared away.'

'Well, in that case I will buy a *gofer*, one of those sugary things the American's call a waffle, the ones that look like a Barrow-in-Furness cast-iron grid, or I may push the boat out in the town and just for a change I will have bacon, eggs and haricot baked beans; "Whip it out, Mr whippy, whip it out, why not".'

'You know they are not the words to the song, Robert and from what I have heard from your lady friend, Miss Gloria Aspinwall, you seem to know a great deal about pushing the boat out.' Alistair chuckled.

'*Och aye*, I *wasnae* amused Alistair, I was *nae* amused.'

'Do you know Robert that since we arrived in Canada; you have contributed naught point blank, sod all to this First World Y.M.C.A. Assembly.'

'*Nae* I *wouldnae* say that, Alistair, I put fifty cents in the offertory box in the 'Church of the Redeemer' last evening and you can buy two cheeseburgers out on the sidewalk for that amount of money.'

'If there is anyone who needs redeeming, it is you, Robert.'

'And while we are on the subject of redeeming, here is a poem extracted from a collection of verses called, "Hovering towards Success", written and put together by one of our Scottish Y.M.C.A. delegates, Quentin Miller Service, and it is called "Songs of a Sourdough".' Robert said removing a scrappy piece of paper from his tight-fitting trousers:

Songs of a Sourdough

"They've cradled you in custom; they've primed you with preaching,
They have soaked you in convention through and through,
They have put you in a show-case; you're a credit to their teaching,
But can't you hear the wild, its calling you.
Let us probe the silent pieces, Let us seek what luck betides us.
Let us journey to a lonely land I know,
There's a whisper in the night wind, there's a star agleam to guide us,
And the wild is calling, calling, let us go.
Have you suffered, starved and triumphed,
grovelled down yet grasped at glory,
Growing bigger in the business of the whole,
Done things just for the doing, letting babblers tell their story,
Seeing through the nice veneer; the naked soul.
Have you seen God in his splendour, heard the text that nature renders,
Have you heard a silent pooh?
You'll never hear it in the family pew.

The simple things, the true things, the silent men who do the thing
Then listen to the wild, its calling you and for us all to do our thing."

'What is the thing, Robert? Just what is the thing?'

'Norma's Kitchen' – route 51 Toronto

Eating burgers is synonymous in Canada and where inspiration had been drawn from the United States of America. More than just a national dish, it is comfort food, a love affair and a dish that promises to warm the cockles after a hard day at the University of Toronto. Being truly patriotic it's not about knowing the lyrics to "God save the King", but about finding the perfect burger bar.

Luckily for the people of Toronto, Norma's Kitchen was one such place, located on the long stretch of Highway, route 427, The Queen Elizabeth Way, and just a short distance from the city centre. This family-run place of mouth-watering refreshment had been a burger house for nearly eleven years and was completely destroyed by a wild bush fire in the September of 1931.

Their burgers were fresh and tasty and their ribs perfectly roasted, bursting with flavour. They also made incredible homemade Californian pizza as well as fish and succulent French frites to die for.

The colourful doughnuts, resembling round rubber lifebelts and be-speckled with hundreds and thousands of microscopic balls were a-plenty beneath glass-domed display jars; the ones decorated with chocolate, marshmallow and Royal icing were particularly inviting.

With great food and friendly efficient service, it wasn't hard to see why Norma's Kitchen was often buzzing with customers vying for a table. And if you were serious about your cheese burgers with onion, chilli, sweet corn and caper relish, it was definitely a table worth fighting for.

It was eleven-forty-five when Robert entered the threshold of Norma's Kitchen to enjoy a belated brunch consisting of a hamburger, pineapples and grits; thin triangular shaped wedges of well-burnt potato cake that tastes like shit, but one could live on them.

A friendly Native American Red Indian who Robert later said was from the infamous '*Chuck-um-out*' tribe in Las Vegas, Arizona, Texas, became his waiter during his visit to one of Canada's more historical and adventurous restaurants.

Robert was handed a menu by Tommy Tomahawk, commonly called by the local populace as the six feet two-inch hatchet man with a long grey pony tail and a bowie knife hidden away, tucked down inside the seat of his trousers.

'Hey man, you're sure not from around these parts, are you?' Tommy inquisitively asked.

'*Och*, no, I'm from Scotland.' Robert smugly replied.

'Did you drive all the way?' the waiter continued. 'And are you from the North because you sure as hell talk funny?'

'As a matter of fact, I am.' Robert said pointing his finger in a southerly direction towards Antarctica.'

'Gee, man, I just knew you were from Alaska.' Tommy geographically calculated. 'And what is that thing hiding in your sock?'

'It's called a *skin dhu*, a Scottish knife.' Robert replied, taking the small barbaric-looking weapon from its leather sheath to show the waiter.

'This is what you call a knife.' Tomahawk said, pulling out ten inches of cold-steel from inside the seat of his trousers.

'And, where may I ask, did you get that?' Robert asked, his eyes popping out from their sockets in sheer amazement.

'Probably the same store you bought yours; '*Woolworths*'.

At the end of the meal, Robert got up from the red and white gingham-clad table to find a seat at the 'Maple Leaf Bar', situated in a corner of the restaurant. It was when he was sitting on a high stool drinking a glass of refreshing '*Vichy*' Spring Water, in walked Gloria Aspinwall, the woman whom he now called not fit to shine the shoes of a penniless hobo.

'Hello Gloria, how is the dog?'

'Oh, he is no longer with us.' Gloria precociously replied.

'I wasn't referring to 'Chips'.' Robert retaliated angrily.

'Sadly, its goodbye Mr Chips.' she continued to explain.

'What are you talking about, Gloria? And, why isn't he with you?'

'He escaped from the house yesterday afternoon and was hit by a car belonging to the street railway between Broadview Avenue and Gerrard Street.'

The check for the meal was delivered to Robert by the waiter, Big Chief Tommy Tomahawk, who tried to impress on him that he had known Miss Aspinwall for several years.

'I will pay the bill, Robert, don't you worry about that.' she said with a haughty wink.

'I don't want you to pay for anything, Gloria.' Robert emphasised. 'And, while we are on the subject of paying, at what time did Chips leave your apartment?'

'Oh, it was shortly before midday, when the door was opened by the maid.'

'The maid wouldn't have been Stephan Peabody Junior by any chance, would it?'

'No, whatever gave you that idea?' Angela replied with an emotionless expression.

At that point, Robert paid the bill and hastily sped out the restaurant into Norma's Kitchen courtyard completely fed-up with blonde-haired broads, narrow-minded rednecks, brass necks, worthless greenbacks, half-read hardbacks, bingo gringos and inefficient Poker players who were about to leave Toronto and owed him money.

*

The Farewell Party – Convocation Hall that evening

At nine o'clock there was a photo call in Convocation Hall. The delegates attending the evening of entertainment were asked to sit and stand up in order of size; needless to say, Robert was standing on a form at the back, making him look taller than he actually was.

Before the photographer's head disappeared underneath a black cloth behind his Kodak camera, the Y.M.C.A, delegates, attending from around

137

the world had to sing the Scout's song, "Spreading Chestnut Tree", made famous by Edward, The Prince of Wales during a Scouting Jamboree the previous year.

With actions, arms outstretched overhead, striking knees and tapping of the head, they began to sing:

"Under the spreading chestnut tree
Where I held you on my knees
We were happy as could be
Under the spreading chestnut tree"

A Chinese delegate, Ho Ling from Peking, made comment to Robert, saying that in his country they have water chestnuts, to which Robert replied: '*Agh*, you *can nae* play conkers *wi* them, because they'll explode sideways in front of your wee eyes.'

Chapter Sixteen

Sunday morning, August 2nd – the last day of the Conference

The morning began as usual with the trooping of the colour, the gathering of the clans in The Great Hall in Hart House.

'At ten-thirty this morning, it is going to be our last visit to The Church of the Redeemer in Bloor Street and Avenue Road.' Alistair had to remind Robert.

'Would you like to buy a hymn book, Alistair? And, if you buy a psalm book as well you get the third one for free, a signed copy of the Holy Bible; they are a bargain at fifty cents each.'

'Are you telling me, Robert, that you have reduced yourself to stealing prayer books from churches; whatever next.'

'Or alternatively, would you like to buy a box of fragrant candles; they are perfect when Jane, sorry, Mrs Shipley, turns out the lights and the whole of Wycliffe College smells like a Moroccan *Kasbah*.'

'Now you are really having me on, you know, Robert; I have got to the stage where I don't believe one word you say, but now you come to mention it, I did smell something funny emanating from her apartment in the early hours of this morning.'

'Oh, that would be Mr Shipley's cologne, I can smell it now, it is called 'Innocence'; the dry sweet fragrance of his lotion really gets up my nose and lingers on for days.'

'How do you know the name of his after-shave lotion?'

'I saw an empty bottle lying on top of Shipley's tin dustbin.' Robert convincingly replied.

'Isn't he the one who gets up in the middle of the night to go out fishing?'

'Yes, Alistair, and last night was no exception when Bruno Bateson threatened to hit him with a tin tray.'

'I suppose we had better join the queue for our breakfast because it looks like some of our German friends have taken up residence on the centre table and are about to help themselves to more *bratwurst* and, *bockwurst* sausages, *salami* and *sauerkraut*.' Alistair emphasised.

'Eat what you can today, because it may not be there tomorrow.' An obese delegate from Heidelberg was heard saying before piling up his plate with huge rashers of back bacon and a mountainous supply of baked haricot beans in tomato sauce.

'*Och*, you're still here are you.' Robert said to Klaus Muller, with an air of deliberate self-importance. 'I thought perhaps you would have done us all a favour and thrown yourself off the St, Lawrence Valley Bridge.'

'I am not amused.' Muller stressed. 'I shall report you to the angry as soon as I return home.' he added.

'These guys are going swimming this morning in the pool at the Central Y.M.C.A building in College Street.' Robert said, looking down at a German stomach equal in size to Billy Bunter. 'If he goes in the water, Alistair, half of Toronto will be under water.' he added.

'Half of The Dominion of Canada is already underwater, Robert, from the St. Lawrence Valley to the Pole.'

'*Agh*, it's just a ruse for the Germans to do something else with their time before the wagons begin to roll in the mass exodus tomorrow.' Robert made clear.

'I am going to use the swimming pool next door in Hart House.' Alistair said, helping himself to a huge dollop of scrambled egg and then placing it on top of one of those grid-like Barrow-in-Furness waffles.

'*Och*, it's just an excuse for them to go into Queen's Park and chat up the local tottie.' Robert knowledgably put in. 'The local gals go promenading every Sunday morning with their umbrellas and then, after they have been to church and confessed their sins, they go out and do it all over again.'

'And, it's not raining, Robert; not even raining.'

'You will probably find that in fifty years' time, a quarter of the population of Toronto will have blond hair and blue eyes.'

'They already have, Robert, you only have to look at your friend, Kurt Schmidt, to realize that.'

All eyes were on the centre table where, *"Das Fatherland"* became the number one song at breakfast time when two of the German delegates, dressed in tight-fitting *lederhosen*, leather short pants with horizontal and vertical strap-like braces, long white socks and a hunter's hat, complete with feather duster got up from their seats to stand on the table to render a slap dance.

'Do you know, Alistair, I can envisage a time when those people sitting there and along with the Japanese will try to take over the entire world.'

'Robert, just because the Japanese delegates hide Samurai swords down the insides of their trouser legs and the Germans carry Hitler Youth knives inside their back pockets, it doesn't necessarily mean they are hell bent on cutting people's throats; it's just that they are better than anyone else at chopping wood, catching fish and lighting camp fires, that sort of thing.'

'Does that include dropping bombs on London from several thousand feet from German '*Led Zeppelin*' Airships?' Robert put in.

'Next, you will be telling me again that the Japanese Imperial Navy is systematically building up their fleet to make ready for a possible attack on America; you are like a bloody parrot, Robert'

'*Och aye*, I *wouldnae* trust them as far as I can throw them; for example, take a look at that fellow sitting at the centre table, Alistair, he *didnae* get that scar cutting himself shaving.'

'They are into fencing, Robert and probably belong to a Youth Club.'

'My father is into fencing; it's to keep the Douglas's in, and the Campbell's oot.'

'As you know, Robert, I belong to a Youth Club, and in later years, I hope to become its oldest member.'

'You mean like Dr. John R. Mott, the president of the World's Alliance Young Men's Christian Association, Russel G. Dingman or that strange fellow who looks like someone from a 'Madame Tussaud's' waxwork museum?' Robert concluded.

'Yes, they do look a motley crew, don't they?' Alistair agreed as he looked inside his Y.M.C.A. handbook to see their black and white non-photogenic portraits depicted on the second page.

During the course of having to dispense tea from a copper urn positioned in the centre of a six-foot wooden table, one of the Cantonese

Y.M.C.A. delegates, the leave it with me dog handler cum coolie with a flair for exploding bubble gum, asked Robert whether he knew of a respectable Chinese restaurant in the town? Robert's answer was no, but, however, he once knew a Chinese in Rose Street, Edinburgh where he called in and had a meal afterwards.

'How far is Edinburgh from here?' Michael asked, as he waited in line to fill up his personalized bone-china cup with insipid tea, sliced lemon, Mandarin oranges and pink lotus blossom petals.

'*Och*, not very far, just turn right at the traffic lights and keep on walking.' Robert said, his finger poking into the nape of someone's back as he shuffled his way down towards the front of the queue.

'Yesterday, I was in the library and I just happened to listen into a conversation between two gay delegates from Austria.' Alistair said to Robert. 'One of them said that Oscar Wilde wrote in his prison cell, "Women have more holes than a Swiss Cheese".'

'Ironically, I've been down many holes in my passing years and Toronto is of no exception.'

'I bet you have, Robert; I bet you have.'

The next song at the ping-pong table on the centre court was the wartime favourite called, "Lily Marlene", commonly known as "Underneath the Lamplight". The lyrics to the song were written as a poem by school teacher, Hans Leif from Hamburg in 1915 and later popularized by the German actress and singer, Marlene Dietrich. The single recorded and released by 'Decca' in 1945 was an instant success, particularly amongst the German troop movements in Europe.

A Bavarian delegate from Salzburg had the presence of mind to bring his squeeze box, a huge accordion with a keyboard resembling a mobile baby grand piano and, with what seemed to be a network of black shiny buttons not dissimilar to a telephone exchange.

'*Agh*, I *cannae* stand *nae maer* '*o* this, come on Alistair, let us *ga doon in ta* the town and get some fresh air into our *wee* lungs.'

'What a good idea, Robert; apart from commuting from Wycliffe College every day, this will be the first time I have ventured out into the town.'

At this high-point Robert, recited one of his poems which was created and penned on board the T.S.S. *"Athenia"* after a bout of throwing up when he and Alistair observed an iceberg passing by the ship.

'Mindless Adventure'
"Ta nae maer gan oot, tis such a shame
The Y.M.C.A. they are *ta* blame
Nae maer the crags and crevasse to ponder
Awa we go oot, vast rolling hills to wander."
In ta the Lakes and in ta the Prairies
Some would say, *tis awa we* the Fairies"

'Tell me, Robert, are you alright? and is this some kind of foreign language you are speaking because, I think you are going through a phase of learning Esperanto, or a dialect bordering on the periphery of the Outer Hebrides or the Arctic Circle, I don't really know.'

'Och, *tis* only a *wee* Scottish poem, I knocked up in the lavatory this morning.' he fibbed.

'Do you know, Robert, with your attitude, you could change the whole course of the entire universe.'

'Yes, I know!'

'Since we've been in Canada, you and I haven't been doing much conferring at the World Conference, have we; in fact, apart from taking breakfast and having the occasional coffee break together in Hart House, I haven't seen much of you at all.'

'No, it was supposed to be an education, a culture course designed to develop and broaden one's mind, Alistair, but from where I have been sitting in the Convocation Hall, I haven't seen very much culture, and as for the Russian delegation, they would be quite happy eating sawdust sausages, cockroaches, fag-end broth and bowls of rope soup.'

'Do you know, Robert, I am quite looking forward to the visit into the town; that in itself will be a real culture course because of the monotony of being regimented into things you really don't want to do, and I think the congregation in the Church of the Redeemer could be lacking in numbers this morning.'

'Now, you are talking sense, Alistair.'

*

'The Covered Wagon Café', Ball Street, Toronto

"Going for a Stroll"
"This is the park where young ladies discover
The timely deliverance of a long-awaited lover
They stroll along paths towards heavenly bliss
In order to steal a much-needed kiss
Down a leafy glade where there's no one around
This is the place where they sit on the ground
They are not here to soak up the sun
But to have fun 'neath a large currant bun"

'Here we go again, Robert, you never let up, do you: it is like going out with Lord Byron?'

'We are here to soak up the sun underneath a large currant bun.' Robert said trying to make light of Alistair's futile comments. 'You don't seem to understand the meaning of verse, Alistair, and more importantly, you should also realize, it gives one a licence towards meaningful expression.'

'I have a licence, Robert; it is for my dog, and it runs out next month.'

'What runs out next month, the licence or the dog?'

'Very funny, Robert.' Alistair said dryly, 'I don't see any tightly-laced bodices hanging around here; maybe the young ladies you were referring to are all suffering from late-night hangovers caused by popping too many pills in the night clubs of Toronto.'

Robert and Alistair chose to sit at a table outside where they could command good panoramic views of the picturesque city park.

A gay pock-marked and-well leathered Native American Redskin of a waitress called, Randy Crowfoot, and apparently an expert in throwing knives in Wild West travelling shows, came over to their table and asked:

'Are you guys going to order something, or are you just *gonna* stare at the scenery all day?'

'Can't we do both?' Robert replied in his usual sarcastic way.

'And why is he wearing a frock?' she further asked him.

'It's because Alistair is from Scotland and the kilt is his national dress.' Robert explained.

'Gee, you guys, Nova Scotia sure is a long way from here and you have both come to the right place.'

'*Och aye*, we drove all the way.' Robert uttered.

'We would both like to order two pepperoni pizzas and two strawberry milk shakes.' Alistair said to the waitress with more lines on her face than a 'McVitie's' ginger-nut biscuit.

'Would that be with chillies, Cayenne pepper or red hot Indonesian black pebble-dashers?'

'We would like some tomato ketchup; just tomato ketchup.' Alistair replied, asking for the order to be prepared sensibly.

'Would you both like to eat French fries, jacket potatoes or muffins with your meal?'

'I think the pizza will be quite enough, thank you.' Robert said.

'And may I suggest you both change your order for the drinks; 'Canada Dry' Ginger Ale or natural spring mineral water instead of the strawberry milkshake; that would be a far better idea; we don't want to have any accidents, do we?' Randy put in.

'We would like two Coca Cola's; both with ice and a slice of lemon.' Alistair said to the waitress before she suggested something quite different and disgustingly rude.

'Hay man, what is that thing dangling on a chain in front of your skirt?' the waitress asked Alistair, inquisitively.

'It's *ma wee* sporran, *tis* where I keep *ma spense.*'

'You guys sure talk funny; and don't forget to turn your money over this evening; you may get lucky *cos* there is going to be a new moon.' Randy explained.

'What happened to the old one, and to whom are we going to turn our money over?' Alistair asked.

'Rosie Lee; he is the local fag around here, and he may just be your cup of tea.'

'*Och aye*, tonight is the night the Red Indians dance around camp fires waving multi-coloured feather dusters to make it rain.'

It was when the waitress had finished taking the order, an enormous raven flew over the 'Covered Wagon Café', to make a splodge on to the folds of Alistair's kilt; its wingspan similar in width to a Boeing 747 and its beak resembling what seemed to be the nose of a British Airways Concorde.

'There you are.' Randy said, with a facial expression which looked like a carved effigy on the side of a ninety-foot totem pole; 'I said to you guys it was going to be your lucky day.' she added. 'The Thunderbird is my friend and she is called Jacqueline Daw, she visits me every Sunday morning and then later, after my shift, she visits me again inside my tepee wearing brown leather calf-length boots, a raw hide jacket and a ten-gallon Stetson.'

'Does she have any sisters?' Robert hastily enquired.

'No, but she has a brother called, Raymond, and he is the YO-YO man around these parts; he appears in the Café every afternoon to do his thing.'

'What is the thing?' Alistair asked, looking rather puzzled.

'He demonstrates his whirly thing that goes up and down which reaches the floor.'

'Come on, Alistair; let's get the hell out of here.'

'What are we going to do about the knives, Robert?'

'Don't worry Alistair; I will pull them from out of your back and, as for her Indian magical religious mumbo-jumbo thing, I don't believe a word of it.'

'*Agh*, do I feel a few spots of rain?' Alistair said.

'That's all we need, a bent café and an umbrella shop which is closed for the season.'

'You wouldn't think, Robert that in 1749, Toronto began as a French and Indian trading post and now has a population of well over eighty-thousand inhabitants.'

'Well that is truly impressive, Alistair, but where is the population this morning because they certainly aren't around here.' Robert replied, attempting to rotate his head three-hundred and sixty degrees.

'Give them time.' Alistair advised. 'The bells have not started to ring yet to summon the Anglicans, Presbyterian and Catholics to church; most of them are probably all at breakfast eating their Quaker Oates, Kellogg's Corn Flakes and Spaghetti Bolognaise.'

'*Och aye*, along with the pill popping this could explain three of the reason why the gals are not here in the park this morning.' Robert said, resigning himself to the fact that the 'Rialto' cinema in Hardware Street, could be his last chance of meeting a young lady before shipping out to Cleveland the following morning.

'And who may I ask is going to be on the big silver screen.' Alistair asked.

'I suppose it will be that man with his big gong.'

Chapter Seventeen

Farewell to Mrs Shipley, Monday 3rd August, and it was also goodbye to Toronto, French fries, maple syrup and Chopin. It was to be hello Cleveland, Ohio, USA where they have George and Ira Gershwin, big Sirloin steaks and hamburgers with the works.

The Closing Session the previous evening took place in Alumni Hall after the delegates dined for the second-last time in Burwash Hall and Hart House. The theme of the session was 'Fire and Friendship' with the emphasis towards not killing each other before clambering on-board the Steamer "*Chippewa*" built by the Niagara Navigation Company in 1894 and was bound for Queenston, Lake Ontario, early the following day.

The journey from Toronto to Cleveland, Ohio, in total was two-hundred miles, taking in a short train ride to Niagara, New York state, USA, where some hours were spent sight-seeing and getting wet before proceeding on Monday evening by rail to Buffalo thence another Steamer to Cleveland, arriving in the early hours of Tuesday morning.

The conference in Cleveland was to begin on Tuesday August 4th until Sunday August 9th, and then to begin their return journey home, via Washington and New York by rail, lodging in the main Y.M.C.A. building in Central Manhattan for four days following a rigorous outward-bound course in Camp Reynolds, Pennsylvania.

The Steamer destined to take the Scottish delegation back to Glasgow from New York was to be the 'Anchor Line' vessel the T.S.S. "*California*", sailing at noon on Saturday 22nd August 1931. Ironically, on the eleventh of September 1943 the troop ship, painted in grey, was attacked by enemy aircraft, three-hundred and twenty miles west of Oporto, Portugal. The ship was damaged and set on fire and finally torpedoed and sunk by an escorting destroyer belonging to The Royal Navy.

Robert was to mention several years later when he was an L.A.C, a leading aircraftsman, based at RAF Kirkham, Lancashire: 'Just to think that all those sterling silver teaspoons that one could buy in the souvenir shop, are now lying at the bottom of the Atlantic Ocean.' And equally ironic, was that the troop ship RMS "*Aquitania*", a sister ship of the

'Cunard White Star Line' RMS "*Mauretania*" was scrapped in Scotland in 1950. Both steamers, the RMS "*Mauretania*" and the RMS. "*Aquitania*" were almost inseparable, and after the war in Burma they repatriated dedicated war brides and their children to Canada from Singapore and carried thousands of emaciated troops back to Liverpool via Australia and New Zealand and, of course L.A.C Robert Bruce Hamilton-Brown, who, according to his journals was the busiest airman in Burma and indeed, the Far East.

Alistair was noted as saying that when rockets were invented, his so-called friend, Robert Bruce Hamilton-Brown, was definitely not in the firing line, but still remained a target for criticism when he remained in bed for a long time after everyone had got up to feed their faces in Hart House.

It was at seven am precisely, when Robert's compact '*Smith's*' travelling alarm clock sounded from underneath his cosy six-foot military style bed; the flannelette sheets and two feather-down pillows, reeking of cologne, were acting like magnets to entice a five-minute snooze. Appearing to be unsteady on his feet following a late night sing-song around a harmonium in Convocation Hall, a last cocoa supper in the Quadrangle, and an altercation with an English delegate concerning the ownership of a bar of '*Pears*' soap, Robert ventured out from the dormitory to take a soapless douche.

All the Scottish and English delegates, packed and ready to go, moved out at six-thirty from Wycliffe, to take breakfast in Hart House, prior to their long-awaited journey to the United States of America.

Mrs Shipley, as if by magic, appeared in the dormitory carrying a box containing a huge chocolate gateaux and an assortment of muffins in individual ruffed grease-proof paper doilies.

Robert, interestingly noticeable, was wearing white cotton long johns, an undesirable pink rubber shower cap to match my favourite hot water bottle, and a pair of black canvas pumps which had been laced up in two different ways to confuse any prospective Japanese Y.M.C.A Samurai swordsman, who may have had an idea to kill a British delegate by crawling on their hands and knees during the hours of darkness.

'I have brought you a few things to eat on your travels, Robert.' Mrs Shipley said with an air of sadness. 'And, please take that rubber shower cap off; you look like you are about to enter into a Miss Canada Pageant, or Mary Pickford who has finally decided not to end her life chained to a railway sleeper, but to jump into the deeper waters of Lake Ontario.' she added.

'You do realize, Jane, I could have been knocked unconscious by a tin tray your husband was carrying; it so happened, my Canadian friend, Bruno Bateson was the recipient of his wrath when the university campus was systematically blacked out by catapulted projectiles.'

'Yes, I know, I heard all about it from Wilber, he is just as confused as you are, Robert.' Mrs Shipley said trying her best to hand over the unwanted box.

'I could have been taken to hospital and remained there for several weeks not knowing when I would be coming out. I wouldn't have been able to continue with the Conference, or indeed the remainder of the trip, but I suppose, that may have been a blessing in disguise because when I return home to Glasgow, I am going to end up in one anyway.'

'What do you mean, Robert?'

'*Agh*, it is Morag, my girlfriend in Scotland; her brother, Alistair, is here with me in Canada and he is threatening to spill the beans to her, if he hasn't already done so; he says she will have my head on a pole.'

'There is an abundance of totem poles around here Robert, most of which are totally occupied.'

'There are plenty of Poles in Scotland as well, Jane, they are mainly of the same ilk as the "monkey see, monkey do's", mainly imported from Warsaw to fix the tiles on someone's roof.'

'Oh, by the way, while we are on the subject concerning monkeys, Wilber, has decided to leave me; it was shortly after the farewell party on Saturday evening when young Mr Bateson said he was going to sue him for grievous bodily harm.' Jane said when she eventually handed the black square cake box over to Robert.

'*Och*, I'm so sorry to hear about your husband, he was such a quiet man.' Robert said, tongue in cheek.

'Yes, and I cannot think of any reason why he should want to abandon me?' Mrs Shipley replied with what could only be interpreted as a sigh of relief.

'Do you know, Jane, I deserve a medal for some of the things I've been through since arriving in Canada.'

'My father was awarded the Congressional Medal of Honour by the American State Department for outstanding diplomatic services in Egypt.' Mrs Shipley took pride in saying.

'And my grandfather was awarded the 'Grand Order of the Whistle'.' Robert responded.

'Don't you mean, 'The Grand Order of the Thistle', Robert?'

'No, he was the station master on Moffat railway station. We are heading for Cleveland and Akron, Ohio, this morning, Jane,' he went on to explain, 'where the Goodyear Zeppelin Corporation, build the world's largest airships pass in the night; they also collide with each other, bump into pigeons, explode, and back into Rocky Mountains; they should concentrate on what the company started out to do, and that is to produce rubber tyres.'

'Yes, I do know where Akron is situated.' Jane mentioned before saying: 'My husband, Wilber and I, frequently see them passing overhead; they don't half make one hell of a noise and the vibrations caused by the engines make our apartment shake; do you know, Robert that my bath was underneath the window when it was installed and it is now behind the bathroom door.'

'*Och aye*, vibrations, they play havoc with your nervous system.' when Robert's knees began to tremble after Jane asked him if there was anything else she could do for him before he departed.

'I am going to give you an extra present, Robert; it is called "*Innocence*", my husband's favourite cologne, it's very fragrant, aromatic and comes from the Orient.'

Robert soon learned that, Chang Wan, the Chinese laundry and pyrotechnic expert had sold several bottles of the highly inflammable liquid to the Scottish delegation before leaving the campus.

'You will write to me, won't you Robert, it will give you the opportunity to get rid of the sweet smell of innocence.'

When Robert made his way out of the building, he threw the lotion into the same garbage bin and for it to join the empty bottle which had previously been discarded by Shipley; it was good riddance to bad rubbish he told Alistair at breakfast.

Mrs Shipley kissed Robert passionately and said: "My Sweet Embraceable You"; 'the words written by George Gershwin and the lyrics by Ira.' she would insist on telling him.

Robert's words were: 'Which football team did he play for, Motherwell or Hamilton National Chemicals?'

'And don't forget your pipe, Robert; I will sure miss that aromatic smell wafting down the hall.'

*

Breakfast in the Great Hall, Hart House

'Late for breakfast again, I see.' Alistair said when Robert walked into the Great Hall to take breakfast. 'Don't tell me you tripped and fell over the cat and what is that impression of a pair of lips doing on the side of your cheek?'

'*Agh*, it was Mrs Shipley, she wished us a pleasant journey and gave me a box containing one of her homemade chocolate cakes and an assortment of muffins.'

'*Och aye*, I just knew it was something like that Robert; *ya cannae* leave it alone for one minute *can ye?*'

'I *can nae* leave what alone, Alistair?

'Those things we men have got in our trousers.'

'Oh, you mean *ma* poetry; *och*, I've run *oot* of things *ta* say.' Robert made clear.

'Well, you do surprise me, Robert; does this mean we are all going to experience a quiet crossing between Toronto and Queenston this morning?'

'Well we might.' Robert said being not entirely sure of what he was saying.

'Why, what are you expecting?' Alistair asked curiously.

'If I told *ya* the truth Alistair, you just *would nae* believe *ma*.'

'Go on, Robert, try *ma* patience.'

'Are *ya* ready for this, my friend? There is a party of girl guides who will be on the steamer this morning and from what I have heard they are right little floozies, ready for anything.'

'Well in that case, Robert, you won't need any breakfast because later, you can have as much as you want on board the Steamer *"Chippewa"*. I can remember when you were chucked out of the boy scouts for money laundering on Johnson's farm during the summer holidays; no wonder the tally man went off his head when he realized there was a discrepancy between the sacks of hand-picked new potatoes and the wages at the end of the day; bob-a-job week was never the same after it had all been spoilt by yet another Hamilton-Brown misdemeanour. I can remember you telling me, Robert, that the girls you were picking potatoes with didn't come cheap, but from where I was sitting at the back of the tractor, this wasn't necessarily the case. And, by the way, here is a letter from Morag, it was sent inside the same envelope as mine and judging by the size of the envelope, it should take you less than a minute to read it.'

'Thank you, Alistair you certainly know how to start the day off with a sense of foreboding and an apparent lack of happiness.'

'Don't mention it, Robert; don't even mention it.'

Robert began his breakfast by tapping his ten-minute boiled egg with a dessert spoon, the curvature being twice the size of its oval construction. He gave everyone, who was unfortunate to be sitting at the same table, a rendition of two of his revamped Boy Scout camp fire songs which went:

"Ging gang, goolie, gang bang!"

"I'm a little brownie dressed in brown see my knickers hanging down".

"Dib dib, Dob dob; have no fear, my name is Rob"

*

153

Bay Street Toronto, eleven am the same morning

The morning had arrived when Robert Bruce Hamilton Brown said: 'A town has never looked better looking back.' when the steamship service *"Chippewa"* pulled away from the quayside of Toronto's busiest passenger maritime harbour.

'Hi, my name is Maryanne Demetrious de Bono-Grech from busy Chicago, Illinois.' one of the innocent-looking seventeen-year-old girl guides proffered to Robert as he strolled along the recently swabbed deck which was in dire need of a coat of brown yacht varnish.

'Hi, haven't you got any more names I am to call you? My name is Robert Bruce Hamilton-Brown and I am from Bonnie Scotland.' he replied, giving her the idea he was a descendant of the famous *wee* Jimmy; the Scottish clan hero called, Rob Roy.

'Pleased to meet you Rob, we are on our way home from a two-week summer camp which is pitched somewhere to the north of Quebec.' Maryanne said, blowing down the front of her blue open neck shirt to keep her cool. 'I have been living in bell tents, collecting firewood and joining in with outrageous Boy Scout camp fire songs every night since we arrived in Canada; I think I will take a rain-check on it next year, the camp was a bloody hell hole.' she added.

'I know of someone who is into rain checks and just may be able to help you.' Robert had to mention.

'You are from Scotland, where they wear kilts and throw things up in the air; I learnt that from the front of a *'Scot's Porridge Oats'* box; my dad calls them 'tossers'.' she, so diplomatically put in. 'My family are from Rhodes in Greece and my father is a shipping magnet in Athens and owns many ships.'

'When I was at school we had magnets as part of the course, and I can remember an incident when I dropped a bottle of mercury on to the floor inside the science laboratory; I spent most of the morning on my hands and knees chasing the bloody stuff around the room; "knees bent, arms stretched, rah, rah, rah" you know how the scouting song goes, Maryanne, don't you?'

'Yes, and if you play your cards right, you may just end up on your knees all over again.' she so eloquently put it.

Maryanne was sitting alone on a long wooden deck seat which was also lacking a coat of paint.

'May I sit down next to you?' Robert asked knowing what the answer was undoubtedly going to be.'

'Please do, and make yourself comfortable, Rob.' Marianne said, positioning herself at an angle in the corner of the seat where she could see his profile more clearly.

'When we arrive in Queenston, the Scottish delegation is to take a short train ride to Niagara to see the falls; will you be going there as well?'

'No, I've had enough of waterfalls and rapids because we have done that already; I volunteered to walk underneath Niagara Falls and gotten myself all wet.'

'Oh, what bad luck, such bad luck, but if you play *your* cards right, you could do that all again.' Robert said looking round to see a bulkhead door which led down to the baggage hold.

'However, we are sailing from Buffalo to Cleveland this evening on the Steamer "*City of Detroit III*" and I, sorry we, will have a cabin all to ourselves until the early hours of tomorrow morning.' Maryanne said, rubbing her hand up and down the sleeve of his grubby white shirt.

'*Och*, that sounds good *ta* me; it sure beats the hell out of sleeping in a bunk bed specially designed to fit inside a torture chamber,'

'But, first of all.' Maryanne said slowly. 'You can show me where you keep your bag.'

*

Queenston Harbour, Ontario, Canada

'I see you have scored again, Robert: 'Glasgow Rangers' seven, 'Forfar Bridies' nil.' Alistair said to Robert, the ship's regular Rudolph Valentino. 'And, what was that noise I heard coming from the baggage hold just now?'

155

'Oh, that would have been me making a sigh of relief when I found my travel bag.' Robert replied with a not so difficult to understand answer.

'The bag would not be blue, have big tits and wearing spectacles, would it?'

'No, no, Alistair, as you can see *ma* bag is brown, I bought it from 'Woolworths' in a sale.'

'Do you know, Robert that one day you are going to get it plenty.'

'*Och, aye, tha noo*, you've either got it or *ye have'ni.*'

'*Weel, tis* hoped that *ye have'ni*; Morag is the pity.'

Chapter Eighteen

Niagara Falls, New York State, U.S.A.

The hour had arrived for Robert to be subjected to a hazy cascade of water, falling one hundred and seventy-seven feet, the spray failing to cool him down in the intense heat radiating from the sun. The cold water penetrated his brain and like a child being christened for the first time, he yelled at the onlookers who were standing in the wings of the American falls as if they were waiting to go on stage.

The total volume of water in the Niagara Falls is two hundred and ten thousand cusecs, of which about ninety-percent flows over the Canadian Falls. The United States Falls has a total width of one thousand and fifty feet as opposed to two thousand four hundred and sixty feet on the Canadian side.

The spectacular falls form a major tourist attraction and, Niagara Falls on the United States side claims to be the 'Honeymoon' Capital of the World, contrary to Robert the 'Bruce' Hamilton-Brown, who said that Gretna Green in Scotland far outweighed the American tourist industry in the two towns on both sides of the river Niagara.

America, this was the land of dreams and where they were made, the land of steak and honey and where the Stock Market seemed to crash every five minutes. The land of big cars, big ideas and big sky-scrapers and like the sun, without fail, concrete and cement set every day.

'*Agh*, another umbrella shop closed for the season, Alistair.' Robert said before taking on the role of leader of a newly formed Scottish Y.M.C.A. pathfinder group which was to walk along the base of the United States side of the Horseshoe-shaped Niagara Falls. 'How is it, one can buy a bowie knife, a Niagara Falls baseball hat, a toy pistol, a catapult, a kiddie's bow and arrow with a sucker on the end, but not an umbrella.'

'*Och aye*, while we are talking about suckers, I can remember, Robert when we used to visit the golf club to look for stray balls in the rough and in the burns so we could sell them to the clubhouse shop for extra pocket money. And can you recall the time you fell into the water when you attempted to tickle a trout that had probably escaped being hit by a number six iron belonging to Bing Crosby.'

'What has that got to do with umbrellas, Alistair?'

'Have you forgotten? I used one, in metaphor, to fish you out of the burn; wherever you went, you always appeared to act wet, Robert. I mean, just look at you now, you look like a drowned rat.'

'Do you realize, if I were to fall into the water, Alistair, I would be in Cleveland *afore ye*?'

'Yes, it did cross my mind, and why don't you do us all a big favour and jump in the river.'

'*Agh*, if I was to do that, Morag would *nae* have the pleasure of *ma* company when I return to Glasgow.'

'I *didni* think she would want *tae*.'

'And, *didja* see that James Cagney, "You dirty rat" mouse trap in the joke section of the souvenir shop, Alistair; it had 'Merry Christmas' written on the side by a small lump of artificial *Emmental* cheese.'

'*Och aye*, I did see the damn thing, Robert; it was displayed next to the itching powder and something that could only be described as lavatorial and positively disgusting.'

'*Agh, ye cannae* take a joke, Alistair. For brunch, I am told we are going to a place called 'The Loggers Inn', where one can eat *Chevrolet*, bison and buffalo steaks, grilled to perfection on top of a flame. They also have succulent beef burgers to go and if that isn't enough, there are three feet long 'Snake in the grass' hot dog sausages as long as your arm.'

'Well, Robert, you should feel at home there, and as for eating a grilled *Chevrolet* on top of a flame, well, this could be the start of *ye* getting burned or prematurely going *ta* the dentist because the breed of cattle you were referring to are called *Charolais* and not *Chevrolet*; a *Chevrolet* is the name given to a car manufactured by the General Motor Company in Detroit City, Michigan, where by day they make the cars and by night they make the bars.'

'Well, how come some models have a cow with a pair of horns sticking out from the top of the radiator?'

'You always have to have the last word, haven't you, Robert?'

'*Och*, come on, Alistair, this is the beginning of ma holidays; *ye cannnae* call being in that penitentiary in Toronto a holiday when one had to listen to pontificating old farts, who so happened to drop in at the University for a quickie with Jane Shipley.'

'*Aye*, well you should know. Robert, you should know.'

'Do you ever get that feeling someone or something is watching *ye frae* a distance.' Robert said when he saw a crow sitting on top of a telegraph wire.

'I was only thinking this morning, how long it would be before your girlfriend, Gloria Aspinwall, would show up and follow you around the American continent?'

'*Nae*, Alistair, it *cannae* be her; she'll still be in her bed.'

'Just how long will it take us to get to Buffalo by train?' Alistair asked.

It was when Robert proceeded to put a light into the bowl of an upside down counterfeit *Meerschaum* pipe, he divulged that Mr Swanson had told him that the short journey would take just thirty minutes from Niagara Falls Railway Station to Buffalo and then another five minutes to take them by bus to the D&C Steamship Company office at the quayside; and by the time the Scottish delegation arrives in Cleveland the following day they will have travelled no less than two-hundred miles, most of which would have been nautical.'

'Yes, I can believe that, Robert, especially when we board the ship and you get your hands on that young lady in blue, Maryanne what's-her-name.'

'*Agh*, we'll be up playing cards all night, Alistair.'

'Are *ye* saying we will be playing bridge, tonight on board the ship "*City of Detroit III*"?'

'Is this one of your better puns?' Robert asked having just purchased a brand-new pack of playing cards with risqué photographs depicted on the back of each one.

'I suppose your idea of a game of cards tonight will no doubt be, 'Strip Poker'.'

'Tell me Alistair, what do you think of these? They are stink bombs; I bought them in the souvenir shop this morning, and they are guaranteed to get rid of unwanted company and are far more effective than insect repellent.'

'And, where may I ask, do you intend to use those chemical and biological weapons of mass destruction?' Alistair asked looking rather puzzled.

'Why, 'Camp Reynolds' of course, Alistair; I have heard there are lots of mosquitoes dancing around inside the log cabins at night.'

'You will have your little jokes, won't you Robert, and I have a little joke for you. Remember when you disappeared before the host announced the winner of the raffle at the farewell party?'

'*Och aye*, I had *ta gan oot cos* Wilber Shipley was on *ma* tail.'

'Well, Robert you won first prize; a five-hundred-piece jigsaw of the new Empire State Building in New York.'

'Well where is it?'

'Bruno Bateson claimed it before he went home with a sore head.'

'Typical, that's bloody typical.' Robert said angrily. 'I could have sold it *ta* one of those so-called clever Japanese students; they are into *hari-kari*.'

'Don't you mean *Origami*, the Japanese art of paper folding?'

'*Aye*, they are experts at that as well.'

'Tell me Robert, what you think of this *wee* poem I knocked up this morning, it is called, "Balls *ta* Niagara Falls".'

"Balls *ta* Niagara Falls"
"Underneath a waterfall dry as dry can be
I lost my umbrella when it floated *oot ta* sea
Far in the distance and in *ta* dark sunset
A cloud *cam oot fray* the horizon
And then I got bloody wet"

"Listen Alistair, are you taking the piss, because if you are I will.....'

'... what will you do, Robert catch the next Zeppelin back to Bonnie Scotland from Akron tomorrow?'

'*Agh, ye cannae tak* a wee joke Alistair.'

'Come on let's go and have that meal, I am beginning to feel hungry.' he suggested.

'Och *aye*, I *cannae* wait to remove the horns from a *Chevrolet*, dust it down and then place it next to a plate full of chips.'

'Don't you mean French *Fries*, Robert?'

'*Aye*, Alistair; if they are on the menu as well I *would'ni* mind.'

*

"The Loggers Inn" Restaurant, Brunswick Street, Niagara Falls, New York State

Six tables which had been previously booked at the 'The Loggers Inn' were set for the thirty-six members of the Scottish delegation including their wives; hitchhikers and stowaways not included.

Seated at one of the wooden tables in a tiny alcove were Robert Hamilton-Brown, Alistair Campbell, Alexander Smith, John Tindal, Hugh Cameron McLaren and William Martin, all at the unbending mercy of an insufferable Irish American waitress called Brigitte Callaghan from County Wicklow.

Mr Thomas Swanson, a senior member of the delegation appeared at the table to congratulate John Tindal on his seventeenth birthday. It was then a loud applause came from one of the top tables where an employee of 'Tindal's Gloves and Accessories' in Glasgow turned the moment into an ideal opportunity for him to seek promotion, needless to say Robert Bruce Hamilton-Brown, contrived to join the company six months later having torn up a shoddy slip of paper to which an I owe you five pounds from the Chief Executive's son, John Tindal had to be repaid.

It was later during the proceedings and after one of Robert's stink bombs had been accidently been trodden on causing everyone to go out for some much-needed fresh air, a birthday cake was delivered to the table. The pastel shades of red, white and blue which covered the square-shaped sponge cake had been baked in the University kitchen by Mrs Patricia Lightbody, the wife of Henry Lightbody, the most senior member of the Scottish delegation during the Conference. The seventeen candles, purchased from the souvenir shop, had the ability to stay alight once they were blown out; however, Hugh Cameron McLaren came to the rescue when he put them out with a powerful outer-space water pistol, specially designed to put out obstinate fires and Roman Catholic incense burners.

'Did you have anything to do with the purchase of these candles, Robert?'

'No, and who put that idea in *ta ya heed*, Alistair.'

'It's a wonder why they *didni* explode.' Alistair said with great relief.

'*Aye*, I must have misread the writing on the side of the box.'

'*Agh, ye* shall reap all the sins *ye* have bestowed upon *ma*, Robert, that is for sure.'

At this point the waitress asked what they would all prefer to order. Robert, hell bent on striking up an in-depth conversation with Brigitte, began by him asking whether they served steak. She, after listening into another conversation concerning American cars, sarcastically said, 'Would that be a Mustang, Chevrolet, Cadillac or a Studebaker; either way they all have horns, some louder than others.'

'I would like one that fits comfortably on a plate; I so hate big plates and small portions.' Robert said, putting her mind at rest when she concluded he was an absolute buffoon who wore odd socks and spoke with a funny accent.

'I have a better idea, sir, why don't you go outside and play with the traffic.' she so eloquently suggested in a New York accent which for several years had been confined to the Bronx.

Roberts's meal consisted of macaroni cheese on toast, spinach and half of a sun-dried tomato, a baked apple with cinnamon and sultanas', meanwhile everyone else ate succulent beef burgers, flaming steak and *tutti-frutti* side salads.

'Before I leave the restaurant, would you care to give me your full name and address, lassie?' Robert asked building up the *repartee*.

'My name is Brigitte Callaghan and I live in Niagara Falls, New York State U.S.A.' she replied hoping her unwanted luck was soon to walk out through the door.

'Thank you, lassie; you must find it extremely wet and damp; furthermore, you will be hearing from my lawyer in due course.'

'But you haven't got a lawyer, Robert.' Alistair said looking vacant and totally mystified.

'Agh that is today, Alistair, but tomorrow will be a different story.'

'*Och*, the waitress was only trying to do her job, Robert; two of the orders were delivered to the wrong table; the macaroni cheese was meant for Alison Duncan on the top table; Brigitte sent your *Charolais* steak back to the kitchen because Mrs Duncan is a vegetarian.'

'Well, in that case, I think I will have no choice but to demand my money back, Alistair.'

'Tell me, Robert, how can *ye* demand *ya* money back, when *ya didni* pay for it in the first place.'

'*Agh*, but there's still such a thing as redress of grievance and I will expect an apology.'

In the words of the proverbial prophet, Alistair said shaking his weary head: 'Where are we going?'

'Don't you know, Alistair; we are going to Cleveland, Ohio; the place where dreams begin and then come to an abrupt end once we reach a boot camp called 'Camp Reynolds'.'

*

The D&C Line quayside in Buffalo Harbour, the same after afternoon

The D-III of the D&C Line in 1931 plied the Great Lakes; the Detroit-Cleveland run. The D&C Line at that time was one of the most important passenger package freight lines operating upon the inland waters of the United States.

People flocked to the docks to watch the steamer *"City of Detroit III"* belching stacks of thick black smoke into the atmosphere and its massive paddle wheels churn as it pulled away from the quayside to make her way across Lake Erie; if it was a first trip, it would awestrike a young person beyond comprehension.

The ship was big and if you were going to Cleveland or Detroit for the first time, it would be like going on one of the old ocean liners.

After boarding, passengers would step into the hardwood-panelled lobby and go to the purser's office window to grab keys to their room. Then it was up the staircase into the Grand Salon, it was an impressive sight as you came to the top. There, passengers were wowed by seven large mythology-themed murals on the ceiling and a large painting on each of the two staircase landings, the work of William de Leftwich Dodge of New York City.

The promenade deck was built of the finest imported mahogany, while the upper and gallery decks featured painted panelling. There were also three moon-shaped, or "lunette", panels in the dome which arched high over the staircase.

The D-III had twenty-five staterooms for society's upper crust, lavishly outfitted in hardwoods with private baths and a veranda from which to enjoy the fresh air and beautiful lake views; however, there were twenty-one slightly less opulent semi-parlours featuring private baths; an extra buck would have got you a spot in one of the luxurious state rooms. The vessels less lavish accommodation had four hundred and seventy-seven staterooms, measuring only about seven feet in which were crammed an upper and lower bed, a sink and, if you were lucky maybe a fold-down stool; all staterooms sported telephones, hot and cold running water and clean ventilation.

Meals and top-shelf service were offered in the colonial-style dining room, which seated three-hundred and fifty people and was located at the rear of the boat on the main deck. The more high-brow travellers dined in mahogany and gilded private rooms some distance away from promiscuous Girl Guides, Boy Scouts and Y.M.C.A., and 'Jack the Lad' persons.

The Palm Court was a popular spot for guests to relax and unwind in wicker chairs as the boat chugged along. It was located on the upper deck at the rear end of the ship and show-cased a fountain, flower boxes and ivy, the vines climbing the walls. The dome covering over the Palm Court's open light was full of leaded glass and like the ill-fated passenger liner "*Titanic*"; it was the ship of dreams and a credit to the engineers of

Detroit, Michigan who were responsible for building such a beautiful and colossal machine.

The smoking lounge wasn't the only room decked out in elegant detail; the ship also had a bar modelled after a seventeenth-century style Rhine wine cellar; the atmosphere, beauty and charm of this room won praise for its decoration and designers from many states and countries.

Newlyweds, following the prohibition, would visit the bar and the Palm Court when they sailed along Lake Erie on their way to Niagara Falls via Buffalo.

For Robert Bruce Hamilton-Brown, this was to be a journey of a lifetime; or so he thought.....

Chapter Nineteen

The Paddle-Steamer *"City of Detroit III"*,
Buffalo docks - all aboard

"Paddling along on the crest of a wave" was the song for the moment. And for the young men of the Y.M.C.A. Scottish delegation, it was to be the journey of a lifetime, travelling on-board one of the world's largest and most luxurious paddle-wheeler with an overall length of five hundred and nineteen feet bow to stern, forward and aft, just shy of two football fields.

The one-hundred and fifty-one nautical mile journey was to take in some of the most scenic and picturesque views imaginable as they sailed along Lake Erie towards Cleveland, Ohio.

At five the ship pulled away from the D&C Line quayside, gathering up momentum for the first time as a surge of white water cascaded anti-clockwise inside a labyrinth of copper-plated iron paddles, rotating and churning around inside two massive partially-covered paddle-wheels on the port and starboard side.

From the moment Robert began to walk precariously up the ship's gangway, gripping on to a knotted rope attached to an old wooden stairway, he said to Alistair, he could feel a presence as he made his way to an entrance door situated just below the main deck. He was quite correct in his assumption when at the purser's desk he was tapped on the shoulder by the unmistakable and unsinkable, Miss Maryanne Demetrious de Bono-Grech, the lady with the pigtails and a space wide enough to drive a bus through her teeth.

'Hi Robert, well if it isn't your regular Scots person.' Maryanne said to Robert, jingling a set of keys to her cabin in front of his face. 'Well, big boy, aren't you going to take me up on that special offer you promised me this morning?'

'What special offer?' Robert asked making her believe he had forgotten the contents of a conversation he had with her earlier.

'You know the one where we play poker and take off our clothes.'

'Sorry, I don't seem to know that game.' Robert said, looking at a crowd of business men who were about to set up a card school in the Palm Court. 'I was told that the staterooms had two beds, an upper and a lower in which to sleep.' he added.

'That is correct, Robert, but you see the girl I was supposed to share a cabin with will suddenly disappear into another one while we are getting down to business.'

'You seem to know a great deal about business and special offers, don't you?' he said to her.

'Yes, this is why I'm a Girl Guide; I steer people in the right direction, however, I will meet you in 'The Marie Antoinette' drawing room on the gallery deck before we have dinner but first, I must change out of these stupid clothes. Would you care to join me, Robert?'

'Thank you for the special offer, Maryanne, but I have to change into some fresh clothes myself.'

'Oh, that is a pity, I could have done it for you.' she said trying to be helpful. 'Tell me, Robert,' she added, 'what is that man doing inside your trouser pocket?'

'*Och that* will be *ma* pipe; *tis* a *wee Meerschaum* John Brown classic.' Robert replied.

'You guys from Scotland don't half behave and sound funny; he doesn't look small to me.' Maryanne said looking at the protrusion sticking out from the front of his cavalry twills. 'From now on, Robert, I shall call you Sherlock Holmes.'

'He had a pipe too.' Robert said pushing the hand-held furnace deeper inside his *trews*.

'Yes, I know, but it was not as big as yours!'

'*Agh* but, *ye have'ni* seen it.'

'I will, Robert, I will.'

As the D-III headed out into the Lake, it was full steam ahead. There was now a gathering of people standing at the quayside waving and shouting farewells to passengers who were now leaning over the ship's port bow to reciprocate.

Suddenly, members of the Scottish delegation burst into song with

167

"Riding on the Crest of a Wave". This didn't, however, go down very well with the bourgeoisie type of passenger who said they sounded like a cat's chorus and demanded a refund on their ticket.

"All hands aboard boy, all hands aboard boys,
The ship is calling for more.
We're getting ready, now for a steady,
To pull away from the home shore
We are off to find adventure any how
Because we know that now
We're riding along on the crest of a wave,
And the sun is in the sky,
All of our eyes on the distant horizon,
Look out for passers by
We'll do the Hailing!
When all the ships around are sailing,
We're riding along on the crest of a wave,
And the world is ours"

'Hey, you guys, you will keep the noise down to an absolute minimum, won't you?' the D-III's first officer, Andrew Davit-Morgan shouted, bellowing out from the bridge situated high above the ship's fo'c'sle; the raised forward deck.

'Aye, aye, captain.' A delegate shouted to him waving a pole with a Camp Reynolds pennant stuck on the end.

'I am going to our cabin to change my attire.' Robert said to Alistair.

'You mean, once you've arrived in Akron, you will be able to compare yourself to a '*Goodyear*' rubber tyre or an obese '*Michelin Man*'.'

'I have been invited for cocktails in the ship's bar this evening; it is modelled after a 17th-century-style Rhine wine cellar.' Robert said, his ambitions now beginning to run away with him.

'Was she modelled in the 17th-century too?' Alistair asked with a hint of jealousy lurking beneath it all.

'Are you referring to Maryanne Demetrious-Give the dog a Bone....?'

'Stop it, Robert, you know I don't like Greek Cypriots, one of them ran off with my cousin's girlfriend who now lives in a one-room apartment on an island called Lesbos.'

'Don't worry, Alistair, I won't be abducted and sent to a Greek island.'

'Why not, indeed, I will pay for your ticket.'

'Tell me Alistair, who are these well-dressed people hugging the lobby?'

'They are business men who are returning to Chicago probably having bought half of Canada.'

'*Och*, this will explain why they have guns bulging out from inside their coat pockets.'

'One of them, so I have been told, is called Mr Harry Weismann.' Alistair was quick to mention. 'And, apparently, he has the monopoly on most of the pawn-broker shops in North America and made his fortune during the depression; he is the man with the 'Golden Balls'.

It wasn't long after his voyage to Cleveland Robert penned a poem in remembrance of Weismann who took all his money when he lost that evening playing poker. The poem was called "The Man with the Golden Balls" and began....

"He sits inside his shop
It is an Aladdin's Cave
Full of Artefacts and beautiful things
Most of which he wants to save
He puts beauty inside his money box
And can't afford the door
That hides away the jewellery he dearly wants to store
When he goes out from his well-padlocked flat
You'll find the key underneath the well-trodden mat
He keeps a close watch on Stock market falls
He is the man with the Golden Balls"

Weismann may have been the man with the Golden Balls but, Hamilton-Brown was the man with the Golden Gob.

'And who is the other Herbert standing in the corner, Alistair? It is truly amazing that after only twenty-minutes, you seem to know everybody on-board the ship.' Robert curiously asked.

'He looks antagonistic to me.' Alistair said reducing the sound of his voice to a lower level.

'Is that similar to one of those non-believers?' Robert said, chuckling like a gibbering water hen.

'They are agnostics, you fool.' Alistair said; 'The type that sneak into churches, listen in to confessions and steal the contents of the offertory boxes when the verger isn't looking and, if I may add, this conversation extends to people who pinch candles as well.'

'*Och aye*, I wondered when you'd get around to saying that.' Robert said, looking up the staircase leading to the Grand Salon. 'I paid my whack you know; I left one or two cents in the tin. *Agh*, I have *nae* sympathy *wi* that lot, the Catholic church; they will insist on leaving their places open long after the congregation have been chucked out and it is *nae* wonder why the priest finds half his things missing on Sunday mornings. Well, Alistair where does this Gunsel come from, and what names does he have?' Robert asked.

'He is Sicilian and lives in New York; his name sounds like Al Cappuccino.' Alistair hastily replied.

'But, on the other hand, his name could be Donald Smith from Doncaster.'

'Yes, well, I suppose so, he could be.'

'Do you know Alistair; you must be the world's biggest gossip and I suppose every ship has one.'

'Yes, and Morag would agree with you.'

'Well, I will take a private bath now.' Robert said, and it will be so relaxing to pamper oneself without any interference from the rest of the passengers.'

'Don't be too sure about that, Robert, from what I have just heard the stateroom is a tight squeeze, measuring only about seven by seven feet and passengers have to go down the hall to use the bathrooms. However, all four hundred and seventy-seven staterooms sport hot and cold running water, clean-air ventilation and a telephone in which to call your lawyer.'

'Bloody hell.' Robert said.

'And be careful, Robert, don't drop your soap.'

'*Agh*, that reminds me, Alistair, I lost my bar of '*Pears*' soap to an Englishman in the washroom in Wycliffe last evening.'

'It could have been worse,' Alistair conveyed to him. 'He could have been a Japanese Samurai swords person who could have removed your head when you bent down to pick it up.'

'*Aye*, you're right, Alistair; it's not often you are correct in your assumptions, but I could have been walking around the ship with my head tucked underneath my arm.'

'Well, Mary Queen of Scots; she still walks around with her head tucked underneath her arm, and it was the English who asked her to bend down in the Tower of London three hundred and fifty years ago to enable her head to fall into a basket.' Alistair said.

'*Och aye*, but she said I'm not bending down until you put some jewellery on the floor first.' Robert replied with a cheeky grin.

'She, *didni* get *ta* France from bonnie Scotland *ta* find a new romance, and Queen Elizabeth the First of England was responsible for that' Alistair so knowledgably pointed out and, at the same time, reminding Robert not to forget his roots.

'Anyways, she was a Catholic, and as you know Alistair, I have *nae* time for that lot. Well, I must fly and spruce myself up for this evening's entertainment.'

'When you are flying, Robert, just beware of those Fokkers who occupy the parlour staterooms on deck 'A'.

*

The 'Marie Antoinette drawing room' on the gallery deck at seven pm that evening

Robert stepped into the drawing room with an air of familiarity and confidence as if he had always been used to this kind of luxury; the plaster and carved exquisite woodwork, balustrade staircases, gorgeous paintings, mural ceilings, candelabras and chandeliers adorning the interior.

Maryanne was waiting for him to arrive. She was sat regally on what seemed to be a high-back red velvet Chippendale occasional chair, the type with hundreds of brass studs hammered into the seat accentuating the elegance of this type of furniture.

It was evident that Miss Maryanne de Bono-Grech had gone through a transformation because of the way she was now dressed. A cloche hat with a brown net veil was covering half of her heavily powdered face; the pencil-lined contours of her purple lips inviting any would be admirer towards them. A simple two-piece outfit consisting of a knee length skirt and a waistcoat with gold cotton thread embroidery, typical of the nineteen-twenties hugged her shapely figure with an adornment resembling one of Hollywood's greatest film actresses, Mary Astor. Under the waistcoat, she was wearing a coffee-coloured silk blouse, unbuttoned provocatively at the top to allow men of a taller position to stare and gaze inside. The transformation had continued with silk stockings and a pair of expensive American '*Blake and Black*' high-heeled shoes, the colour being two-tone beige and brown. And, in total contrast to her heavily stained khaki Girl Guide back-pack, she held a sequined purse which reflected the light shining down from one of the chandeliers. Around her neck, hanging gracefully was a small twenty-two carat gold jewel-encrusted Greek Orthodox crucifix which slipped and disappeared down her cleavage with embarrassment when she leaned forward to light a cigarette.

Robert, however, was wearing a white shirt, black bow-tie, patent leather shoes and a borrowed tuxedo; his black shiny trousers having tram-lines wider than the San Francisco Street Car railway.

It was amazing that passengers who were having drinks in the bar or dining in the top-shelf service colonial-style dining room, compared Robert's outfit to the waiters because they all looked exactly the same.

'Hi, Robert, we meet again.' Maryanne said on his approach to her. 'I thought you guys all wore skirts, carried handbags and had pen knives tucked down their socks and blew on piccolos?'

'*Och, aye wi do*, but tonight some of us have, and some of us *hav'ni.*'

'Gee, Rob, you sure don't half talk funny, and can you not put this conversation into some *kinda* language we can all understand?'

'*Aye*, I can *nae* but try.'

'Shall we go into the bar before we have dinner on the main deck?' Maryanne suggested.

'Yes, that would be very romantic seated amongst three hundred and fifty people during the ship's first sitting' Robert replied.

'One has to eat, Robert; there are no camp fires or Buffalo grills on-board this boat, it is all top-shelf service, and don't you worry about the bill; my father has an account with the D&C Line in Detroit.' she emphasised.

'Well, that sounds okay, suddenly I'm feeling a wee bit hungry.' he said wantingly.

'When *we* girls arrive in Detroit, *we* will be staying at the prestigious Wayne Hotel in the busy transportation hub which is situated along Jefferson Avenue and Third Street. I have stayed in the Wayne Hotel many times and the lavish Wayne Gardens and its Pavilion, auditorium and concert hall are a delight to visit; they are a like the Tivoli Gardens in Copenhagen; have you been there Robert?'

'No, but I once went to Brighton during my school holidays and walked around the Grand Pavilion there; it was there I had all my money confiscated when I was caught bending the wheels on a fruit machine in a Penny Arcade on the pier.'

'You cannot be serious, Robert?'

'I also recycled empty soda-pop bottles and returned them to their rightful shop owners for two-pence each, and that's how I travelled back to Glasgow with more money than when I started off.'

'Gee Robert, you are some guy.'

'Well, it sure beat the hell out of getting *ma* feet wet retrieving golf balls and having *ma* arse kicked in a field for stealing sacks of new potatoes.'

'Oh, my God, you should be in jail.' she said.

The Detroit III's cool and comfortable cocktail lounge excellently reproduced a three-hundred-year-old drinking room. The room was covered in Pewabic tiles and fashioned with massive, hand-hewn oak beams with a large oak bar at one end and behind the bar was a mural of a gnome painting a frog. Also, behind the bar were heavy oak doors leading to the liquor and wine storage chamber. Travellers would kick back on heavy leather-covered settees or sit on the fine leather benches which lined the wall. The light fixtures were of wrought iron and patterned after old European candleholders, and in keeping with the motif, a little critter, simulated spider webs and bats festooned the ceiling and walls.

'I'm going to have a '*Gin Sling*' on the rocks.' Maryanne said after climbing up the side of what seemed to be a six-foot high bar stool to peruse the menu. 'And what are you going to have, Rob? And, may I recommend the 'Monkey's got a Gun', it is a patriotic concoction of fudge-infused Tennessee whiskey, chocolate bitters and Innis and Gunn oak aged beer from bonnie Scotland.'

'*Agh*, I think I shall have one of those complementary glasses of punch from that *wee* bowl, I *can nae* stand anything that's been interfered *wi* from different parts of the world; *ma* father used to make a bowl every Christmas day after all the guests had arrived with presents, fruit, whisky and bottles of wine from Spain and Australia.'

'Ah, that was nice of him to do that, Robert; my father on Christmas day was usually smashing plates; he said it was his way of being banned from the kitchen after drinking far too much Ouzo; it is a Greek tradition to smash plates, you know Robert?'

'Would *ya* like *ta* listen to one of my poems, Maryanne?'

'No, not now, Robert, I would sooner listen to Charlie Rubenstein playing George Gershwin's "My Sweet Embraceable You" on the piano.'

The '*Gin Sling*' after being shaken to death by the bar tender was placed at an arm's length distance in front of Maryanne Demetrious de Bono-Grech, together with a generous glass of *Sangria* destined for Robert's insides and concocted from Spanish red wine, French *Muscadet* white wine, thinly sliced apples, oranges, bananas, limes and a hint of Canadian Club whisky; a selection of savoury nibbles, minute curried to death things on sticks and popcorn were in evidence to liven the taste-buds of the sterner sex, who dared to venture into the cocktail bar to share its beauties with other passengers.

'Tell me, Robert, when you arrive in Akron, will you be going up in one of those balloons?' she asked, twirling a wand around inside a blue crystal cocktail glass with a delicate stem.

'I don't think so, Maryanne, I want *ta* get back home *ta* Glasgow in one piece. Do you realize there is more explosive in one of those Zeppelins than Guy Fawkes had hidden down in the basement of the Houses of Parliament in London?'

'Who is Guy Fawkes, Robert?'

'*Agh*, he was another one of those English mercenaries who is still walking around with his head tucked underneath his arm.'

'Oh, was he double-jointed, Robert?'

'*Och* no, but the situation could have been worse he could have ended up sitting on the top of a bonfire.'

'I hear from one of the Y.M.C.A. boys, that you are a very good artist, Robert and after dinner would you like to come back to my stateroom and draw a sketch of me?'

'Yes, but first I must retrieve my crayons from my suitcase in the hold.' Robert said as she hastily finished drinking the cocktail in anticipation; her long purple fingernails grasping the rim of the glass, momentarily teasing him when she licked the end of the wand with her tongue.

Robert had inadvertently left his saucy playing cards down there as well, and as luck would have it when he thought he could turn the situation into a double-whammy.

The colonial-style dining room was fitted out in white enamel-painted woodwork and ringed by windows, a practical yet new innovation on steamships at that time.

Robert and Maryanne chose to circumnavigate the *smorgasbord*, a cold buffet located in the centre of the room consisting of fresh-water salmon and *fruits de mer*, an assortment of seafood Oysters, prawns, mussels, crab meat, whelks and small pots of lower grade caviar; an assortment of rabbit food; salad concoctions, consisting of lettuce, carrot and baby radishes soaked in a garlic and white wine *vinaigrette* was to hand.

Meanwhile, the other members of the 'Y.M.C.A. Scottish delegation' and 'The Girl Guides', the Chicago Ventura's, were impatiently waiting on the main deck to enter the restaurant's second-class sitting.

After Maryanne had made a point by criticizing the egg mayonnaise by saying it looked positively disgusting and tasted like puke, they both got up from their seats to make an exit from the restaurant and to walk down the hall to her cabin.

'I would like to listen to your poem now, Robert.' Maryanne hesitantly conveyed to him.

'It is called "Stevenson's Rocket",' he was quick to say, 'and goes like this:

Stevenson's Rocket
"A rocket driven by steam
Was Stevenson's ultimate dream
Abraham Lincoln was soon to scoff
He said this bloomin' thing will never take off"

'Is that all you British Y.M.C.A. guys can talk about, trains, boats and planes?' she asked with a hint of patriotic Anglo-American disapproval.

The stateroom was in a bit of a tip to say the least. In evidence, were greasy mess tins lying in the sink and a make-shift washing line stretching the full width of the bedroom on which to hang recently washed camiknickers, bras, long stockings which were stained and holed brought about by trudging along the rugged plains of the North West Frontier.

'*Agh*, this cabin is much larger than ours.' Robert said as the door slammed firmly shut behind him. The one Alistair and I have to share isn't big enough to swing a cat around.' he added.

'Gee, I'm sorry about the mess, Robert, but me and my partner, Angela, would not want to enter into the Wayne Hotel in Detroit smelling of a recently extinguished Girl Guide camp fire. Now, where would you like me to sit, and please tell me now if you would prefer me to remove my clothes? It is extremely hot this evening and so I will turn on the *ventalateur*, the electric fan on the ceiling, that will stop the steam from coming out from your ears.'

'If you wouldn't mind posing for me in the nude stretched out on the *chaise longue* smoking *ma* pipe.' Robert insisted, placing his sketch pad on his lap directly in front of her.

Maryanne's sumptuous undulating body nervously quivered with every intake of Robert's aromatic '*American Black Cherry*' tobacco; the rings of smoke rising constantly towards the ceiling before it was redistributed by the fan all around the stateroom.

'Have you finished, Robert?' Maryanne asked wiping some of the perspiration from her forehead with a red and white striped neckerchief she had just pulled down from the washing line. 'Because, if you haven't, I will surely die of asphyxiation.' she went on.

'*Och, aye*, I think it is finished, we're on track.'

Maryanne rose to her feet to look at the masterpiece displaying what she had hoped to be the perfect portrayal of her delicate and vivacious body.

'What the hell is that, Robert? I've been lying on this bloody settee for over an hour.' she screamed.

'It is the seven forty-five express train from Moffat to Glasgow.' he explained.

'Goodbye Robert, Maryanne said to him, 'I'm not sorry I didn't know you.'

Chapter Twenty

The smoking lounge later that evening; the road to ruin and Akron

The Grand Salon became the focal point of the ship's artistic and mythological theme. Again, artisans had meticulously carved the woodwork inside the smoking lounge and a seductive siren was painted on the ceiling by William de Leftwich Dodge; grand ladies posed and pirouetting precociously on top of the staircase; a trident-wielding baby Neptune held court under the wistful gaze of cupids and nymphs. The idea behind all this vulgarity was to distract poker-players when they glanced up towards the ceiling to see a half-naked wood nymph lying down coquettishly on the grass next to a fifteen-foot long python.

Robert had found the ideal opportunity to win some money playing poker with the big boys on-board the ship.

Sitting at one of the gaming tables was Harry Weismann, the man with the golden balls. He was smoking a half-corona Havana cigar, the type which seem to burn forever. His gambling skills had already cleaned-out most of the wealthy attendees in his card schools and going to bed early was not on his list of daily events. 'Operation Clean Out' was a favourite past time played at the tables which consisted of whist, brag, poker, aces high and a cut of the playing cards to finish and this would have taken Robert possibly a day and a half to learn and less than an hour to lose all his money. Poker was Robert's better option as he knew the game already and this could have cleaned him out in half that time.

Everyone, except for a few unlucky stragglers had now retired to their beds to dwell on their losses. There were no torn up 'I owe you' demands, life insurance policies or snapped- off indelible pencils in sight and one could assume that most of the upper crust passengers may have handed over their wrist watches and jewellery to clear their gambling debts; it was apparent that Harry Weismann was the man with the most money and he called the shots.

Robert walked into the ship's smoking room with an air of confidence, hoping he could release some of his efforts and energies at one of the tables.

'Hello, young man.' Harry Weismann said getting up from his high-backed chair to greet him. 'Please take the seat opposite to me; it should feel quite warm as three different people have sat on it tonight.' he added.

'Good evening, sir, my name is Robert Bruce Hamilton-Brown, and may I have the pleasure to play poker with you and anyone else who feels he is going through a gambler's lucky streak'. Robert said smugly.

'It is ten bucks to start.' Weismann demanded and looking at the square-face of a recently acquired diamond encrusted Cartier wristwatch. 'Can you afford to open with ten dollars, young man because later, it may cost you two-hundred to withdraw from the game.'

'I have only got Canadian dollars and need to get them exchanged.' Robert said.

'Oh, that is no problem, I will exchange that Mickey Mouse money into American 'Green-Backs' for you at a reasonable rate and should you win tonight it will prevent you from visiting the *Bureaux de Change* in either Cleveland or the 'Rubber City' Akron tomorrow.'

Seated at a rectangular table were four card players; Robert Bruce Hamilton-Brown sitting in an uncomfortable position to the south, Alfonso Gambachino, who was sitting to his right, Harry Weismann, facing north and Lorenzo de Roberti to his left.

It was within the space of five minutes when Lorenzo retired from the game, followed by Alfonso Gambachino, leaving Robert and Weismann to continue. The game ended when Weismann won, by paying to see Robert's cards and as luck would have it the Ace of Spades had the upper hand.

'Tell me Robert.' Weismann asked with a curious look on his much lived-in face. 'What happened to that fine-looking young lady you were cavorting with this evening?'

'*Agh*, that would be Miss Maryanne Demetrious de Bono-Grech from the Windy City, Chicago; she tossed *ma* pipe *oot* through one of the port-holes inside her cabin. *Ye wouldni* be interested in buying one of *ma* drawings of the seven forty-five express train from Moffat to Glasgow, would *ye?*'

179

'I know a children's nursery rhyme, Robert, it has something to do with a "Little Miss Muffet" sitting on her tuffet, chewing her curds and whey, along came some spiders and sat down beside her, she frightened them all away; sounds very much like you Robert. Tell me,' he asked, 'with a name like that what is she doing living in Chicago?'

'*Och*, she is the daughter of one of those shipping magnets you will find gun-running and people trafficking in the Mediterranean; from Athens to Sicily and from Lisbon to North America, that's where he operates'

'You mean one like this? Alfonso Gambachino said when he allowed Robert to see his piece of equipment, an Italian *Berretta* fully automatic pistol he kept in a holster close to his chest.

'*Och aye*, I have heard that in New York the *Mafia* carry 'Saturday Night Specials'.' Robert said to Gambachino.'

'Not me.' Alfonso replied. 'I carry a different one for every day of the week.'

Penniless and broken, Robert made his way back to his stateroom. Alistair, who was in his bunk waiting impatiently for him to return, asked: 'Where the hell have you been until this ungodly hour?'

Robert explained to him in great detail how he had lost all his money playing poker and to make matters worse he had also lost his pipe when it fell out from his mouth when he leaned over the ship's rail to throw-up over the side.

Alistair, having no sympathy whatsoever for Robert said: 'Well, that's what you get when mortals play with the gods.'

'And, that's what you get when you can't have what you want.' Robert retaliated.

'Would that be the Ventura Girl Guide, Miss Maryanne de Bono-Grech?'

'*Och no*, she went *ta* bed early with a stomach ache because of a dodgy egg mayonnaise.'

'Good night, Robert, and let us all hope you will be happier in the morning.'

'Happiness is not a competition, you know, Alistair.'

'Good night, Robert.'

It was when Robert was queuing up for breakfast outside the dining-room he was approached by Harry Weismann who gave him an envelope containing his losses.

'It makes me wonder who the Christians are around here.' he said, fumbling around in his waistcoat pocket to find something else of lesser importance. 'Oh, and by the way, I have deducted the cost of the envelope. And, don't tell anyone about this charitable refund will you, Robert?' he added.

Weismann had found what he was looking for; it was Robert's *Meerschaum* pipe which had been given to him that morning by Maryanne Demetrious de Bono-Grech.

'It would seem it wasn't thrown out of a porthole after all. And do you know Robert; I would have preferred to play poker with the devil than to have played along with you.'

'Why should she have given it to you and, how did she know it would end up back with me?' Robert asked inquisitively.

'Like you, Robert, the answer is quite simple; I could see her profile in the mirror when we were playing cards.'

'So, who was responsible for returning some of my money, you or Maryanne Demetrious de Bono-Grech, Mr Weismann?'

'It was me, Robert, who had the responsibility for giving you back some of *my* money.'

After the nervous conversation had come to a close, Alistair appeared to join Robert in the queue. He had purchased the morning edition of the "*Cleveland News*" newspaper and couldn't wait to read it alone at one of the breakfast tables.

'Tell me Robert, why are you so happy, you are looking as if you have just lost a shilling and found a pound.'

'*Och aye*, I've just found a Scottish five-pound note in *ma* back pocket.'

'And *didja* find your pipe as *weel*, and why are *ye* no wet?'

Robert being a slow learner and a fast forgetter forgot that he had mentioned to Alistair earlier about his pipe falling from his mouth into the moonlit murky waters of Lake Erie.

'Do you know, Robert that one day you will be recognised as the teller of the tallest stories and tales in the world?'

'*Och aye, tis* a fact that one day I'll be famous, Alistair, but on that day, it will be far too late.'

'Well on that day, I'll bring in a thousand pipers from Braemar *ta* pipe *ya oot.*' Alistair said bringing the subject to an abrupt end but by no means to a close.

*

Cleveland, Ohio Tuesday 4th August "The D&C Line" docks at ten that morning

The "City of Detroit III" berthed at the D&C Line quayside to allow some of its passengers to disembark before it moved off again to its final destination, the City of Detroit on the Detroit River.

Meanwhile, Maryanne Demetrious de Bono-Grech, Harry Weismann, Lorenzo de Roberti, Alfonso Gambachino, together with a multitude of Girl Guides from Chicago and members of the American Y.M.C.A. delegation from Houston in Texas, stayed on-board the ship to alight in Detroit.

Robert could not help but hear the Texan Y.M.C.A. lot he so politely called them, singing the Vaudeville song "Pasadena" in the background.....

"Oh, you railway station
Oh, you Pullman train
Here's my reservation
For my destination
On the Western Plain
To see my home in Pasadena
Home where grass is greener
Where honey bees hum melodies
In the breeze

I want to be a home sweet homer
And there, I'll settle down
Beneath the moon in someone's arms
In Pasadena, town"

And, during the voyage that morning he was heard, saying that if he were at the Michigan Central Railroad Station in Detroit he would buy all of their tickets to go back home to Texas.

He also conveyed to someone that he knew why one of them sang in what seemed to be a bashed-in red fire bucket when it was used to simulate a megaphone to enhance the sound.

And, so this was Cleveland, the largest town in the State of Ohio U.S.A. It stands on the south bank of Lake Erie at the mouth of the Cuyahoga River and provides access to the Atlantic for its hinterland by way of the St Lawrence Seaway.

In the *"Cleveland News"* newspaper that morning it exalted D&C as one of the most important passenger and package freight lines operating upon the inland waters of the United States, but things started to slow down because of the rise of the automobile industry and for steamer passengers to lessen their journey time by travelling by road. The sun was beginning to set on the golden age of passenger steamers on the Great Lakes.

D&C managed to stay afloat through the Great Depression, though it lost more than two point-eight million US dollars from 1930 to 1935 and about forty-two million US dollars when adjusted for inflation; it was the end of the line, the age of the great paddle-wheelers had come to an end.

Robert and Alistair, prior to their arrival in Cleveland, were given envelopes which contained an Introduction Card to a Host and an Automobile Assignment Card which had a Number fourteen written on the top in sepia ink. The instructions on the lower half of the card were to ensure that they had secured their hand baggage and then afterwards to proceed at once to the automobile, bearing the abovementioned number.

The Introductory Card was to introduce the Official Delegates, Robert Bruce Hamilton-Brown and Alistair Campbell to a guest house proprietor, a Mr M.B. Vilas, living at Number 2289 Stillman Road, Cleveland, Ohio, from the 4th August until the Monday morning of August 10th.

*

The Old Union Station Akron

The railway station in Akron was built in 1891 and demolished in 1951. Akron's second Union Station was located between East Market and Park Streets (called "Amelia Flats). The Akron Old Union Station served Buffalo, Cleveland and Erie and had offices nearby in East Street next to the Hotel Pendleton; the Amelia hotel was also nearby in Park Street.

At three-thirty pm buses were waiting in Park Street to take the members of the Scottish delegation to Akron's magnificent Young Men's Christian Association Central Building prior to it being dedicated, inaugurated and opened to the public that day.

The building, situated at number 80 W Carter Street, Akron, looked every inch like a nineteen-forty Bakelite radio, had three main elevators which, from the outside, had the appearance of modern-day graphic equalizers running vertically up the side of its facia.

The latter part of the afternoon was spent meandering around Akron's Y.M.C.A. Central Building with both its elaborate inside and outside architecture not dissimilar to the New York Stock Exchange on Wall Street and the Empire State Building in Central Manhattan.

The swimming pool, libraries, study and conference rooms were still to be occupied and the brand-new show-case gymnasium still had shuttle-cocks, rackets, table-tennis bats and balls in cardboard boxes waiting to be unpacked. There was also a magazine and tuck shop without any wares; the shelves devoid of contents and a metal case bubble gum dispenser was standing alone, looking sadly like an empty aquarium without the tropical fish.

The ceremony began in the Public Auditorium at eight with a prelude by the Y.M.C.A. Orchestra playing Handel's Messiah, followed by words of welcome by Stacy G. Carkhuff, President and Presiding Officer of Akron Y.M.C.A.

This was followed by a hymn, "A Mighty Fortress is our God".

An Invocation was put forward by Soichi Saito, the General Secretary of the Y.M.C.A., Tokyo, Japan, representing Asia; the dedicatory address was given by Francis S. Harmon, the President of the National Council representing America and the service of dedication was led by Keith A. Falconer of New Zealand, representing Oceania.

Leader of the dedication began – 'Having been prospered by the hand of God and enabled by his grace and power to complete this noble character-making temple, let us now in His Holy presence, dedicate this building: "Except the Lord build the house, they labour in vain that build it."'

Response – We dedicate this building.

'And, if you can understand that, you are a far better man than I, Gunga din.' Robert had cause to ask Alistair.

Leader – "To the widening of horizons and the lengthening of our vistas so that they shall share in the world-wide interest and endeavour to make the brotherhood of man and the fatherhood of God everywhere a vital, determining, dominating principle."

Everyone, with the exception of Hamilton-Brown, responded in unison – We dedicate this building.

'What in God's name is he talking about, Alistair?' Robert asked. 'I wish the President of the National Council would put the dedication into some sort of common language we can all understand. The mortar and cement on the seventeenth floor of this new art-deco building seems still to be wet, and I don't want to be around when it all decides to collapse and fall down around my ears.'

'The building has sixteen storeys, not seventeen, Robert.' Alistair said with what he thought was the end of the matter.

'*Och aye*, but *ye canni* discount the roof, Alistair; *ye canni* discount the roof.'

'I, like you, Robert, cannot understand one word of what he is saying.' Alistair said, shrugging his shoulders in total bewilderment.

'It matters not one wit when one has to put up with all of this shit.' Robert said, poetically describing Keith Falconer's ranting and incoherent burbling.

To conclude the ceremony a dedicatory prayer was said by Hugo Cadegren, the National Secretary of the Y.M.C.A., Sweden, representing Europe. This was followed by a hymn – "All Hail the Power of Jesus' Name" by Audience Standing, and the benediction was given by, Naguib Kelada, the Secretary of the Egyptian Y.M.C.A., representing Africa.

After the over-the-top mumbo-jumbo was completed and a Roman Catholic priest, who Robert described as being a religious maniac from Outer Mongolia, ran out of Holy water when he anointed the building from every angle with his anointing stick, a black and white baton which looked every inch like David Nixon's magic wand, it was back to Cleveland by train for a well-deserved cocoa supper in Stillman Road.

*

The Goodyear Zeppelin Corporation at Akron, Ohio Saturday 8th August 1931

On Saturday 8th August, the members of the Y.M.C.A. Scottish delegation were invited to Akron to witness the launch of the helium-filled United States Navy airship, USS Akron, the ZRS-4, from its manufacturing base at Akron, Ohio.

The Akron was launched floating out of the hangar door and was christened by Mrs Lou Henry Hoover, the wife of the President of the United States of America, Herbert Clark Hoover. Unfortunately, its fate was predicted, and on 4th April 1933 it crashed off the coast of New Jersey killing seventy-three of the seventy-six crewmen and passengers.

It was for Robert and Alistair a day to remember when they saw one of the world's largest airships, the USS Akron (ZRS-4) approach its mooring, the mast towering one hundred and fifty feet above the ground.

Robert was in his poetical mode that morning when he penned a poem which he thought to be poignant and significant for this special occasion.

The poem was called, "Magnificent Men and Women".

Magnificent Men and Women
in their Flying Machines

"A pilot had to get it right
When he flew Transatlantic Flight
British Airways were to bear the brunt
When they said he had to fly his plane
With only two up front"

Like all good things, they eventually have to come to an end and Cleveland, Ohio was no exception.

Monday morning had come around once again and it was time for Alistair and Robert to say their farewells to Mr Vilas who had painstakingly accommodated them at 2289 Stillman Road, Cleveland for the past six days of their memorable visit. However, Mrs Lavender Rose Vilas, the deaf and dumb landlady and the wife of Mr M.B. Vilas was sitting in a wheelchair outside the front door. She accentuated her invalidity by using a brass ear trumpet, wore gold-rimmed spectacles and couldn't help showing them her tonsils every time she opened her mouth in an attempt to speak.

It was farewell to the wild-life parks, the friendly red squirrels, ever-greens, and the fresh water lakes of Cleveland, Ohio. The salmon, the trout, the hot dogs, the walnut trees and endless walks through the conifer glades and forests, the fishing, the canoeing, the pony trekking and hiking; all this had suddenly come to an end as the members of the Scottish delegation clambered on-board the Pennsylvania Railroad train to travel the thirteen-hour journey to Washington DC.

Chapter Twenty-one

The Y.M.C.A. Building, Central Park West, Manhattan, New York City a week later following Camp Reynolds

Robert had all but forgotten about Miss Victoria Brunswick, the not so level-headed school mistress he met on the good ship T.S.S. *"Athenia"*, the banana lady who lived in an exclusive apartment block on Fifth Avenue, 59th Street in a prestigious quarter of North Manhattan, New York.

They were neighbours, living just a stone's throw away from each other's front door. How wise it all was of him to have been cocooned amongst his fellow delegates within the heavily fortified battlements of the almost impregnable Y.M.C.A. Building in Central Park West.

It was on Monday the 17th August when Robert arrived in New York from Washington State. To him, checking in at the Y.M.C.A. in uptown Manhattan was probably like Maryanne Demetrious de Bono Grech staying at the prestigious John Wayne Hotel in Jefferson Avenue, Detroit after roughing it in one of Canada's popular Rocky Mountain playgrounds where "six-foot two, eyes are blue" bum bags are seen posing as buffalo hunters and would certainly have been arrested by Sergeant Gordon Copper Nickel Junior for stalking underage Girl Guides before carrying them off to a hoedown somewhere between Hamilton Ridge and Gay Gordon's Keyhole to the north of Quebec.

And, so this was New York. I can recall a poem, "Find Strength through Lennon", written by a friend of mine, in memory of my favourite singer and song writer, John Lennon, who died walking along an icy street close to his apartment block in 1980, and it begins......

"In New York City's Central Park
Where the New York light fades into dark
It was a place out of sight
Where "Blackbirds sing in the dead of Night"
It was here he hoped to find
Imaginative thoughts and peace of mind

In Central Park West it was a *kinda* madness
To see it turned into a place of sadness
And in the morning
The squirrels slept and the Willows wept
He's still alive amongst the trees
Where once they shed so many leaves"

Hamilton-Brown, now almost penniless and on the brink of contracting a cold when he almost fell into a duck pond in Central Park after he had observed the four stowaway passengers, Mr and Mrs H.J. Donaldson and Mr and Mrs G.O. Norrie, climbing into a horse-drawn landau, a type of pony and trap with large wooden wheels. This was for Robert, his lucky day when he approached Herbert Donaldson and asked him for an advance on the money which was to be paid to him on their return to Glasgow. He also mentioned to Donaldson that if he paid him half in dollars and the other half in pounds sterling on-board ship, he would not report Steven Boswell, the organiser of the trip to the Y.M.C.A. authorities for unheard of misdemeanours.

The day progressed; it was long and pleasantly warm when Robert, having salvaged seventy-five pounds found himself in the company of a local good-time girl, Bubble gum Samantha Avitov and the gun-packing Gunsel from Broadway who had a brain the size of a *petit pois* garden pea.

'At least the hotdog was free'. Robert remarked later when he told Alistair a whole new batch of lies to configure out. 'Here is the money I owe you, Alistair; I think you will find the debt is now sufficiently repaid'.

'I thought during breakfast you didn't have two pennies to rub together.' Alistair said when he glanced down to see a huge wad of 'Green Back' banknotes spilling out from Robert's brown leather wallet. 'I also thought it was the recipient of the ill-gotten gains, namely the broad on Broadway, who was supposed to benefit from the money and not the other way around?'

'*Agh, ye cannie* be too careful, Alistair; the man with the gun must have been a magician because when he pulled the trigger a miniature flag bearing the stars and stripes popped out from the end of a snub nose.'

'Just where did you get all that money from, Robert?' he asked, hoping to get a reasonable and honest response to his question.

'*Agh, I didni cam oot* on the last banana boat, Alistair, there were a few English guys who settled their 'I owe you' debts, and with the compound interest, I decided to buy myself a hot dog.'

'I thought you said the hot dog was free?' Alistair curiously asked.

'Well, the first one ended up on the sidewalk because it was far too big to put into my mouth.'

'*Och*, I *can nae* believe that, Robert, *you* could fit the magnitude of the New World Metropolis, the new Chanin Building at forty-second Street and Lexington Avenue into that big mouth of yours.'

'*Och*, you *can nae tak* a joke, Alistair; you *can nae tak* a joke.'

'And, who may I ask bought you the second one?' Alistair asked.

'Oh, that would be Bubble gum Sam, she felt a *wee* bit sorry for me when I had to clean someone's shoes after they had been splattered with tomato ketchup, hot chilli peppers and mustard.'

'And, by the way, a lady was looking for you shortly after breakfast; she looked remarkably like the woman who was dancing provocatively to "Black Bottom" on the T.S.S. "Athenia".'

'Oh, no, it's that bloody school teacher, Victoria Brunswick from Brooklyn.' Robert said, shaking his head in disbelief. 'Can't anyone have a quiet life around here?'

'She is not from Brooklyn, Robert; she lives just across the road on fifty Ninth Street.' Alistair said as he pointed up to a window on the twenty seventh floor of the fifth Avenue apartment block. 'Where is your camera, Robert? Don't tell me you have sold it to keep your head above water.'

'Are you being funny, Alistair? As a matter of fact, it is in my Bergen rucksack which I have left in my room.'

'Also, if I may ask, what has happened to your gold ring; the one with your initials embossed in the centre.'

'Agh, I lost that this morning when it began to rain.' Robert sadly explained in a long drawn-out detail. 'You see, when I was walking towards Times Square, there was a sudden down-pour and I had to put my umbrella up, and because of the quick, sharp and sudden movement of my hand, the ring came off my finger and was projected far into a maddening crowd on Eighth Avenue.'

'Well, in that case, how come I found it lying on top of a washbasin in the washroom this morning?'

'*Och*, I *cannie* be in charge of everything, Alistair, and I must have forgotten I was wearing it at the time during the *wee* downpour.'

'This is the second time you have lost your signet ring. I can recall quite vividly an incident last week at Camp Reynolds, when an honourable young English gentleman found your ring at the bottom of one of his mess tins, and this was when you said to me, he would have been far better off panning for gold in the Klondike Valley. And this, quite honestly, was a crass remark to make, Robert, and I think you will eventually go down in history as one of the most outrageous persons who has ever lived.

'If *ye havni* lived, Alistair, *ye* don't know anything.'

'Why is it Robert, you keep on having a go at every nation in the world except for Scotland? It was only yesterday you called the Catholic Church a haven for sinners and said the Pope is a monster who should be flung from the roof of the Vatican.'

'Well, Alistair, the delegate who found my ring is from England and you know what the English are like; he is from Luton, which is somewhere down in the Southern hemisphere, bordering on the periphery of London, so I am told. Shortly after we had arrived at Boot Camp Reynolds he was to mention: 'Camp Reynolds,' he said. 'What a load of shit, this place *innit*.'

'You told me *ye didni* like Camp Reynolds because of the altercation you had with a local poacher when his fishing line became entangled with your walking stick and then after buying one of his fresh water salmon which had leapt out of the lake into his camouflage backpack, you successfully resold it to the camp chef for supper.'

'That's true, Alistair, you've got to speculate to accumulate.'

'Is this why a number of the Y.M.C.A. English delegation went down with stomach ache after learning the fish had been dead for at least two weeks.' Alistair remarked.

'Did you know, Alistair, salmon after spawning can find their way into the sea, swim half-way around the world and then come back to die where they were born?'

'The salmon didn't happen to come back last week did it?' Alistair curiously asked,

'*Och, nae*, it was the week before, Alistair.'

'Do you know, Robert, it is amazing how much knowledge you have stored up in that tiny brain of yours.'

'*Och aye*, I don't know how I do it for the money.'

'If voices came out from noses, you would need a bigger handkerchief.' Alistair said in great sincerity.

'*Agh*, there are people with bigger noses than mine down-town, Alistair; they all seem to be wearing ankle length black overcoats, Fedora hats and sport long grey beards.'

'That will be the Jewish lot, and, like you Robert, they have all got long arms and deep pockets; the better for peeling oranges without people noticing, wouldn't you say?'

'And what type of activity will you be getting up *ta* this evening, Alistair?' Robert asked transferring the rhetorical barracking over to him.

'I think after dinner, Robert, I will try to relax in the library where it is hoped I will be able to take in a modicum of intellectual stimulation, something which is currently lacking around here.'

'Try reading Rudyard Kipling, Alistair; when we were at school, he was good at writing Barrack-Room Ballads, Poetry, and Other Verses, that type of thing, he will stimulate your brain alright. I once read out a poem, penned by him, when I was a pupil at Moffat junior school; it was called "Mandalay"; written in March or April 1890. The poem had six verses and took almost half an hour to read out; my fellow pupils, the teacher and the pet goldfish had all but fallen asleep by the time I had finished. Needless to say, Malay Malik, an Indian classmate of high-cast status, stayed the distance and was awake all through the proceedings only because he wanted to go to the toilet.'

'But Rudyard Kipling wasn't at your school in Moffat, Robert; he is now sixty-five years of age and would hardly have sat beside a classroom full of head-shaking misfits and a *punkah wallah* from Bengal, would he?'

'*Agh*, but his father is a Scottish army officer serving with the Bengal Lancers; he also plays cricket for the 'Bengal Tigers' in Rangoon, Burma.'

'And what happened to the goldfish, Robert, did it wake up?'

'*Och, nae*, it died of boredom when it leapt out of the fish tank and ended up on Miss Allison's table.'

'And this Malay what's-his-name, did he have a red spot?'

'*Och aye*, Alistair, he had dozens.'

'No, Robert; did he have a Hindu symbol of divinity painted in the centre of his forehead?'

'*Och aye*, everyone in the school thought it was a gunshot wound.' Robert replied in all seriousness. 'It was a hoot on carnival day when he turned up sitting on the back of an elephant.' he added.

'What does a Hindu, Robert?'

'I don't know, Alistair, what does a Hindu?'

'It lays eggs, of course.' Alistair replied in retaliation. 'And what, may I ask are you're plans for this evening, Robert?'

'I may have a stroll down Eighth Avenue and take in the sights, namely, the theatres because the Y.M.C.A. has special deals for its members providing you book early.'

'Would you like me to come along with you, Robert? I would enjoy going to a theatre review on Broadway.'

'No, I don't think so, Alistair; your idea of a good play is sitting in the front row of a theatre and being deafened by an out-of-tune upright piano.'

'And I suppose your idea of a good play, Robert, is to sit alone in the back row to utilize your efforts and energies with a dirty raincoat resting in your lap.'

'Well, you must admit, the buxom and curvaceous Hollywood actress, May West, is worth going to see; she always gives one the impression she suffers from Saint Vitas dance and cannot keep still for at least one second.'

'Tell me, Robert, don't you feel a *wee* bit vulnerable when you wander down town all on your own?'

'Well, it's like this, Alistair, one has got to give one the impression when you walk along the streets and sidewalks that you own the place because New York City is full of jokers.'

'Are you including yourself in these numbers, Robert?'

'On the corner of fifty-third Street,' ignoring his sarcasm. 'You will find a Burbank Co-operative store where you can buy things from home, for example; 'Jacobs' cream crackers, 'Walkers' Highland shortbread and 'Baxter's' Royal Game, Oxtail and cock o' leaky soup.'

'Don't tell me, Robert you can buy 'Arbroath Smokies' and 'Forfar Bridies' as well?'

'Och no, Alistair; they seem to have sold out of those for the time being.'

'And, just what are you supposed to do with all that bloody stuff, Robert?'

'Buy it and sell it to the delegation for twice the amount I will pay for it, and do you know, Alistair, they have 'OXO' cubes to make a beef tea? I read somewhere that an 'OXO' cube, in relation to other popular household commodities was the least expensive consumable item on the shelf of a grocer's shop. At three forty-five,' he continued to pontificate not waiting for Alistair's response, 'there is a sing-song with tea, coffee, sandwiches and cake in the Recreational Hall.' recommending a little light entertainment and refreshments, similar to a tea dance in New York's exclusive Waldorf Astoria Hotel. Anyway.' he went on, 'I will be attending the afternoon tea session and I hope to try one or two pieces of those delicious Battenberg, Black Forest Gateaux and coffee walnut cakes if I am going to utilize all my efforts and energies sitting in the back row of the cinema.'

'I thought you said it was a theatre, Robert?'

'*Och aye*, but you see Alistair; a cinema is darker when they dim the lights and you have only the fleas to keep *ya* company for a *wee* while. And pray tell me, how did you know Victoria Brunswick lives on the twenty-seventh floor of that monstrous high-rise apartment block across the road?'

'It is because when she returned from not having seen you, Robert, I saw her hanging out her underwear; a white corset with more whale bones than "Moby Dick".'

'Wow, whatever next?' Robert said before beads of perspiration became rapidly evident on his forehead.

'Maybe a pair of silk stockings and a set of multi-coloured French cami-knickers, as seen on the T.S.S. *"Athenia"* the night of July 17th, or should I say in the early hours of the following morning.' Alistair replied shockingly.

'How did you know that, Alistair?'

'The cabins, if you remember, have big keyholes, Robert; all the better for spying on unfaithful young men who purport to be your friends and take delight on cheating their girlfriends.

'You *didni*, Alistair?'

'*Nae laddie*, like your mother's milk, you swallowed it again. You know, when we return to Glasgow there are a few holes to be filled in, and you Robert might be sitting on the tarmac.'

It was when Alistair and Robert were strolling along the main corridor on the ground floor of the Y.M.C.A. building they spotted Miss Victoria Brunswick heading towards the reception desk from the glass-fronted double door and before she had time to squeeze particles of information from the receptionist regarding Hamilton-Brown's whereabouts, she caught sight of him.

'Hi, Robert, I have kept my promise to call in and show you our wonderful city.'

'Well, if it isn't the dancer, Josephine Baker, the lady with the bananas.' Robert replied looking at a woman who was now wearing summer holiday-type fashion. 'Tell me, Victoria, do you always hang your smalls outside of your window to dry?'

It was at that high-point Alistair, did a quick exit and left the couple to deliberate inside the lobby.

Chapter Twenty-two

The Y.M.C.A. in New York opened in 1896 in West 57th Street and was relocated to Central Park West in 1930 before relocating to their current address at 5 West 63rd Street.

The conversation between Robert and Victoria Brunswick in the Y.M.C.A. Lobby continued with.....

'He seems to have left in rather a hurry, Robert; has he a train to catch or something?' Victoria asked in her eloquent unmistakable New York accent.

'No, we were about to join in a sing-song in the Recreational Hall before having afternoon tea.'

'Do you always have to sing for your supper? I can remember it was a bit like that when we were sailing the high-seas on-board the T.S.S. "*Athenia*"; you and your tartan-clad cronies gave me a headache when you all sang "The bonnie, bonnie banks of Loch Lomond" and before you personally ended up inside my state room in those early hours. Tell me, Robert, everyone around here is wearing a kilt; why is it you are not wearing yours?'

'It is because I hadn't time to retrieve it from the dry cleaners in Montreal.' Robert replied tongue in cheek.

'Oh I see, well better luck next time.' Victoria so naively remarked.

'Are you not working today?'

'No, I'm still on vacation, Robert, and so I will take this opportunity to invite you out to dinner tomorrow, that is after we have taken in a show at the Mansfield Theatre on forty seventh Street West of Broadway. The play, a fable by Marc Connelly, is called "The Green Pastures" and it is an attempt to present certain aspects of a living religion in the terms of its believers; the religion is that of thousands of Negroes in the Deep South.'

'That sounds very interesting, Victoria, is May West in it?'

'No, it's not that type of play, Robert; this one explains the unburdening of the American Negroid people who compared themselves to educated theologians, and by accepting the Old Testament as a chronicle of wonders which happened to people like themselves.'

'Do the usherettes walk up and down and sell ice cream, popcorn and 'Weenies' during the interval?'

'Now come on, Robert, you will have your little joke.'

'I often wondered how the usherettes managed to do that.' Robert said puzzlingly.

'How the usherettes managed to do what?'

'Walk down the aisle backwards with a '*Pifco*' torch without falling over and then dispense ice cream, cigarettes and take people's money beneath an illuminated lamp.'

'It is the Mansfield Theatre we are going to, Robert, not to see the silent movie actor, Buster Keaton, performing in a flea pit on Seventh Avenue.'

'On Thursday morning, the Scottish delegation will be going to see the New York Stock Exchange at number sixty-eight Wall Street.' Robert made clear, just in case she had designs on kidnapping him.

'Yes, I do know where The New York Stock Exchange is; I pass by the twenty-two-storey building five days a week on my way to 'All Saints' Proprietary School in Brooklyn; the entire city block of property is bounded by Wall Street, Broad Street, Exchange Place and New Street. Nebuchadnezzar walked the roof of his new place in Babylon and looked haughtily down on more humble homes. Pride, as well as economic needs raises the skyscrapers where from upper floors, occupants may sometimes look down on phantom cloud fragments.'

Like a typical school mistress, Victoria went on and on about her dream world, a city in fairyland, the towers, domes, business temples and turrets piercing the clouds forming landmarks to aviators flying above. America, she thought, was the land of plenty, the land of opportunity, the land of dreams, big cars, and more recently "Mr Ed" and "I love Lucy"; where television sets, refrigerators, toasting machines and Bakelite radios still existed in the nineteen-nineties and looked as if they had been salvaged from an abandoned "Dr. Who" film set, and he thought this was the epitome of a land of '*Milko*', '*Bilko*', '*Homo*' and Perry Como.

'You know two weeks ago, I was in Cleveland,' Robert said, 'I observed Zeppelin airships from Akron flying over the City on their way to Europe. One day, a misguided sky rider, as if on a magic carpet, will forcibly have to change course and the airplane could horrifically fly into one or two of your so-called business temples and in a New York minute, everything could change.'

'No, I don't think so, Robert, these skyscrapers are built to last for a thousand years, the pyramids are still in evidence after four thousand years and so will the Empire State Building.' she was confident in saying.

'*Agh*, but not dissimilar to the pyramids, they are built of sand and are crumbling as we speak and like most things, Victoria, things do not last forever. The Rockies may tumble, Gibraltar may crumble; they're only made of clay.'

'It was only last year,' Victoria explained. 'I travelled to Egypt in the footsteps of Agatha Christie and during the voyage to Cairo, the ship, the R.M.S. *"Carinthia"* stopped off in Gibraltar to take on-board extra produce; oranges, lemons and sword fish as we sailed into the Mediterranean. I can remember my handbag being stolen by one of the monkeys when I was sitting on a bench seat by the Rock.'

'And did you see the ape carrying it away?'

'No, Robert, but I was told later that lots of American tourists have their bags snatched in Gibraltar.'

'*Agh*, it was probably a sailor from Britain's Royal Navy who took it; they are noted for that sort of thing, especially in Portsmouth, Plymouth and Southampton.'

'Well, how come, when my bag was recovered, everything was intact apart from a banana that was meant for my brunch?'

'Tell me, Victoria, was this a container ship you were travelling on or a fruit and vegetable van?'

'It was neither, Robert, the ship was a *"Cunard"* cruise liner, commissioned in Nineteen twenty-five and was similar to the *"Queen Mary"*, but noticeably faster.'

'It must have been terribly difficult to navigate a ship of that magnitude up and down the River Nile.'

'No, no, Robert we sailed down the River Nile to the temple at Abu

Simbel in a dhow and paddle-steamer and on the return journey, we travelled by train.'

'They say, Karnack and Abu Simbel are sad places, especially after six o'clock in the evening.'

'I suppose, you could say the same thing about New York's Y.M.C.A. building, especially at three-thirty in the afternoon.' Victoria quickly responded.

All of this reminded Robert of a poem, written by his school friend, John Hargreaves, who he had the pleasure of associating with at Clydebank Grammar School.

The poem was called "It's Murder on the Nile" and begins:

It's Murder on the Nile
"The tourists step on board the boats
Each with a pocket book inside their coats
On deck chairs they all sit
Trying to find out which one did it
The boats sail down, there's a lot to see
They find more interest in page three
As the sun sets it's a beautiful sight
To see them all go to bed
And turn out the light"

The steamship, R.M.S. "*Carinthia*" was sunk during World War Two by a U-46, a German submarine, in 1940, and interestingly, the "*Queen Mary*" was laid up and decommissioned in 1930 because of the world-wide economic recession.

It was at this low-point Victoria said to Robert, 'Don't you think you should go and have some tea and shortbread or something because now I have to go to a hair-dressing salon on 42nd Street and I shall be sitting on a chair underneath a hair dryer for at least half-an-hour.'

'Would that be gas or electric?'

'You are in New York now, Robert; we are all connected to the grid.'

'And so was Mary Pickford.' Robert put in.

'Gee Robert, you are so funny. I will have a cab pick you up at seven tomorrow and then we can go for coffee, cake and ice cream at *'Childs'* and be at the Mansfield Theatre just in time for curtain-up at eight-thirty sharp.'

'I can't wait.'

'I think I may have overstayed my welcome.' Victoria said as she caught sight of Alistair hanging over the banister rail to see what was going on. 'I will say goodbye for now, Robert and I will see you tomorrow at seven.'

'Welcome to the land of the living.' Alistair said with a little boy's smile. 'What is the matter, Robert, you are looking extremely vacant.'

'You mean like a toilet.' Robert replied.

'If you insist on comparing yourself to a lavatory, Robert, then yes you look like a toilet.' Alistair said.

'*Agh*, but then I could be engaged.' Robert said and continued to successfully get Alistair's gander up.

'But it won't be to my sister that is for sure.'

*

The Mansfield Theatre, showing Lawrence River's production of "The Green Pastures", Wednesday evening 19th August 1931

The reviews following Monday's opening night were quite favourable. One critic, writing in the "*New York Amsterdam News*" said it was a refreshing and dignified play explaining the plight of the untutored black Christian, but it was dashed when an opening line was interrupted by a loud thunderous noise which sounded like one of the jokes a member of the Y.M.C.A. bought at a souvenir shop in Niagara Falls. Interestingly, a fire notice which was put together by the Fire Commissioner, John J. Doorman read, "Look around now and choose the nearest exit to your seat in case of fire; walk and don't run to the exit. Do not try to beat your neighbour to the street". However, the tobacco fumes permeating inside the auditorium likened to a Southern County penitentiary gas chamber, where loud coughing could be heard from three blocks down the street; '*Lucky Strike*', '*Chesterfield*', '*Spud*', '*Murad*' and '*Camel*' cigarettes had recreated a Somme-like World War One battlefield

The audience was respectfully requested to accentuate the importance of being seated in time to witness in its entirety the first scene which takes place in the Sunday school of a little Southern Negro church where Mr Deshee, the earnest superintendent undertakes with the limited resources at his command to expound from the Scriptures the order and significance of early sacred history.

'Please take to your seats now ladies and gentlemen.' the master of ceremonies said to the audience before they scuttled into the auditorium to find their allotted sleeping compartments.

'I hope this is not going to be one of those plays when a knocker-upper comes and pokes you with a stick at half-time.' Robert said, seconds before the lights were dimmed and the curtain went up.

'Robert, this is not a 'Chicago Bulls' ball game.' Victoria said as a half-pound box of "*Moonlight and Roses*" dark fondant and praline chocolates fell from her lap on to the floor. 'See, what you have made me do, I cannot find a single one of them; they have all rolled down towards the front row.'

The geography of the seating arrangement wasn't complicated, and Robert and Victoria were sitting on the upper level of the auditorium next to an aisle just behind the crossover and in full view of Exit Number fifteen, where a quick getaway could be made should the need arise.

'Would you like some of my toffee popcorn, Victoria?' Robert proffered, passing over a red cardboard bucket which wouldn't have been out of place inside a New York, South Manhattan fire station.

'No, Robert, I think I will wait until half-time and have a Popsicle, one of those things on sticks.'

'Why wait until the interval, Victoria?'

It was when the Conductor of the Mansfield Orchestra raised his baton to start the proceedings and Victoria had punched Robert in his rib cage with her elbow, the bottom fell out of the bucket and the contents, a more than ample supply of genetically modified maize, spilled out on to his knees ending up on the recently vacuumed heavy-duty floor covering.

'You know, Robert, you are not safe to be let out.'

When the lights came on to herald the intermission, it was if all the stuffing had been knocked out of the red velour seats, there was toffee popcorn chocolate and fag ash everywhere.

'It's a *wee* bit like Smokey Joes in here, Victoria.' after she had produced a six-foot long telescopic cigarette holder from inside her handbag and proceeded to light up a '*Black Russian Sobrani*' cocktail stick with a measurement twice as long.

'Tell me Robert, have you still got your pipe?'

'Well, only just, Victoria,' Robert replied. 'I had to salvage it from the bottom of Lake Ontario when I capsized a rickety old canoe and then it fell from my mouth into Lake Eerie, as I leaned over the rail of the "*City of Detroit III*" paddle steamer; *agh*, and afterwards, to make matters worse, I had it shoved down my throat by one of my friends.'

'And by the sound of it,' Victoria had cause to put in. I'm very surprised you've got any friends, Robert.'

'*Och*, they're all back home in Scotland probably sitting at a table eating *haggis*, *neeps* and *tatties*, a venison pudding, turnip and mashed potato, as we speak; oh, how I remember happiness.'

'Somehow I don't think so, Robert, because the time in Scotland is around five-thirty in the morning and I can't see them eating that stuff for breakfast.'

'*Agh*, they are a hardy lot; that is why we gave the English a hard time at the battle of *Bannockburn* in 1314.'

'Don't you like the food in America, Robert?'

'*Och aye*, it tastes like puke, but one can live on it.'

'And so, you won't want to go to the 'Flaming Steakhouse' on Eighth Avenue.' Victoria put in. 'You can have a traditional sixteen-ounce rib-eye, jacket potato and a hot muffin, and afterwards we can visit the Top of New York and observe the magnificent views from the Empire State Observatory. We can also enjoy a cool refreshing drink, listening to George Gershwin's tunes being played on a grand piano at the World's loftiest soda pop fountain, it is a never to be forgotten experience.'

'I must say after looking inside The New York Magazine Program, Victoria, and learning that the final scene is called "Another Fish to Fry", I was starting to feel quite ravenous.'

'The final scene is called "Another Fish Fry", Robert; you need to borrow my spectacles. Fish Fries are the words used in a Negro terminology to explain angels from heaven taking earthly public holidays.'

'Oh, that's interesting.' Robert commented. 'Does that include Glasgow Fair, Club Days and Wakes Weeks?'

'Do you know, Robert, if the aperture of the exit door was smaller on our way out than when we came in, you would find it difficult to make your way into the street.'

The penny finally dropped, and the conundrum solved when Robert realized that Victoria wasn't joking when he unwittingly banged the top of his head while walking out through the auditorium door.

'And so, you are ravenous, are you Robert Bruce Hamilton-Brown. Well, after being in America for several weeks, what do you desire the most?'

'Don't tell me that flaming steakhouse has got a chip pan as well?'

'Oh, you will have your little joke, Robert; I meant later, we go to my place for a cocoa supper.'

It was when Robert was looking out from the Empire State Observatory, he asked: 'Why is there a bundle in the distance that looks like brown paper packaging tied up with string?'

'Oh, that is The Statue of Liberty; she is currently being given a new lease of life because visitors to our wonderful country are beginning to get the impression that Liberty is a bit past its prime. She is in the process of being brushed and scrubbed and a new elevator is to be installed. A new lighting system will also be in evidence to stop a rumour that the statue has a double chin, hollow cheeks and a runny nose when being observed at night.'

'Well, I suppose that dispels my idea of it being posted back to France, which is where it came from in the first place.'

The time neared one am when Robert and Victoria summoned a cab in Wooster Street to take them back to her apartment on Fifth Avenue,

59th Street, Central Park West.

'If *ya* play *ya* cards right, Victoria, I will give you a good run for *ya* money.' Robert said with confidence when he was being elevated up to the seventeenth floor.

The cocoa supper lasted for at least a couple of hours when Robert clocked a picture placed high up on one of the walls depicting a one-legged ballet dancer rehearsing nude in front of a mirror.

'That particular work of art you are admiring,' she informed him, 'was painted by a Russian artist, called Hervey Purvey and rumour has it he was a choreographer in the Bolshoi Ballet Company in Moscow before getting himself a steady job to become an artist in New York City.'

'Is that so, Victoria?'

'You know, Robert, for a young man who is bordering on the edge of puberty, you do very well.'

'*Och aye*, yes I know, shall we do it again?'

'Do you want to cut the cards this time, or shall I, Robert?'

Chapter Twenty-three

The departure 12.00 noon, Saturday 22nd August

The Good Ship T.S.S. *"California"* slipped away from New York's Anchor Line Warf on time; it's magnificent and colourful paintwork reflecting splendidly in the Hudson River, which was at that time a temporary home, and berth, for The T.S.S. *"Cameronia"*, The T.S.S. *"Transylvania"* and The T.S.S. *"Caledonia"*, The R.M.S. *"Aquitania"* and the S/S *"Tuscania"*.

The return arrangements were as follows: "Vessels on the return journey usually sail from New York about noon. Delegates are advised to call at the Anchor Line Office, 25 Broadway, New York directly they arrive in that city – certainly not later than first thing on morning of sailing. They will thus be able to check time of embarkation, secure their cabin numbers which have been reserved, procure a supply of baggage labels and be generally advised on all details.

Customs Permit. All passengers embarking at United States ports require to be in possession of Customs Permit prior to embarkation. These are obtained at the Barge Office, The Battery, New York, but consult the Anchor Line officials. The object of the Permit is to satisfy the authorities that no American Income Tax is chargeable. There is no trouble attached to securing a Permit, but it must be done personally.

The *"California's"* single funnel billowed black smoke from the engine room, the furnaces being fiercely stoked with coal to enable the ship to travel on a three-thousand and thirty mile non-stop journey to Glasgow, passing by Quarantine, the peninsula; the Ambrose Lightship, the Fire Island Lightship before sailing into the wide and deep expanse of the Atlantic Ocean, where icebergs roam like ghouls to collide with ships that sail into the night. No one can hear the voices from a silent grave, but just a ripple from an incoming wave. A poem, "Mansions at the bottom of the Sea" written by an uncle of mine, William James Hodgekiss, whose father died serving as a steward on-board the "Titanic" wrote that it was written in respect of the passengers and crew who lost their lives during the early hours of Monday morning 15th April 1912", and began as follows:

"Rolling along in the breeze I thought
There are ships out in the seas
Some are surged and some sub-merged
Some with masts and some with pasts
They all have sailors, let them be
In their mansions at the bottom of the sea"

This was a message for all adventurous deep-sea divers, so-called salvage experts and pilots of submersible and amphibious craft everywhere, to heed the poem of moral respectfulness; for those who have lost their lives travelling on the high seas, who deserve the right to be left in peace without having to suffer fast moving technology travelling at an unstoppable pace disturbing their place of rest in order to gain profit.

Robert and Alistair were standing by the rail on the port side waving goodbye to Victoria as the ship moved slowly away from Anchor Line Warf into the less congested waters of the Hudson River. Alistair was adamant he wasn't going to return to America because he said that apart from Canada being a lot of to-do about nothing in particular, America is a long, long way away from reality, where money seemed to look as if it had been recycled more times than a second-hand toilet roll.

'There is a possibility I will return one day and give Miss Brunswick a call.' Robert said and forgetting once again to remove the lens-cap from his camera to take a photograph of another tearful event.

"Oh, what a tangled web we weave when first we practice to deceive". Alistair said, quoting Sir Walter Scott's poem penned at the battle of Bannockburn.

'I can recall her saying, Alistair, take this, it will bring you good luck.' Robert went on to say, showing him a sixty-carat gold Saint Christopher pendant suspended on what seemed to be a five-mile sixty-carat gold rope-chain which she had especially bought for him in a Catholic Holy

Willie Store in an Italian quarter in down-town New York.

'Well, I hope your talisman works when we are sailing the high seas, Robert, because a couple of rogues have been spotted off the coast of Philadelphia.'

'There seem to be a lot of rogues on-board this ship too,' Robert said when he saw Herbert and Alison Donaldson, Graham and Trish Norrie, the intrepid Y.M.C.A. stowaways, poking their heads out from around a door of a first-class state room. I can feel my talisman is beginning to work already.' he added without explanation.

'Just what did you get up to on Thursday afternoon, Robert, I am longing to know.'

'Well, as you know very well Alistair, on Friday we were confined to barracks because of us shipping out on Saturday, and the Y.M.C.A. in Central Park West didn't want to be preoccupied in rounding up stray Scottish delegates who had designs on going absent without leave in New York City. And so, on Thursday afternoon, following our educational visit to The New York Stock Exchange, Victoria invited me to have lunch with her in an Italian restaurant called Giuliani's.

'According to the story,' he laboured on, 'Frankie Giuliani, who now is the proprietor of 'Frankie and Benny's' Restaurant in Edinburgh, Scotland, was ten years old when he and his Mamma and Poppa left Sicily and landed at Ellis Island, New York in 1924. It was of no surprise when the family opened a restaurant; everybody helped with the building and cooking, each of them having a favourite dish to contribute.'

'And, what did you eat in this house of culinary expertise because I had to make do with a cheeseburger out on the sidewalk.' Alistair pointed out as a bell rang out sweetly in the ship's dining salon to alert passengers it was time to go in for lunch.

'Victoria and I started with the tiger prawn skewer which features four large tiger king prawns in their shells, served with roasted shallot, beetroot, a sweet chilli dip and rocket.'

'Well, that will make a change for you, Robert.'

'What will make a change, Alistair?'

'Having a rocket placed up your backside.'

'And to follow,' choosing to ignore his rudeness, 'we had Mediterranean vegetable risotto which would satisfy even a devout carnivore. I was about to order the fillet of beef but then I remembered the sixteen-ounce rib-eye steak I ate in the 'Flaming Steak' diner on Wednesday evening and so I decided to give it a miss.'

'You really do enjoy rubbing salt into the wounds, don't you Robert?' Alistair said looking at his watch. 'You don't need to tell me what you had for desert.' he went on. 'You can explain to Morag when you see her.'

'And for desert Victoria and I shared 'The Godfather'; Giuliani's iconic desert, a mountain of warm chocolate brownies, crunchy malt balls, red berries and cream.'

'I think we had better go in for lunch now, Robert, because I am feeling quite hungry after you explaining to me in great detail what you managed to put down that grub tunnel of yours on Thursday afternoon.'

'But first, before we go in to eat,' Robert interrupted. 'I would like to silence that English Sassenach lot standing against the rail at the stern who are singing: "Home on the Range", the Canadian Boy Scout song; they are fast giving me a headache, especially that one banging on a native North American Red Indian tambourine complete with feather dusters.'

"Oh, give me a home where the buffalo roam
And the deer and the antelope play
Where seldom is heard a discouraging word
And the skies are not cloudy all day
Home, home on the range
Where Boy Scouts suffer from mange
It's where many a tune
Is played with a spoon
Under the light of the moon
Home, home on the range......"

'I would be careful if I were you, Robert; one of them has a bowie knife that stretches half-way down his leg.'

'Oh, is that what it is, I thought it was......"

'.... you know, Robert, you really are the pits, and a rebel without a cause.'

'*Agh*, I *wouldni* say that, Alistair.'

'It's just as well and a great pity you can't turn the ship around and do a retake of the scenery.' Alistair said with a much sort after smile.

'What do you mean, Alistair?'

'You forgot to take the lens cap off your camera again, Robert.'

'*Agh*, these new-fangled Kodak cameras that look like a concertina really get up my nose.'

It was when they were walking into the dining salon Alistair, with an air of curiosity, continued to give Robert the third-degree about his antics on Thursday afternoon and during the evening.

'Well, I can tell you explicit sex is in its infancy in Glasgow, Alistair.'

'*Ya didni*, Robert, *ya didni?*'

'Only the once, Alistair, only the once because the photographic studio heavies threw me out when they discovered I *didni* have a film in *ma* camera.'

'And where was Miss Victoria Brunswick when all of this was going on?' Alistair asked, the conversation now bordering on conclusion.

'*Agh*, after we had emerged from the subway in Greenwich Village, Victoria hailed a yellow taxi cab back to her apartment because she had a severe migraine and needed to lie down.'

'Well, that was a shame, Robert, a real shame.'

'What was a shame Alistair?'

'You could have escorted Victoria back to her place for a late cocoa supper; I'm sure sharing warm chocolate brownie cakes would have done wonders to dispense with her myopic illness.'

At this point a steward began to bang on a mobile brass gong with a hammer to alert passengers that it was time to sit down at their allocated tables and, dependent on who they were, it was the ship's policy to have them situated geographically in order of importance; it was needless to say, the gong looked remarkably similar to the one stolen in the Chinese quarter of down-town Manhattan the previous day.

'You know, Alistair, if that pock-marked steward doesn't stop making that insufferable noise, I shall report him to the captain.' Robert said with angry deliverance.

'But he is the captain, Robert, it is an Anchor Line policy to welcome the passengers on-board their ships, the *"California"* being of no exception; they do this before giving their opening speech.'

'Well, in that case, I shall ask him to do it a wee bit quieter.'

'Yes, it is just as well, Robert, because we don't want to be rowing back to Glasgow in one of the ship's life boats, do we?'

'*Agh*, you're right, and we don't want to miss an opportunity to possibly sit at his table.'

'I don't think we are in any position to do that Robert because we are not placed high enough inside the 'Bee Hive'.'

'And what, may I ask, are we doing inside a bloody bee hive, Alistair?'

'It is a terminology used to describe the British social class system which was derived by some lunatic in the eighteenth century, Robert, royalty at the top and the armed forces at the bottom.'

'And what about thieves, vagabonds and murderers?' Robert asked, knowing there would be an outrageous answer to his question.

'Oh, you had better ask the Duke of Wellington that, Robert; he was in charge of them all at "Waterloo".'

'*Agh*, it's amazing the amount of 'Bees' that hang around in the concourse of that railway station.'

'And like you, Alistair, they probably have a bee in their *wee* bonnets.'

The boys and young men of the Y.M.C.A. Scottish contingent were seated well out of the way of refinement and tables reeking of money.

Robert and Alistair where allocated places in the salon directly above the engine room and this was where the crockery and cutlery seemed to rattle and roll along rhythmically to the ship's vibrations. They were seated next to a senior delegate, Mr Hamish Gavin, who had the previous week, gone through a traumatic experience at Camp Reynolds when one night he was attacked by an angry and disgruntled wild boar which was pig-sticked with a tent pole and it is of little consequence to tell you that Gavin had to sit on a small rubber life belt throughout the voyage because a large chunk had been removed from his backside.

It was just before the steward came with welcoming handouts of piping-hot soup, dishes of hearty Irish stew served with pieces of bread which had been sawn-off from a sixty-foot baguette, Alistair mentioned that the numbers in the delegation had suddenly increased by four people and that he was puzzled as to why this came to be?'

Robert, in his infinite wisdom added to the confusion when he explained to Alistair that Herbert and Alison Donaldson, Graham and Patricia Norrie would be going on ahead to join two Anglo Scottish Canadian Y.M.C.A. delegates, Professor Jas S. Thomson and Mr. John S.M. Thomson in Toronto after they had arrived in Quebec.

The evening sky was pitch-black, and after the eighth knell of the bell tolled, Robert and Alistair strolled around forward of the main deck. This was when Robert turned around and looked up towards the crow's nest and shouted to the ship's two mizzen mast men: 'I hope you haven't forgotten your binoculars, we don't want to bump into any icebergs, do we?'

*

The Gathering of the Clans - Princess Dock, Glasgow, Monday morning, 31st August 1931

Morag was waiting impatiently on the quayside of Princess Dock to observe the T.S.S. *"California"* sail slowly into its murky waters before dropping anchor to allow passengers to lose their sea legs and walk down the gangway on to Glaswegian *terra firma*.

The weather that morning was somewhat inclement, and the rain was coming down in bucketfuls, splashing down on the top of the oil-based Clyde River making prismatic circular ripples of all the colours that make up a rainbow.

Robert and Alistair stepped on to the quayside and walked over to a high metal barrier where Morag and family were waiting to give Alistair a welcome home hug once the formality of going through the customs and port authorities had been cleared. However, Robert was treated somewhat differently when later he was asked if he had a present for her in his tucker bag.

The customs and excise were not that over friendly either when they asked Robert about his rather large gold Saint Christopher medallion which was hanging loosely around his open- neck shirt so that everyone and his dog would be able to admire it, especially at the Sunday Church of Scotland table tennis championships which took place the following week.

'Where did you get this, sir?' a customs and excise officer asked Robert.

'It was given to me by a lady friend of mine in New York; she bought it as a going away present.'

'Yes, very nice, sir; it has *'Macys Departmental Store'* stamped all over it.'

'Do you mind,' Robert said, shouting hysterically. 'she bought it from a souvenir shop at the 'Church of the Holy Family' in Brooklyn; that's in New York City, you know?'

'Yes, I do know where Brooklyn is, sir, but you could have at least taken the tag off before putting it on.'

'Bloody Hell, just where are we going?'

'Into the office, young sir, and after your item of jewellery has been weighed and the hall-mark verified it will cost you at least fifty pounds to stop it from being confiscated by the Inland Revenue.'

'And what about this,' Robert said angrily. 'I have a ring around my arse, would you like that too?'

'Now, sir, we don't want any aggressive behaviour, do we?'

'*Agh*, you can keep the damn thing, for what it is worth, I'm not into Catholic 'mo-Joes' that don't work.'

'As you wish, sir, you can pull your trousers back up now.'

'Have you brought me back something nice from America, Robert?' Morag asked following a small peck on the cheek.

'*Och aye*,' Robert replied, handing over a small white paper bag containing two souvenir spoons connected with his voyages to and from America. 'They are good for adding sugar to your tea, porridge and impressing your friends, that sort of thing.'

Morag, disgusted with his generosity, hit him with her umbrella which had been previously packed with a ton of Accrington bricks.

'Here is your Saint Christopher, sir.' the customs officer said to Robert when he handed back his pendant. 'I've had second thoughts.' he went on to say.

'What have you had second thoughts about; my Saint Christopher pendant or my arse?'

Chapter Twenty-four

Mobilization at RAF Kirkham, Lancashire Monday October 25th' 1943, the day Robert Bruce Hamilton-Brown declared war on his so-called outside world, going in the wake of Marshal Joseph Stalin's "Great Red Army".

As seen and experienced and, at times, imagined and exaggerated, by the 'great man' himself; namely, Robert Bruce Hamilton-Brown:

On the morning of Oct 25th, 1943, I was informed by telephone that an overseas posting had just been received for me from records. I accepted the announcement on the "square" having anticipated "depreciation" in this direction for some time and I preceded immediately for dental and medical examination. By five pm, I was pronounced fit, on draft number 5606, and instructed to begin our fourteen days leave the following day. I spent Monday evening compiling various parcels of oddments collected over my long stay at Kirkham. These I mailed home. I travelled north to Moffat on the five thirty-one from Preston on Tuesday, and pulled in about eleven pm. The first part of my leave I spent travelling to and from Glasgow, squaring various assurance accounts, and endeavouring to put my house in order generally. During the week, Norma and I decided to be married and so on the Friday evening, we called at Dalziel High Church, to arrange the bans, and the wedding for the following Tuesday afternoon. Norma's residence being in Holytown however, we found it necessary for the bans to be called in Barfin Church.

On Saturday Oct 30th, I travelled to Moffat to invite my people to Motherwell on the following Tuesday afternoon. On the following Monday, I went to Airdrie to visit aunt Maud and on returning about six pm, I discovered I had been recalled by telegram for 07.30 hours on that day Monday Nov 1st. Since this was impossible, I prepared to travel South on the 11.25 pm and consequently, was married that evening by the Reverend J Henderson-McKenzie at Barfin Manse.

On reaching Kirkham early Tuesday morning, I discovered that the telegram should have read 07-30 hours on the 3rd Nov and on the strength of this, I was granted an extension to 07-30 hours on the 4th Nov, and travelled North again on the ten thirty-three am, arriving in Motherwell about three-fifteen pm.

The wedding reception, which commenced on my arrival, was very pleasing although attended by only a few friends. I returned to my unit on the 11.25 pm on Wednesday, when my Uncle Gregory and Auntie Annie waved me out.

At two pm on Thursday 4th November, I had finally cleared myself from Kirkham and left them in full marching order with two others; aircraftsmen, Sydney Bowden and Victor Hughes for 105 P.D.C. Blackpool; we were now on draft 5599. The sun shone brightly, in a vain endeavour it seemed, to have us feel cheerful.

We reported about 3.30 pm and were allotted billets at No 17 Soap Street, a full penny tram ride from the P.D.C.

The house was situated behind the central pier in a third-rate locality, nevertheless, we were glad to find ourselves there and to dispense with our kit which by this time, was unbearably heavy.

After tea, which was a very satisfactory meal we enquired about washing accommodation, but alas the old "kitchen sink" was all that was available. Later in the evening, I had some supper, wrote and mailed a few letters home. At 08.20 hours we paraded on Alexandra Road; five or six hundred strong and marched about a mile and a half to the "Black Hangar". Here we were arranged in squads and lectured on the necessity of strict secrecy regarding (concerning) all draft matters. In the afternoon, we had a gas equipment parade and, where necessary, dress replacement. I was soon to learn that Blackpool was totally unsuitable for a P.D.C. in that each depot, where equipment was stored was often situated over a mile apart. This meant unnecessary hours of marching and reduced the working day to three or four hours at the most. Had the equipment been stored in one or two hangars, the whole function of equipping a draft could have been completed in two days at the very outside. On Friday evening, I phoned home and wrote a few more letters.

Our landlady, Mrs Richardson, proved a very kind and good woman and at 08.30 am on Saturday, we again paraded at Alexandra Road with certain home-scale kit for handing in purposes. This done, we duly proceeded to draw a full tropical kit, with an extra kitbag. All this gear had to be marked with number, rank and name, etc., and most of Saturday was spent in this way; from time to time between parades, we found the many Blackpool cafes very welcome indeed.

Sunday brought us a surprise from the blue. We paraded at 09.00 am and were informed that those who only had seven days leave would proceed on warrant from after duty that day till 23. 00 hours on Wednesday. Our kits, however, had to be handed into the orderly room and this meant a hurried dash back to our billets; carrying two well-filled kit bags was no joke, and needless to add, all of us were glad to finally drop them on the deck.

I did not receive my rail warrant till one pm, and consequently missed the 12.55 pm for home. I travelled north to Carlisle however on the 16.17 pm where I rested at the "Citizens League" hostel before catching the 4. 30 am train for home.

I spent the afternoon in Glasgow and, in the evening, went through to Crawford with Norma. Monday and Tuesday were delightful; the sun shone brightly on both days and the hills of home, were never more attractive. The good food and general relaxation proved a great tonic but, alas, the hour glass had run low and consequently at 10. 00 am on Wednesday saw me on my way back to Motherwell. I left again that afternoon at 16.10 pm for Blackpool, pulling in about 10.30 pm.

In a matter of eight days, I had covered approximately fourteen hundred miles by rail between Blackpool and home. At 8.20 am on Thursday, November 11th, we were on parade again at Alexandra Road. The situation obviously had deteriorated and the inevitable was fast approaching. I collected further kit and had a lecture in the afternoon by the Padre. On Friday, we marched with our deep-sea kits to the fateful "Black Hangar" and deposited them there for shipment. In the afternoon we collected our sten-guns, ammunition belts and magazines, and an inspection followed. I phoned home in the evening announcing developments and talking farewell. At 9.00 am on Saturday. 13th

November 1943, we paraded in full kit and marched to the "Black Hangar". Here we boarded trucks and were conveyed to the Central Station where we entrained eight men shared each compartment, and the conversation all the way South was very speculative. Our port of embarkation, and final destination, were constantly reviewed. We arrived in Liverpool about noon and changed somewhere outside the City to the electric rail systems, which conveyed us to the quayside; here, we had another two-mile hike in full kit, to the actual point of embarkation.

The "*Reina del Pacifica*" looked a goodly ship, with at least a twenty-thousand-ton displacement. We clambered on-board and were allocated to A4 mess 159. Alas, already the romance had developed a tendency to pale. We were well down and were soon to realize the worst. The mess itself measured approximately twelve yards by thirty-four yards with a total height of seven feet. This accommodation had to be shared by one hundred and fifty men for both eating and sleeping purposes. All kit had to be stored in the pipes and gratings overhead. Each mess consisted of seventeen men who were accommodated at long tables with fixed forms on either side. Above this table, we slept in hammocks slung from hooks overhead. When every hammock was slung, they totally filled the horizon, giving one the impression of being in a field of yellow grain standing about six feet high, with the sky touching the tops of the ears. The heat was oppressive, and the whole scene one of total chaos. Many slept on the floor and on the tables. Our hammocks were stowed at the end of our mess and once all port holes were sealed, our only lighting was from wall lights, situated about eight feet apart.

They arrived in all their glory, the senior medical officer, the captain, a Wing Commander, the Officer Commanding troops etc. In two minutes, the inspection was over, and everyone satisfied except the men who were condemned to live this environment for an indefinite period. Few of us could prevail. We realized that we were on a troop ship and expected to rough it, but yea gods, this exceeded our expectations. About five pm our orderlies, now appointed, proceeded to the galley to draw tea for the mess. Some kind of stew came back with white bread, and a portion of margarine.

The ship was crowded with troops of various regiments from whom there was no escape. We stood on deck long after dark, gazing at the dim lights of nearby shipping, and Liverpool beyond. Few in that motley crowd did not think of home and the future, not once, but many times. At last the time came to go below to the "hell hole", as we now called it, and prepare for bed; a grim fight for hammocks and sights was in progress, when we arrived, and chaos prevailed and when we undressed, we had no place to lay our clothes. After sailing however, we turned in fully clothed each night save for our coats and tunics. About nine pm, I with others had the misfortune to be detached for guard. This duty consisted of standing on a stairway two hours on, and four off, for the purpose of reporting fire, smoking below decks, and keeping the stairways clear. I was all-in after our heavy days' training and slept on my feet more than once during the night.

Breakfast was rough, as were all the meals for the first few days out, until rigorous complaints somewhat improved the situation. No doubt someone from above made a fuss apart from the "grub takers", fresh water was very limited, and could only be had between six-thirty am and eight- am, and five pm and six pm.

The washing accommodation was totally inadequate, and it was a common thing to stand sixty minutes for a wash.

We had an officer appointed to look after our interests, but he was of the "be good boys" strain and proved totally unsuccessful. Sunday was a tiring day on board, without even moderate service comforts, and settling down was a difficult job indeed. We soon learned of the first-class food being served to the commissioned ranks on-board, and a great wave of discontent swept the ship. It was obvious that we had already established a miniature England on-board, with the war lords and merchants surviving on top, living in luxury, and away deep down in the bowels of the ship, the serfs and hirelings eating from communal pots, sang bawdy songs, and smoked duty-free cigarettes.

It was a topping set up, with the usual awfully, awfully, ga ga, with teeth on top and below, the groans and curses of the damned. The corking-good ship's cat was eating better food than we were.

At eleven am on Monday 15th November, we left our berths and prepared to pull out. The tugs took charge, and at two pm we were in the river under our own steam. With various other shipping, we made for the estuary and proceeded to sail south. After a few hours on this course, we did an about turn and sailed north. Ere midnight, I felt a dreadful sickness overtake me and I was glad to lie flat out for the night. The general conditions, and the hectic time I had at Blackpool did not keep me in anyway.

Tuesday 16th November 1943 dawned cold and wet, with a very heavy sea running. I was now all out, and during the day suffered violent sickness. I never remembered feeling so ill or generally miserable.

On Wednesday, 17th November, the ship was somewhere East of Iceland. We joined a few more ships and under a heavy escort of five destroyers, and two cruisers, we headed south again, this time West of Ireland.

Thursday, 18th and Friday 19th November were heavy sailing indeed with high winds. I feel very unwell, and for four days, did not eat or drink.

Saturday 20th and Sunday 21st turned a little warmer, and we discovered we were sailing round the Azores, to turn north again, and follow the African coast. A convoy at sea is indeed interesting to watch, and while time dragged, changing course, signalling, etc, etc all helped to keep us interested. We had lifeboat drill at least three times per week and wore our lifejackets at all times. Cigarettes were cheap at one shilling and three pence for fifty, and these were drawn in bulk with a bar of chocolate per man per day. Biscuits were on sale at night from the day canteen, and in view of the poor food, were in great demand.

Blackout was strictly observed on deck and finding one's way about, was both difficult and dangerous. About this time, I made contact with four clear thinking, progressive, left wingers. I found their company and knowledge very heartening. Each day the army went on parade, with the usual inspection and accompanying nonsense. The general moral was poor, and everyone openly expressed disgust about the circumstances and the war in general. The men generally, were the usual type, totally disinterested in anything, especially politics. They spent their time wandering round the ship aimlessly and playing cards.

Monday 22nd and Tuesday 23rd at sea was warm with hours of sunshine. We were now sailing north toward Gibraltar.

Wednesday, 24th dawned perfect and here I will write a letter to be mailed home. The evening approached with unspeakable grandeur and the whole world seemed aflame with evening's sacred shades of peace. How ironical it all seemed in that hour, everything so still and peaceful, with hidden death lurking all around. About eight pm the Spanish coast came up on the horizon and twinkling lights could be seen from time to time. As we approached the straits, darkness fell, and with mixed feelings we gazed northwards to the nearby Spanish coast and as being neutral, was ablaze with a myriad of lights. Most of us had not seen a city lit up since war broke out four years ago. Occasionally, we would see the headlights of an automobile on the coast road, and one wondered who the occupants might be. Most conversations on-board were about home and happy by-gone days. With my two left wing comrades, I discussed fascist Spain under the "butcher" Franco, and the hope for the establishing of socialism there at some future date.

Some of the troops sang as we passed Gibraltar and on one occasion, the "Red flag" and "Internationale" were voiced with gusto.

Thursday, 25th was warm and pleasing with hours of sunshine. We sailed close to the African coast, which looked quite like the north of Clyde save that the mountain peaks appeared much higher. I spent the night on deck till about nine pm, as I did most nights. I could not tolerate the heat or the confinement of our mess.

Friday, 26th dawned clear and bright with much sunshine and accompanying warmth. I was detailed with others for ship's guard duty, and at four-fifteen pm we paraded on E deck aft. At four-thirty pm we reported to the guard room on D deck aft, and were arranging shifts, when "action stations" pounded; about five minutes later, we were attacked by anything up to a dozen bombers. They flew high and circled the convoy before going into action. Our ships sent up all they had and, on-board the sound of gunfire was terrific to the point of driving one mad. A great quantity of HE's, high explosives, kept falling, and all around one could see huge water spouts. We had an escort of three fighters, but two of them hit the drink. One bomber, by this time, received a direct hit and blew up. Then, two HE's came our way, one about twenty-five yards on the port bow, followed immediately by another as near on our stern. The sensation defies description, and all of us felt the end had come. On completing each attack, the bombers circled into the now setting sun. Our fire seemed short of them by hundreds of yards and only the cruisers guns seemed to find the range. About 5.10 pm, three enemy craft came in on our starboard beam. We already saw with our naked eyes, three radio-controlled rocket bombs drifting in our direction. Sailing abreast of us, was a ten thousand-ton East India liner, now in direct line of fire. Before we could grasp the situation, she was hit amidships, on her starboard quarter. Her whole superstructure simply flew into the air, in a million fragments, and in a second, she was totally enveloped in steam and black smoke. She listed badly, fell out of line, and looked a total loss. A destroyer pulled abreast of her beam and they both fell astern. We learned later, that she was towed to a North African port, probably Algiers, which we passed early in the morning. The attack lasted till about six pm and was in all a very unnerving experience. I was disappointed in the range of our guns and felt that throughout most of the action, we were at the mercy of the attackers.

About seven pm in the evening, we had another attack, but fortunately, this only lasted about thirty minutes, and no damage was done.

Saturday 27th, was dull with low clouds and at times heavy showers. We all welcomed this change of weather and the uneventful day it assured us of. We passed several unchartered islands today and reckoned we must be near Pantelleria. I spent many hours over the map, calculating our exact position. At no time was any announcement made as to our progress or, indeed, our final destination.

Sunday 28th was warm and pleasant with many hours of sunshine. We passed a few more islands today but could not account for them.

Monday 29th on-board, was washing day, and we had fresh water available till noon. I washed three pair of socks, a collar, a handkerchief and my towel. In the early afternoon I sat on deck and darned two pair of socks, a task which to my amazement, I performed very well indeed.

At five we were all seated in our respective mess decks, having tea when "Action Stations" again sounded. Almost immediately we were attacked. All of us, not being on duty, were confined to our mess decks. We immediately prepared for any emergency and wore lifejackets, tin hats, water bottles and ration packs. The heat in the dimly lit mess was terrific, and the atmosphere was very tense. We could hear the sickening thud of HE's and our own gunfire. A few minutes after the action had commenced, we were attacked by fifteen bombers, in waves of three, five, five and two. The "stuff" imploded again on our starboard, with a terrific report, and the whole ship rocked. A dynamo, or perhaps a pump which had run ever since we left Liverpool, stopped for a second, spluttered, and started off again. I felt sure we were hit but held my breath. Soon after, the bridge announced on the speaker how we had been attacked, but that they had been driven off with one bomber losing height.

A second attack followed, but without recording any hits. We were now opposite Crete and fully expected this sort of trouble. I spent the remainder of the night on deck thankful for the fresh air, and the knowledge that up to the present, we were safe.

Tuesday, 30th dawned bright and clear. Our mail box was about to close in view of nearing Port Said, and so I busied myself writing a few letters. An alert was sounded about noon, but the all clear followed almost immediately. No doubt the enemy had sent out a scout to mark our position. About ten pm, we heard a number of depth charges go down with a sickening thud followed immediately by the signal "full speed ahead". We lay, prepared for any event, but fortunately there were no further developments.

Wednesday, 1st December was bright and warm. We changed our position in the convoy for the first time, but after an hour's sailing reverted to the old order. The position regarding the changing of money for going ashore was discussed, and it was suggested we each exchange half a crown. It was hoped to send cables home and a sheet was issued with the usual code numbers.

Thursday, 2nd dawned hot and still. Port Said was now clearly established on the starboard bow. The sun shone brilliantly, and the smoke haze from the convoy, now sailing in single file, travelled hazily upwards.

About eight-thirty am we were sailing through Port Said itself, with the city on either side of us. The gaily coloured buildings, some of Eastern structure, were a very welcome sight after sixteen days at sea. We towered above the city and the spreading palms seemed dwarfed below us. One could already see the native population, in many coloured robes, hurrying about their business. The waterways were simply teeming with shipping from a Red Cross liner, about fifteen-thousand tons, to sailing craft, sailing back to the earlier Egyptian times. At nine am, we were on deck doing P.T, physical training, much to our disgust. Gradually, under our own steam, we approached the narrows leading to the Suez Canal. As far as we could see, the land structure on either side of the canal was purely a vast area of sand flats without any sign of vegetation.

The heat was fierce, and the surrounding land simply blazed with colour and brightness. At many points on the canal banks, one could see military settlements. The sea in this narrow channel was now a distinct shade of green, a contrast to the indigo blue tone of the past few days.

A rail track ran on either side of the narrows. One train passing north was filled with troops. The natives in coloured gowns, or sometimes in khaki shorts, tunics and red-coloured fez, stood on the canal banks and waved or clapped their hands. Many were bathing completely naked. The sun at this time of day was really hot.

About three-thirty pm, we passed a very large settlement surrounded by many trees and pleasing stretches of green grass; all a very decided and welcome change to the endless expanses of burning sand further north. At lunch-time all our port holes were opened for the first time. We passed several ships in the narrows with only a few feet to spare. At four pm we sailed into the vast expanse of water known as the 'Bitter Lakes'. Great disappointment was felt on passing Port Said. All had hoped to get ashore for a few hours at least. At night the lights on shore were a welcome sight. Total blackout was observed on board, but we were allowed to smoke on deck. The moon came up very bright, and as we lay at anchor waiting to pass through the lower reaches of the canal in day light, many of us thought of home and the unknown future. Many of the troops spent the night singing popular songs. This time when the "Internationale" was sung, a voice in the darkness called a halt. It may have been a service bred NCO, a non-commissioned officer, hoping for promotion, or perhaps an officer from the top deck.

On our way below, we came across a group of men singing, "The sash my father wore". I began to give things up then. It appeared on orders today that with effect from tomorrow, Friday, all Royal Air Force personnel would wear khaki shorts and shirts from 09.00 hrs till lights out, and regular service blue. You can well imagine what the troops thought about this.

Friday, 3rd dawned bright, but fortunately the sun never seemed to penetrate the heat haze, and consequently the day was comfortable. About nine am we lifted anchor and with the rest of the convoy proceeded south to the second channel, which varied little from the first. The general brightness of things seemed quite unreal. The sand appeared a burning gold, the sea an almond green and the sky a perfect azure blue. Passing the ancient Egyptian sailing craft had one imagining biblical times had established themselves in the present. We passed a submerged vessel on the way down which left us with but inches of clearance. Camels now appeared on the canal banks from time to time. About four pm we were approaching Port Suez. Here we left the narrows and took up a position in the bay where we dropped anchor. Tenders came along side with vegetables and water, others bringing out various military people. Our mail went ashore but we were unable to send cables home.

The troops threw coins and cigarettes to the native crew on the tenders who playfully fought amongst themselves for such humble treasure. The night was clear, while from the shore, the lights from Port Suez twinkled.

Saturday, 4th December dawned clear and warm, and the sunshine was brilliant. Some of the troops went ashore here, probably bound for the Middle East somewhere. I went sick this morning; dull hearing in my right ear. After lunch, we finished off taking on-board fresh water and supplies.

About three pm, we lifted anchor and headed south for the Red Sea. The night fell early without a moon. We retarded our watches an hour, the second since we left home.

At four pm I went on guard on the first shift 4.30 to 6.30 pm. The heat became intense despite the fact that we were now doing a good eighteen knots. I went on deck about seven-thirty pm, in the hope of a breath of fresh air. Alas, however, the surrounding deserts were having their effect. I felt miserable all night and kept wishing, as I had always done, for a posting to Iceland. I had a short chat with Brian, late buyer of Arby's robe dept; he reckoned we would make Aden about Tuesday.

Sunday, 5th December brought us the same intense heat, with no wind whatsoever. Roll on the Indian Ocean. I finished my guard at 2.00 pm and immediately after had a cold salt water bath. This, however made little difference, and in about ten minutes, I was as bad as ever.

At night a high wind arose but being hot it brought no relief. It was arranged for twenty-five per cent of our mess to sleep on deck each night commencing tonight (Sunday). I went up with ten others. We slept on one blanket with one on top, but even so the heat was still intensive. At six am, we had to lash up and stow, to allow the crew to wash the decks. I did not feel over-well this morning.

Monday, 6th December; the heat seems now to be telling a tale. We are still doing about eighteen knots and should be in Aden tomorrow.

I may wash a few garments today after lunch. Most of the troops are grumbling about going to India although some are happy at the thought. I did not feel well again all evening. The moon came up white accompanied by a very high south wind. I slept below decks where the heat was simply beyond description.

Tuesday, 7th December. The wind remains very high for which I am thankful. The sun and general heat continue unabated. I kept in the shade all day and will continue to do so throughout my tour overseas.

I arranged to have my ear syringed this afternoon at three pm. Sydney and I lay on deck after lunch and chatted about home conditions in general. He is a confirmed socialist and detests the thought of serving imperialism in India. I slept on deck at night. The wind remained high.

Wednesday, 8th December. About five am we were approaching Aden. The coast line appeared rugged and very mountainous, no vegetation could be seen, and from first appearances one could readily compare Aden to any of the slag hills or ash bungs to be seen anywhere in Lancashire. The only difference was that instead of being grey the peaks of Aden came up in burning tones of bronze.

We lay in the roads awaiting the signal to pull into Aden itself. Here we moored against an oil pipe fed from tanks on the hill side. Preparation was then made by the native barge crews to refill our oil tanks. We already observed near the shore many military establishments. Aden itself looked tired and parched. Many of the natives here wore bright red turbans. At breakfast we were informed that on no account would anyone be allowed ashore. I had fully expected this and was not disappointed. This is a real "hell ship", reeking with cant, class distinctions, and red tape. The food continues to be awful and yesterday in the "Red Sea" we had steaks and potatoes.

I now have a number of small bites visible and painful. These are caused no doubt through lack of greens and proper feeding in general. I sat on deck after tea with Syd and Vic. The moon was bright and directly overhead. About nine pm the men began to lay the hammocks and bedding on deck. Soon the ship was a mass of human bodies, all half naked and lying at all angles and in all positions.

Thursday, 9th December; the day dawned bright and clear as usual. Strange to relate however, we had a shower of rain which lasted about four minutes. I arranged mess duties this morning and sent two more nominal rolls up to the orderly room. Lunch today, was a more appropriate meal for a change, consisting of cold meat and potatoes with peas. We finished off with steamed stewed apples for a sweet. Having to eat each course from the same plate without washing most certainly detracts from the meal.

This afternoon, I dared the sun and watched the Indians at work on the oil barges. It appears that the oil taps are also underground as well as floating on buoys.

Today the tide left us aground and the oil pipe connection had to be severed, in view of our developing a very severe list.

This afternoon, pipes were led from under water taps so that we could be in deeper water. An Iranian oil official, in white topee and shorts directed the operation. The natives kept running about chanting as they hauled the ropes etc, etc. During the peak of the activity, one Indian knelt on his prayer mat, no more than a piece of rag, and removing his shoes commenced to indulge in prayer, bowing from time to time, and touching the mat with his forehead. I had many strange thoughts at this time. I remembered Adam Malone and of the time he spent in Persia on oil. I thought of Macintosh and his totally indomitable outlook. I also reflected on how I might have been pleased had I gone to China for Tindal & Grey Ltd, and by God, I thought of home. I am now feeling totally sick of this present life. The food, the conditions, the type of men, and the total lack of culture wear me down.

Friday, 10th December. The day dawned dull and generally conditions were much cooler. We are still in port without any sign of pulling out. I did some washing today but lost about five pounds in perspiration. At night, Syd, Vic and I sat on deck, with the oil official drinking pots of tea and sharing each other's melancholy.

Saturday, 11th December. The sun came up bright and hot, damned hot. We were issued with four air graphs per sixteen men later in the day however, and I was able to secure one which I shared with Vic drinking tea in the bright moonlight.

Sunday, 12th was another hot day. At four pm, I went on guard again. The men are now showing signs of restlessness. Remaining so long in Aden in the heat, and not being able to get ashore, now seems to be having some effect. An RAF dance band from a local station came on-board tonight. The officers apparently expected to have their services confined to themselves but a somewhat ugly encounter with the troops altered things slightly.

Monday, 13th dawned bright and clear. At eight am we were moving at last and sailed out to join the convoy in the bay. At 9 am, we were all under way and Aden lay astern. The sun remained hot, but a heavy breeze sprung up and the sea rose heavy. I came off guard at four pm feeling tired and not too fit. I sat on deck at night with the old pot of tea and a few biscuits purchased at the canteen. At nine I went below and slung my hammock. We now appeared to be doing about twelve to fourteen knots.

Tuesday, 14th December. The weather continues bright with a heavy breeze blowing but despite this slight respite from the intense heat, also that we are on the move again, the men are very discontented.

The commanders are being lectured daily on how to avoid tropical ailments and are also making a study of Japanese expressions of a military nature. The general conditions here are something fearful and one cannot sleep for the terrific heat. The food is vile and in consequence feelings run very high. Some of us are now less fit and natural energy is a thing of the past. For tea last night we had stew again, the very sight of which turned the men sick. Cheese and pickles for tea is not normally considered a luxury meal but is received with tears of thankfulness. Total blackout is now observed.

Wednesday, 15th December. The weather continues favourable with bright sunshine. Night falls fast and the moon does not rise till about 9 pm. I did some more washing today. I feel tired and much in need of a rest and some good food. After tea, Syd and I wandered down to the engine room, and by appearing totally disinterested were able to see quite a part of the machinery. We sat on deck in the evening drinking tea and discussing the present political issues. Syd is a confirmed communist and is good to listen to. In himself he is very refined, well-mannered and most considerate of the other fellow.

An aircraft carrier joined us today, and we had "Sea Spits" and "Swordfish" kites flying around all day. A number of ships left the convoy today and sailed south. I presume bound for South Africa. I wish I had been on-board one of them.

Thursday, 16th December.

Another bright and pleasing day with a good breeze blowing; the library books have now been recalled, our canteen closes tonight, and our webbing comes out of the hold today. These items appearing on orders suggest we are now nearing our destination. Since we sailed, I have heard rumours of our going to the Azores, Algiers, the Middle East, Turkey, Aden, South Africa etc, etc, but it now seems as I first thought, we are bound for India. Today brought us the real highlight of the whole trip. We were served with a hot lunch again today, and as a sweet, one single bun without custard or sauce. The result was instantaneous. The men refused to eat any of the meal and marched in hundreds to the galley, demanding decent and appropriate food. Feeling ran very high indeed and war was very definitely in the air. By official rumours, each mess even fore and aft, were kept in touch with the situation, and one-hundred percent unity prevailed. Hell itself rained among the men who were now in a fearful temper. The "Red Flag" was sung with great gusto, much to my delight. I did all I could to introduce the political aspect with great success. The officer commanding troops, the captain etc, were dug out and asked in good English, what the hell they thought we were. A tall marine and a red bearded sailor led them on. Two Commando sergeants and a Regimental Sergeant Major were placed under close arrest.

We were all led to the bridge, to witness cat food being thrown out from the fridge. It was of little consequence to learn that Felix, the cat had gone AWOL, absent without leave, and was last seen paddling his way back to Scottie Road, Liverpool.

Complete triumph was soon ours and at three o'clock they served tea, bread and cheese. Today has proved our success beyond doubt as we had eggs for breakfast, cold meat, roast potatoes and fruit for lunch and cheese and pickles for tea. I enjoyed the show immensely and had hoped to see some of the commissioned swine pitched overboard.

Friday, 17th December. I learned today that when we reach Bombay, this ship is due for repairs. It seems in the last raid we sprung several plates.

The "City of Rangoon" the commodore of the fleet when we all set out, left us at Port Said in similar conditions. We had another mock attack on the convoy today by the aircraft carrier. The "Spits" dived on us from the clouds, attacked amidships and then rose almost vertically. One "kite", almost jumped the carrier on landing. The "Spits" were assisted by a Bristol Blenheim V bomber aircraft from No 8 Squadron, based at RAF Aden. The RAFs role primarily, was to operate in and around the Gulf of Aden, the Indian Ocean and the Red Sea; their main aim, to protect British convoys and to ward off any prospective Italian submarines lurking off the coast of East Africa, however for the convoy they didn't pose a threat as they had previously surrendered to the British a few weeks earlier.

As usual, I spent the night on deck drinking tea and chatting with Syd. We all feel brassed- off, especially at the thought of doing time in India, the last stronghold of British Imperialism.

Saturday, 18th December.

Another bright and warm day; we packed our kits at the cost of "buckets of sweat", general preparations are now being made for going ashore.

The food continues poor and I feel miserable with hunger. We had another mock attack on the convoy by the "kites" from the carrier. Great speculation prevails about going ashore. We retarded our watches another half hour, making a total now of five and a half hours. Chatted with some troops on the deck in the darkness and contacted two more socialists. I did not sleep on deck tonight, in view of a high night wind.

Sunday, 19th December. It was a delightful morning and the coast of India came up on the horizon about noon, shrouded in mist, and undulating in appearance.

At 1-30 pm we could see the City of Bombay, with its many colourful and attractive buildings. A great deal of shipping lay in the bay. The heat was now great.

At four pm we lay alongside the wharf, and almost immediately some of the army personnel prepared to go ashore. Indian stevedores came on-board and commenced to unload. The city was fully lit up in the evening, a feature which was very welcome. Great activity prevailed on-board. I clambered into my hammock at about 11 pm in view of reveille at 4-30 am.

Monday, 20th December. After breakfast, I went on deck, and watched the general activity. The morning was cool, and dawn did not break till almost eight am. At 9 am we were assembled on deck fully equipped, webbing, kit bags (quantity two), blankets and sten gun. Four-hundred rounds of ammo, khaki shorts, shirt, hose, tunic and topi.

We scrambled ashore and assembled outside the wharf. Here, I met an RAF policeman, an SP (Shore Patrolman) on duty with his dog, Rex, both of whom were with us at one time in Kirkham. Oranges and bananas were freely being sold at one or two *annas* each. I bought a few oranges and thought of the many millions at home who had not seen either of these fruits since the war began. We were conveyed in trucks to 'B' Camp at Worli. What we saw of Bombay was very pleasing with primitive and modern life moulded side by side.

American cars were numerable, as were wagons drawn by oxen. The avenue of palm trees and the many modern flats presented a pleasing picture. The camp was situated in a semi- residential area about five miles out of the city, on the sea front. There were no wired surroundings as we know them in home command. We slept in long high stone dormitories with open windows and red tiled roofs. The space which we now find ourselves with was more than welcome, after the terrible conditions of the past few weeks.

We handed in our rifles and ammo, and then drew a few more items of kit including a mosquito net. I did not really enjoy my lunch, but no doubt in time we will become more accustomed to this type of food. In the afternoon the C.O, the commanding officer, delivered a general lecture on terms of service, regulations, mail etc, etc. About 4 pm I had a shower, changed into long pants, which must be worn after sundown, and then had tea. I slung my mosquito net from cross wires overhead, and underneath, made down my bed. We walked down to the sea front about seven pm and witnessed one of the most amazing sunsets I have ever seen. The sea appeared deep indigo in colour and the sky brilliant red and orange, fading into a pale azure blue.

We spent an hour in the canteen, one of three attached to this camp. These canteens, all spacious places, generally painted white, have a staff of Indians who serve whatever maybe ordered. A grocery bar is usually attached where one can buy almost anything from Camp coffee, Gillette razor blades to Carr's water biscuits. I devoured some fruit and had a few soft drinks. We then visited some of the nearby shops, or shacks, as they were, where I purchased a pair of slacks and a tunic. Bartering with the natives over prices and articles can be a very interesting and demanding experience.

The darkness falls early at this time of the year with little twilight as we know it at home. The evenings came in cool and pleasing. We had no light in our billet and had to use candles. I retired under my mosquito net for the first time in my life.

Tuesday, 21st December. I rose about 6-30 am in darkness and had the usual wash and shave. We had a good breakfast of porridge, bacon and egg, tea, bread and butter. We paraded at 8-45 am and made our registration cards. Natives collected our laundry for washing. In the afternoon we had another lecture in the camp cinema by the padre. At night, I then walked along the front to one of the canteens and had a soft drink later, at what was known as the "Chinese Restaurant" where we had bacon and egg for supper. In season, eggs in India are cheap and plentiful. The evening was cool and quiet save for the chirping of the crickets.

Wednesday, 22nd December. I rose early and had the usual shave and shower. About ten am we were paid fifteen Rupees. The sun now shone brilliantly.

In the afternoon we were free to go to Bombay, and naturally all the camp pulled out on this expedition. We went by bus to a nearby railway station at which we boarded an electric suburban train. Bombay is indeed impressive with many gaily coloured flats situated all along the sea front. The streets are very picturesque with delightful shopping centres, studded with stately palm trees. The myriad of natives, of all types, who throng the city, are in themselves, a thrilling study. Some are dressed in primitive costumes while others are almost European in appearance. We drove along the sea front in an open carriage, admiring the many coloured modern flats and the brilliant sunshine. We had tea in a very select rating house resembling those of Paris or Brussels; we enjoyed, beyond words, a meal of chicken, salad and a peach melba with cream and coffee.

However, everyone had to observe No 5 article of a Part One Order relating to Discipline and Brothels.

ALL Brothels (including native brothels) are out of bounds to ALL ranks.

With this in mind at eight-thirty pm we returned to camp by rail and bus, passing on the way a native funeral party, carrying the dead body aloft on a stretcher. Syd and I had supper at the *"Mary Lee Bone's Kitchen"*, the Chinese Restaurant, before retiring.

Thursday, 23rd December. Last night I received eleven air mail letter cards from home. They were more than welcome. I clambered out from under my mosquito net, lit a candle, and read at least half of them before turning in again. Today, we went on deficiency and exchange clothing parade. I wrote a number of letters this morning and spent the evening in camp. We had supper at a nearby cafe and played snooker.

Friday, 24th December, Christmas Eve.

Today, we had an inspection by an air chief. At 8-45 am, the whole camp paraded and marched to the promenade, where we were inspected. The whole ceremony lasted only about an hour and a half, for which we were very thankful. After lunch, I went with Syd and Vic to visit a nearby mill, on the strength of an invitation we had a few days before. We were received by the under-manager, a Parsee who walked us all round the mill. We saw the total process from the cotton bale, passing through various methods of cleaning and separating, to the finished cloth. Each stage, cleaning, stretching, twisting, winding on reels and weaving was most interesting. This was the beginning of the demise of the British cotton industry as we knew it.

The mill, "Edward Sassoon" covered a tremendous area and contained hundreds of thousands of pounds of machinery. We were introduced to the manager, a stately Indian, who greeted us with reserved dignity. We had tea before leaving. The under-manager had a very highly developed political outlook. He insisted that the British Industrialization had attracted much too much wealth from India, even to the extent of bringing about dire poverty among plenty. The Indians found the USA troops much more democratic in their ways than us and admired them.

He outlined the total unity among the coolies during "Index", the last "Quit India Campaign". There was no doubt that had Russia not been at war, India would have been communist. A definite hatred for Churchill and Anderson prevailed. If the Hindu's and Moslems were to unite, he reckoned it would be a matter of twenty-four hours for the British in India.

Saturday, 25th December, Christmas day. I spent the morning letter-writing. We had our Xmas dinner of turkey, plum pudding, minerals, etc; etc. The dining halls were decorated for the occasion. I slept all afternoon and awoke feeling very hot. After tea, we walked round the shops and I purchased a writing case. About nine pm I had some supper, and after a shower I retired for the night; this being the most joyful part of the day's festivities; "Happy Christmas" everyone!

*

Saturday, 1st January, Worli Camp, India 1944

A poem written by an R.A.F. airman in December 1943 began:

The tropical day is born
In shades of pink and blue
Till the sun comes over the horizon
Bringing his mightier hues

The pastel shades retire
With grace and perfect main
The sun now high in the heavens
Is torrid to extreme

The trees they give protection
The labourer rests in the shade
All life awaits the Western trend
Of this blinding cavalcade

The shadows now they lengthen
Soon night will conquer day
Perhaps with this new triumph
Contentment will hold sway

We wait alas in vein
The night brings no relief
With insect and stifling shadow
We are tortured beyond belief

East of the Suez with Kipling
Fills a colourful book
But give me Service's Yukon
Or a murmuring Scottish brook

L.A.C. Robert Bruce Hamilton-Brown's diary continued with:

Went sick with my ear again and had inhalations before reporting for duty to the armoury. Received my posting chit this afternoon for Chiringa, where I have to join the Intelligence Section 261 Squadron R.A.F. India Command.

Chapter Twenty-five

The road to Mandalay Sunday 2nd January 1944 and for Robert Bruce Hamilton-Brown, it was paved with bad intentions.

Sunday, 2nd January. I left Worlie at two-thirty pm by truck for the station. The R.T.O, the railway transport officer, appeared dull and disinterested. Eventually, I was latched on to a party of about ten, all bound for different destinations. I am the only one for Chiringa and made an issue of one hour's travelling expenses. At 4-30 pm we pulled out for Calcutta travelling third class, recommended of course by the G.I.O, the group intelligence officer.

After leaving Bombay astern we were soon out into open country which rolled away north and south of us, as far as the eye could see. Palm trees and other types appeared in numbers, a striking contrast to the brown glasshouse on which they grew. Mountain ranges appeared from time to time looking tired, and like sandstone creations. About seven pm I had supper in the dining car which was not connected to the train by the normal corridor and consequently could only be reached when the train pulled into a station. I had a very satisfactory meal for one rupee. After sun down, the darkness fell rapidly and the countryside vanished into darkness. We closed the windows about this time to keep out the mosquitoes and all other insects. I lay down on the wooden seats in an endeavour to sleep, but all in vain.

Monday, 3rd January. I rose about seven am and on finding a tap near the floor of the convenience, had a wash of sorts. At the first stop, I went forward to the dining car for breakfast, which was a very satisfactory meal of porridge, egg on toast, tea etc, etc. At 9-30 am we pulled into Raipur, where we had a thirty-minute break. The electric train system terminated here, and we proceeded on steam. The native vendors certainly made the most of our company, selling fruit, tea, cigarettes etc., etc. A native barber stepped on-board and in about ten minutes had shaved three of our men at the cost of three ammo sacks. In all parts of India one sees the natives carrying bundles on their heads and a station is no exception. We watched one coolie carry two trunks and two kitbags on his head all at once.

The countryside between Raipur and Gondia was flat and well cultivated. Oxen and cattle could be seen in thousands. A surprising number of trees could now be seen, even though the land seemed dry and parched. We pulled into Gondia about noon and had lunch at the "upper-class dining room". Before pulling out, native women carrying baskets of coal on their heads walked up gang planks and filled the engine tender. Later in the afternoon we stopped and had tea at a W.R.V.S. venue, "The Women's Royal Voluntary Service" stall. We were served by American and English ladies who looked very wholesome in their coloured prints in the powerful sunlight.

A poem dedicated to these magnificent women was later penned by an unknown Lancastrian poet and began:

WRVS

"If you're down in the dumps and feeling the blues
There is always the lady with the hat and court shoes
With lots to do whatever you choose
A quick game of 'Poker' you have nothing to lose
If you fancy a dabble
She comes up with the 'Scrabble'
And if you are tiddly after some drinks
It's on to the sofa for a quick forty winks
She talks in strange foreign languages
It sounds like tea and cucumber sandwiches
She smiles all the time, there's no-one finer
Sporting a scarf drives a green Morris Minor
She's into 'Allsorts'
The round ones are best
Those hundreds and thousands don't *arf* stick in your chest
She wears lots of make-up and cares not a damn
If you're familiar and don't call her ma'am
If she has helped you then she has succeeded
Her services worldwide are forever needed"

About seven pm we made for Raipur and had supper at another upper-class dining room. All along the track we passed Indian villages with houses made of dried grass, few stone buildings were to be seen. The people seemed poor beyond words, obviously living on the land. At each stop young children came on to the rail track begging for free food "(*buckshee*)". Some no doubt were professional beggars, a well-known feature in India, but most were desperately poor.

Tuesday, 4th January. About 7-30 am we stopped at Khargpur and had tea with bread and butter at another W.R.V.S. stall. The temperature has now gone down considerably, for which I am very thankful. At noon we pulled into Calcutta and were eventually conveyed to a transient camp about two miles out of the city. Here we were accommodated in an old college. Calcutta at first sight seemed larger than Bombay, perhaps more commercial and certainly suffering poverty. Signs of the famine were obvious from time to time. At night, we went down-town by street car to Dalhousie (de lousie) Square and had supper at the International Service Club, and then looked round the shops.

Wednesday, 5th January. We paraded at 9 am and were instructed to pull out for Chittagong by rail that night at 10 pm.

In the afternoon I went down-town in a gharry, a four-wheel horse-drawn carriage, at the cost of six annas. I did some shop-gazing and ended up purchasing a book in which I intended to rewrite my diary. About five pm I had tea at the International Service Club and returned to camp by street car about eight pm. At 9 pm I drew my sten gun from the armoury and prepared to pull out for Chittagong. We left at 10 pm by truck for the station. The railway transport officer was too tired to even look at us and eventually we found accommodation in a parcel van. We had no lights and the interior accommodation was filthy beyond words. I created hell and called Imperialism for everything it was worth.

Eventually, a British army warrant officer threatened to put me under close arrest. We pulled out at eleven pm and soon after, I lay down on one of the wooden racks. The night was cold and I did not sleep.

Thursday, 6th January. About 6-30 pm we pulled into Goalundo, where we embarked with a struggle on a river steamer bound for

Chandpur. Our party carried our own dry rations and consequently all I had for breakfast was a mug of tea and a slice of bread and marmalade.

We sailed along the banks of the estuary of the Ganges River all day, and at 7-30 pm we were in sight of Chandpur. Strangely enough, the weather was cold and overcast; a vast contrast to the sun of Bombay. No food was available here where we entrained on the final lap. I feel miserable travelling now, without a proper wash or food. The night was again cold, and I did not sleep.

Friday, 7th January. At five am we reached Chittagong and were conveyed by truck to this transit camp. Here we were accommodated in bamboo huts or '*Bashas*', and afterwards one lay out in the open until breakfast. The surrounding lane was wooded and swampy and consequently mosquitoes flew about in their thousands. This is indeed a grim part of the world. About ten am, I was informed that I would pull out that day for Chiringa. Later in the afternoon, however, the arrangement was cancelled in view of the road being closed following two days of rain. In the evening I decided to give Chittagong the once over. The town reminded me of a Middle West settlement. Most of the shops and houses were wooden erections built at all angles. The main street was a dust track. Refuse and all kind of filth lay on the roadside. The town and district is a noted hell hole for all kinds of disease. I had tea at the Y.M.C.A and walked back to camp under a white moon and from out of the nearby jungle came all kinds of weird night sounds.

Saturday, 8th January. I wrote a few letters and generally rested. In the evening I went over to the Y.M.C.A again and had a pot of tea. I chatted with the secretary there and he noted particulars regarding my Y.M.C.A. connection. He seemed anxious to have me join the Indian Y.M.C.A., in his own capacity, provided the service would release me. I fear this is wishful thinking, however.

Sunday, 9th January. At four am I pulled out by truck with five aircrew men for the station where we entrained for Wohazari. The morning was cold, and the train seemed full of mosquitoes. About seven am we arrived at Wohazari which is more or less a military terminus. There is no real habitation here but near to the station I discovered a cafe where I had breakfast of tea, egg on toast.

The road to Chiringa itself is a Burmese hamlet consisting of a number of thatched bamboo huts scattered among the surrounding jungle. The squadron was situated in a clearing. I was well received and made to feel at home instantly. Rank and distinction hardly exist, and we dress as we feel fit. The men live in '*Basha's*' scattered among the trees. The living is rough and almost a touch of Robin Hood and his merry men of ancient Sherwood Forest. Every department is accommodated with a *Basha* and we have no hangars. We have a reasonably good canteen and club room where all kinds of entertainment is conducted; however, there were no Maid Marians in site. We also have an open-air theatre which has great possibilities.

Each *Basha* has a bearer who makes our beds and fetches water. We wash at tables outside in the open. Our mail comes up each day in a Tiger Moth and takes off in the same fashion. About ten miles north east stretches the Chinfoot hills which always seem blue in appearance. They are thickly wooded and remind me of home. The food is really good under the circumstances, with eggs in plenty. We now see more corned beef, however. I pulled in about 10 pm feeling very tired after a week's travelling.

Monday morning, 10th January. I commenced work this morning at about 8 am in the Squadron's Orderly Room. We are surrounded by palm trees here and I find it difficult to refrain from sitting gazing out on the jungle. *Loofahs* grow here on a small plant. They first appear in a green covering like a small marrow and when this decays the *loofah* remains, to be dried off before use.

I was issued with another blanket today and a pair of mosquito boots for wear after sundown. Fireflies and crickets abound at night to say nothing of the screeching night birds, mice, rats and the whining coyotes.

Many different kinds of snakes varying in length from two to six feet can be found in this area. The jungle itself teems with *pukka* animal life and we often go out shooting wild hog which makes good eating.

Tuesday, 11th January. I am slowly settling down to this new life. I have written two articles for our magazine, the "Menace", and one poem.

I have also been appointed assistant editor. I take part in debates each Sunday and am booked to speak on "America and ourselves".

I received three letters, two aerographs and three bundles of newspapers today. One of the letters was from Ernie Lingard, a colleague of mine at John Tindal's Gloves & Accessories. He wishes me well and informs me that my job will still be there on my return from the war. And, being declared as a hero, I thought, was going a *wee* bit too far, but I suppose if that's the way their misinformed minds work, then so be it, Amen. Ernie has also despatched a magazine cutting of the Hollywood film actress, Jane Russell showing lots of leg and more. He says, the picture will help relieve some of the stresses and strains of my being here.

One of our pilots bailed out with engine trouble and landed in the jungle. A search party was sent out and all returned safely to the camp two days later. The Japanese captured one of our airstrips with a kite on it and commenced to invite other aircraft to land. And, together with another shooting expedition, my "sten" is in good working order.

We had two warnings today. Our kites were flying all afternoon, Waikato's, Spitfires and Hurricanes in plenty. There were six heavy explosions about twenty miles south between 22-30 and 23-30 hrs; a perfect moonlit night for a fight.

I played poker with two South African mercenary pilots who had flown in during the afternoon. Their de Havilland DH.82 Tiger Moth aeroplane is currently being stretched with dope and an extra gun is being installed around a back seat. The two likeable chaps were called Stephan Rosenberg and Karl Van Hagen and hailed from Durban, a city on the south east coast of Africa. Karl Van Hagen was, in metaphor, the back-seat driver and was an expert in shooting down stray and unwanted Japanese Zero aircraft. Meanwhile, Stephan Rosenberg, an Anglo-American Air force war veteran and fighter pilot, professed to play a mean game of cards with me in the club.

My luck was in and I cleaned him out. Stephan had no money left to play and so the only way he could reduce his losses was to hand over three paintings which he had brought with him from South Africa and were kept in a side pocket inside the cockpit.

"On purchasing a trunk" in Calcutta

Ever since being up-country, I had decided to purchase a stout metal trunk. This was not just a "pale kneed just over" fancy, but rather a classic necessity. In the first place, the ants played havoc with my kit bags. Secondly, my clean clothing was always creased and damp when unpacked. More important still, my writings, pictures, paintings and valuable works of art, which I had carefully collected, were subject to crude unrealistic pressure, and were liable to become damaged.

With all this background of reasoning behind me, it was not surprising that my first city contact found me in the bazaars seriously concentrating on trunk assets and liabilities. My national disposition, coupled with my uncanny instinct of knowing just what is right, caused many of India's commercial sons to arrive from the accustomed Eastern Square position in the hope of doing business with the white Sahib.

At last my eye alighted on what, from the very start was what I had visualized in my mind, more by instinct than reason.

The Eastern merchant with high hopes and many salaams dragged my choice under the mellow rays of his oil lamp in order to convince me finally. The trunk measured three feet by two feet by two approximately and was bottle green in colour. I held him firmly to sixteen rupees and while it was more than I had intended to pay, the quality and general stout construction justified the price. It was warm work; I removed my topi and was now sitting on a bale of cloth awaiting the total cohesion of all my faculties engaged in the transaction. It was a deal, "Have a lock fixed, and get a bearer to carry it out to the street." I was in fine fettle now, my cautious financial outlook had been conquered, the purchase was yielding me no end of pleasure, and the cost was already forgotten.

On reaching the street, I hailed a rickshaw and started off towards the Service Club. Night had now fallen, and the city's myriad of twinkling lights seemed to vie with the stars. City trams thundered past and the streets were thronged with a native population clad in loose- fitting colourful robes.

The night was warm, and the scene of the East was overpowering. I sat back in the rickshaw, seeing everything, hearing above the *charwari* and the patter of the rickshaw man's feet on the hot streets. And the bus bell that rattled on the shaft warning jay-walkers of our approach. My sixteen-chip trunk was a treasure and I was glad of his caution; the whole scenario similar to obtaining a jewel in an Englishman's crown.

*

Sport's afternoon at R.A.F. station Chiringa. Wednesday 12th January.

It was a delightful morning. I went by bus to Coonoor in the afternoon where I met Flying Officers, Garner and Grey. We had coffee and cakes outside the club house prior to playing eighteen holes; neither of them are good players. Played again in the afternoon but unfortunately, I was feeling dehydrated due to excessive haggling in the bazaar, and after tiffin, I retired early to my bed at five-thirty pm; it seemed a long way back to July 1940, when I walked through the gates of Podgate for the first time.

I dreamt of a poem, written by Fred. W. Holton, it was called London: April 12th, 1942 and begins:

In Whitehall they sell primroses
And in Trafalgar Square
People stop by close-set trays,
And then carry everywhere
Gold of Spring in poses shining
Through the towns grey morning air
But all those neat-tied bunches by the dozen lying
    there
And all the people in Whitehall and in Trafalgar
    Square
I'd give for this far better thing, and give without a
    care

One early primrose bright against the dark wave of your hair

Chapter Twenty-six

Demobilisation looms on the horizon, December 1945

Saturday, 1st December 1945. I had a busy morning in the Orderly Room, listening into the 'Home Service' frequency in two 'stags', two hours on and four hours off.

I had three letters from home and one from Syd Bowden informing me of Victor Hughes being put under close arrest by the RAF Police in Madras; the charges are one of treason and the others, insubordination towards his Commanding Officer and political beliefs detrimental to the interests and well-being of the nation.

This is the moment I want to lay low, preferably hidden behind a net and underneath a blanket, out of sight and out of mind, and when all evidence of my existence in 261 Squadron and, latterly, 185 Squadron have gone and I have followed on in the wake of the "Red Army"; only then, will I emerge victorious from this contraption the RAF call a bed; a 'donkey's breakfast', a straw-filled palliasse mattress reminiscent of a Palladium cinema seat in Preston.

My thoughts are with those two brave South African pilots, Van Hagen and Rosenberg, who were shot down in flames by the Japanese during the successful attack on Rangoon by a 261 Squadron Hurricane Mk II in September 1944.

My thoughts continued, going back to a month earlier when I was on duty in the Orderly Room, 'Silent Peeping', listening into some *'Pukka Gen'*, genuine news, broadcast on the BBC World service and taking down notes in short-hand of various happenings at home. I can recall it was around six pm, India time, on the 23rd of August, when disaster hit a village in Lancashire at ten-thirty that morning with sixty-one fatalities, including thirty-eight children; a recently refurbished American consolidated B-24H Liberator bomber had crashed into the Holy Trinity School in Freckleton during bad weather on approach to the airfield at RAF Warton. Ironically, my previous RAF Station at Kirkham was situated less than two miles, a cabbage patch distance away, and the *Sad*

Sack Snack Bar, where I ate hot dogs and American burgers a-plenty was completely destroyed.

A memorial garden and children's playground were opened in memory of those lost, the money for the playground equipment having been raised by American airmen at the nearby Warton airbase.

*

LAC Robert Bruce Hamilton-Brown, the man with no faith, no hope and little charity had stashed away three valuable works of art in his trunk, presumed to be painted by Vincent Van Gogh, and estimated today, to be worth around thirty million US dollars. During the outbreak of war in 1939, they were removed from their frames by their Dutch owners in Amsterdam and discreetly hidden inside rolled-up newspapers and quickly despatched to Durban in South Africa where Stephan Rosenberg was appointed sole custodian.

Ironically, the trilogy and legendary trinity, supposedly named *Faith Hope* and *Charity*, the three Gladiators, flown by a division of 261 Squadron RAF and based in Malta became history when the unit was disbanded on 13th September this year.

*

Today has been one of strange reactions. All morning, I had in my heart, a bitter hatred for men back home who go on leave in full uniform complete with ribbon.

I know them so well, wallowing in cynicisms, basking in the lesser glory.

Last evening, I was catching up with a few things I had neglected to add to my scrap book; even my 1945 diary was fast depleting in pages and lacking in words; how I hate this place, it is really getting me down.

I flicked through the pages quickly and found a page where I had unwittingly made an entry twice; it was Monday the 3rd April 1944. To my surprise I had pasted the same newspaper cutting of a theatre preview side-by-side; and in ophthalmic terms, it was a classic case of double vision when Bette Davis appeared simultaneously, again and again in front of my eyes. My writings to accompany this were:

"Tonight, I saw Paul Luras and Bette Davis, the screen's first lady, in a Warner Bros, Triumph, "Watch on the Rhine" at the E-L-I-T-E theatre in Calcutta; the delectable Bette Davis in the role that demanded her artistry, her understanding; a story that tells forever of woman's tender bravery and gallant courage. I no longer hate those who only know the meaner choice. All hate is sin and cannot therefore be of mightier things. The goodness and the glory of the truly great things have their being, their creation, their sustenance, a way above this type, who wilt before such a background. The immortal triumph of the really great things, the only real triumph is assured, in time, because they are of the Christ. Only the humble have eyes to see, they alone will sense the crowning hour."

At the top of the page I pasted a cutting, by ANY SCOTSMAN, and reads:

"When *ye're* smoking *ye're ain baccy, ye're* thinking of the awful expense, and when *ye're* smoking *anither* body's, *ye're* pipe is *rammit sae* tight it *willna* draw."

And written in Chiringa, Burma in February 1944 is my poem "Ode to Light" which I sent to Flight Lieutenant A. Cummings, the Editor of the "Journal of the Air Forces" and was published at the General Headquarters based in New Delhi. The poem begins:

Ode to Light
Far in the East, assembling fast
I see the armies of night,
Gathered in strength, a frowning mass
Poised to assault the night

Fast and in silence,
With certainty supreme,
They cross the vault of heaven
The territory between

Bright shafts of Light announce the clash
And soon the armies meet,
Death looks on in triumph
Prepared to steal and cheat

The conflict grows in fury
Filling the tortured heavens,
T' is blow for blow on either side,
With no thought of quarter given

But night rides on, *t'is* destiny will
Days champion must give ground,
He fights in breathless courage yet,
Scorning his many wounds

Alas his rear guards, drenched in blood
Are forced to yield the skies
And soon above, and all around
Nights triumph fills our eyes

Exploit your hours of glory
You warriors of the night
Your triumph is a fable
And will die with the morning light.

My reaction to some of the reactionaries who read the poem was of complete and utter disdain knowing they were of the lesser type, and probably couldn't string two sausages together, never mind words.

*

Labelled a crazy misfit, a joker and pronounced totally *doolally* by the RAF, Robert Bruce Hamilton-Brown was later heralded with the title of hero at John Tindal's Gloves & Accessories Ltd, to which he was later appointed head buyer for the company, distributing leather gloves which transformed into slippers, rain hats which magically turned into a shopping bag and flat packs containing six foot fold-up cardboard sentry boxes.

*

Extract from my letter I sent home on 26th March 1944

I now feel in a better position to offer you a little more general information on India. I find that the average Indian, there are many different races, is a bright, intelligent creature, considering he has not been allowed to progress as we in the West.

Many of his methods are primitive as consequently are to be expected, but he is anxious. The majority are of docile disposition and accept orders without question. It is obvious they have been subjected to this sort of thing for generations.

In the Indian himself, there exists great possibilities; unfortunately, his whole country is subjected to extreme exploitation both from outside and in. The Parsee class, equivalent to the western Jew, controls factories and most real business. There also exists the vaunted Indian Prince class and many other born exploiters.

I have not yet observed the various religious handicapping progresses but no doubt they do to a considerable extent exist. Indians generally, are keen merchants and will sell you almost anything. They enjoy reasoning with a prospective buyer over a price.

As you know, there are many languages spoken here, and I have listed these in order of importance. Hindu, Urdu, Bengali, Tamil etc., etc. To obtain a post with the Government i.e., Railways, Office Departments, or in a factory of almost any kind, an Indian must speak perfect English and, in most cases, have a degree. All street signs and adverts are written in English.

Sanitation is very bad all over India. In the country, where a tremendous number of Indians live, it does not exist, and in the cities, such as Calcutta, it is fourth rate.

Everyone seems much, far too much, interested in business, big and small, to worry about sanitation. In most cities, thousands of people sleep in the streets. This is quite accepted in Calcutta and Bombay; there must be millions of Indians unaccounted for by any Government department. The mosquito menace is tackled in the white sections, but I fear the National Policy, if there is one, has not yet functioned; again, there seems little interest. The services merely look after in a mild way the area which interests them. At least eighty per cent of the native population don't have mosquito nets and consequently, are subject to malaria every night of the week. The cost of a net is well beyond the Indian pocket. Only one type of mosquito, the female, carries the germ. Prostitution is very bad indeed and venereal disease haunts the whole country.

There is still traffic in selling women and young virgin girls. Most women are employed in manual trades such as building etc, etc. So much for the Indians' India.

In the hot season, which is now approaching, white people suffer from prickly heat; a painful rash caused by the pours becoming exhausted through continual perspiring, and foot rot is also known in Bengal. Here the flesh actually rots away.

*

Calcutta 1944

Had it not been for the Indians, LAC Robert Bruce Hamilton-Brown would not have been based in India, or indeed had the privilege to go and see Bette Davis twice in one day. One of his fellow NCOs asked him why he always carried three handkerchiefs around in his pockets. His answer to this was, the red, white and blue silk handkerchiefs were called Pip, Squeak & Wilfred, the nicknames of the three British medals instituted at the end of the First World War; "Where one was, the other two were sure to follow", reminiscent of the inseparable characters of a Daily Mirror newspaper strip thought up by Bertram J Lamb in 1919.

'What a load of bollocks, double bollocks, triple bollocks.' Senior Aircraftsman Gary Cooper remarked. 'I would have thought the real reason was that you used them in cases of emergency sitting in the back row of the E-L-I-T-E cinema.

'*Agh*, yes, I must admit it is a *wee* bit dark in there, and the ice cream does have a tendency to splash all over the place.' Robert was quick to remark, nodding like one of the donkeys walking along Blackpool beach.

'Tell me Robert.' Cooper asked him inquisitively. 'Why do you always carry a Union Jack flag in your thirty-seven-pattern side-pack?'

'It is because, if we were to be captured by the Japanese, they may be able to afford a modicum of leniency towards us.' he replied, knowing his attempt to emulate Stanley would result in himself and the flag falling on to stony ground.'

'Do you know, Hamilton-Brown,' SAC Cooper went on to explain. 'This is the biggest load of bullshit I have ever heard in my life, and, if I may add, Robert, if the Japanese were to capture you, they would decapitate you and have your head placed on top of a pole, and then, to make matters worse, alternatively, they could tie you down having shoved a bamboo shoot up your arse; how does that sound?'

'Well, I think I'll leave it behind tomorrow when I go into town because I can't visualize being tied down and a bamboo shoot being stuck up my backside.'

'Don't worry, Robert, we are about twenty-two miles away from any hostilities and supposedly, just supposedly, the Japanese did decide to invite themselves to a late cocoa supper, then there are plenty of guns and ammunition in the armoury to do you and us all a great favour.'

'Do you know Corporal Cooper, this is truly amazing.' Robert said enthusiastically. 'Last night I caught a deadly five-foot snake; it was beautifully marked, red white and blue, similar to a Far Eastern Wrestle viper.'

'Oh, that would be Charlie, we patriotically painted him three weeks ago and he is harmless.' Cooper disclosed.

"Dressed-up like a million-dollar trooper, trying hard to look like Gary Cooper", Robert sarcastically sang as he left the canteen with everyone falling about in loud mass hysteria.

*

Tuesday, January 6th 1946.

It was a beautiful sunny morning and Calcutta was lovely at this time of year. I had lunch with Ian McGregor and spent the remainder of the day walking around the city and eating good food for a change. I collected my trunk from Cox & Kings depository, and then repacked and rejected all the kit of little use and then had supper at Noodles, a Chinese restaurant in the centre of the town. I retired about eleven pm.

The following morning, I was at last given my marching orders. I paraded at ten am this morning and have been detailed to pull out at nine am tomorrow. I duly left Calcutta by military train at twelve noon, and at 1.46 pm flew the sixteen-hundred-mile journey to Singapore by a wing and a prayer inside an old RAF Dakota transporter aircraft.

On arrival it was like going from one jungle to another when I saw thousands of British, Australian and Canadian, men, women and children, sleeping in tents waiting to be shipped out, back to their respective homelands.

The Changi nine-hole golf course which, up until September 1945, the previous year, had been played by the Japanese and now resembling a Boy Scout jamboree with hundreds of bell tents erected and scattered on the surface of the once immaculate and well-kept tropical greens.

Chapter Twenty-seven

The Arrest of LAC Robert Bruce Hamilton-Brown of No 185 Squadron RAF on Wednesday, 7th January 1946

Wednesday, 7th January. One cannot begin to describe the nature of this place; hundreds of emaciated troops with sunken faces, looking pale beyond description, waiting anxiously to embark on troop ships to take them home; many of them suffering from mange, rickets and a lack of a good diet.

For these men, the only solution was to circumnavigate the globe, to be fattened up, well fed and brought back to normality to avoid unwanted embarrassment among the military authorities who are sitting comfortably in their ivory towers in Whitehall.

Some of the British veterans of the Commander, Lieutenant-General William Slim's Forgotten 14th Army, found themselves in places like Hawaii, America and Canada before leisurely sailing back to their various and respective demobilisation points in England.

How I hate this place; how I hate being here. I have no friends, no colleagues, no comrades in arms to talk with, not even Cooper or my Squadron, who are now down to twenty men in number when I left Calcutta this afternoon, and apart from the 'Weaver's Woman' an upper-middle class, snooty-nosed WRVS dragon, called Heather Hartington-Withers, whose looks are enough to frighten children, dispenses cocoa from a bucket and scares mice away from cheese. She has no time to hand out the draughts because there are enough coming in from underneath the tents.

I was so glad to have been able to send my well-padlocked trunk to Scotland. The MFO, the Military Freight Organisation in Calcutta allowed me to hand it to a native bearer, who put it immediately on to a ship which was bound for Liverpool this evening.

My purchases in Calcutta consisted of a length of Indian cotton curtain material, a Kashmir *sari* and a lady's wrist watch for Norma which were all carefully wrapped in tissue paper with a couple of small lime stones to stop them becoming damp in transit.

The post office had been opened to receive and send letters, parcels and telegraphs, but unfortunately it was some distance away from the camp and after I had complained to a Sergeant Major of a British army tin-pot regiment, he impertinently told me to mind my own business and to dip my head into a jar of 'Brylcream'. It was interesting to hear that the following day my complaint had been substantiated and a sub-post office had been opened in a marquee, two putts away from the ninth hole, but due to a temporary hiccup, I was unable to deposit my letters home.

Oh, how I hate this place, the entire atmosphere is beginning to wear me down.

I am writing two letters home. One to the duchess, Norma, and a reminder to my former colleague, Ernie Lingard that Tindal's Gloves & Accessories would again have the pleasure of employing me but, however, this time it would be in a capacity of a directorship or executive role. I emphasised that it would take some time for me to adjust and it would be at least six months before joining the company following disembarkation leave and the all-important demobilization.

The time is nearing four pm and a visit to the *chogey wallah*, who serves corned beef curry which glows on a wooden plate and is hotter than a stoker's shovel. He combines his lucrative catering business by selling dirty postcards depicting Japanese golfers hitting their balls sideways into the rough. The make-shift corrugated metal shack with crude-looking wooden tables and bench seats was reminiscent to a soup kitchen I had the misfortune to stumble across years ago in downtown, Seventh Avenue, New York.

Another misfortune I was faced with on my way back from "Fortnum & Masons", was a few lines from a Christian Psalm read by the resident 'Sky Pilot', Captain Chris Harrison, a British army chaplain with a warped sense of humour, who would insist on telling us that it was a "Long, long way to Tipperary".

A two-ton truck arrived carrying Red Cross parcels, albeit almost two weeks late.

I was hit in the chest with a box which was projected by a shortsighted 'Slop Carrier', an Australian Army Service Corps lance corporal, who was sitting cross-legged on the back of the tailboard.

Ye Gods!

I opened the parcel to find gifts of the type one would give to someone who had just come in from the cold, having been stranded in minus zero-degree temperatures on a snow-capped mountain in Chinese Outer Mongolia or the ice tundras of Russian Siberia. The contents of the parcel contained a scarf, pullover, gloves, an assortment of festive nuts, five 'Woodbine' cigarettes, a small bottle of medicinal Indian brandy, a tin of Kendal Mint cake, a bar of Cadbury's plain chocolate, two sheets of thin writing paper, a *"Cunard"* White Star envelope and a pencil complete with an eraser, just in case one changes one's mind in order to address the envelope to someone else. To conclude, there was a red flimsy paper hat to wear to put you into the Christmas spirit; the fact that Christmas had all but gone and, for some, had never arrived in the first place, was by this time neither here nor there.

The next item on the agenda for the afternoon's free entertainment was to have a haircut inside one of the bell tents which was full of Royal Australian Air Force. The barber was an Indian migrant who sharpened his cut-throat razor backwards and forwards along the side of a shiny leather strap; it is of little importance to tell you, his appearance looked similar to a Sikh who probably had an aptitude for dismantling heads from British Army *Pongos*; his black-waxed moustache, on the face of it, looked as if it had just come out from a theatrical make-up box and was stuck on with adhesive because it twitched and reacted independently to the rest of his face.

At six pm, I was about to call it a day and retire to my tent which I shared with two non-commissioned officers from the 1st Battalion the Loyal North Lancashire Regiment and six hardy troopers belonging to a Chindits platoon attached to the 3rd Indian division, led by General Orde Wingate's Force in Burma. For them, this place was no different to the jungle, and it mattered not one wit when one had to put up with shit.

I was alone when three Regimental policemen arrived on the scene to take me away. I was not surprised at this, knowing the temperament of

Aircraftsman Victor Hughes, who had been arrested by the RAF police and was now shopping socialists, communist sympathisers and right-wing extremists for fun.

My hands were tied, forced together around the nape of my back, aided by a six-foot RAF policeman with the biggest pair of rusting handcuffs clasped around my wrists; the chain attaching one grip to the other looking similar to what one would find securing the *"Queen Mary"* and the key resembling a large diameter butterfly water bottle stopper.

'We are going to put you where the birds won't shit on you.' The provost sergeant bellowed out, in an accent which could only be described as incoherent, and that only a Welsh Rhonda Valley pit pony would be able to understand.

'And does this place, have a decent shower, breakfast room and a receptacle in which to post my letters?'

At this low point, the provost sergeant took away my two field canvas mail sacks containing my diaries, scrap book, Union Jack Flag and various oddments belonging to my overseas collection. I was pleased that my trunk had not been confiscated and was now being conveyed to bonnie Scotland across the high seas as he muttered the words:

'What is going on here?' You cannot be serious; I thought you comics had hammers and sickles on your red flags?'

'Well, it all depends on who's coming up your backside; the last thing I would want is to wave a horizontal green and white coloured flag with a fiery dragon in the foreground, and there was no need to take that attitude.' I said, knowing I would have to pay for that particular remark later.

I was placed under close arrest; the charge being 'Top Secret', "Information and material, the unauthorised disclosure which could be detrimental to the interests of the nation".

'What a load of bullshit and Tommy-rot.' I disclosed, but it didn't stop them from banging me up for several weeks inside Changi's most exclusive and prestigious, albeit notorious, hotel.

The day came for me to be transported under lock and key back to Liverpool, which was where my journey to the Far East began.

Ironically, it was the RMS *"Mauretania"*, the flagship of *'Cunard's'* White Star Line, which, still in her grey paint scheme, transported me back to Liverpool via the Cape, the Horn of Africa.

Travelling first-class down inside the brig with only a Sergeant at Arms to keep me company throughout the journey, I was forced to lie on a straw palliasse and fed on porridge, stale bread, dripping and water; on occasion an all-important apple was thrown in just to keep the doctor inside his sick bay.

I had no pen or paper on which to write home and the only medium I had to recall the diabolical events which unfolded and conjured up by these pathetic hooligans in uniform, was my brain.

The only advantage of my being down inside this hell-hole, was to sleep up against the bulkhead which was next door to the engine room where the heat was generated from the ship's huge boilers.

There were no windows through which I could look out and it was difficult to calculate the time as two of my wristwatches had been taken from me. My only wish was for Neptune to appear and puncture three holes into the bottom of the ship with his trident but alas, this *was nae* to be because legend has it, he is confined to the depths of one of the equators and it had always puzzled me how he could be in three places at the same time. However, I left this one to chance and hoped that a black Neptune would appear somewhere around the coast of Africa.

It was interesting to note later that year, the RMS *"Mauretania"* on the 2nd of September 1946, returned to Liverpool after further voyages, was released from Government service and immediately went to Gladstone Dock to be reconditioned by Cammell Laird & Co. for return to *'Cunard'* White Star service. I only wished I could have been banged up earlier because the shipping company would have saved me a rather expensive train fare home.

The voyage to Liverpool took just over one month. I was immediately put into solitary confinement somewhere in Walton Vale, pending a court martial; the only difference concerning the accommodation was that every day I was offered a plate of *'Scouse'*, a disgusting concoction of Liverpudlian Irish stew, consisting of vegetables, mutton and red cabbage and, after I had eaten this muck the military had the audacity to call food, I was allowed freedom of movement by stretching my legs as I walked around a dismal courtyard talking to the pigeons and the laughing cow which dispensed cigarettes from its backside.

On Monday, the eleventh of March 1946, I was taken to a place in Liverpool where I was accused of being a communist and a subversive element operating inside Britain's Armed Forces. The judge said at the trial, that if it were not for a senior member of the diplomatic service, namely my father, I would have been incarcerated for life inside the tower of London, and then he would have instructed a Beefeater to throw the keys away.

'However, in this particular case, I will grant you leniency.' Judge Sir Stanley Turner said with reservation, 'I sentence you to two years' imprisonment'. This pronouncement was to be his last and final offer.

'You will also be systematically stripped of your Second World War medals; namely, the 1939-45 Star, the Burma Star, the War Medal 1939-45 and the Defence Medal.' James Macefield, the Queen's Councillor for the defence recommended. 'Your diaries and scrap book will be handed back to you only when we feel fit to do so; the incriminating evidence which was extracted from these journals will be kept by the military for an indefinite period.' he concluded.

'I uphold your recommendations.' the judge, Sir Stanley Turner said to the barrister before checking on the time to break off for his lunch. 'LAC Robert Bruce Hamilton-Brown, you will now be despatched to a place of penalisation, and it is hoped that when you are eventually released you will become a far better person.'

'And does this place, where I'm supposed to be going have an eighteen-hole golf course and 'Forfar Bridies'?' I said to a red-headed prison officer, Mathew Kelly, as I was escorted down towards a door with the usual pair of handcuffs gripping my wrists.

'We have a famous golf course called the Royal Birkdale in Southport, if that is any comfort to you.' Kelly said with an air of sarcasm. 'And, if you are looking for someone to relieve some of your tension, then I would suggest that in your dreams, you take up with Jane Russell.'

'Well, I could always get used to a crazy golf putting green, copper knob.' I said to Mr Kelly underneath my breath.

*

During his time inside H.M Prison, Walton, Hamilton-Brown's wife, Norma died of consumption and had been constantly informed by the authorities that he was still serving in the Far East on special military duties, i.e., intelligence work for the British Government. Only his father knew of his leanings towards the Soviet Union, and not one word was mentioned to either his wife, Patricia or indeed Norma Anne Mulholland, the long-suffering wife of the controller and manipulator Hamilton-Brown.

Chapter Twenty-eight

The Aga Saga at No 4 Waverly Court, Westminster, London, England Friday, 18th December 2015

'Something has just occurred to me, Henry, I've never mentioned this before; in fact, I'd completely forgotten about it until, well, I suppose when we went through all of Robert's paraphernalia.'

'What is the something?'

'It's about the time he took mother to Jersey for a couple of days; you may remember, it was about twenty-five years ago, and the first day they were there, they went along to one of the banks, she never told us which one, probably, knowing him, it was the Royal Bank of Scotland, anyway, this is the odd part; he told her to wait outside on the pavement while he went in and conducted whatever he had to.'

'Really?'

'Yes, it does make you wonder, doesn't it?'

'Are you thinking what I'm thinking Liz?'

'I think so; obviously he didn't want her to know anything about his finances, or I should say, his investments-'

'-*ill-gotten* gains, I would say, especially after what we've been reading in all of his ramblings. And, if we're talking offshore banking, don't forget the Isle of Man, another tax haven.'

'He really wasn't a nice person, Henry; he really wasn't, and to think, thank God, mother never ever knew what he was like.'

'I know.'

'A stepfather from hell and wasn't the full taper to light up his pipe, that is what he was, Henry.

'Yes, I know Liz, but hatred and anger rots the soul.'

'And, I suppose Henry, by going to these places to try and find his money would be just like chasing rainbows.'

'Yes, dear, as usual, you are absolutely right.'

'Do you realize,' she went on, 'it's eight months since Christopher brought all those items of interest, and all those months we've been completely absorbed in our writing. Alright, the book is nearing completion now, but I feel we should have a break; in fact, we deserve a break.'

'I was thinking exactly the same this morning and I was going to suggest we treat ourselves to a day off.'

'That's a great idea, what do you suggest we do?'

'What do I suggest?' he repeated.

'Yes, give me a clue?' Elizabeth asked.

'Well, I suggest, we paint the town red or in this case, red, white and blue.' Henry said, adding more suggestions to his list of priorities.

'Now you're talking, and what do you suggest we should do with some of these things; we've finished the book now so they're no longer any use to us for research purposes. Okay,' she added thoughtfully, 'we'll keep Robert's diaries, but the paintings; we don't want them, do we?'

'Probably not.' he agreed.

'Shall we just shove them in the Aga, then?'

'Why not, Liz; best place for them, just amateur stuff, if you ask me.'

'It's been a great day,' Elizabeth said to him when they returned home later in the afternoon. 'but somehow, even when we were pushing our way through all those eager-beaver Christmas shoppers in Selfridges, and then when we had that fantastic meal, I kept thinking about what we've learned about Robert; I just cannot get his hypocrisies out of my mind. He used to say that Christmas-time brings hypocrisy to its maximum level.'

'Really, I know what you mean, but there's still something missing here, isn't there?' Henry said looking somewhat puzzled.

'Do you mean those two years when he came back from India?'

'Yes; where the hell was he?

'Maybe the laughing cow which dispenses 'Woodbine' cigarettes from its backside may be able to tell us.' she said.

'And, how come Robert always came back from the January sales sporting a black eye?' Henry wantingly asked.

'Oh, that was because someone was fighting over a bargain. I can remember an incident when he took on the role of Jesus and up-tipped some of the tables inside Debenhams department store in Oxford Street; my mother had to convince the police he was completely mad and would be returned to a psychiatric hospital in Streatham immediately.'

'I can remember him continually slapping his thigh as if he were Roy Rogers, galloping off on his horse, Trigger.' Henry said, doing his best to imitate his late father-in-law.

'That was after he had checked all his investments and "I owe you" slips which he kept in his trouser pocket.' Elizabeth put in before saying: 'He used to give me ladies' sample leather gloves every Christmas. I called them 'Robert's Specials' because the stitching and lining came apart. Also,' she continued, 'he would have this habit of calling me Elizabeth Taylor, which I thought was very complementary, and as for Christopher and Leonora, he called them Elvis Presley and Beatnik Annie which didn't impress her much I can tell you! Patricia, however, came out better in my estimation when he called her a Dorothy Perkins coat hanger. Do you know, Henry, this afternoon was reminiscent of the time we used to go to the Opera Room in Charing Cross Road, especially in December when we could buy hot roasted chestnuts from a 'Pearly King and Queen' vendor on the pavement outside.'

'Yes, those were the days, Liz, you can still buy them, but one has to trudge along Baker Street to find them these days, and it is not so pleasurable when it is freezing cold, snowing and one is subjected to a dozen or so Father Christmas look- alikes in the street.'

'And, this afternoon visiting the Imperial War Museum in Lambeth was exceptionally good,' Liz said. 'Can you remember that painting they had on one of the walls after we had seen a De Havilland Tiger Moth aircraft, suspended from the ceiling, giving us the impression it was flying above us. The painting was very like the one we found in Robert's postal sacks showing an RAF Bristol Blenheim III aircraft in action over somewhere or other; perhaps it is a pity we disposed of it to light the Aga.' she added.

'Well, there's no need to cry over spilt milk; anyway, its gold frame will come in handy' Henry replied with glee.

'I used to particularly enjoy the meal in the Japanese restaurant, 'Sushi

Sue's' in Old Crompton Street.' she said. 'And, the assistant manageress, Alice Entwistle, was exceptionally helpful when she said: 'It's nice here innit; if you need anything else, just clap your hands twice and I will be there tending to your requirements in a jiff.'

That evening Henry was watching BBC television; the programme was called "The Lost Treasures" and the theme for that particular evening's entertainment was about lost art work painted by Vincent Van Gogh and, along with several other pictures which he had painted in the late nineteenth century, there were three which looked vaguely familiar; namely, "View out to Sea at Scheveningen", "A vase of red tulips" and a "A bowl of Fruit".

'Henry?' Elizabeth said as she switched off the bedside lamp.

'Yes Liz?'

'The ghost has been finally exorcised.'

'Yes, my dear, at last.'

Other titles by Michael Alty:

The Guildford Boys – ISBN 978 1 84549 428 5

The Ghost of Latchford Hall – ISBN 978 1 84540 528 2

The Bells of Saint Clements – ISBN 978 1 84549 620 3

27 rue Mortain – ISBN 978 1 84549 686 9

Lancaster Grill – ISBN 978 1 84549 728 6

Published by arima Publishing.

www.ingramcontent.com/pod-product-compliance
Lightning Source LLC
Chambersburg PA
CBHW071132260626
47162CB00003B/762